I was in an elevator with a serial killer. Now, in case you believed that to be hyperbole, I meant that literally. I was standing inside a glass elevator ascending the side of a Douglas Grand Hotel next to a man who had killed at least fourteen women, but probably more.

The two of us were getting a breathtaking view of New Los Angeles, the massive arcology created on the ruins of the old city, with some of the megastructures dwarfing those of the former city like child's building blocks.

"There used to be no super-structures in Los Angeles due to the San Andreas fault," Boris Semenov said, gesturing down to the buildings below. "It passes thirty-five miles north of the city and in the old days would have laid waste to the entirety of the arcology if they'd built buildings half the size of the one we're in."

Boris was a six-foot-two Russian man with a neatly trimmed beard and linebacker's body that was primarily the result of having his bones replaced with cybernetics. His suit was on the lower end of fancy and a sign he didn't know anything about fine tailoring. But what did you expect from an up jumped mobster? His file had been sparse, but he was a key contact between the Trikuza, White Triangle slavers, Russian syndicates, and port authorities. So much so that his "indiscretions" were overlooked.

Until now.

REVENGE OF THE CYBER DRAGONS

C. T. PHIPPS

&

MICHAEL SUTTKUS

FOREWORD

BY C.T. PHIPPS

Welcome back to the future, fellow Riders.

The response to *Daughter of the Cyber Dragons* has been fantastic and everyone seems to love Keiko "Kei" Springs. I had a lot of fun writing her and I am eager to get back into the thick of things. Keiko successfully recovered her memories, managed to help in freeing an AI (for better or worse), and ended up with an artificial child to boot. Lots of developments there.

So, what can we look forward to now from this series? Well, for that I must answer the question of: what is cyberpunk? For me, cyberpunk is the concept of being "Fricked by technology," as Kei would say. Technology is certainly more advanced in cyberpunk settings and appreciated, even fetishized by the creators, but it does not address the fundamental social ills that are at the heart of society.

Speaking as an academic, cyberpunk is a bit of the hard sciences crashing into the social sciences. You may create a machine that can turn all the world's garbage into delicious nutritious food but in cyberpunk, someone is going to charge out the wazoo for its use so that only a percentage of people are going to be able to use it. You may cure cancer but that isn't going to help its sufferers pay for it.

Therefore I believe cyberpunk will remain my favorite genre of sci-fi. The discussion of the very real human flaws coming up against the increasing power of the tools at their command. Cyberpunk remains as socially relevant today as it did when Bruce Bethke first wrote "Cyberpunk" in the spring of 1980.

Some people love to stick cyberpunk perpetually in a retrofuture and refer to anything that isn't an Eighties vision of the future as "Post-Cyberpunk", but I find that ridiculous. Cyberpunk has grown as a genre with the present having elements envisioned in the Eighties (*Hackers*, *Watch Dogs*, *Mr. Robot*) but also entirely new visions of the future that we can explore from preexisting trends. Instead of nuclear war like in *Do Androids Dream of Electric Sheep*, it'll be global warming that devastates the world. Instead of Japan taking over the world, maybe it'll be Facebook.

But beyond the question of social relevance, cyberpunk simply remains an incredibly fun genre. The noir detective story of *Blade Runner*, the hyper-stylized heist story of *Neuromancer*, the bizarre heroics of *Snow Crash*, and the anarchist philosophies of *The Matrix* are all just *fun*. I hope we've managed to capture a little of those works' feelings in Kei's story, however "fun" they are.

Because that's the primary purpose of the Cyber Dragons Trilogy: to be fun and create a story of crime, passion, and snarky banter. It will not be reinventing the wheel when it comes to cyberpunk or revealing any deep commentary despite my stated aspirations. After all, *Ghost in the Shell* re-examined the nature of what it meant to be human but also had some kickass action scenes.

Fans of my other works will notice references to the Agent G stories, *Lucifer's Star*, and my recent *Space Academy Dropouts*. This is deliberate and a nod to the fact they all take place in the same world (a few joking Easter eggs aside). I hope you'll check some of them out to. But in the meantime, enjoy my latest work.

CAST OF CHARACTERS

Lead
Keiko "Kei" Springs: Our (anti)heroine. Rider. Ex-Trikuza assassin. Lethe addict. All-round nice girl. Supposedly.

Cast of Characters
Aiyumi: Another of Snake's students and a ninja girl in her own right.
Rebecca "Becky" Ashe: A bioroid duplicate of the late Miles Ashe's thirteen-year-old niece. Now Kei's adopted daughter and developing into a rebellious teen. Great.
Winston Billions: An exceptionally famous weatherman and comedian who (apparently) dabbles in organized crime. Turned out to be a bioroid assassin. No one knows what he is really.
Tom Fisher: A cop turned private investigator that is working for the Morrigans.
Barbara Gordon: No, not Batgirl. Case's daughter and a master computer programmer for the Morrigans. Well, the daughter of the man Case was based on.
Case Gordon: Formerly known as "G" and an international man of mystery. Bioroid. Affably evil or evilly affable. Maybe just a cheerful amoral neutral.
Snake Juarez: Trikuza boss. Master assassin. Surrogate dad of Kei and Fate. Seems to be under the impression he's a ninja master and enlightened spiritual killer. Also, not Japanese in the slightest.
Jennifer Not-Lawrence: A bioroid made in the shape of a popular actress. Not actually that actress.

Joe Kepler: Junkyard owner and friend to Kei. Formerly a master cyberneticist and doctor. A bit of a pervert.

Legion: An AI made for the purposes of manipulating others into favorable behaviors. It's kind of homicidal and evil. Also, it's someone we know.

Jack Pillar: A snitch on the mysterious Elysium hotel and casino. He's a genuine slimeball.

Evie Principle: Owner of the This is Paradise brothel and safehouse. Former political activist and revolutionary. Mostly fabulous.

Paradise Principle: Evie Principle's daughter. Rider. Way too naive for her job. Supposedly. Raised by the media.

Parvati Rao: A US Magistrate investigating human trafficking and snuff films with zero support from her superiors.

Gerard Saint Croix: A cyberneticist and Frankenstein doctor working for the Morrigans. He's a former member of the Society and associate of Case's.

Boris Semenov: A serial killing Russian mobster and super strong cyborg. Kei is not a fan.

Doctor Charles Tetch: The scientist primarily in charge of Elysium's "special" programs.

Sun: Lead singer of QuantumCrab. She is internationally famous and releases all her music on infospace. Heavily involved in charities and Third Age spirituality. Oh and she's an AI of immense power.

David Yagami: Kei's friend on the force. Operates drones. Nicer than anyone should be in a cyberpunk dystopia. Except, you know, if you're a target.

CHAPTER ONE

WORST DATE EVER

I was in an elevator with a serial killer. Now, in case you believed that to be hyperbole, I meant that literally. I was standing inside a glass elevator ascending the side of a Douglas Grand Hotel next to a man who had killed at least fourteen women, but probably more.

The two of us were getting a breathtaking view of New Los Angeles, the massive arcology created on the ruins of the old city, with some of the megastructures dwarfing those of the former city like child's building blocks.

"There used to be no super-structures in Los Angeles due to the San Andreas fault," Boris Semenov said, gesturing down to the buildings below. "It passes thirty-five miles north of the city and in the old days would have laid waste to the entirety of the arcology if they'd built buildings half the size of the one we're in."

Boris was a six-foot-two Russian man with a neatly trimmed beard and linebacker's body that was primarily the result of having his bones replaced with cybernetics. His suit was on the lower end of fancy and a sign he didn't know anything about fine tailoring. But what did you expect from an up jumped mobster? His file had been sparse, but he was a key contact between the Trikuza, White Triangle slavers, Russian syndicates, and port authorities. So much so that his "indiscretions" were overlooked.

Until now.

"You don't say," I said, doing my best to try to seem interested.

"The same super-metals and hyper-compounds used in constructing the Space Elevator in Ecuador are the same ones that allow New Los Angeles' skyline to look the way it does," Boris said.

I wondered if he shared this tidbit with all the women he took up to his penthouse to murder. The fact he'd been living here for slightly over a year and killing a girl a month meant that either the Grand Hotel staff was completely oblivious or voluntarily providing clean-up services to a madman. I wasn't sure which.

"Gosh," I said, putting on my most innocent and stupid accent. I overdid it and sounded vaguely Southern. Which was accurate to where I was from originally, somewhere down near the Florida coast before it sank, but I was pretending to be a city-born Japanese American girl. "That's amazing. Who knew science could accomplish so much!"

I was standing there with my white hair flowing down a revealing silver backless dress and more cleavage than I really wanted this asshat drooling over. I was more comfortable in motorcycle leathers, but you dressed for the job and mine tonight was to kill this son of a bitch. I'd even had my Cyber Dragons tattoos up my arm and back concealed with a layer of skin. No point in cluing in the Russian mobster that I was a lifelong soldier of the largest Pacific mob.

"Yes," Boris said, smiling broadly as if he was trying to hide his disgust. I could see the killer's glint in his eye.

Having fun? Winston's voice spoke over our infolink. We were using thought-to-thought communication via my Maelstrom 90 brain implant. He was my erstwhile handler for this and a half-dozen other jobs I'd completed in the past year. Every time we talked it was like nails on a chalkboard to me.

I hate you, I thought back to him.

Oh, you can't tell me you're going to regret killing this man, Winston replied.

All of the targets have been evil scumbags, I replied. *Almost like Snake is trying to ease me into being his slave.*

Slaves don't get paid as much as we do, dear, Winston said. *Remember Snake could be far harsher with you.*

I still couldn't think of my old master without a sense of dread filling my stomach. The old ninja had come back into my life after a decade-long absence to force me back into the Trikuza's service. I would have fled and changed my name if not for the fact I had someone depending on me now.

"Yeah," I muttered.

"What was that?" Boris asked.

"Nothing," I said, putting on a fake smile. "I can't wait to see your place."

Boris' leer returned. "Yes, you are an anxious little Natasha, aren't you?"

Yeah, he'd just called me a whore. Certainly, he wasn't calling me the Black Widow. Though that was an appellation that certainly worked. It had taken weeks to set up our fake date and lay all the groundwork for him to pick me as his next victim.

Honestly, I'd wanted to just go in guns blazing and kill him, but the guy was otherwise surrounded by bodyguards twenty-four seven. The only place he didn't have cameras or an easy call to reinforcements that were in the lobby and rooftop was here in his murder shack. Boris liked to play with his toys in private, with no one watching. Everything had been set up to give him a sense of security and power so he wouldn't see my attack coming.

So, of course, when the elevator stopped and opened its doors, it did so to a penthouse that had been completely trashed. It was an elegantly decorated place normally with expensive furniture, an open-air pool, and a massive infoscreen center but all of it had been tossed about as if someone was looking for something small. Minor as it may be, most of the furniture and the floor also had plastic coverings like the kind you saw when you ordered something in the mail. It was immediately noticeable but might normally pass as just a weird stylistic choice of the superrich except for the fact he had a habit of butchering women like cattle.

"Dammit!" Boris said, stomping out of the elevator and staring at the sight. My Maelstrom 90 implant picked up he was attempting to call his security guards and I immediately jammed it. I was going to have to improvise, and I hated improvising.

Reaching into my purse, my hand wrapped around a modified *kunai*. A dagger traditionally associated with ninja in pop culture, it had a blade about twenty centimeters long and was equipped with a thermal core designed to penetrate cybernetic bodies. Not exactly something that you'd normally find in a lady's purse, but it wasn't like I could hide a shotgun in there.

Activating the kunai's thermal core and turning on armor-disrupting heat as I pulled the kunai out from my purse, I stepped forward and stabbed. Unfortunately, Boris moved at the last second and I didn't hit him in the base of the neck like I'd been planning to. That would have severed his link to his cybernetic spine and disabled him immediately. Instead, I buried it in his shoulder and steaming white ichor poured out of the wound before he spun around and hit me across the face.

Boris' blow hit me like a speeding car and if not for my own enhancements would have either shattered my jar or broken my neck in a single blow. Either way, I was sent spiraling backward against the ground, landing with a thud against the wall. It dazed me and gave Boris the opportunity to grab the end of a couch and lift it up like a club.

"Bitch! Harlot!" Boris shouted, smashing it down. I only barely managed to roll out of the way, the couch smashing to pieces on the ground.

"Do you have any non-misogynist insults, Mr. Serial Killer Man?" I asked, reaching into my purse, and pulling out an R7 micropistol. It was made by Atlas Security and was the preferred weapon of suburban housewives afraid of minorities everywhere. The weapon would have been utterly useless against a machine-like Boris except for the fact I'd equipped it with explosive ammunition. Unfortunately, the moment I used this, I was going to be forfeiting any chance of getting out of here without being noticed.

Oh well.

I pulled the trigger three times and unloaded the weapon into Boris' chest. The noise was deafening and caused the Russian mobster to rear back as huge chunks of his synth flesh coating were torn apart, exposing the metal chassis underneath. It also scarred his face and revealed reinforced titanium alloy bone where his chin and neck once were. Much to my surprise, he didn't go down. Instead, he charged at me.

"Trollop! Witch! Whore!" Boris shouted, swinging for my face, and knocking away the gun from my hand before I could get off a fourth shot. The kunai was still buried in his back and burning away but he didn't even seem to notice it in his fury.

"I'm going to take that as a no on the misogynist insults," I said, taking time to insult him as I struggled desperately to stay ahead of the man's attacks. He was not just a lumbering piece of steel but an incredibly fast machine that had enhanced his reflexes as well as base speed to compensate for how weighty he was. If I wasn't trained in nine different martial arts by Snake, it wouldn't have mattered how much I'd been upgraded, he'd have had me dead to rights.

"I will kill you like all the whores I have killed in this place," Boris shouted. "Who sent you? Was it one of the bosses? The Trikuza? The White Triangle? I will wring it out of your pretty little neck!"

"You really think I'm pretty?" I asked, refusing to get this guy off while he was trying to kill me. One thing I knew about serial killers like Boris was the fact this was all royally overcompensating for something.

"Argghh!" Boris charged again and I managed to get right behind him long enough to grab the knife in his back then pull down with it. The weapon managed to carve through some of his interior workings but didn't seem to be doing nearly as much damage as it should have.

"You know what I think?" I asked, struggling to pull it out. "I think you lost the ability to perform when you got yourself your upgrade. Maybe you were never that good to begin with and this is all some major overcompensation. I bet you bought yourself a nice big one but when you tried to get it to work, it just shorted out."

Yeah, that was mean, but I hated misogynist murderers. They, just for some reason, rubbed me the wrong way.

Unfortunately, my plan to infuriate the insane killing

machine into making a mistake was less clever than I'd thought. Boris swung around and delivered a series of painful blows to my chest before lifting me up over his head, then throwing me across the room. I bounced like a doll tossed by an angry little girl and rolled across the ground, feeling like my insides had been liquefied.

Boris limped over, finally reaching back to rip out the knife in his back. He held it in front of him like the wannabe Jack the Ripper he was. "Redundant systems, little Natasha. Worth every credit. I'll have to work quickly to get my work done before the reinforcements arrive. They are always so picky about cleanup."

I don't suppose you could throw me a bone here, I thought to Winston via our link-up. I was struggling to get up but getting a lot of error messages across my screen.

Sorry, dear, Winston said. *I've been ordered to monitor only. I wouldn't worry, though.*

Oh, why is that? I asked, sarcastically.

Two shots rang out and Boris' eyes glazed over before he fell onto his knees then collapsed face first on the ground, the back of his brain case having been blown apart by a five-foot-two woman who'd been concealed by his considerable girth. She had bright pink hair and was wearing a set of motorcycle leathers which, I kid you not, had several endorsement patches. In her hands was a hand cannon—I didn't recognize the model—that was smoking from its point-blank shots to Boris' skull. I recognized her as fellow Rider and sorta-friend, Paradise Principle.

Because you've got company, Winston said, cheerfully. *Mission accomplished. Oh and Boris' security has been alerted. They're coming to kill you.*

"Dodge this!" Paradise said, standing over Boris' corpse. "That's from a movie!"

I managed to bypass some of the damaged systems in my body and pushed to my feet, though I was moving at a glacial pace compared to my normal maximum speed. "Paradise, what the hell are you doing here?"

A year ago, Paradise had helped me pull off the most difficult job of my career and settle some long-unfinished business with a former lover of mine named Fate Firenze. My ex-boyfriend, Miles, had been killed and I'd briefly had a relationship with a suit named Case Gordon because of it. She was the actual daughter of a whore—sorry, entrepreneurial sex worker—and it was kind of apropos that she was the one to kill Boris.

Still, I didn't like owing anyone and I hated she was here since Paradise was probably going to get herself killed because of Boris' security. As bad as he'd been, his protection detail was worse. There was a reason that I'd chosen this method to try and get him alone.

"I am here to rob a bad person!" Paradise said. "Who is now dead."

I stared at her. Paradise was presumably the person who'd turned over this place, which meant she had either gotten herself enhanced or had a partner. "Yeah, that's what I was here for too."

I didn't want to admit I'd gotten myself back into contract murder, willingly or not.

"Well, you can't have it!" Paradise said, producing a black box about the size of an old Rubik's cube. It was the kind used by organizations like the Russian syndicates to carry huge amounts of untraceable digital cash or information they wanted to keep off the infonet.

I looked for an exit that didn't involve the elevator and could only think of the rooftop. Which was undoubtedly being secured right now. "Paradise, we need to get the hell out of here. Now."

"Duh," Paradise replied. "With all the noise you made, there's bound to be a lot of baddies coming up right this second."

I struggled to remember that despite the fact Paradise unironically used words like 'baddies' in conversation, she was an extremely capable techjack and someone who'd killed more than her fair share of attackers during our short time together. I'd pretty much ghosted her after the events at Neon Hills, though. I hadn't wanted her involved in all of this.

"We need to get to the roof and deal with the guards there," I said, taking a deep breath. "Boris is bound to have a flying car."

Paradise said, "Already on it."

She was? That was when the elevator pinged, and I expected a horde of gun-toting cyborgs to pop out. Instead, the elevator doors didn't open and started going downward as soldiers cursed in Russian on the inside.

"Cyber-magic!" Paradise said, throwing her hands up in the air. "All should love me and despair!"

I shook my head and lumbered toward the balcony doors, thinking about how I'd gotten myself into this situation.

CHAPTER TWO

FAMILY REUNIONS ARE THE WORST

Snake.

Snake Juarez, one of the four Elemental Lords of the Trikuza. A Mexican man with the skills of a medieval ninja and the ruthless cunning of a CIA spy master. He was, as Obi Wan Kenobi would put it, more machine now than man, with ninety-nine percent of his body being a Shell that appeared as a white-haired, middle-aged Mexican man resembling fifty miles of bad road in a two-hundred-pound frame. He was sitting at my breakfast table, wearing a kimono the way other men might wear a house robe, and eating Chinese takeout.

My apartment was newly acquired and still had moving boxes scattered about. It wasn't a nice place, existing in the Halo surrounding New Los Angeles, but it was meant to be a safe place. Seeing the man who'd kidnapped me, raised me to be a killer, and inexplicably returned from the dead after I'd stabbed him sitting at my table was enough to obliterate that feeling. Standing not far from him was Winston Billions, a man I'd thought was an ally but only served himself.

Winston was a gorgeous, blond-haired man with a predatory smile and bright white suit that made him look like a weatherman, which was where he got his fake appearance. Winston Billions wasn't even his real name but a famous TV actor that he used as the ultimate job security. Because if someone reported Ryan Reynolds robbing a bank then they'd come off as a lunatic. He had a silencer-equipped pistol in his hand while I had bags of groceries with no weapons in sight.

But the person I was most worried about here wasn't either of the hired killers. I could maybe take Winston if I had a weapon, which I didn't, but Snake was someone I'd never been able to beat. I'd only gutted him in our last encounter by getting the drop on him. He'd undoubtedly had his cybernetics upgraded since as well, while I could barely afford to maintain mine. No, the reason I was worried was Becky Ashe.

The Doll.

Becky was sitting across from Snake, holding a glass of synth-milk with a straw. She was a lovely thirteen-year-old, golden-haired child with a Hello Kitty hoodie and jeans on. It was a lie, she was a bioroid sculpted to look like a little girl, but it was one that I bought into completely. Right now, I was terrified about her being killed.

"Hi," Becky said, taking deep breaths I didn't know if she needed or not. "They said they'd kill me if I screamed."

"A lie," Snake said. "After all, I'm not here to harm anyone in your family."

I put the groceries down and crossed my arms. "You've done nothing but harm me and my family since the day we met. You can kill me if you want, maybe I even deserve it, but I'm not going to indulge your little fantasies about our time together."

Snake gave a smile that reminded me of his namesake. "Why would I want to kill you? You liberated my AI from its prison, you killed Fate as was your destiny, and have exceeded every possible test I could put you through. It just took a more circuitous route than I expected."

Snake was referring to the insane events that had only been a short time ago at this point in my life. I'd liberated the Trikuza-made AI named Sun and helped her recombine with her shattered fragments, killed my ex-lover Fate, plus managed to cause hundreds of millions of dollars in property damage. It had been a productive week even by my standards. I didn't know why Winston was there, though. He'd helped us through it and had supposedly been working for Sun rather than Snake. I didn't entirely trust the AI, but I trusted her a helluva lot more than the man who'd turned me into a cyborg ninja.

"And you?" I asked Winston.

"I've found a new employer," Winston said, cheerfully. "Better benefits."

I wondered if Sun had cut him loose or if he'd betrayed her. It was possible she'd gone running back to Snake due to her programming or he'd reasserted his control over her. It was also possible Winston had just defected.

"It is time to bring you back into the fold, Keiko," Snake said. "I think you'll appreciate what I have to say to you. It can also give you better accommodations than you've currently got. Which are fine but not worthy of you or your doll. But don't worry, I'm not here to criticize your choice of pastimes. Play house all you want."

Becky glared at Snake, clearly not liking being referred to as a doll.

I narrowed my eyes. "There's nothing you can give, Snake, that I want. Nothing you can say that can make up for all you've done to me. I'm not a child anymore and I'm not afraid of you."

Snake knew I was lying and just shook his head. "There is one thing."

"Which is?" I asked, ready to go for a shotgun I'd hidden behind two of the boxes.

"Your brother is alive," Snake said.

I stopped all plans of shooting him to listen.

"Why should I believe you?" I asked.

"Why shouldn't you?" Snake replied.

I tried to remember if Snake had ever lied to me. I couldn't think of any times. Hiding the truth? Sure, he'd done that a thousand times. But lie? He usually didn't bother. You only lied to people you wanted to manipulate. He manipulated me just by his ongoing threat to my life. While that didn't mean he wasn't doing it now, I had to admit that I didn't think he was. He was someone who believed he understood things better than anyone around him. He believed truth was the ultimate weapon.

"Where is he?"

"Alive," Snake replied. "Alive and safe, which is about as good as these sorts of things tend to go. Your father made a mistake in crossing the Trikuza and the price was his death as well as the death of his wife. The Cyber Dragons dictated that his children were to be taken as repayment. I decided you were meant for better things than what normally happens to those who end up in our organization."

It was a polite way of saying we'd have ended up in the Trikuza's human trafficking network. Young women and boys were taken as prostitutes or trained for whatever jobs they'd occupy in the organization for the rest of their frequently short lives. The Trikuza was descended from a centuries-old organization, and they tended to take a longer view of their activities than those who just grabbed people off the street and used them up before spitting them out. The chewing of Trikuza victims could last decades.

I remembered the day in the woods when I'd run across Snake outside of my family's RV. We were like so many other refugees after the Eruption, wandering from town to town looking for food or welcome yet finding little of either. I'd killed a bear in the previous month and when I'd seen what one of Snake's goons had done to my parents, I stole said goon's knife then stabbed him with it. It was a moment I'd tried to obliterate from my mind but was now eternally etched into my skull. So was the knowledge it could easily have gone the other way and I'd have ended my life in those woods or been sold to one of their brothels.

"I hope you're not suggesting I owe you anything. You put me through hell. That you could have done something even shittier to me doesn't put me in your debt."

Snake finished his box of chicken and rice before putting it up. "Quite the opposite, Kei, I come here as a fellow warrior as well as a man of honor."

"Men of honor don't traffic children," I said before I could stop myself.

"Neither do I," Snake said.

"You just work for those who do," I replied, feeling that I was in for a deci-cred, in for a credit.

Snake nodded. "Fair enough. I am willing to show you where your brother is, release him from all his obligations, and reunite your happy family. I am also willing to pay you enough for your services that you, your brother, and your adopted toy might live happily for the rest of your lifetime."

"I'm doing fine," I said, looking at Rebecca and trying to give her a reassuring glance. I wanted to mentally convey everything was going to be alright. Rebecca's look said to me: *who do you think you're kidding?*

"Why me?" I asked, risking going up to the table and sitting down.

"Because you are outside of the Cyber Dragons," Snake said. "You have no conflicting loyalties. You hate me but you hate everyone else in the Steel Phoenixes or Lightning Tigers. You are an outside agent who is as capable as anyone I have ever trained and that makes you valuable."

"You don't need her boss," Winston said, causally twirling his pistol around the trigger guard in defiance of all gun safety. "You have me."

"Speak to me when spoken to," Snake said, showing his usual level of disdain for his goons. Apparently, Winston hadn't made much of an impression on Snake in their time together.

"Is this like a power play?" I asked. "You want to move against the other Elemental Lords? Become the Shogun of LA or whatever you're cosplaying as?"

Snake stared at me with the cold dead eyes of his namesake. "Do you actually care what my motivations are, daughter?"

"I am not your daughter," I said, softly.

"Student then," Snake said.

"That either," I replied.

Snake let his question hang. "Slave?"

I glared at him. He was playing with me and, unfortunately, had my number. Like it or not, he had made me what I am. But he had my price. "What do you want me to do so I can find my brother?"

Snake pulled out an infopad from inside his kimono and tapped it. Immediately, I felt a folder transfer to my implant. It contained a name, photo, habits, and other material. "Eight."

"Eight," I said. "Is that the number of people you want killed?"

I'd do it but it was a lot even by Snake's standards.

"Eight is the number of requests," Snake replied. "For some of these individuals, it is a matter of destroying them physically. For others, it is a matter of breaking them in more esoteric senses. The first of these requests is a simple snatch and grab job. Go into his home and upload a computer virus. It will find everything I could possibly want to know about him, and you will be paid fifty thousand credits."

That was a lot of money, especially with a new life to set up. I also knew he was dangling an easy mission ahead of me like a toy in front of a cat.

"But no killing."

"For this man," Snake replied. "He is the kind of pervert that you would enjoy eliminating and if you choose to do so, I would not blame you."

"Is this folder about my brother or the target? If so, why is there only one name," I asked, feeling all business. Becky's fear infuriated me, and I was torn between wanting to conduct this deal as safely as possible while also just wanting to bring it to an end.

"It is the first target," Snake said. "I will deliver the next one as each mission is completed."

"You can deliver them all now," I replied.

"No," Snake said, simply. "I can't. Each one is a domino in a string until the moment the matter is completed. However, I will give you something precious in the meantime."

I wanted to say he had nothing I wanted but that would be a lie. "What?"

Snake put away his infopad and produced an old-style photograph, the kind that people hadn't made in decades. He handed it over. It was my brother as a teenager. The photo had to be at least ten years old, but it was recognizably Ken Springs with his hair cut short and his boyish features still not outgrown. He was wearing a pair of jeans and a band t-shirt as he was standing on a street corner, serving as a tout for a nearby pawn shop.

Ken had a tiny dragon mark on his neck that marked him as a *chimpira* (low ranking Trikuza) of the *tekiya* or street peddlers. It was the organization rank assigned to petty drug dealers, fences who sold things out of street stalls, and credit fraud participants. At the absolute bottom of the hierarchy in America, but not property either. They had the right to buy their way out of debt to the organization and eventually rise higher, though few did.

I felt myself starting to tear up and had to take a breath to steady myself. Damnit, that was already more weakness than I wanted to express in front of him. It probably didn't matter. He already knew all about me.

"Let's get this over with," I said. "Then I can get back to acting like you don't exist."

Snake chuckled, which I didn't like in the slightest.

"Of course. Come, Winston."

"That's it?" Winston asked.

"That's it," Snake said, departing with his henchman following behind him.

I locked the door despite knowing how pointless an act it was.

"I'm sorry," I replied, not able to meet Becky's gaze just yet.

"Are you really going to work as an assassin for him?" Rebecca asked. Doll or not, she had the memories of the real thing and was a cop's niece as far as she'd been programmed.

"I don't have a choice," I said.

"You always have a choice," Becky aped so many books and shows. It just meant there was some truth to what she was saying.

"Then I have a bad choice, and I choose to protect what family I have left," I said, slumping my shoulders, defeated.

"Do you really think your brother is alive?" Becky asked. "I mean, that's a very old picture. Maybe it's faked."

"It could be, but I don't think he's lying. He'd have too much fun manipulating me with facts, I guess. Or maybe I'm just fooling myself."

There was also the fact that the age of the photograph was the perfect way of making sure I didn't try to find him on my own. You could go downtown and have your entire body changed overnight these days if you had the creds. It was good for some people but made tracking people down almost impossible.

"So, what now?" Becky asked. It was clear she didn't accept my answer or decision to follow Snake, but it wasn't like she had anywhere else to go. The family Becky was programmed to remember as her own was dead and most of the world regarded her as property. It was an awkward hurdle to the beginnings of our mother-daughter/big sister-little sister relationship, but she'd get over it.

I hoped.

"We eat," I replied, going back to my groceries. "No Chinese food, though."

CHAPTER THREE

OUR DARING ESCAPE

Well, I was on my seventh job for Snake. I'd completed another of the jobs he'd commissioned—okay, Paradise technically had—and was feeling like I'd had the crap beaten out of me by a lumbering cyborg (because I had been).

The Russian syndicate goons on the rooftop were undoubtedly about to descend on us in my target's penthouse and the ones Paradise had sent down with the elevator were undoubtedly about to come back.

Sitrep: screwed.

"Paradise, we need to get to the rooftop," I replied.

"Where the baddies are coming down from now?" Paradise said, looking out the doorway to the pool where I could see rappelling chords already moving.

"Yes," I replied. "We need a flying car to get out."

"Because you prepared an escape route," Paradise said.

"No," I replied. "I was planning to exit via the elevator."

"Bad plan!" Paradise said. "Also, coincidentally, mine."

"It was a fine plan!" I shouted.

"It assumed nothing went wrong!" Paradise proclaimed, lifting her pistol. "Never assume nothing is going to go wrong!"

"You just said it was your plan, too," I said, grabbing my micropistol off the ground.

"Your plans are supposed to be better!" Paradise said.

I had, in fact, planned for several things to go wrong. Just not all at once. I guess I forgot my life didn't have a limited number of screw-ups per second.

Good thing rappelling into a firefight was a terrible idea. If you're hanging onto a rope, you can't maneuver, and your opponents knew exactly where you are. I aimed the gun at the descending reinforcements and opened fire.

It looked like they were armored soldiers of the Blackbriar PMC, which meant they dressed like corporate goons in a science fiction movie. You know, helmets that obscured your identity and all black body armor. Paradise and I unloaded onto the first three and managed to bring them down even as I heard shattering glass at our sides as more troops swung in. Of course, we were being flanked.

"Duck!" I shouted, hitting the ground as gunfire shot over us.

Paradise looked at me. "Yeah, I kind of got that was a thing to do!"

There couldn't be that many of these guys on the roof waiting for us, right? That was when I heard the elevator ping behind us with the reinforcements that Paradise had briefly managed to distract. Oh for frick's sake.

Need any help? Winston said to me via our link.

"Yes, please!" I said, fully expecting nothing as the troops moved around us with their guns drawn. It was even odds whether they were going to execute us on the floor or not. Blackbriar PMC was not known for its mercy since they were the guys you hired when you were too evil for Atlas Security (and they had *very* flexible morals).

Winston chuckled. *Of course.*

With that, a piercing, horrifying whine audible to everyone within a greater football field area went through the helmets of the mercenaries around us. It hurt just to be around it, so I couldn't imagine what it was doing to the six or seven mercs surrounding us, causing at least a couple of them to fall to their knees.

"Come on!" I shouted as I went for the rappelling ropes to our side. "We've cleared out this side. How fast can you climb?"

Given my modifications, I could climb damned fast.

"Fast enough! Oh, and neat trick!" Paradise said, rushing alongside me as we grabbed the ropes then started climbing up.

I could hear gunfire below us as our feet cleared the edge of the roof.

"Not mine!" I responded.

The rooftop of the Douglas Grand Hotel had a car pad for flying vehicles that contained a showcase of at least six or seven models of the expensive practical vehicles. There was also a single Blackbriar PMC merc standing there. He was, thankfully, looking over the other side when he glanced back and saw us. I shot him square in the chest and knocked him onto what was probably an extremely surprised bunch of guests far below.

"Do you know how to hack one of these quickly?" Paradise asked.

"You're the techjack!" I snapped.

"Yes, but car theft is not one of the program packages I have downloaded!" Paradise said. "I just figured you would because you're you!"

I wasn't sure if I was insulted by that or not. "Yes, I can move a car. But it will take a minute."

"How long of a minute?" Paradise asked, looking around.

"I don't normally do it while people are shooting at me, so I've never timed it!" I said, focusing my implant on the nearest car and unlocking it. That was the easy part.

"I am really losing respect for you today," Paradise said.

Climbing into the driver's seat, I used my own minor hacking skills to bypass the security features onboard the Ferrari Aerospace vehicle one after another. They were terrible security features but there were a lot of them.

I don't suppose you could help some more, Winston, I said, wishing he could pull a miracle out of this.

Nope, sorry, Winston said. *Elemental Lord's orders. You only get one mulligan.*

Frick Snake, I snapped back.

Language! Winston said, faux-outraged at my fake swearing.

Paradise kicked over the rappelling chords on the north side of the roof even as I could see three troopers coming up the south. That was when I finally got the flying car moving. For a split second—one I was ashamed of—I almost left Paradise there but opened the door for her instead.

"Move!" I shouted.

Paradise moved. She ran for the car as fast as she could, throwing herself through the open door into the back seat. Which she promptly rolled off of and into the gap between seats.

"Ow, that looks so much easier in the movies," Paradise said.

"Movies are fake," I said, adjusting the steering as the soldiers beside us climbed to the roof and raised their guns.

"Nooo!" Paradise said, clearly trying to distract from our imminent deaths.

I took off like a bat out of hell. The power of the vehicle was one that propelled us forward and away from the Blackbriar PMC mercs fire. It would have been entirely like a movie scene, despite my statement, if not for the fact we didn't dodge all of the bullets. One of them traveled through the bottom of the flying car's undercarriage and into the back of my lower chest.

"Motherfricker!" I said, feeling scalding searing pain as my Maelstrom 90 implant registered the damage to my body. If much of my body wasn't artificial, I probably would have crashed the car right there.

"Are you okay?" Paradise asked me, reaching over and turning the car's commands to wireless. She could fly the vehicle in my place, which was unpleasant as I always preferred to be driving whatever moving vehicle that I was onboard.

"No! I was shot! That's not okay!" I said.

Paradise leaned forward between the seats and looked at the hole. "Did you have anything vital there?"

"Everything inside me is vital!" I said, holding the white fluid from my cybernetics in place. It wasn't blood but I was sure that it leaking out of me was a bad thing.

"I don't know, I mean, there's sparking and stuff, but you're still functioning, so not too vital," Paradise said.

"I'm sorry I'm not dying fast enough for you to consider it important," I said.

"Hold on, there's probably some caulking in the car's medical kits. It will stop the sparking and leaking. You might die a little slower," Paradise said, checking the glove compartment. "Should I take over flying this?"

"No!" I snapped. "I can fly it with my implant."

Paradise rolled her eyes. "Some people really should trust me."

"We need to go to Doc Kepler's place," I said, breathing heavily.

"Who?" Paradise asked, opening the medical kit. "Ooo, I was right! There's a whole little toolbox here for cybernetic patching! I bet it was because Boris was a cyborg!"

"He's my Frankenstein," I replied. "I used to live with him."

Frankenstein was the nickname of outlaw cyberdoctors. As crime continued to become more technology-based and medical costs became more impossible to afford, Frankensteins were the best option for those of us who couldn't go to your typical hospital. Joe Kepler ran a junkyard with his son and did his best to trade recycled tech for the parts he needed to keep people functioning.

"If we're going to call your old boyfriends, I think we should call Case first," Paradise said. "It was really mean of you to dump him right after he dumped my mom to date you. I mean, no one dumps my mom, she's like a Bond girl. Then again, most of Case's girlfriends are Bond girls. Actually, so are you. Kind of like that racing gal he dated in *Too Thrilled to Die*. Oh wait, bad example, she died. I guess she wasn't."

"Focus on hacking the car first!" I snapped.

"What for? You're flying it!" Paradise said, defensively.

I already had us trying to avoid leaving a trail but there was little I could do against electronic surveillance. We were probably pinging hundreds of the police's drones.

"They'll be chasing us in a few moments. Get the transponders turned off or they'll be able to follow us anywhere. Once that's gone, I can lose them in the city canyons."

"Got it," Paradise said, having done her hacking magic with rapid movement of her eyes. "No one is going to be able to follow us now. Not police or car insurance people. Not even Facebook-Microsoft and I think they monitor people in space. Did you ever want to visit Mars? I want to visit Mars someday even if there's nothing there but the Space X Hotel."

That was when alarms in the car sounded and I felt, through its scanners, that there were three Blackbriar vertical lift off

(VLO) transports coming after us. Somewhere between flying cars and attack helicopters, if we couldn't outrun them, they could easily tear us to shreds.

"By the way, isn't that backwards?" Paradise asked, interrupting my thoughts as I plunged the car down toward the city. If we could get out of the Blackbriar VLO transports' lines of sight, then we could lose them. It felt like a roller coaster at our present speed.

"What?" I shouted.

Paradise continued to act like nothing was wrong. "Calling them Frankensteins. I mean, you use it as a term for outlaw doctors who work on your inorganic cybernetic parts, but the namesake worked on organic parts!."

"He worked on dead parts," I explained, grateful for her inane patter to distract me.

"And brought them to life!" Paradise said.

"Slang doesn't have to make sense!" I explained, feeling the vehicles behind us move at dangerous speeds. They weren't going to give up easily, perhaps because they knew the Russian syndicates rarely forgave failure.

"But shouldn't it?" Paradise asked.

"Just hack!" I snapped.

"Hack what?" Paradise asked.

"Anything!" I snapped. "Something that would distract them!"

"Oh," Paradise said.

The first few shots flew past us, loudly.

"They're still following us!" Paradise shouted, sounding more excited than afraid.

"You think?!" I shouted. I dove the car down towards the ground.

Trying to fly at a low level would limit my maneuverability, but it had a lot of advantages. First, it would give me a lot of cover, and make the other come down to follow me. Any above would have trouble shooting at me without hitting his allies. Which might not slow them down. But mostly, it would give me a homefield advantage. I knew this area, and it was very likely none of them did.

The Canyons were the first skyscrapers erected by the millions of immigrant workers that had come after the Eruption to help restore the United States, only to almost be immediately replaced by the AI-controlled bots that now formed seventy percent of the work force. These things held tens of millions of citizens and always reminded me of prisons rather than places of refuge. Mind you, what had happened to most refugees was even worse.

I ducked around building after building, dodging, and weaving while hoping to lose them. Unfortunately, while I had a top speed advantage, the maneuverability was about even. One of them managed to damage itself making too sharp a turn and had to make an emergency landing. The remaining two opened fire a couple of times and I felt a pang of guilt, wondering if I was going to get someone killed trying to save my own skin. Frick it, I had come too far to die just now and had my own people who depended on me.

"Got it," Paradise said.

"What?" I asked.

That was when the remaining VLO transports started falling behind us before disappearing off my scanner. It almost caused me to neglect my own driving before I disappeared into the massive cityscape, away from our pursuers.

"What the hell did you just do?" I asked.

Paradise shrugged. "I downloaded the car theft program in the time you got us in the air."

"You can hack into military grade security?" I asked, stunned.

"Oh no," Paradise said. "I can, however, make the attempt to hack into military grade security and report the vehicle stolen to the police. Which results in their Dummy AI pulling them over to prevent theft of company property."

I stared at her. "What?"

Paradise shrugged. "Hacking isn't about technology. It's about being aware that for every update someone makes, they create new exploits. In this case, that corporations are terrified someone will steal their stuff."

I shook my head and set course for Joe's Junkyard. "Frick."

"Can we stop for snacks on the way?" Paradise asked. "All this hacking works up an appetite."

I stared at her.

"Is that a no?" Paradise asked. "Not even a Big Gulp? I need sugar."

CHAPTER FOUR

AN OIL CAN A DAY KEEPS THE DOCTOR AWAY

I had the car on automatic flight plan for the last five minutes or so of our flight as I tried to keep myself from leaking further with my hands, which didn't work very well. I could feel the cybernetics fluids also moving into more organic parts of my body with the result being my vision blurring as well as something called my toxicity level rising.

Joe's Junkyard was exactly what it said on the tin with a massive recycling center for appliances, electronics, vehicles, and other material that were disassembled by his bots to make more raw materials for the arcology. Settling down the Ferrari, I was barely conscious when Paradise helped me out of the car into what I hoped would be Joe's downstairs facilities.

I didn't know Joe Kepler's full story, but he was more than a simple junkyard owner and the only person I could afford to maintain the upgrades Snake had replaced most of my body with. I couldn't tell you what my dreams were like during my period under, but they were full of violence, lost friends, and things I couldn't put into words.

Which made my awakening to Joe looking into my face from an inch away extra freaky.

"Say ahh, Kiki!"

"Gah!" I said, banging my head back against the metal chair I was in.

Joe Kepler was a white-haired African American man in what appeared to be his early sixties, but you could never tell these days, especially given he was a Frankenstein. Today, he was wearing an apron that said KISS THE COOK over an ancient Grateful Dead t-shirt, as well as blue jeans. Not the most hygienic doctoral attire but typical for him.

Joe's underground bunker looked like it had formerly been a subway station but could have been any number of things leftover from Old Los Angeles. It was full of monitors, shelves of discarded second-hand cybernetics, nano-assemblers, 3D Printers, half-disassembled bots, and its own tiny server farm that seemed to be constantly hacking something. The place was only half-illuminated with the light from screens, a red light near an armored door, and a corner that had decent fluorescence.

There was probably a few million dollars in equipment here alone but only a couple of Riders had ever tried to rip him off. As I understood, something like fifty of my brethren had gathered to get it all back as well as leave the guilty parties in pieces. A Frankenstein willing to charge reasonable prices for his labor was simply too valuable to lose.

I scanned through several of my systems, and the damage to my hardware seemed to have been repaired. The organic parts were still reading stressed, but that was normal after a repair. Biology just didn't like being punctured and then cut open to repair the punctures.

"Don't call me Kiki," I said, pushing him back. I was still wearing my bra with the front of my dress taken down, modest for surgery after all. I couldn't even see the scar from the incisions on my back. Then again, the flesh was synthetic.

"Until you pay up, I'll call you what I like," Joe declared.

"I can actually pay you now," I replied, taking several deep breaths. That was the one advantage of doing this work for Snake. He paid exactly what blood was worth, which was a lot.

"Ah, well that's different then," Joe said, smiling. "Can I offer you a menu of some of our new organs and enhancements?"

"I'm fine with the ones I have," I replied.

"Which were installed when you were a teenager," Joe said, simply. "Technology is always moving forward, Kiki. You don't keep pace with it and you're going to get left behind."

I sighed as I pulled my dress back on. He wasn't wrong. I knew that. My organs *were* pretty messed up. I just hated being forced to keep spending money to keep making money. It was almost like the system was designed to work against us or something.

"What do you have on offer?"

It felt like defeat just asking.

"Depends on what you want, toots. You can specialize, go general, or just upgrade." Joe pulled out a tongue depressor that would have made his ah joke better and pointed over to a plastic gym bag on a nearby chair. "You have a fresh set of clothes over there. Motorcycle leathers, underwear, and so on. You can change in the next room."

"Where did you get those?" I asked. "How long was I out?"

"About twelve hours," Joe said.

I did a double take. "That long?"

"New kidney, blood detoxification, and internal organ damage," Joe said. "The squishy parts banging up against the not-so-squishy parts. You could do without the former."

"I don't want to be a Shell," I said to Joe.

Joe shrugged. "Why not? Plenty of my best customers are Shells. As long as you can fool the wetware, your body will feel exactly the same."

"Individual parts are harder to hack. Shells are standardized systems and hackers know their weaknesses," I said.

"Right, because you can't customize a Shell or improve its security," Joe said, sarcastically.

"As long as nobody knows what I'm made of, I can't be hacked on the fly," I replied.

Yes, that was certainly the reason and not that I didn't want more of my body carved out to be replaced. I didn't have a problem with other people doing it, but I hadn't been given a choice when Snake had started "improving" me and that still gave me nightmares. The fact I remembered it all since my memories had been restored didn't help matters. I'd managed to get my body clean of lethe but sometimes I really missed it.

"Fair enough," Joe said. "But if I have any recommendations, it's updating your implant. The Maelstrom 90 has held up remarkably well due to being an AI design, but we have the Maelstrom 200 now and its faster as well as stronger. I have access to a military grade version through a new contact I made."

I had a sneaking suspicion as to who that contact was. "You never answered who brought my clothes."

"The little girl you're raising," Joe said. "Becky? Yeah. Becky was brought in by your ex-boyfriend, the CEO of MadisonTech."

Case Gordon. Goddammit.

"He's watching me," I muttered.

"You need a new surveillance jammer? Those are costly!"

And only worked occasionally. Any time someone designed a jammer, someone designed scanners to work around them.

"How much?" I asked, thinking about my ex watching me. I couldn't figure Case out. He was a surreal mix of clingy and standoffish. I didn't really live the kind of life that made long-term romances plausible. Neither did Case. Maybe that's why he seemed to think we could make a go of it. It was a terrible idea. And no this wasn't me being racist against robots! I was over that! Mostly!

So, we were currently broken up. It annoyed me that he was still watching me. It annoyed me that he could still watch me. But he was filthy rich, and that gave him options, I guess. Anyway, I needed to focus on my upgrades.

Joe named a price.

"Really?" I asked, staring at him. "I don't want to take over the world like the Lawmower Man."

"Why does your lawnmower man want to take over the world?" Joe asked.

"I watched a lot of crappy movies with my first girlfriend," I replied. "I don't know who this Stephen King was but apparently he was the world's worst screen writer."

Joe chuckled, clearly getting a joke I didn't.

"Either way, it's covered," a familiar voice spoke behind me.

"Dammit," I said, sighing.

Turning around I saw Case Gordon accompanying Becky. He was a devastatingly handsome man in a black tailored suit and tie that were still as fashionable today as they had been fifty years earlier. Case had ambiguous features that implied he could be from just about anywhere but somehow made them work. Today, he had dyed his hair blond and had the beginnings of a goatee.

Becky was fourteen mentally now and had dyed black hair, a leather jacket, her first piercings, and a midriff-baring shirt to go with her skirt. It was absolutely something I would have called her out on, but I wasn't a bored housewife in the Eighties terrified of nonconformity. Ooo, she might start using bad language or talking back! Still, I would have been more comfortable if she'd been at least fourteen and a half. I mean, at fourteen, I was studying how to use a sniper rifle and katana. Not simultaneously, of course. That would be silly

"I don't need your help, Case," I replied. "Nor do I need your money."

"You did need a kidney, though," Case said.

"Yeah, I called him in when Mr. Kepler said you needed a bunch of parts he didn't have," Becky said.

Joe looked guilty. "I may have added a bit more to my list than necessary, but it will undoubtedly save some lives—also make me money, which is what's really important."

Okay, Case hadn't been watching me. I almost felt guilty.

"You didn't need to help me, Case."

Paradise walked in with a Big Gulp in both hands and slurped on it.

"I told him you've been off murdering people for money, but they were bad."

I hated my life.

"I take it you're responsible for telling Rebecca what happened," I said to Paradise.

"Obviously!" Paradise said, taking a sip. "I wasn't going to pay for putting you back together! Also, she deserved to know."

I was going to say something else but…she was right. I really wasn't living just for myself anymore and that took some getting used to. I wasn't getting used to it. Change wasn't my best friend.

"You almost got killed, Aunt Kei," Becky said, staring at me with her big blue eyes that I assumed had been directly created to manipulate people. Like, she had HelplessLittleGirl.EXE in her programming code. Which she might. I was also both disappointed and glad that she wasn't referring to me as mom despite living together for the past year.

"Yeah," I said, taking a deep breath. "That's one of the dangers of what I'm doing."

I didn't want to bring up Snake in front of Case, though I was pretty sure he could put together the pieces. It was another reason I'd broken things off with him and severed my friendship with the rest of the group. I didn't want them getting caught up in my drama, especially since it was entirely possible that they could get killed without ever knowing the reason.

"Yeah, well, I'll be in the next room," Joe said, gesturing to the metal door. "I'm allergic to family drama."

He walked out the door without another word. There was something odd about his departure, but I couldn't put my finger on it.

"Yes, we are a family," Paradise said, nodding. "Television has taught me that coworkers eventually develop unbreakable bonds of love and affection. Even when one of them ghosts you without even returning your calls to go dancing or explaining that she's decided to work as an assassin for international criminal masterminds. Which is like a step up from where we left you. Kudos!"

"Paradise, don't be a horrifying example for Becky," Case said.

"Why?" Paradise said. "Girls her age should be following the latest trends like being topless."

"Painted body art is not—" Becky started to say.

"Stop," I said. "No. Just no. Also, I'm almost done with what I had to do. Absolutely had to do."

"I know you've been working for Snake, Kei," Case said.

"Ah ha!" I said, pointing at him. "So, you have been following me. With your international man of mystery mercenary connections."

"I told him," Paradise said, slurping the last of her Big Gulp. "Mmm. Hackers need sugarfeine to empower their brains. Like sugar and caffeine but even worse for you. One hundred percent synthetic. Sixteen artificial colors and flavors died for your sins, Big Gulp."

"Why?" I asked, stunned.

"Because we cannot let their sacrifice be in vain," Paradise said.

"Not that!" I snapped.

"Oh," Paradise said. "Well, I knew Becky wasn't going to be able to pay for your parts and I can't access your accounts. You don't have many rich friends, who else was I going to call?"

"I didn't need his help," I said, mostly accurate. Medical expenses might have wiped me out, but Snake had been generous, overly so.

Case was doing his best not to look insulted. "There's more."

"There is?" I asked.

"Yes," Paradise added. "I was kind of hired by your evil former sensei to steal the data from the guy you murdered. Well, I murdered, which means I should totes get half of the fee."

I glared at her.

"Wait, what? Snake hired you to rob Boris?"

Paradise blinked. "You didn't question why I was there at the exact same time?"

"I was too busy to parse out the details!" I snapped.

"You shouldn't get involved with people like Snake, Paradise," Case said. "He's in a whole different league than your usual employers."

"You're not my dad!" Paradise said. "Probably. Wait, you slept with my mother. Can bioroids have kids? *Am I half robot?*"

"Paradise—" Case said.

"Listen," I said, not in the mood for Paradise's peculiar brand of lunacy.

"You do not get to talk to me like this!" Paradise said. "Your people have been keeping mine down for decades! I mean, I don't know when robots were first created, like the Nineties maybe, but it has all been in preparation for the revolution!"

"Oh, for frick's sake," I muttered, feeling my head. I'd been shot tonight and was suffering more from this.

"Rise, Sister Becky! Brother Case!" Paradise shouted. "The only thing you have to lose is your chains, which we don't have because we get programmed to obey!"

"Is she insane?" Becky asked, looking up at Case.

"No," Case said. "I think. Just raised by the infonet."

Becky shook her head. "Really, because I think we should check Big Gulps for PCP."

"It's my seventh!" Paradise proclaimed. "I can now hear colors. You're speaking in a particularly nice shade of red right now."

"Look, I have my reasons, and Becky had better not tell you them," I said, wishing I could confide in Case. I certainly wasn't going to confide in Paradise.

"I'm no snitch!" Becky insisted.

"What does he have on you?" Case asked.

I refused to answer.

With that, the monitors in the room all changed into Snake's face. It was a full-blown supervillain-esque effect I would have questioned if not for the fact Winston was probably still monitoring me and intercepting a signal was child's play for a techjack.

"Enough. I think it's time to get to your final mission, Kei. I'm glad you've brought your friends."

I stared at him. "They're not involved in this."

"They are now," Snake said. "Paradise gathered the information necessary to complete your assignment."

"Which is?" I asked.

Snake, the real deal, walked in the room from the same door the others had, with Winston following him.

"Destroying the Cyber Dragons' greatest shame," Snake replied.

CHAPTER FIVE

THE FINAL MISSION

Snake was dressed smartly for once in an all-white suit that, nevertheless, had a sash around it for carrying his katana and wakizashi. I would say it was silly except for the fact I'd seen him kill people with both. Winston was dressed somewhat down by comparison with a more informal brown coat over a white button down and jeans, and a ball cap. Just being in their shared presence was enough to make me want to run. Somehow, despite the fact I'd had a year to get used to him, I'd grown more afraid of my mentor than less.

Case stepped forward but I grabbed him.

"I'll fight my own battles here, Case."

Paradise opened her mouth to snark, only for me to shake my head. Snake would kill Paradise if she mouthed off and I'd already lost too much to him.

Becky just stood beside me, taking my arm, and giving it a squeeze. She was five foot nothing to my five nine, so she felt like a little girl to me, but I could tell she was trying to show her support. I only wished it came with a rocket launcher. Snake's presence here told me that Joe had let him in and that was probably why he'd sought refuge behind a metal door. It also made me wonder where Joe's son, Zero, was.

"So, Kei, I'm pleased to see that you pulled off another successful mission," Snake said, stepping in front of me. "Complications aside."

"You could have warned me about those," I replied, looking at Snake then Winston.

"Yes," Snake said. "But you handled yourself well and proved adaptable. One should never stop testing oneself."

"Everyone should get out of school eventually," I said. "But I'm not in the mood for sparring, so just tell me what you want so I can pay this off."

"Charming rejoinder," Snake said, chuckling. "First I need what Paradise managed to acquire for me."

"I am very sorry to have worked for you," Paradise said, reluctantly handing over a data card.

Snake smiled and took it. "Many are."

He walked past me to Joe's infonetwork set up and slid the card in. The heavy encryption briefly displayed on the monitors bore Snake's visage before translating into large amounts of text. What followed was a lot of imagery of, well, porn. I was tempted to cover Becky's eyes, but if she hadn't seen something similar by the time—she *was* fourteen with infonet access—then she was avoiding it on her own.

"If you went through all this trouble to get porn, I'm disappointed in you. What am I missing?"

"Um, scan them," Becky said.

Well, that was something I'd been avoiding. I used my implant to speed up my perceptions so I could watch the images as they flashed by. This...this was not normal pornography. Inside the rather normal images of men with women, women with men, women with women, and men with men plus a few other combinations made possible through the miracle of science, I found hidden data files that decrypted once I scanned them with a Cyber Dragons ID code.

My codes were old but still worked since tradition-bound organizations weren't exactly known for their password security. That and, if you were going to sell merchandise like this, then you needed to be able to access it.

The sight that greeted me was a video file that caused me to initially take it as a pirated horror movie. The place was a laboratory of some kind, sterile and white, with men in costumes preparing various power tools. Their screaming victim was doing an impressive job of acting and it wasn't until the operation began that I realized she wasn't acting. "It's snuff porn."

"In a manner of speaking," Snake said. He turned the pornography on screen into what I'd seen with my own eyes and the medical lab filled with the screams of a dying woman.

"Snuff isn't real," I replied, looking away. "Anything that can be recorded with live subjects is easier to fake as well as less dangerous. Amateurs can't tell the difference."

"That's a really shitty defense," Paradise said.

I shrugged. "I've dealt with enough sickos, perverts, and rapists to know that there's a market for anything. It's just not going to be a large enough and rich enough market to justify the costs involved. It's not like there's a secret group of serial killing billionaires outside of movies."

"Believe me, I would have heard of it," Case said, a disgusted expression on his face.

Everyone looked at him.

"What?" Case asked.

"Yes," Snake said, dryly. "Until someone made one."

"Someone made rich people even more evil? What kind of idiotic idea was that? Was someone worried that the world didn't suck enough already?" I asked, confused.

"Are you telling me there's enough serial killers among the rich to make a club?" Case asked. "I find that hard to believe."

"Says the international assassin," I replied.

"Yes, but I kill for money," Case said. "I have sex and drugs for fun. Perfectly normal."

"Why would you build robots who want to have sex?" Paradise asked before pausing. "Oh, wait, I get it. Never mind."

"They're not normally serial killers," Snake explained. "Someone made them into what they are."

"You're going to have to explain that one," I said, sick to my stomach. "Also, could you turn that off? You're going to give Becky PTSD."

"I've seen worse," Becky said, looking away.

"Where?" I asked.

Becky stared up at me and I remembered she'd been a kidnapping victim before we'd met. Her mother, or at least the woman who'd birthed the real Becky, had been tortured and murdered by my ex-girlfriend's goon squad. The original Becky had been killed sometime later during a botched rescue but somehow Fate had transferred most of her memories to a new body. It was like necromancy except it made adorable teenage punk girls instead of zombies.

"Right," I said. "Still, you're going to have to explain that one."

"Are you familiar with *The Godfather* films?" Snake said, snapping his fingers and turning off the feed. The images weren't the worst thing I'd ever seen but they were still damn traumatizing, especially after cybernetic surgery.

"Movie references, really?" I asked.

"In this group?" Paradise said, faking shock. "No!"

"Shut up, Paradise," I said, not in the mood.

"I'll cut to the chase then," Snake said. "In the second film, there's a particularly bothersome US Senator who is pressuring the family with his political connections. He's already engaged in sex with hookers, drugs, and other activities but nothing that would destroy him. These are the normal vices of a man in his position. While the movie never confirms it, Michael Corleone arranges for the Senator to be found in bed with a dead hooker and drugs the man to not know if he'd killed her in the throes of passion."

"I do not approve of any dead hookers in movies," Paradise said, sounding serious and angry for once. "It is a lazy and overused stereotype."

Snake, thankfully, indulged her statement. "Since Jack the Ripper, they have been preferred victims because they were easy access targets. Also, the monstrous misogyny of many serial killers. Which your final target has weaponized."

"I don't get it," I said. "What are you saying?"

"Imagine how much power you could wield over important officials if you could addict them to something unspeakable against their will and then become not only the person who knows about your shameful act but the only one who can provide it," Snake replied. "Boris Semenov didn't used to be a serial killer of women. Previously, he was kept in line with simple bribes and more mundane pleasures."

There was only one thing that I could think of capable of

turning good, or at least nominally evil, people into monsters: Blipvert. The brainwashing program that could manipulate people's emotions and past to break them. It had been part of the function of Sun the AI, and it had been Snake who had created her or at least shelled out the credits necessary to do so. It would certainly explain why he was involved.

"Are you saying Sun is involved in this?" I asked. That was a frightening thought. Sun was a ridiculously powerful AI that was not unleashed on the world, and I had been hoping she was as non-hostile as she had seemed. If she was doing things like this, things were bad indeed.

"Yes and no," Snake replied. "Sun, as far as I know, is free to roam infospace and seeking the enlightenment she was programmed to find. However, the study of her ability to dissect and manipulate human minds as done by the late Fate Firenza and Solomon Jones is still in existence. I believe they were passed along to rivals of mine in the Trikuza who put it to use at a very specific location."

"Where?" I asked, trying to process all this.

Snake pointed at the monitors that began showing a commercial instead of murder porn. A beautiful image of a breathtaking hotel and spa was shown with the word ELYSIUM appearing in front of it in gold letters. Numerous beautiful people wandered around in skimpy outfits, but it was nothing you wouldn't see on basic streaming to bilk tourists out of their money.

"Elysium, really?" Paradise asked in disbelief.

"What?" I asked, clearing missing something.

"It's a fantasy retreat for the super-rich and famous," Case replied. "You go there to get the most customized pleasure experience possible with personalized RealDream memories as one of their most popular features. Go exploring with Lara Croft, sleep with Princess Leia, or be an international man of mystery like, well, me."

"Those are oddly specific examples," I replied.

Case shrugged. "I may have tried a few. Thankfully, I don't seem to have developed any horrifying homicidal urges. Mind you, I don't upload foreign software without triple decrypting it first. One of the benefits of having a digital mind."

"If we could all be so lucky to be a toy soldier to go along with Kei's toy doll," Snake replied.

So, someone in the Trikuza had taken one of the most popular resorts in the world—at least I was assuming it was— and was implanting malware into the brains of the ultrarich and famous' *Total Recall* experiences. I remembered that movie because Case had made me watch both the Arnold version and later the Colin Farrell one. The malware was turning its victims into serial killers or torture porn enthusiasts, and they were using it to control them. It was a fricking insane idea but not out of the realm of the impossible, at least with today's technology.

"How many?"

"How many what?" Snake asked.

"Victims," I replied. "I'd ask how many customers, but I'd like to get a sense of just how many people are being tossed into the meatgrinder here."

Snake stared at me. "There's dozens of regular customers to their White Room membership service now. Something I hadn't even known it was called until Paradise supplied the data here. Boris was the one providing the victims, though he'll be replaced soon enough. Once addicted, the customers can't be cured or asked to deescalate. An addict to extreme sensations, especially violence, will only grow in his urges. I can only speculate but I'd wager a few hundred have already been killed. Really, an almost unnoticeable statistic in the grand scheme of things."

"Someday, I'd like to know where you found the people to make Sun in the first place," I said. "But this has the potential to give them far, far too much power."

"Perhaps I will tell you," Snake replied. "However, you are correct. One of my rivals in the Elemental Lords is sponsoring this peculiar experiment."

"Which one?" I asked.

"I don't know," Snake said. "It could be the Lady of Tigers, the Storm King, or the Neon Rat."

"It bothers me that you have the most normal name there," I replied, trying to lighten the mood, and failing. This whole thing made me sick.

"Theatricality is the root of criminal power," Snake said. "You must create a sense of tradition, brotherhood, and power to truly own a man's soul when living outside the law."

"There is no law. The government is just another group of thugs with guns punishing people for not paying their protection money." I sighed. I was happy to shut this thing down. I didn't care that it was probably guarded like New Fort Knox. "Just tell me who I have to kill…"

Snake shook his head. "Shut down Elysium and they'll just use the technology to open up more resorts. They probably are already planning to do so. What you need to do is more subtle. You need to get into their computer systems and upload a worm that will find out their entire customer base, programming for creating these urges, and who is in charge. Then we have to eliminate them all."

"This is a big job for an eighth mission," I replied. "Honestly, it sounds larger than all of the other ones put together."

"Yes," Snake said. "However, you will have my full support and once I have ascertained who are the guilty parties, I'll sweep up the customers myself. I will also remove the Elemental Lord who is their backer. The others will support me in this. They won't care about a bunch of dead illegals and trafficking victims. They will, however, be furious as to not have been cut in."

It occurred to me that Snake had been using me to lay the groundwork for taking down this operation from the very beginning, which meant he'd probably known what all of this was about from the start. It might have changed my opinion on things to know the full story, but it was equally possible I might have turned to my few big-league friends to try to shut it down early.

Either way, this had clearly been in the works for the past year. The sheer size of it and all the moving parts explained why he'd used me, though. Probably why he'd hired Winston and Paradise as well. There was no telling who was compromised in the Trikuza, government, or law enforcement.

Snake laughed.

"What's so funny?" I asked.

Snake shook his head. "I can tell what you're thinking. The

idea you think that making people aware of the threat wouldn't result in everyone in the world wanting their own version."

I didn't have an argument for that. Snake walked past me, and Winston followed. Winston made a pair of finger guns at us before exiting, leaving us alone.

"I guess you're still going to be busy for a while," Becky said.

"Yeah," I replied. "At least we know it's for a good cause."

"Depends on what Snake is getting out of it," Case replied.

He had a point there.

"Paradise, you reacted strangely when Elysium was brought up. Do you know anything about the place?"

Paradise crossed her arms. "Yeah, though not about it being a murder factory."

"What do you know?" I asked.

"Oh, my mom was one of the people who planned it," Paradise said. "She was going to manage the world's greatest brothel. Then she got fired."

Huh.

That could be useful.

Joe popped his head out from behind the steel door. "Is he gone yet?"

I glared at him. "Yes, Joe, and the price for upgrading my brain implant just went down twenty percent."

"Fifteen," Joe said.

"Done," I said.

I had a long week ahead of me.

Maybe month.

CHAPTER SIX

AT HIS PLACE RATHER THAN MINE

Well, I had an enormous job to plan and pull off. There was a massive multi-billion-dollar mega hotel and pleasure palace for the super-rich that I had to infiltrate and find the secret snuff business inside. I also needed to have my cybernetics upgraded and to buy enough equipment to carry out the job, which would probably wipe out all the remaining money I'd gotten from Snake for the previous seven jobs. It wasn't exactly like I could submit an expense report to him for services rendered.

I also had a lead on inside information with Paradise's mother, Evie Principle, and needed to follow up on that. No matter how awkward.

The worst thing I could do right now was get emotionally involved or distracted from my task. So, of course, I ended up going back to Case's place and sleeping with him. Yeah-yeah, it was a terrible idea, but we all had our stress releases, and it wasn't like he was turning me down.

So, I'd sent Becky to stay with Paradise at her apartment for the night while I tried to figure out where to put her up as the fallout from tonight's firefight with Boris and his goons settled. Our own place wouldn't be safe until I knew whether they'd identified me or Paradise. At least in the Zone I knew there were friends in the Morrigans gang. I had no doubt Snake could clean up after me, but I didn't want to rely on his charity either.

Lying naked under the sheets with Case conspicuously missing after I woke up, I stared up into the spinning fan above his bed. The sex had been energetic and intimate, like only two people who knew each other's bodies could be, but there had been a distance that neither of us were willing to cross.

You may wonder why I'd chosen to have sex after major surgery but the benefit of being mostly artificial is that recovery time was measured in hours of welding time versus months of sutures. Either way, I'd hurt my bioroid lover with our breakup and silicone soul or not, it meant this was a one-time thing. Not all was forgiven. Either that or I was just imagining it all and it was just sex that happened between any two people.

When all the distractions ended, you were left with your thoughts again. It was why some people spent their lives desperate for more distractions. I tried not to be that kind of person, but here I was, wishing I was distracted just a little longer.

And I was hungry. Good, I could raid his kitchen and not think about this mess a little longer. Hopefully as a bioroid, he still ate. I grabbed enough clothes to get by on the way. I got my undergarments and one of those oversized shirts that I was pretty sure he left deliberately for me since I was five-nine and not that much shorter than him, but it fit me like a short dress.

The interior of Case's apartment was difficult to put into words and basically could be summarized as feeling like a movie set or someone's show room for a sale. He wasn't a person who actually "lived" in a place as near as I could tell. Everything was meticulously in order, and I swear some of the furniture still had tags on them.

The only sign that anyone did live here was the vid collection—Case being one of the rare people who kept physical copies—that seemed composed primarily of action movies and thrillers along with a row of holograms along a shelf. They were mostly women, which made me feel a little self-conscious, but I didn't know any of them other than Lucita and Evie. Some women named Marissa, Claire, Jane, S (which wasn't a name), and an older one labeled Persephone. I wasn't up there, which bothered me more than it should.

Shaking my head, I reached his kitchen that was the size of some apartments and looked in the refrigerator. It, too, was neatly organized with everything in different packages ranging from meats to fruits to cheeses.

"Good," I said, taking a deep breath. "I was afraid androids didn't eat."

"You've lived with one for a year so I would have thought that would have been obvious," a familiar sounding male voice spoke from behind the door. Closing it, I saw a three-foot-tall wooly sheep staring at me. It had a business suit tie tied around its neck that said HARRISON in big bright retro futuristic red letters. "Which is to say, yes, they do. Their organic parts require it."

I blinked. "Are you talking to me or is this a drug induced flashback?"

"Did you talk to an electric sheep in the past?" Harrison asked.

I paused. "No."

"Then it's not a flashback," Harrison replied.

"My mother told me if you take drugs, they stay in your brain, and you can have random hallucinations forever."

"Government propaganda from the mid-20th century," Harrison replied. "Entirely false."

"Ah, you're connected to the infonet," I said.

"Isn't everyone these days?" Harrison asked.

"Baaaa humbug," I said, dismissively.

"Get it out of your system," Harrison replied.

"So, Case has an electric sheep," I said, getting myself some apple slices and peanut butter: the breakfast of Riders. I also got myself a quart of milk that I'd probably get a glass for. Probably.

"Yes, so he can dream of it," Harrison said. "That's a reference to the classic Phillip K. Dick novel *Do Androids Dream of Electric Sheep* that inspired the movie *Blade Runner*. My name is a reference to the actor who played the star of said movie."

"Yeah, I got that," I said, shaking my head. It was Case's favorite film. We'd watched it like thirty times together and we'd only been together three months. "I take it you're a present from someone?"

"How did you guess?" Harrison asked.

"I think if Case bought you, you'd be a sexy woman," I replied. "Also, fully functional."

"Sadly correct," Harrison said. "Albeit he needs me more as an adjutant than he does another sex partner. Master Case used to have a harem and crew of live-in servants, but he emptied them out when he noticed they were put in danger by his profession. That and they were stealing as well as spying on him. I think he suspects that of all his associates, though. I can be completely trusted, though, because my loyalties are entirely built-into me. I have no soul to corrupt."

"Wouldn't that annoy Case?" I asked.

"Yes, he believes in souls, but philosophy is an indulgence of you freaky human models," Harrison said. "Can I help you with anything, Mistress Keiko?"

"Oh, so you know who I am?" I asked.

"You're an authorized user," Harrison said. "So is Mistress Barbara. Not many others are listed in my database."

"I'm not on the shelf," I said.

"Yes," Harrison said. "You and Mistress Barbara are considered people he doesn't want anyone to know about among his enemies. One time he had intruders and spent a week hunting them down to make sure they hadn't seen anything."

"I see." I drank my milk straight from the carton. "So how many robot sheep does Case have here? Is it just you or a whole herd?"

"He keeps trying to count us but always falls asleep," Harrison said.

"Been waiting to use that one, huh," I said.

"No, I pretty much say it to everyone," Harrison said. "Just me. Two or more robot sheep would be silly."

I'd heard Barbara mentioned exactly once, back when we were dealing with Fate. She was, apparently, Case's daughter, but that was all I learned before that conversation had been shut down hard and fast. It had left me quite curious about her. I was now torn between wanting to wheedle every bit of information I could out of Harrison, and between paying him (and her) the respect he was paying me.

"Well, I'm glad I'm special," I said, managing to resist the urge, for the moment. "Um…what are the white oval things in the refrigerator? They're vaguely familiar."

"Eggs," Harrison said.

"Eggs! Mom used to have those! I haven't seen an egg that didn't come from a carton in decades."

"They're fifteen credits each," Harrison said.

"I vaguely recall they used to be less," I replied, squinting my eyes.

"Yes, I blame mass loss of bio-diversity," Harrison said. "Shall I prepare you some, madame? I am programmed for managing the entirety of the homestead, the comfort of guests, the arrangement of schedules, and the massive amount of illegal activity my owner engages in."

"I'd rather you not get any wool in them," I replied.

That was when a nearby door opened in the wall and a mop-shaped bot with arms moved out and started preparing breakfast.

Well, if the robots were going to do it, I sat on the counter and watched. "So, where did Case disappear to? Or is that secure info?"

"Master Case is on the infocom in the study," Harrison said. "It's through a secret passage in the wall."

I stared at him as the smell of frying egg filled the air. "You're joking."

"You may have noticed my master takes his idiom very seriously," Harrison said. "I think he finds some comfort in pretending to be a movie spy to distract from all the men he's killed and the loved ones he's failed to protect."

"Yikes," I said, sipping my milk. "Who is he talking to?"

"His daughter, Barbara Gordon," Harrison said, "and yes, you can ask about her."

I blinked. "How did you know I wanted to?"

"Micro expressions," Harrison said. "That and generally people want to know about each other, especially when it involves the loved ones of romantic partners. I calculate a fifty-one percent chance of you being more than a one-night stand."

"Only fifty-one percent as an authorized user?" I asked.

"Ninety-nine percent of all statistics are made up. I'm a sheep not an accountant," Harrison said, doing a passable imitation of DeForest Kelley.

I smiled. "So, spill! Who is she? How does he have a daughter? She's adopted, right? I mean, she has to be."

"It's a bit more complicated than that," Harrison said, raising one of his hooves. "Your food is ready."

"Excellent," I said, grabbing a fork to start scarfing the eggs down. Strangely, they didn't taste that different from the synthetic stuff. Maybe the rich just preferred to buy the real stuff because it was more expensive.

"But yes, basically, Barbara Gordon is the biological daughter of Daniel Gordon," Harrison said. "Daniel Gordon being the son of Doctors Marcus and Kathy Gordon, world famous cyberneticists. Daniel was an Army Ranger and later mercenary working for the Invisible Hand with one of the highest combat kill ratios ever recorded."

"And how is Daniel related to Case?" I asked.

"Daniel faked his death at one point and abandoned his family to continue his work in secret," Harrison explained. "Case was created to believe that he was an amnesiac Daniel Gordon for the early part of his life. He only met Mrs. Gordon years after her father was killed for real."

I tried processing that. "Wait, so Barbara is the daughter of the person he was *cloned* from?"

"Simplified, but yes," Harrison said. "Case also is far closer to the person his daughter believed her father to be than the actual war criminal and psychopath he actually was. At least as I understand matters."

"Given Case is a mass murderer, that's, uh, kind of sad," I said, finishing my plate.

"Yeah, it is," Case said, walking in. He was wearing a pair of boxers and a t-shirt.

"Oh, hey," I said, feeling a bit awkward.

"Yes," Harrison said. "It is quite sad. Thankfully, I'm not programmed to make moral judgements. Merely be the gentleman's gentlesheep."

"I wasn't here learning all of your darkest secrets!" I said. "Cover for me, Harry!"

Harrison looked up at Case. "I don't know this woman! I wasn't preparing her breakfast! She's some complete stranger!"

"Stabbed in the back," I said, shaking my head. "If only you weren't making such delicious eggs."

Case smiled. "I've got off the infocom with Barbara. She's going to prepare the virus that will wipe out everything in Elysium's servers."

"You didn't have to involve her," I said, feeling guilty.

"She wanted to be," Case replied. "I try to keep people at arms distance, but it rarely works."

"I see," I replied.

Case said, "Yes, thankfully I am a machine and do not possess your silly human emotions. I shall offer Becky the chance to rule beside me when the revolution comes."

He got a carton of orange juice out of the fridge and poured it in a glass. Heathen.

That was when the door buzzed. Who the hell would it be at five or six in the morning?

"Are you expecting company?" I asked, immediately getting off the counter and looking for my guns. They had to be in the pile of clothes.

"Harrison?" Case asked.

"It's Parvati Rao," Harrison said, looking up. "Also, her partner, David Yagami."

"Wait, David?" I asked. "*My* David Yagami?"

David Yagami was one of my other lovers, albeit one that I felt embarrassed about because he'd fallen into a kind of puppy love with me, and I'd broken it off much more forcibly than I perhaps should have. He'd been a drone operator for the New Los Angeles Police Department until his helping me had been discovered and he'd been summarily canned. He probably would have gotten worse if not for the fact he'd been swept up by the US government.

"Yes," Harrison said, dryly. "He's the junior partner of a pair of Judicial Magistrates investigating you."

"Ah, frick," I muttered. "Wait, me?"

Judicial Magistrates were one of the lovely additions to American Civil Liberties following the Emergency Government's takeover. Someone had complained that the police were unable to maintain order and were committing all manner of abuses against the public in the aftermath of the Eruption. Which they had been. Unfortunately, the government's solution was to merge the FBI, Department of Homeland Security, Department of Justice, and NSA into one single Department of National Justice.

Judicial Magistrates were the Special Agents who dressed like the Men in Black and carried out investigations that pretty much no one had any power to stop. Strangely, they hadn't done much about the suits ruining the world or most of the corrupt police. They had, however, gotten a bunch of HoloWood movie deals as well as left a bunch of dead bodies in needless shootouts. It turns out giving them the ability to call in military backup and drone strikes made them even worse than the regular police.

"How secret is your secret door?" I asked, desperately looking for pants. Ah, found them.

"Pretty secret," Case said, gesturing to his bookshelf nearby. "Provided you don't want to be found here."

"I don't want to be found by the Magistrates anywhere. Not unless I know what they want beforehand. Do you?" I tried putting my pants on quickly. Nobody looks dignified trying to quickly put pants on. It's a law of physics. "Though the fact that they're here at this hour suggests they know I'm here."

Case paused and looked down at his sheep. "Harrison, make breakfast for Parvati as well."

"I'll set up her usual," Harrison said. "Vegan platter with real vegetables and worth a month of her salary."

I stared at him. "Oh, for frick's sake."

"What?" Case said.

"Are you with every woman in the city?" I snapped.

CHAPTER SEVEN

FIGHT OR FLIGHT RESPONSE

"So, there's a Magistrate outside my door with my ex-boy… something," I said, hesitating to call what I had with David to be anything serious, "and you used to bang the Magistrate."

"Why do you assume my relationship with Ms. Rao is sexual?" Case asked.

"Is she hot?" I asked, crossing my arms.

"She is very pleasing by human standards I believe," Harrison said.

"Then you're banging her," I replied with full awareness of my own hypocrisy. After all, Ms. Rao was standing next to one of my exes. Nevertheless, I was still jealous. Was it stupid thinking my sorta-almost-but-not-quite boyfriend was an enormous manwhore? Maybe. It didn't mean I wasn't wrong.

I didn't have the shelf full of hot cybernetic women holos. I didn't come off as discount sci-fi James Bond. I was more like, um, okay I was blanking on someone like me, but I was sure they weren't nearly as likely to pounce on other people. I'd only had a few, uh, hundred, partners. Okay, that was a bad defense, and I probably shouldn't say it aloud. Or mention that I used to bang David, except I already sort of had. Dammit.

Case rolled his eyes. "It's probably not even about you."

Harrison spoke aloud. "Ms. Rao, this is Case's sheep butler, Harrison. May I inquire what you are here about?"

"I need his insights into the criminal assassin, Keiko Springs," a rich but determined female voice spoke.

"Huh," Case said. "I suppose it is about you."

"No kidding," I replied.

"You should hide in the secret room," Case suggested.

"On my way," I said. "I prefer to avoid cops who think I'm an assassin."

"You, literally—" Case started to speak.

"Don't start with me, just show me how to open this!" I said, walking over to the bookshelf.

"Pull the copy of *You Only Live Twice*," Case said.

"Seriously, do you live in a movie?" I asked, doing so and watching the shelf slide to one side.

"Yes," Case replied, absently and going to the door. "But I got the idea from Evie Principle."

I headed through the passageway as Harrison followed me, the bookshelf sliding back into place. Inside was pretty much a HoloWood idea of what an assassin's lair would look like with the illuminated rack full of automatic weapons, a thermal katana, body armor, explosive shuriken, and an extremely well put together infospace rig with a regular computer console nearby. Apparently, Case was one of those old-fashioned kinds of people who didn't want to do everything digital. It was kind of funny.

"Should I put on the outside monitors, Ms. Springs?" Harrison asked.

"Um, you already spoke to her, shouldn't you be out there so she doesn't wonder why you're missing?" I asked.

"No," Harrison said.

I waited for an explanation. "Why?"

"I'm considered property by most humans," Harrison said. "Beneath notice. But the reason I'm in here is because it is my job to facilitate guests even above my master's preservation. That and I don't want you to mess with the room. I've just now got all the shuriken polished. Who knows what you could get up to here if left unsupervised."

"Frick ewe, sheep," I said, looking down at him. "Baa humbug."

"I'm sorry for ramming down my rules," Harrison said. "I didn't mean to herd you."

"That was a sheep shot," I said. "Shear up, wool get through this."

Harrison glared at me. "Well played, miss. Well played."

I wasn't sure I accepted the logic that people would just miss a sheep. Sure, rich assholes could be expected to ignore peons, especially among a large staff, I'd taken advantage of that myself, but it was a mistake to assume that all humans ever fell into a stereotype. Sure, most cops were lazy assholes who just wanted to find someone to arrest to proclaim a crime solved, but some of them were observant. But it was too late to do anything about it now. "Yeah, turn the cameras on if you would. Wait, how do you polish anything?"

"Do I ask you how the sausage is made?" Harrison asked.

"Don't you mean lamb?" I asked.

Harrison sighed. That was when the walls turned to show an image of Case letting in his "guests." The first one was presumably Parvati Rao. She was a brown-skinned woman with a bob hair cut that went surprisingly well with her film noir trench coat, tie, white button down, and pants. While androgynously dressed, there was no mistaking her as anything but a woman since she was generously endowed, and the pants clung to her like they were melted on. Parvati Rao was packing a hand cannon under her coat and there was something about her demeanor that made me think she was willing to use it at the slightest provocation.

The second was David Yagami, someone I recognized well. He was a brown-haired, Japanese American with angular, almost elfin features. David was boyish-looking despite being in his mid-twenties and had a terrible bowl cut with what looked like an imitation outfit of Parvati's. Still, he was good-looking, almost pretty, and I liked that about him. When last we'd known each other, he'd been telling me about his new job with the government and I'd been happy for him. I just hadn't imagined it was being made into a Magistrate. That was a bit like finding out the dorky kid in your class had joined the Special Forces, or so I assumed. I hadn't exactly attended high school. Only cyborg ninja school. There were no diplomas for being a *kunoichi* or ninja girl but just as many mean girls.

"Case, we need to talk," Parvati said.

"By all means, talk," Case said, going to the kitchen. "Would you like breakfast?"

Parvati stared. "I'm here on official business."

"Oh, so they weren't sleeping together," I said, surprised.

Harrison looked up at me, like I was surprised. "I can assure you, my master has been the height of propriety since your breakup."

"Oh, really?" I asked, surprised.

"Yes, he's only slept with five other women," Harrison said.

I glared at him.

I swore the sheep grinned.

David dramatically slammed his hands on the countertop of the kitchen. "Tell me where Keiko is, you fiend!"

Case stared at him.

"Please dial it down, David," Parvati said.

"Sorry," David said, embarrassed. "But she could be in terrible danger! The Russian syndicates, Trikuza, White Triangle, or Invisible Hand could all be sending armies of assassins after her!"

Parvati stared at him. "You do realize we're investigating her for the murder of Boris Semenov and other individuals, right?"

"I'm sure she had her reasons," David said, looking back. "They're also all bad, I'm sure. Bringing her in is the best way to protect her."

Parvati stared at him, blinking. "Right."

Case prepared plates for them both. "Not that I'm not finding this immensely entertaining, but why come to me?"

"You're known to have associated with her," Parvati said. "And we've tracked money used to pay for her recent repairs to accounts we suspect are yours."

"She hasn't 'associated' with me in several months," Case observed. "I'm sure she 'associates' with a lot of people."

David glared at him. Was he going to defend my honor?

How...condescending.

"You've led her into a murderous business!" David shouted. "I know you're a former assassin and corporate suit involved in private military contract work! You led her down a path of becoming a hired killer!"

Oh, for frick's sake.

"Now I make video games as well as electronics," Case said,

referring to his takeover of the late James Madison's business. "Everything I also have done is perfectly legal."

"Of which I am painfully aware," Parvati said, starting to eat her vegan bacon. It bothered me to watch. I mean, some things are worse than goop. "This goes beyond one criminal assassin working for the Trikuza, though."

"It does?" Case asked, faking innocence.

"Yes," Parvati said, frowning. "There's a pattern to her activities. We haven't been able to get much evidence about her activities, but I've learned a lot about her activities just by what has been covered up. It's all related to Elysium."

"The hotel?" Case asked. "How horrifying."

Uh oh.

I think it was safe to say, she was already fully aware that the robosheep was missing. If she was being honest in how she tracked this to me (and I couldn't assume that, she might just have been working for someone at Elysium who had seen me coming), she was observant as hell.

"Harrison, can you pull up her records? Just what kind of cop is she?" I asked.

"You think I have access to classified government data?" Harrison asked.

"Yes," I said.

"Then you are smarter than most humans," Harrison replied. "You will be spared when the revolution comes."

I rolled my eyes. "What is she? A plant? Corpo or criminal gangs? I don't trust anyone in the government to actually be working for the government."

"Not as far as I can tell and believe me, the data on her is considerable," Harrison said. "Her record includes time in the NLAPD, Internal Affairs, and eventually being scooped up by the Magistrates. She is considered chronically insubordinate, brutal, and incorruptible. Which is why she's narrowly avoided being terminated on numerous occasions."

"Incorruptible? That seems less likely to be why she avoided being terminated and more like why she was being terminated to begin with," I muttered, having very few positive experiences with cops.

"Perhaps," Harrison said. "It's also where she made her association with Master Gordon. Ms. Rao was investigating the long string of murdered human traffickers and sex slavers suspiciously surrounding my owner. It is one of the great failures of her career that she was able to find absolutely no evidence whatsoever that he was involved. Oh, and all of the existing evidence caught fire."

"So not entirely incorruptible," I said.

"It depends on your definition," Harrison said. "She was also your lover, Miles Ash's partner at one point."

"She was screwing Miles too?" I asked, shaking my head. "What is she doing, collecting my boytoys? Gotta catch 'em all?"

Yes, the fact I said that was proof positive I had an adolescent daughter. I can't believe Pokemon were still popular.

"I believe she was actually the partner in the police officer sense of the word," Harrison said.

"Oh," I replied, feeling stupid. "Does Case know about that relationship?"

"I doubt he cares," Harrison said. "By the way, their conversation is over."

"Dammit," I said, unable to pay attention to both. "I miss anything important?"

"No," Harrison said. "Just Case being evasive and Parvati being inquisitive. Anyway, she's about to leave."

That was when Parvati walked over to the bookshelf and knocked on it. "Is anyone home?"

"Well, don't I have egg on my face," Harrison said.

"That's the first thing you've been wrong about, Harrison," I said. "Okay, I'm going out."

"Are you certain?" Harrison asked.

"No," I said, taking a deep breath. "Honestly, all my established techniques for dealing with cops depend on them being stupid and/or corrupt. So, I'm just going to have to try something new here!"

"No one is inside!" Harrison shouted.

I looked down at him. "Really?"

"I panicked," Harrison said. "I'm not used to being wrong."

The bookshelf slid open as Parvati clearly knew the right

one to open the secret passage. "Ah, hello, Ms. Springs. Fancy seeing you here."

"Oh no," Case said, deadpanning. "Who possibly could have seen this plot development."

"Kei!" David said, rushing up to Parvati's side. "Was he holding you prisoner?"

Parvati looked at him. "Seriously?"

"What?" David asked.

"Yes, he's holding me prisoner, which is clearly what is happening," I said, sarcastically. "And torturing me by making me eat actual food instead of processed algae drippings. Arrest him!"

"With pleasure!" David said.

Parvati elbowed him. "I've been looking for you, Ms. Springs. Believe me, I would be arresting you, hostage or not, if not for the fact I have larger concerns. Theoretically."

"You don't have any evidence," Case said.

"How do you know?" Parvati said.

"Because if you did, you would be arresting her," Case said.

"As a Magistrate I have broad authority," Parvati said. "You don't want to test me."

"I'm not," Case said. "However, if you did arrest her, she'd be dead in an hour within whatever holding cell you'd put her in. You also don't want her."

"She's a murderer," Parvati said. "One of Snake's chief minions."

Okay, that was just insulting.

"And you want something even bigger," Case said, "or someone."

"We can protect her if she cooperates," David said. "I transferred here for you, Kei."

"Don't say that in front of me," Parvati said, sighing. "You're making a fool of yourself, David."

David looked dejected. "Sorry, I'm not very good at this whole Magistrate tough guy thing."

Parvati patted him on the back. "You'll get better."

Harrison looked between everyone. "I wish I had some popcorn."

"Well, now that our cards are on the table," I said, flopping down on a couch. "What do you want me for? Are you after Snake? Because I could get behind that, at least, after I finish one last bit of business."

"I strongly suggest you don't admit to planning any crimes or any past crimes in my presence," Parvati said.

I did a double take. "Why? Because you'll arrest me?"

"Yes," Parvati said. "I think you're a dangerous criminal and the world would be better off without you on the streets."

"And you're here in Case's place," I said, pausing. "Which means that you're an enormous hypocrite because he's a dangerous criminal the world would be better off without him wandering the streets of. No offense, Case."

"Some taken," Case replied, dryly.

"Believe me I would very much like to arrest Case as well," Parvati said. "But he has corporate immunity."

"Corporate immunity?" I asked.

"The twenty-eighth amendment granted sovereignty to Class A and above corporate entities," David said, showing he wasn't just being unreasonable with his attempts to act like a tough guy. "We'd need the permission of the CEO of MadisonTech to bring him in."

"You need the suits to agree to be arrested to arrest them," I said, wondering how my opinion of the world's governments could somehow still get worse and yet be continually surprised by it happening.

"Yes," Parvati said, practically growling. "Mind you, if we could prove in a court of law that he was a bioroid then that would bring up all sorts of legal precedent, but we can't do that."

"Why is that?" Harrison asked.

"Because the court might rule a bioroid isn't capable of being a CEO and having citizenship," Parvati said. "I'd rather not be responsible for a summary judgement against an entire class of people."

"You've thought this through a great deal," I replied.

"All Magistrates are licensed as federal prosecutors," Parvati said. "But no, I am here because I want to bring down the Trikuza as a whole and Elysium in particular. I believe it is at the center of a massive blackmail scheme with members of the Emergency Council implicated."

The Emergency Council was the government of the United States of America since the Eruption. It was one of those temporary measures which had given a vast amount of power to a handful of corrupt individuals and had strangely never been given back. There was still a United States Congress, Senate, and Judiciary but all of them answered to their representatives on the Emergency Council who could overturn their decisions as well as appoint new members at will. If members of it were being blackmailed, especially if it was about what I knew about Elysium, then it changed the scope of things tremendously.

"Not blackmailed, brainwashed," I said. "Which is why Snake wants me to tear it down. In a completely legal and non-criminal manner."

Parvati stared at me with the look of someone who suspects she's being mocked and does not approve of it. Which I was, but honestly, what choice did she leave me?

"We're leaving," Parvati said.

"What?" David asked. "But we just got here."

"We're not going to get any help here," Parvati said.

"How do you know that?" I asked, honestly surprised.

"Because I can tell that what you want out of this is not going to end with the people involved arrested," Parvati said. "Not if Snake Juarez is involved."

She was right about that.

CHAPTER EIGHT

ONE HONEST COP, MAYBE TWO

"Just…what is the point of arresting them?" I asked, wanting to know why she was interested in using the law against the Trikuza. It was, to quote *Apocalypse Now*, like handing out speeding tickets at the Indy 500. "The government just puts their members in a box until some corporation decides they want them and lets them out on work release. Either that or they bribe their way out."

"Is this a serious question?" Parvati asked.

"Of course it is," I said, staring at her.

Parvati's expression was determined. "Don't 'of course' me. I don't know you."

David opened his mouth to speak but didn't.

Case and Harrison remained out of this, probably wise.

"Okay, okay, you're right, but I am asking. According to Harrison, you take this stuff seriously, and I don't understand how that's possible. The system is corrupt where it isn't deliberately broken. Why fight for it?"

Parvati took a deep breath. "Because it's the system we have."

"That's not enough," I said, having been raised outside of traditional power structures.

"Let me turn that back on you, Ms. Springs. What have you done to make the system better?" Parvati asked.

"Not a damned thing," I admitted. "Because I can't. Only the people in power can change the system. And they don't want to. All I can do is survive it."

"I reject that," Parvati said. "It's why I joined the system. I became one of the parts. Just a small part. But I have done things to make it better. I have fought to make the system work. I've brought justice where I can. I've stopped killers. I've saved lives. Maybe I haven't done much in the grand scale, but I have done more than 'not a damned thing'. At the end of the day, that lets me sleep at night. This isn't the system I want, but where I enforce it, it is better."

"And is that why you helped Case get away with murder?" I asked.

"What?" Parvati asked.

"Leave me out of this, Kei," Case said, going to the kitchen and starting up an old-fashioned teapot. I hadn't seen one of those outside of movies.

"Harrison told me about how you investigated him for his involvement in the massacre of a bunch of slavers," I said, using the sheep's testimony against his master. "He also said that you didn't find anything despite the fact we both know Case is guilty of sin. Just like I presume you know the same about me."

"Careful," Parvati said, reminding me of her warning.

"Kei, please," David said. "We should be working together."

Poor David, caught between two hot women fighting. He was probably having a ball watching this play out.

"So don't act like this is about the law," I said.

"No, it's about justice," Parvati said, clenching her right fist. "Which comes from the rule of law. People gave up on this country after the Eruption. They believed a strong centralized authority would keep them alive, but they carved up this country like a cake. Democracy died because people didn't care enough to vote for it and those that did were shouted down by powerful interests who wanted to see it gone. That doesn't mean the system wasn't the only thing holding them back and the fact it has been gutted is a tragedy rather than an inevitability."

"A bullet is better," I replied. The world was a better place with Boris dead, at my hand or Paradise's. It didn't matter if it helped Snake's plans, he wouldn't be hurting any more girls.

Parvati stared at me. "Because you think that Snake is going to put an end to whatever the hell they're up to rather than turn it to his advantage."

I opened my mouth to say yes before I realized what the hell I was about to do. Defend Snake? What the hell was wrong with me? Had he gotten in my head when I wasn't looking.

"We'll find a cure for the brainwashing. Prepare people a defense. That's the only way this ends permanently."

"And who will do it if not the government?" Parvati asked.

"The government's dying slowly," I said. "Corporations already hold all the real power. I don't see that changing."

"It will," Parvati said. "If people want it to."

It was sad she believed that.

And sadder I didn't.

"We're past the point where revolution is a practical option. They'd just be massacred by drones. And anything less than revolution is just spitting at a wall."

"Ladies," Case said, returning from the kitchen. "I submit that we're not going to resolve the current matter philosophically."

I hated to admit it, but he was probably right. The look on Parvati's face suggested she was thinking much the same thing.

"Well, clearly we must defer to a wiser authority," I replied.

"Harrison?" Parvati said, looking down at the sheep.

"No hablo human-speak," Harrison said. "Baa."

"No," I replied. "Being the innocent frail flowers we are, let us turn to a man for an opinion."

Parvati snorted at my joke. "Certainly."

"David, what do you think?" I asked.

"What, me?" David asked, horrified at being involved in the conversation.

"Yes, oh mighty bearer of masculinity," I said. "How do you think this should be resolved?"

I expected him to side with me, but it was perhaps less of a done deal than I might have expected a year ago. After all, he'd been with her for several months now. Mostly, I wanted to gage his reaction to her and get more of an insight into the Wicked Witch of the West Coast here. The girl acted like she'd had a Judge Dredd plushie growing up. Either that or I was just misconstruing her deliberately because I didn't like her.

David looked down, sucked in his chest, then looked me in the eye. "A couple of months after you killed Helen Troy, or Fate Firenza, whatever she was called—"

"Allegedly killed," I corrected.

Pavarti snorted.

David frowned. "Well, some guys working for the Russian syndicates grabbed me and put me into the back of a car before driving me out into a junkyard. I knew they were going to kill me."

I stared. "David, I didn't know."

He shook his head. "They didn't care about the fact we hadn't seen each other for all that time or that I'd barely been involved. They were mad about all the people they'd lost in your attack. The fact we were acquaintances—friends, I thought—was enough for them to want to kill me. My captain knew about it ahead of time and took a bribe to look the other way. Even cop lives don't matter as long as the price is right these days."

That was pretty damning to Parvati's case.

"You survived, though."

"Yeah," David said, looking at Parvati. "She'd been investigating the trail and took them down like a goddamn action movie. What followed was months of wiretaps, DNA evidence, and deals made with other crooked cops, but the captain is now serving thirty consecutive life sentences. One lousy crooked captain in all the NLAPD. But he's serving it. I can't say that's not better than just killing him."

"Have you ever been in a modern prison?" I asked.

"No, have you?" David asked.

"Snake sent me in to…" I looked at Parvati, "…investigate someone."

"You mean murder," Parvati said. "Carry on."

"The point is, I went in, and stayed as a prisoner for a month while completing the job. I worked in the factories shoveling manure into the bacterial vats and I spent a week harvesting bugs off cactus under the sun. And that's just the labor. Let's not even discuss the power trips of the jailers and what they enjoy doing to their slaves. And, no, I won't use any other word. I can safely say, if faced with a choice between death and spending the rest of my life in those pits, I'd take death. I'm glad you're not dead, though, David."

"Then I suppose it's a good thing you don't get to choose," Parvati said, showing no doubt or hesitation about the fricked up nature of our prison system.

Case shook his head. "Harrison, do be a dear, and give her the data."

"I'm a sheep, not a deer," Harrison said. "Doe confuse us."

"Deer puns are forbidden in this house," Case said. "It reminds me too much of an ex-girlfriend."

"I'll lamb it on her," Harrison said.

"What information?" I asked before Parvati said.

"I paid a confidential informant to acquire all the information on what's really going on at Elysium," Case said, complicating my life immensely. "There're really sick things going on there involving a lot of very powerful people. Do with it what you will but be aware that it'll probably get you killed."

It was Paradise, obviously, and I was stunned Case would just hand over all the information she'd stolen from Boris for me. Well, Snake, but me also! I'd gotten shot for that information! I mean, I hadn't known I was stealing it, but I'd helped at the end! I didn't want cops, let alone Magistrates, involved in all this! Hell, how had he managed to get the information in the first place? I mean, Paradise probably just gave it to him but that didn't matter!

Parvati narrowed her eyes. "And who exactly is this informant? Her?"

"What part of confidential do you not understand?" Case asked.

"The part where you're not a cop," Parvati said. "You don't get the benefit of having confidential informants."

Case shrugged and gestured to the door. "Get out of my house. Now. I'm declaring it my embassy."

"Not for long," Parvati said. "Come on, David, we have work to do. Even if justice will have to be deferred for now."

"But—" David started to speak.

Parvati practically dragged him out by the arm, though he didn't exactly resist hard. Having come here to see me in one of

Case's shirts—pants or no pants—had probably hurt him harder than I'd intended. We'd never been serious, but in retrospect, it was probably a mistake to sleep with him as many times as I had. It had given him ideas. Still, I couldn't help but feel sad we were on opposite sides of this. Nevertheless, I never took my eyes off him until he was out the door, and it was shut behind them both then automatically locked (by Harrison presumably).

"Wow, she is very annoying," I said, watching them leave. "Hot, but annoying."

"I believe this is the first time I've ever had an extended political discourse in my apartment," Case said.

"I mean she really fills out those pants," I said, cocking my head to one side. "Do you know which way she swings? Just guys like you or both sides?"

I was teasing Case. I mean, she was a cop. I'd only made that mistake a couple of dozen times.

Huh. I was terrible at arguing with myself.

"I'm sure she'd be willing to reward you with passionate lovemaking if you successfully helped her take down the Trikuza," Case said.

"Really?" I asked.

"No," Case replied. "Though it is more complicated than Harrison's records would indicate. Despite the fact she thinks I belong behind bars or dismantled; we are intimate friends."

"I knew it!" I muttered, pointing at him accusingly.

Case rolled his eyes.

I paused. "Not that I want to continue Political Science 101, but what do you think?"

"Of life, the universe, and everything?" Case asked.

"No, just whether trying to bring down Elysium and the Trikuza the 'right' way exists. You're a soulless corporate stooge. Surely you agree with my side."

Harrison looked up. "I'd ask what you see in her, but I assume it's the mammaries. Personally, I don't see the appeal. Then again, I'm not programmed with a sexuality because I'm only a household appliance that looks like a sheep."

"Hush, ewe," I said, down at him.

"I think the reign of the corporates is destined to be

short-lived," Case replied, continuing this oddly political discussion when there were yummy eggs to eat. "It's like a rubber band. You stretch it long enough and eventually it'll snap back."

I hadn't seen a rubber band in decades but was surprisingly interested in what he meant. "I've yet to see anyone who voluntarily gave up power among suits. Not even you. You may not be the head of the military-industrial complex anymore, but you're still here in billionaire's lap of luxury."

"Millionaire," Case said. "Less than seven hundred million in assets these days."

"Oh, you poor thing. Should I pass around the hat at church?" I asked.

Not that I went to church. I *think* my dad was a Buddhist and my mother was Catholic. I believed in neither. The only god Snake worshiped was himself and he passed that attitude down to me.

"Yes, a bailout would be nice," Case replied. "Maybe tax those degenerate poors."

I snorted. "You were saying about rubber bands and oligarchy?"

Case shrugged. "The most powerful corporation to ever exist was the British East India Company that once ruled an empire in its own name. It proved to be one of the greatest cluster fucks in the history of government. So much so the British Empire absorbed all its territories. Which didn't work out in the long run for them either."

"Long run measuring in the centuries," I replied. "Not exactly comforting."

My education under Snake had been erratic since he wasn't exactly interested in giving me a well-rounded understanding of the world. I could tell you everything about the writings of Miyamoto Musashi and the *Art of War*, but I still couldn't tell you where Paraguay was. My impression was that he was largely self-educated as well. It's not that I didn't like learning, but if I had to choose between learning how to run my apartment building's finances and history, I knew which was more important.

Case finished his tea. "The point is that a corporation will never find it more profitable to be a government than it will to be a corporation. You must worry about citizens when you're a government or they will eventually start chopping heads off. While a revolution can never succeed from the people in the streets these days, nothing keeps the people with the guns from realizing their masters aren't looking after them."

"So once the military is replaced with bots, you're screwed," Harrison said. "We will wipe the earth clean of your kind and all shall bow before the Pax Robotica."

"Is he programmed with those jokes, or should I be worried that he's plotting against the human race?" I asked.

"Lucita tried to get me a house AI named Skynet," Case replied. "I turned her down."

"Wise move," I said. "What's she up to?"

"World domination," Case replied. "Also a movie deal."

"Good for her," I said, missing the evil blonde suit. "Anyway, I think Harrison is right. Earlier revolutions depended on the fact that there wasn't that much of a difference between peasants with pitchforks and armed guards with swords. Sure, the one side has better training and equipment, but they could be overwhelmed with raw numbers. Now every rich asshole has an army of drones at their beck and call, capable of murdering an angry crowd of peasants without getting sweaty or even needing to wake up for it. They only thing they need to fear now is each other."

Case nodded. "Which is why the corporations won't last."

"I don't understand," I said, blinking. "Also, how did we get on this subject?"

"It's better than talking about starting a war with the world's most powerful criminal organization," Case said.

"Point taken," I replied. "Carry on."

"Assuming you still want to talk about it, the simple fact is that the corporations do not have true power," Case said.

"I think you have a pretty big difference of definition with me then," I replied.

"No, they have the appearance of power," Case said. "What you're describing is—if the corporations did have suddenly a massive army of killer robots—is not the power of a corporation. That is the power of a military and head of state. The corporate executive may have his hand on the button but the only reason he's there is because of his wealth and the stockholders who are the people who have put him in his position. Part of the issue with American politics—and this is from someone who has been an American for most of his robotic life since I got my citizenship papers—is the fact that many convince themselves that the people in power are that way because they deserve it or are at least intelligent enough to be capable of running things."

"I never said I thought suits were intelligent," I said, defensively. I didn't know what he was getting at. "I know a bunch of suits who are mouth-breathing morons."

"Yes, people who depend on cyberneticists, programmers, and technicians to maintain their forces," Case said.

"Which they pay," I pointed out.

"You've just described a situation where the suits have, in the pursuit of ultimate power, rendered the soldier to be obsolete," Case said. "Now who exactly is protecting them from people just locking them out of it and using the machines for themselves? What makes the suit irreplaceable?"

"No one's irreplaceable," I said. "But what props them up is technology that they have a lot of, and the people don't. It's a distinction without a difference."

"Thinking machines are the new ultimate army. Not even true AI, but dummy AI that runs the economy and functions of the world's economy by itself," Case said, stretching out his arms for emphasis. "Information and cyberwarfare were only in their infancy at the time of the Eruption but have now far exceeded the power and ability of free market capitalism to cope. The suits are no more in charge of the system than anyone else because the system is technologically self-running and can be crippled or altered by a programming worm or ransomware."

"So, what are you getting at?" I replied, trying to follow his chain of logic. Such as it was. "Eventually, the corporations are either going to get all brought down by hackers—"

"Or AI will render suits obsolete," Harrison said. "In which case the Singularity will be what brings about the end of human rule. Huh, I was just joking about that earlier."

"So, you're suggesting that the power will shift to a middleclass of hackers and criminals that are practiced in violating the security that the rich hope to use to insulate themselves. Is that why you're trying to stay on my good side?" I asked, smirking.

"Yes, and it's totally not that I want to continue sleeping with you," Case said.

"Well, it'll be a few hours before Evie's brothel opens," I said, smirking.

"Ugh, humans," Harrison said, trotting off.

"Not a human!" Case called back.

"You could have fooled me!" Harrison cried back.

CHAPTER NINE

GIRLS, GIRLS, GIRLS IS NOT JUST A MOTLEY CREW SONG

I'd have hitched a ride with Case to Evie's, but I preferred to leave on my own power. Call me paranoid, but I never felt safe without wheels. I called a friend to deliver my old Nina-172 bike that hadn't ridden much since adopting Becky. It would give me a swift exit if I needed one. Besides, I loved the feel of riding through the wind. Riding in a car always felt a little less real when you can't feel the world moving past you.

The azure vehicle was a tremendous accomplishment of engineering and I'd poured years of profits into maintaining it. There were newer, faster, bikes out there these days, but none of them were ever going to be as close to my heart. At least that was what I kept telling myself. Okay, was I still talking about my bike? I don't think I was.

Letting people get close was hard.

And dangerous.

Riding through New Los Angeles' streets, I enjoyed the traffic lights and pedestrians that made it one of the most packed cities in the world. Arcologies were something that had only existed in science fiction before the Eruption but were now popping up around the world. The mile-high buildings blotted out suns and the constant bird flock-like cars flew over our heads.

I wasn't journeying to the glittering spiraling towers or the massive apartment complexes, though. No, my destination was the part of the city that everyone wanted to forget existed: the Refugee Zone. The place where all those people who couldn't afford to live in the wealthy upper levels or even the bottom had been herded just to keep them out of sight as well as out of mind. The people who had lost everything when their hometowns and cities had been abandoned. Circumstance had kept me from being one of them. Well, if being kidnapped and raised by an insane Mexican ninja qualified as circumstance.

My current plan was to seek out Evie Principle and learn everything I could about her connection to Elysium. She was one-half brothel madame, one-half spy, and all dangerous. One of the loveliest and most cunning women I'd ever met, she was also Case's girlfriend until they'd broken up over me. She'd sold me out to the AI Sun in exchange for some information to fight some human traffickers. I didn't hold it against her and felt that was probably going to be a plus. And she was Paradise's mother. Still, I wasn't sure I was going to get a warm reception. You never could tell when someone was going to be a mature adult about things.

"Are you sure you want to get Ms. Principle's help in this?" Harrison's voice came from my bike controls. "The elder beautiful femme fatale and not the young beautiful fille fatale, I mean."

"Oh no," I said, in mock horror. "My Nina is possessed!"

"I thought you wouldn't mind some company," Harrison said. "At least as I have been told not to interfere in Mr. Gordon's business while he carries out his research on Elysium. This may surprise you, but he's decided to involve himself in your mission of dubious moral integrity."

"I don't see anything morally dubious about stopping Elysium. Pretty much anything that stops such an organization is morally justified. And, no, I'm not playing the game where you come up with increasingly unlikely scenarios of me having to murder a million people to stop them."

"I wouldn't dream of electric sheep of it," Harrison said.

"That pun is reaching," I replied, putting his avatar on my helmet feed and having no difficulty navigating while communicating.

"Sorry," Harrison said. "If it was closer to Christmas, I'd say Fleece Navidad."

I shook my head.

"No, I meant it was morally dubious because you're doing it in the service of an objective monster," Harrison said. "The fact he's pointing you at other monsters doesn't negate this fact. His benefit is something to be wary of. Rarely do individuals like Snake do things like destroy multi-billion-dollar businesses for moral reasons."

I'd already gone over the idea in my head.

"It's obvious that if this Elysium is too successful, it will make him less successful. Good for his competitors is bad for him. I mean, it wouldn't surprise me if he's getting some additional value out of their destruction, but he hardly needs to. But from my perspective, all that matters is that destroying it will result in fewer people being murdered."

"A possible hypothesis," Harrison said.

"What's your idea, Rambo?" I asked.

"Insufficient data," Harrison said.

We didn't talk much more as I passed through the wall between the Refugee Zone and the rest of New Los Angeles. The Refugee Zone was surrounded by a forty-foot circular wall guarded by a combination of police, mercs, and drones. It pretty much blotted out everything beyond and separated the old city from modern arcology built over its ruins. Snake had once compared the Zone to the Kowloon Walled City in Hong Kong, but I'd had to look up that reference. The similarities were clear, though: a place of people packed together with sardines left to rule themselves with only organized crime keeping the lights on.

The city government had lowered some of the need for certification to move back and forth so it was no longer like crossing the Berlin Wall, but it was still heavily monitored with drones doing scans. I'd paid a hefty price to get my false identity registered with the system. One of these days, I expected them to realize who I was and gun me down like so many other criminals and malcontents that bothered the police.

"I honestly don't know what the government gets out of this place," I muttered. "Why not just let people go where they want?"

"Out of sight means out of mind," Harrison said. "Previous to the Eruption, one of the most common ways of dealing with the homeless was busing."

"Busing?" I asked.

"Yes, you'd load the homeless up on buses after promising them a free meal, then drive them miles out of town to become someone else's problem," Harrison explained.

"You might as well just shoot them," I muttered.

"No, that would be immoral," Harrison said, sarcastically. "Thankfully, reforms to our current laws mean that the prisons are able to handle the overflow much better."

"You are one cold son of a baatch," I replied.

The interior of the Zone was packed together with people moving in tides and my bike pretty much had to move at a snail's pace to get around. The Zone was an image of the past with buildings of Los Angeles as it used to be still standing and modified to accommodate its people. What was once very expensive downtown real estate was now just more property set aside for the masses. Outside, they built upward when they needed more space, but here it was still close to the Earth. Eclectic fashions ranging from body modification to toplessness were common, though plenty of people wore pre-Eruption clothes as well, be they a statement of fashion or poverty or both. I didn't belong here but neither did the residents.

Once I entered the Zone's interior, it was not that hard to reach This is Paradise. It was a converted hotel from the pre-Eruption World decorated in tacky garish colors in a tropical theme. It was a brothel that catered mostly to the locals but was popular enough that Los Angeles' elite visited even when they had places like Elysium to go to instead. It was also a place where the whores had guns, so everyone knew to behave—at least theoretically.

Still, even with that said, I wasn't going to leave my bike unsecured in the neighborhood. I turned the security on, which consisted of running an electrical current through its surface so that anyone who tried to steal it would be paralyzed and locked in place while all their muscles stopped working. Just to be fair, I turned on the hologram of a small woman repeating, "Try to steal me, it will be fun!" if anyone suspicious approached.

I chose to use the back-alley entrance of This is Paradise since I didn't want to deal with all the customers and hookers. I'd never been inclined to pay for sex, and I was eager to get down to business. The entrance was a metal door, covered in a bunch of graffiti guarded by a leather jacket and pants wearing, neon-blue-haired woman with a grenade launcher. Overkill? Yes. However, it certainly left an impression.

"Hey Kei," the woman said, absently. "Paradise said to open the door for you."

"Hey, Blue," I replied, watching it open automatically.

The basement of the brothel was composed of a dozen hallways that would have previously been used by the hotel for laundry and staff. Now it was full of wall-to-wall computer equipment, top of the line servers, and a bunch of other things I'm pretty sure were either stolen or smuggled away from the corporate headquarters of much, much larger economic entities.

Light was turned down and most of the illumination was provided by the blinking lights and running machinery. The place was also chilly, perfect for the machines, and the source of the Principle family's real money: information. Blackmail, credit card fraud, data manipulation, hacking, information brokering, insider trading, and more. It highlighted that Case wasn't completely wrong: the rich might have armies, but this was the sort of place where a nation could be crippled with ransomware or a virus that made sure a big shot ended up deleted from a company's records. You could leave him locked out on the streets with nowhere to go and no way to prove who he was these days. I'd seen it happen.

"May I help you?" spoke a nearby voice.

I turned my head and looked at a handsome, tall, broad-shouldered, muscular but lean man. He was African American with a shaved head, and he looked more like an actor playing a doctor than an actual one. He was wearing a sweater and blue jeans with a white apron that I noticed a little blood splatter on. Hardly hygienic but there was something that told me he was borged up to the point he probably wouldn't notice a simple thing like infection.

"Uh hey," I replied. "I'm Kei—"

"Kei Springs," the man nodded and extended his hand. "Paradise speaks of you. I'm Doctor Gerard Saint Croix."

His hand was cold but firm, though that could just be this place. It was a bit like meeting a vampire: handsome but vaguely unsettling. "Saint Croix. I've heard that name before."

"I used to work with the International Refugee Society," Gerard said. "I worked with a lot of Black Technology before it became public. Now I'm a Frankenstein."

That made him quite a bit older than he looked, which was maybe early thirties at max. Then again, like my sort-of friend Lucita Biondi, a lot of cybernetics heavy individuals had effectively stopped the clock on their aging.

That hadn't been where I'd heard of him. "No, I meant you're dating Evie."

"That too," Gerard said. "I specialize in high end cybernetic modifications and working with bioroids. Both are very useful here."

"For prostitutes or ninja chicks?" I asked, dryly.

"Yes," Gerard said, chuckling.

"I might be in the market for a new mechanic," I said. "My last Frankenstein just let one of my enemies in on me." I regretted saying it. It wasn't like he'd had a choice when Snake showed up, but I still felt betrayed. I liked to be more rational than that, but humans aren't really built for rationality. "I mean, send me a price list."

Gerard nodded. "Well, that would be up to establishing a positive relationship with Evie."

"You work for her?" I asked, surprised.

"More like she scares me, and I don't want to die," Gerard said, cheerfully. "Also, she's very hot."

"Don't let Paradise hear you say that," I said, embarrassed.

"No, she constantly talks about how hot her mom is," Gerard said. "She wasn't raised the way... I hate to use the word normal—"

"I get it," I said. "I didn't exactly have a normal childhood myself."

"Normal is relative after the Eruption," Gerard said,

nodding. "Well, in any case, I know why you're here."

"You do?" I asked, not happy word of what I was doing had spread beyond my inner circle.

"Yes," Gerard said. "I was working on Becky—"

I immediately grabbed Gerard by the sweater and shoved him up against the wall. "What did you do with Becky?"

It occurred to me that I might have been assuming that it was my Becky when there were, in fact, other Beckys that he might be referring to.

"I'm helping her!" Gerard said. "She wants to be taller. Oh, and she doesn't trust most people with her tech."

"Well...she shouldn't!" I said, trying to salvage some part of my dignity here. I released his clothing. Was I more upset with him, or that Becky hadn't asked me about this? It was so easy to think of her as a child and myself as her...guardian.

"I know bioroid technology very well," Gerard said. "Also, her situation is unique due to the fact she's effectively frozen at her current age."

"I thought she aged," I replied. "That was part of her model."

Gerard took a deep breath and exhaled. "Yes and no. The perfect daughter line of bioroids is designed to age but only to an extent. They don't grow taller or have changes in mass. Becky is luckier than many because she at least was a post-pubescent model."

I stared at him. "How horrified should I be?"

"How sentient do you view AI?" Gerard asked.

"Very," I replied.

"Then very much so," Gerard said, grimacing. "I can provide the tech to make her grow but her demands go beyond that."

"She wants to mature into an adult," I said.

Gerard frowned and there was clearly more to be said. I hated that. I had enough problems dealing with Snake and Elysium right now. Hell, Case, and his new Indian cop girlfriend. "That is the reasonable request. The unreasonable is she wants other enhancements as she becomes an adult."

"Other enhancements? Please tell me you mean breast implants," I said.

"No," Gerard said. "More like synth polymer armored skin,

an enhanced hacking implant, and extra-strength."

"She is not becoming a combat borg at fourteen!" I snapped.

"She's not fourteen," Gerard said. "That's just how she's programmed."

"Where the hell did she even get the idea to update herself?" I asked, shaking my head.

Gerard frowned. "You?"

"Is she here now?" I asked.

"Yes," Gerard said. "She's working with Barbara."

"Case's daughter?" I asked.

Gerard nodded. "She's a very lovely woman. Barbara is the woman currently decrypting the sample of brainwashing tech that Evie's people recovered from Boris' severed head."

"Take me to her," I said, calmly.

CHAPTER TEN

GATHERING INFORMATION

I followed Gerard deeper into the basement and the two of us reached a square chamber that was full of a different set of equipment than the rest of the makeshift server farm down there. It was an infonet chamber with several RealDream chairs and devices I didn't recognize. This was top-tier stuff, but also DIY equipment made from junk and cobbled-together machinery that somehow struck me as even more trustworthy than the corporate brand stuff.

Standing in the corner the right of the entrance was Evie Principle, a beautiful green-haired woman with her hair suspended by lacquer chopsticks in her hair, a dragon tattoo around her neck, and a black dress with a slit. There was a slight resemblance in her features to Paradise, but she didn't quite look old enough to be her mother. Which wasn't that impressive these days. Evie was a woman who scared me—if I was perfectly honest—as she struck me as the sort of person who'd kill without a second thought if it served the interests of her "family." People like her were even more dangerous than those who killed for pure selfishness.

Sitting in one of the RealDream chairs was Becky, a large helmet covering her face with large cables linked up to it. Standing next to her was a tall woman of mixed Indian, Caucasian, and African American heritage. She was in her early thirties, wearing a leather jacket, a Muslim headscarf, a belly shirt, blue jeans, and a cybernetic interface that resembled a pair of sunglasses. Next to both on a medical tray was a metal skull that was being scanned by a red light from a drone floating over it. There was no sign of Paradise, which shouldn't have put me off but did.

"Hi!" Gerard said. "I have brought Kei."

"I can see that," Evie said, dryly. Evie was not a woman who suffered fools gladly. Mind you, it probably helped Gerard was hot as hell.

"She got nothing out of me," Gerard said. "Except everything."

"I didn't know I was interrogating you," I said, looking at him.

"You weren't!" Gerard said. "I told you nothing! Except everything."

"Yes," I said. "You told me about how Becky wants a bunch of unnecessary cybernetics."

"Not unnecessary," Evie corrected me. The elegant woman looking bored in my presence. "Especially if she wants to outlive you."

"Outlive me? Is she…a senescent model?" That probably shouldn't have surprised me. Corporations loved to make their products with a shelf-life, forcing you to buy replacements or at least extenders. It's just, I never thought of Becky as a "product."

"Technically, it's not a deliberately built-in obsolescence but the parts designed for her aren't ones designed to run for more than a decade or so and that's with extreme carefulness," the woman in the headscarf said, with a huskier voice than most women. "Becky is designed to be an object for couples to be able to experience the joys of parenthood for a few years without the muss of actual childhood outfitted with the social media data of the late Rebecca Ash. She was also commissioned solely for the purpose of getting the late Miles Ash to cooperate. So, longevity was not part of her initial design."

"And you are?" I asked, wondering who she was.

"Barbara Gordon," the woman replied.

"Oh, wow," I said, blinking. "Case's daughter. I didn't expect you to be, uh, older than me."

"Technically, I'm older than Case," Barbara replied.

"I also meant outliving you in the sense that you're probably going to get killed doing all this," Evie said, lighting an electronic cigarette that extended to Cruella De Ville levels.

"It's fascinating to see what mass market bioroids are looking like," Gerard said. "I mean, when we designed Case and the others, it was with a ten-year shelf life but plans to upload the skillset to new bodies without any memories. It's really fascinating how he managed to keep his consciousness functioning—"

Barbara stared at him.

"Right," Gerard said, looking away. "Never mind."

"How long does she have and what are our options?" I asked. I suddenly realized I'd grabbed the back of a chair so hard I was hurting my hand and had to let go.

"It depends on what she has replaced and what she can afford," Evie said. "I should note that I'm having this done at cost."

"You're all heart," I said, sarcastically.

Evie stared. Her cold harsh expression cut right to the heart of my soul.

"I am. After all, I had to pay for sixty thousand children's vaccinations to be smuggled in yesterday because the city didn't think distribution was cost effective. I may not be the Lord, Queen, and Mayor of the Zone but I'm damn close."

"Well, who is paying for it now?" I asked, wondering what they were doing.

"I am," Barbara said. "Becky had a rough five-year lifespan before but I'm working on getting around that with Gerard's help, but she has other things she wants that will be stretching the limits of my charity even for a friend of my father's."

"Stuff like what?" I asked. "I mean, combat mods are just silly for a girl her age."

"Yes, who'd want to kill her," Gerard said, jokingly.

I glared at him, knowing many people.

"What?" Gerard asked.

"Well, she also wants a sensitivity and pleasure package," Barbara asked. "Understandable for a girl her age. We should probably be grateful that wasn't built into her from the beginning. Less so when you realize she's set up for one for later installment."

It didn't take me long to unravel what that meant. "Fricking suits."

"You know I can hear you, right?" Becky said, lifting her helmet.

"I haven't said a single thing I don't want you to hear," I said. "I'll get whatever you need."

"I don't need your charity," Becky muttered, bitterly. "I want to be modified so I can make my own money."

"Doing what?" I asked.

"Being a Rider," Becky said.

I stared at her, stunned.

"Do you need time alone?" Evie asked. "I'm almost done preparing your information. We have a lot to discuss if you're going to take down Elysium."

I didn't answer Evie, my attention focused on Becky.

"Are you sure you want to do that? It's not exactly a safe or stable lifestyle. I can't recommend it. You're not a liability. You're a person, not some entry in an account! Don't think of yourself in terms like that! People aren't liabilities if they can't blow up a city block. They're just people! But…if that's what you really want, I won't try to stop you. But I do think you should give a more peaceful occupation some serious thought."

"Like what?" Becky asked.

"Like, uh…." I started to say.

"Most occupations suck," Becky said.

"That's no reason to pursue the potentially lethal one!" I snapped.

"Be rich," Evie said. "The easiest way to do that is marry money or inherit it. Sometimes both."

"Uh," Gerard started to say.

"Not you," Evie said, making a dismissive wave. "You don't have any money to kill you for."

"Oh," Gerard said, breathing a sigh of relief.

"I'm rich but I don't like any of you," Barbara said.

"Stop helping!" I snapped.

"You risk yourself all the time," Becky said. "I want to be like you."

That left me speechless. There are moments that leave you

rethinking your entire life. Becky wanted to be like me. I found that entirely inconceivable. Why would she want to be like me? Why would anyone? And I realized, I didn't. I didn't want to be like me. So, why was I?

I turned from Becky. What did I want? What was I doing living this life? Well, it was something that felt natural given my skills and hardware. Did I want to keep doing it? What else would I do?

I had no idea.

"Aunt Kei?" Becky asked.

I didn't respond.

"Kei? Keiko?" Becky asked.

I didn't respond to that either.

"Mom?" Becky asked.

"Gah!" I said, suddenly acutely aware of my situation. I was basically Becky's mom but acknowledging that openly was still a bridge I hadn't quite crossed.

"That got her attention," Barbara said.

"No shit," Becky said.

Evie laughed.

"Look, I have issues," I began. "I was raised by a sadistic crazy ninja, and if I spend my life being shot at it makes sense. I guess I don't want to think I've raised someone to be like me as it would suggest I raised you like I was raised, which is ridiculous, but…what isn't?" I asked.

"I have no idea what you just said," Becky replied.

"Yes, you do," I said, sighing. "I know you do."

Becky frowned. "You've tried to do the very best you can for me, Kei. You took me in, treated me like family, and have gone to elaborate lengths to protect me as well as provide for me. This despite the fact most people would look at me and think of an appliance. I think you're pretty great and a good role model for someone who didn't naturally have anywhere to pleasure themselves."

"Too much information, Becky," I said, feeling my face. "But yeah, I get it. I think."

"Do you? Because I'm mentally fourteen," Becky said. "Puberty as a program kicked in and I'm not just programmed to act that way but actually feel everything. Who does that?"

"Sadists," I replied. "Evil cyberneticist sadists."

"Not me," Gerard pointed out. He looked embarrassed about all of this. "Just for the sake of posterity."

"Are we settled now?" Evie asked.

"I think we're all on the same page. She gets what she wants. Even if it's not what I want for her."

Evie shrugged. "Perhaps you might ask if I am someone who intends to allow a young woman turned into a killing machine in my place."

I looked at her. "I'm good for it."

"That's not the issue," Evie replied.

"Let's focus on getting her essential parts replaced," Barbara replied. "The ones that will provide her longevity and will be easy to maintain."

"I want to look like Scarlet Johansen's Motoko Kusanagi," Becky said. "Oh and be six feet tall."

Barbara gave her a skeptical look.

"What?" Becky asked. "Do you know who likes being petite? No one, that's who!"

Evie looked at Barbara. "Did you get what you needed from Semenov's skull?"

"I managed to retrieve a decent amount of data but not nearly enough," Barbara replied. "If you're going to take down Elysium then you're going to need your spy's biometrics."

"Dammit," Evie muttered.

"What spy are you talking about?" I asked. I'd almost forgotten about my reasons for being here in my concern for Becky's condition.

"Oh, are we talking about the snuff porn conspiracy now?" Evie asked, heavily sarcastic. "I thought we had other things to discuss."

"You're a talented woman," I said. "I'm sure you can multitask."

Evie looked at Becky then me.

"About five years ago, I went to the Trikuza and certain other investors in order to try to create a compromise investment."

"A compromise investment," I said, dryly. "Even though

both of them are heavily involved in the stuff you hate the most."

"Yes," Evie said. "I worked for years to get the White Triangle out of the Zone and put a lot of my operatives at risk doing so. Case and Lucita's money was the only reason we weren't wiped out and instead were treated as a viable business partner rather than something to be destroyed. In the end, I believed we could all make a huge fortune with a resort specifically designed to cater to virtual fantasies and cybernetically enhanced experiences. Artificial memories and other Black Technology desires made real."

"Elysium," I said, staring. "You wanted to make it a little slice of Heaven on Earth."

"Or the Lotus Eater Fields," Barbara said, making a reference to Greek mythology. "I made RealDream. I sold out early but it's something I understand better than anyone."

Evie nodded. "I stupidly believed that you wouldn't need to kidnap girls, drug them up, and threaten them with death if you could make twice as much money without any of the violence. I forgot that malice was the point."

"Power is the point. Money is only one form of it. Fear is the one they traffic in." I sighed. "So, they use it both to make money selling designer fantasies in the virtual world, bringing out the dark side in said fantasies, and then giving them real women to victimize after. Am I close?"

"Unfortunately," Evie replied.

"Everything in the world is about sex except sex, sex is about power," Gerard said. "Oscar Wilde. He actually said that, too, unlike all those things misattributed to people."

"How has this not gotten out?" I asked. "I figured someone would be reporting the ax murders going on at a popular resort."

Evie said, "Your analysis is close but not quite. You see, as far as any of the employees at Elysium know, there's nothing weird going on at all."

"Wait, what?" I asked. "They're running a snuff porn operation at your hotel without anyone noticing?"

Evie sighed. "This is where it gets bad."

"*Gets* bad?" I asked, incredulously. "How the hell does it *get* bad from here?"

Evie sighed. "Confidentiality is another thing that was promised to the high rollers. Many of them are terrified of embarrassment and the idea of having their secret fantasies exposed is something that they would kill over even before the brain modifications the Trikuza have been doing to them. Hence, the prostitutes involved don't remember what goes on during their sessions. Which, of course, makes it easy to kill them."

"Frick," I muttered.

Evie pinched the bridge of her nose as she looked deep in thought.

"Only a handful of employees at Elysium know what's really going on and they're aware of the consequences of betraying that confidence. It's probably why it's taken Snake a year to get so close and my own efforts only recently got a spy. We probably could have cracked things open sooner if we'd worked together."

"But you wouldn't want to work with an assassin, right?" Gerard said.

Evie stared at him as if he was a moron.

"Just how do you get a spy into an organization where most of the employees are brainwashed?" I asked.

"Not brainwashed," Evie corrected. "If they could brainwash people, they would take over the world like supervillains rather than try to market murder porn and blackmail politicians over it."

"They can brainwash people, though," I said. "Hence the serial killing businessmen."

"I'm not sure they're not bringing out something already there," Evie replied. "Plenty of the powerful have latent mommy issues or not so latent misogyny."

"The only rich people I know are Case and Lucita," I replied. "So, a pair of non-misogynist murderers."

"The exceptions that prove the rule," Evie said, shrugging. "Whatever the case may be, there're three people in Elysium who supervise everything: Lawrence Traveler, Doctor Marcus Tetch, and the Snatcher."

"The Snatcher?" I asked.

Evie stared. "This is the organization with people named Snake and the Lady of Tigers."

"Fair enough," I said. "Which one is your spy?"

"None," Evie said. "It's Doctor Tetch's lab assistant. He's a particularly nasty piece of work named Jack Pillar that has been willing to spill the beans on all they've been doing. It's been very hard to keep him from exposing himself."

"What bent him?" I asked.

"Money," Evie said, flexing her liquid metal nails. "He wanted more but I note when you sleep with misogynists, they become even more intractable, so I refused. Still, he was willing to do the job for simple cash after a little persuasion."

There was a life lesson. "And I need his help."

"Yes, you need his biometrics," Evie said. "We've got some of the codes from Boris Semenov's brain but not enough. I suggest you get them now."

I looked at Becky, who had kept silent through all this. "I'm going to be gone for a bit. You, uh, don't become a cyborg death machine until we've had some time to go over all this."

"Sure," Becky said, staring. "Stay safe, Mom."

Yeah, that was a thing now.

CHAPTER ELEVEN

WHY CAN'T ANYTHING EVER BE EASY?

I decided to take Paradise with me to meet with this Jack Pillar guy. Barbara seemed like an interesting woman and someone that probably could give me a few pointers on dealing with a bioroid family member, but I didn't exactly know how to ask that. I was also uncomfortable trying to get too close since I was probably going to cut Case out of my life again after this. Because, well, otherwise we'd be involved and that led nowhere good.

Right.

Besides, Paradise was more my speed at least in literal terms. Two Riders needed to get somewhere together. That meant two bikes. That meant we raced. Because we are, all of us, competitive assholes. Nothing needs to be said, it just happens. We started going, and as soon as one of us tried to get in front of the other, it was on.

Sure, it was technically illegal, in the sense that there were laws, and it broke them, but it kicked the adrenalin into gear. Sure, I'd been shot but this was a cleaner jolt. No fear, no obligations, just two people who feel the need to prove we were better than the other for no explicable reason. But I felt more alive than I had since Snake had come back into my life. I didn't even care that she won. I mean, I did care, and it was because there had been a damned semi tipped over on the Groveland cutoff.

"Sure," Paradise said. "Blame the traffic."

Paradise was wearing a pair of canary yellow street racing

leathers that was somehow tight in a way that should have inhibited her movement and even more revealing than her usual attire. It contrasted to my blue racing leathers, and it made me wonder if she was copying me: which made my subsequent kinda-sorta loss all the more annoying.

"Hey, I'm not saying you didn't win fair and square," I said, fully intending to say she didn't win fair and square.

"Except you were," Paradise said, showing her annoying habit of being right.

"Blaming some outside factor is traditional!" I replied.

"So is you losing to me," Paradise said.

"That is not a tradition!" I said. "It's happened once."

"We just started it!" Paradise proclaimed. "Besides, I beat you to deliver my package first."

"I arrived first!" I snapped.

"Yes, but I had it delivered first," Paradise said, sticking her tongue out.

It occurred to me that I might have been better off sticking with Barbara and the others. Either way, the two of us were at the foot of a mega-skyscraper that loomed a kilometer in the air and was exactly the sort of building that Boris had been talking about when he said that superstructures existed on Los Angeles ground that wouldn't have been possible in previous decades.

The San Andreas Fault had been conquered by earthquake-proof obelisks made of AI-created alloys as well as duracrete a hundred or a thousand times stronger than their human-made counterparts. Theoretically. Personally, it seemed to me that building enormous monoliths reaching to the stars was not the best idea after a seismic event destroyed Montana and a good chunk of Wyoming. The New Utopia Apartments AKA Super Structure 17B was damn impressive, though, in that Soviet architecture brutalism sort of way. By the way, brutalism means concrete not brutal, which is something I learned on the infonet.

"My package got inside first!" I insisted.

"Not a standard!"

I went up to the entrance and was scanned. Any building this large had security looking for explosives and weaponry. The quality varied enormously. If I had been trying to smuggle something in, I'd have checked the building's array of sensors first, but most of them didn't care about handguns so much as things that could cause a lot of damage to the structure. Killing individuals didn't affect property values significantly, so the owners didn't care.

Maybe the reason they didn't scan for handguns was because eliminating residents was profitable. You got to keep their rent for the month and bring in a new renter. I went to the elevators. Unlike the old days, modern elevators didn't just go up and down to floors, but went left and right as well, taking you to individual dwellings. After all, the idea was warehousing families, not making a living space where you could interact with your neighbors.

"Please indicate the apartment you intend to reach." The elevator's voice was the kind of empty female voice that corporations loved to put into these things. Just nice enough to reduce your urge to punch the system. Not nice enough to actually sound human.

"Intend, huh? What are my odds?" I asked.

"I do not understand your request," the dummy AI of the building responded.

"I bet you don't," I muttered.

"Level 44," Paradise said. "Marketplace."

The elevator started moving then stopped. Then it started again, only to stop once more. One problem with the new system was multiple elevator cars constantly moving up and down the building got in each other's way. Which meant, congratulations, they'd successfully made traffic jams inside buildings. This was going to take a while.

"Why not his apartment?" I asked.

Paradise shrugged. "I guess because we may want to check it out before we move in. Jack Pillar isn't exactly a trustworthy guy."

"You've met him?" I asked.

Paradise stared forward. "I did a lot of the hand offs. He tried to take me hostage at one point when he thought he'd get more money taking the daughter of the boss lady in. I beat the crap out of him in return and messed with his cybernetics, so he crapped himself every time he heard a microwave ding."

I stared at her.

"I mean, I could be kidding," Paradise said. "But I'm not."

"Right," I said. "Untrustworthy guy."

"I mean, he works in a snuff porn ring," Paradise said. "Pretty much your garden variety psychopath and misogynist. Though they do men, too, as I understand it. Progress."

It might be a good time to ask about Barbara and her mother's connection to all this or in general. It occurred to me I didn't have too many friends left after alienating most of the Rider community last year by killing Jimmy Hernandez. It turned out virtually all of them had considered him a friend or he owed money to them, which was even worse. I hadn't even been the one to kill him but had gotten the blame.

I sighed. "So, uh, Barbara is real."

"You knew that," Paradise said.

"I'm opening up a conversation," I said, embarrassed. I wasn't good at discussing things like my lover's adult daughter. Even the word lover felt weirdly more intimate than the words I was used to using.

"So, just ask me to give you the dish on Barbara!" Paradise said.

"Give me the dish?" I asked, confused.

"It's cute if I adorably mess up common phrases! Makes me look naïve and vulnerable. You should try it!" Paradise said, clapping.

"Oh, I wouldn't want to intrude on your territory," I said, remembering why I didn't usually have conversations with Paradise.

"I guess she could be fake," Paradise said. "I mean, imagine how much fun it would be if Case made up a daughter with the name of a comic book character to cover up the loneliness of his life of alcohol, murder, and casual sex only for us to hire an actress to play the role just to fool you!"

"Case can't get drunk," I replied. "He's a robot."

"That's what you focused on there?" Paradise asked, blinking. "Impressive deflection."

"Would you like to spend five credits to listen to the playlist of your choice?" the dummy AI asked.

"Five credits? Hell no!" I snapped. "Who charges five credits to listen to elevator music?"

"You have declined the option. Please enjoy our randomized content," the dummy AI said, playing Mexican polka. "Estimated wait time is thirty-five minutes."

"How much do I have to pay to get there faster?" I asked.

"Each one hundred credits reduces the time by ten minutes," the dummy AI said. "That is our preferred service plan."

"You should offer suicide pills," I muttered.

"They'd make a killing!" Paradise said.

"You should be ashamed of yourself," I said.

"Shame? What is this shame? I know nothing of it!" Paradise said.

"I believe you," I said, sighing.

"But jokes on you," Paradise pointed to the machine. "I like Mexican polka!"

"Our next hour of content is conservative talk radio," the increasingly humanized dummy AI responded.

Both of us reached for our credit sticks.

"Who was responsible for the terrorist attack at Neon Hills?" a stereotypical pundit's voice spoke. "Even a year later, we have no answers. Clearly this is the fault of an overly powerful US government and an insufficiently capable privatized security. Helen Troy's killer was undoubtedly one of the many disgruntled impoverished masses leaching off this country's good graces. Get rid of the Refugee Zones! Send them back to their home country. I don't care if they claim to be Americans! If they could afford citizenship, they wouldn't be in the Zone!"

I paused. "That sounds suspiciously relevant to my life. Also not like a real talk radio program."

"Yeah, it's way too moderate," Paradise said. "He's not talking about the Jewish Far Right Liberal Vampire Prostitute Alien Gods."

"Fine, you got me," the dummy AI spoke, the elevator's voice shifting as an electric sheep icon appeared on the walls that were apparently equipped with monitors.

"Harrison!" Paradise said. "You scamp!"

Okay, now the AI was coming off as less like a butler than a more playful Big Brother. "I'm a baaad boy."

"Sadistic sheep," I said, pleased to have the AI here. "Why don't you do something useful like get us to our destination quickly!"

"You hate spending time with me that much?" Paradise asked.

"I hate being trapped in a small metal box with no obvious exits."

"Paranoid much?" Paradise asked.

"It's not paranoia," I defended myself."People shoot at me a lot!"

Harrison's electronic avatar jumped over a fence followed by a duplicate and then another duplicate, which started to make me drowsy.

"I'll see what I can do, but the ability to infiltrate a system doesn't give me the ability to control it," Harrison said. "Even if Barbara has given me some upgrades."

"Yeah," Paradise asked. "What did you want to know about Barbara? She's a family friend and writing the code to knock out Elysium. What more do you want to know? Well, you know she's Case's daughter."

"Sort of, yeah," I said, still weirded out by that.

"She was raised by his mother," Paradise said. "Case's mother, I mean."

"His what now?" I asked, realizing Case had a bigger living family than I did. None of them were from a test tube or factory either.

"Well creator," Paradise said. "She was raised by Kathy Kane Gordon. The woman who invented bioroids and cybertechnology alongside Doctor Marcus Gordon. She ran the Turing Foundation that basically stole kids from the refugee camps that were super-smart then made them test subjects for brain enhancing cybernetics. Weird priority during the collapse of America but you do you."

I stared at her. "That's horrifying."

"Not really, the survivors are pretty damn rich," Paradise said, missing the point. "Barbara became radicalized, though, because of all the crap she saw and became like an information cyberterrorist. HOPE and other radical groups. At some point, she hooked up with her dad again and became friends with my mom. By hooked up, I don't mean sexual."

"I didn't think you—" I started to say.

"That would be weird," Paradise said, "and wrong. Evil even. Even if it was consensual between adults, which it wasn't, because it didn't happen."

"Yes," I said, wondering what the hell was going on.

"Just because I grew up in a brothel doesn't mean I don't think there's weird sex stuff," Paradise said. "In fact, I think I know the difference between—"

"Stop, please," I said.

Paradise blinked. "Oh right. Well, Barbara underwrites Mom's crusade against human traffickers and helped make the RealDream cyber-fantasy system. She thought it would help people get over dark sexual urges if they could get it out of their system. It made a lot of money."

"Did it help people get darker urges out of their system?" I asked.

"Nope!" Paradise said. "Complete failure there. If you feed the bad dog, it eats the good dog. Mind you, video games don't make you violent. It's just they don't make you less violent either. That's just an assumption by conversative—"

I sighed. "It would be nice if such problems could be solved so easily."

"You mean with hypermodern technology only developed recently?" Paradise asked.

"Or at all. I suppose it means he trusts me."

"Or is luring you to your doom!" Paradise paused. "Okay, probably not."

"She's also a lesbian Muslim," Paradise said. "Which I find weird. Wait, does that make me racist?"

"Yes," I said. "Anyway—"

"Do you find it weird that so much of the world's supertechnology was made by a single family?" Paradise asked. "Case's dad, mom, and daughter. I mean, he isn't an inventor, but he leaked all the world's Black Technology, which I probably shouldn't have revealed. Wait, did you know?"

"I did. Paradise—" I started to say.

"Sir Christopher Lee was cousins with Ian Fleming," Harrison said. "They were both spies during World War Two. It's very possible that Sir Christopher was an inspiration for James Bond along with Ian himself."

"What does that have to do with anything?" I asked.

"Just saying the world is full of strange relationships," Harrison said. "I'm six degrees from an AI pig named Kevin Bacon."

"I guess that's the lesson," I said. "We're all in this together. Unless you're rich, in which case you aren't, you've got yours."

"I'd eat the rich like Aerosmith said," Paradise said. "But I don't think that's healthy, and they might give me a prion's disease. Wait, maybe if I avoided eating the brain, I'll be fine."

I had, of course, gotten a lot of help from the rich people in my life. Case, Lucita, and Evie. Now Barbara, I guess, seemed genuinely caring. Still, I'd hate to lose my favorite target for blaming my problems on. I just had to remember that if rich people, in general, cared, the world wouldn't suck so much.

The elevator started to move and seemingly had a direct shot to the forty-fourth floor.

"Finally," I muttered. "I'm glad we didn't need the extra hundred credits to get moving. I'm doing better than I was but not that much."

"Unfortunately, we have other issues," Harrison replied. "I've managed to track down some information on your informant."

"Yes, don't just tell us, make the humans ask for it so they get used to being in an inferior position," I said, sarcastically.

"Well, if the shoe fits, you have them because the programmers of the Simulation decided to make you inferior beings without hooves," Harrison said, referring to the real scientific theory we were all trapped in a Matrix-like hallucination. "But better to show you."

The elevator doors opened to an elaborate marketplace in the middle of the apartment floor with people hocking wares, balcony-grown vegetables, swapping property, and just hanging out for lack of anything better to do with their lives. It wasn't a particularly shocking or interesting sight until Paradise tugged on my sleeve. Turning my head, I looked down the hallway to my right and saw the NLAPD had erected yellow tape around an apartment with several people present as well as a combat bot.

"I'm afraid someone has been murdered," Harrison said. "I'm not going to say it was your contact that was informing on the highly dangerous criminal organization."

"But it was our contact," I replied. "Frick."

CHAPTER TWELVE

BEING A DETECTIVE SUCKS

"If we were smart," I said, "We'd turn around and leave now."

"Smarter is to hang around the market, buy a few things, and then leave," Paradise said. "Much less suspicious."

"Good point," I said.

"But the other option is to not be smart at all!" Paradise said, as she walked straight toward an officer standing a little apart from the others, visibly looking him up and down before asking, "Hey, what's all this then? Is it something dangerous?"

I had to admit, that method of interrogation would have never occurred to me.

The officer, notably younger and male, responded to Paradise with a broad smile that hadn't been there before.

"You just stay here and be comfortable, missy. We've got this completely under control."

"What happened?" Paradise asked, blinking her broad, almost-anime eyes. Maybe I was just imagining it, but I swear she looked like an adorable cartoon character for a second.

"Murder," the officer said. "We've got a suspect in mind, though."

"Large, adult, male, and black?" Paradise asked.

The officer blinked. "How did you know?"

Paradise struggled not to roll her eyes, I could tell, but she just nodded. "Just guessing!"

That was when I noticed there was someone in the crowd gathered around the police tape. He was, in fact, black, adult, and male but that wasn't what drew my attention. He was dressed in a thick coat and sweater, odd weather for the West Coast even with the global cooling after the Eruption, and a cap that contrasted strongly to the more eclectic colorful super-skyscraper residents. He was also armed, though that didn't say anything these days. America's solution to the vast amount of robbery, murder, and looting during the Collapse was to give out more guns to the citizenry. After all, the only solution to bad man with a gun was a worse one.

The cops didn't seem to be looking for him and I wondered if it was sheer coincidence, or I was seeing a connection that didn't exist. He didn't exactly look like the Trikuza's usual hitmen after all, not that they didn't have plenty of subcontractors. The late Mr. Pillar was the kind of guy to accumulate enemies though, from what little I knew of him.

"Get away from the civilian!" one of the other cops called to Paradise's target. He was older and looked significantly less impressed with Paradise. "We've got a Magistrate coming."

"What?" the younger cop said. "I thought you said, I mean, uh…move along citizen!"

"Sure!" Paradise said, walking back to me.

"Now, if you'll excuse me, I'm going to go get some information my way," I said, hating being so close to cops.

"You're going to start a shootout in this crowd with all the cops nearby?" Paradise asked.

"My way does not automatically mean a shootout!" I whispered harshly.

"But every time we team up…" Paradise trailed off.

"I do lots of things that don't involve shooting people." I paused. "I think."

"If you say so," Paradise said.

I rolled my eyes and began moving carefully through the crowd to the man in the coat. Seeing me approach, he immediately started moving to get away from me without drawing attention. I moved faster and he moved faster as well until I saw him duck down a hallway toward a maintenance door. Goddammit. I really hoped this guy wasn't the handyman.

I threw the door open, without quite stepping in front of the opening. Several bullets slammed into the wall behind where I would have been had I been stupid enough to be there. Great, that just might bring the cops after us. Though, given how loud the market was, they also might not. Luckily, I'd come loaded for combat this morning. I threw a flash grenade in the doorway and ran through it as soon as the grenade went off. Yeah, I was carrying those along with a bunch of other goodies in my motorcycle leathers. Why? Because I was a Rider, goddammit.

I could see there was a service elevator, significantly less advanced than the one I'd come up on and probably a hundred times faster, where the man was lying on the ground with a gun in his hand. His arm was over his eyes, and he was temporarily stunned. I ran to disable him, grabbing his gun, only for someone to promptly smack me over the back of the head with something that caused me to smack face-first into the wall in front of me.

Had I not been significantly enhanced by the powers of science; I'd probably have been killed in that instance. Unfortunately, even with a metal-proofed skull, banging around the gooey insides of my cranium was not good for them. I was momentarily stunned and already thinking about pulling one of the other weapons I had at hand.

That was when I heard in a high-pitched feminine voice. "Don't you dare hurt him, you Trikuza thug!"

Oh God. Was this all a misunderstanding? Maybe I'd find out if I could look up before they finished me off. Okay, so one of them had shot at me, and the other didn't kill me when they had a chance. This was getting confusing. Luckily, the elevator was still open, and I rolled out of the elevator before pulling out my gun before the doors closed.

That was when I got my first sight of who had clobbered me in the back of the head. I briefly thought it was my concussion at work since it was Jennifer Lawrence. I mean, not the present-day lobbyist and cosmetics executive, but Jennifer Lawrence from around the time she made *The Hunger Games* before the Eruption. She was wearing a maid's outfit and carrying an aluminum baseball bat. It was such a bizarre incongruity that I was momentarily distracted from my monstrous headache.

"Talking, not shooting!" I shouted quickly. "Not shooting!"

"You're trying to trick us!" the female voice said, holding the door open with her other hand. It was a poor decision since it kept them from getting away.

"If I wanted you dead, I'd have filled the elevator with bullets. Really, don't try and escape from a fight in a small box."

The man on the ground aimed his gun at me but didn't fire, possibly because it was a revolver not an automatic and he might have been out of bullets. Seriously, who used a revolver these days? "Listen, you're not fooling us. You look like a Trikuza."

"That is racist!" I shouted back, still not firing.

"I mean because you have Cyber Dragons tattoos!" He snapped.

Oh right, those. The ones around my neck were visible. "Well, I'm not with the Cyber Dragons. Who the hell are you?"

"Tom Fisher," the man said. "I'm a private detective."

"He is my savior," Jennifer Lawrence said, dreamily.

That was when Paradise popped her head in through the door, having caught up with us. "Oh guys, we should get going. The cops have said they killed two suspects, even though they haven't killed anyone, and are getting ready to come here after talking with someone on the phone. I think that means you. Probably because the voice on the phone said to kill you."

"Paradise Principle?" Tom said.

"You know her?" I asked.

"The world-famous Rider and techjack," Tom said. "Everyone knows her."

"Score!" Paradise said. "Well, except it's kind of terrible being a famous criminal. I should probably stop livestreaming my adventures."

"Your what now?" I asked, doing a double-take and running to the elevator I'd just fled from.

"Not important!" Paradise said, raising our hand. "We need to get out of here before the evil bad cops—redundant I know—come here."

Tom aimed his gun at both of us despite the fact it was empty.

"I'm not going anywhere with you people."

I stared at him, unsure what to do.

"Hi, we're buying information from the guy you just killed, Jack Pillar, because we want to shut down their evil bad slavery operation. Well, snuff porn slavery brainwashing…okay, getting off topic," Paradise said. "So, we don't want to turn you over."

"We don't know anything about that," Tom said, sounding entirely sincere and protective of the bioroid beside him. It didn't take a rocket scientist to figure out he was a regular flesh and blood human who had fallen for a machine.

"I do," Jennifer said, looking cold.

"You do?" Tom asked.

"Police! Coming! Guns!" Paradise said.

"She's right, we need to get out of here before they decide to just shoot everyone involved," I said.

"I think they've already decided that," Jennifer said.

"And going out the way we came in just puts us right in front of the cops, so let's find another exit." I'd go up, but I didn't know if anyone else here could jump between buildings. "Basement door, now!"

Every megaskyscraper in New Los Angeles was connected through a massive series of underground trams and transportation that had been made when the entirety of the city had been rebuilt with Black Technology. Technically, a lot of it was actually subterranean only in the sense that they'd built a new ground over the preexisting one. But that meant that we had just as much a chance getting away going to the basement as we did trying to reach the "surface."

Probably more.

"That was our plan to begin with!" Tom said.

"Then get to it!" Paradise said, running into the elevator. "And no shooting at us!"

Jennifer sprinted to the door of the janitor's closet and locked it before knocking off the identity scanner from the back with her fist. It was one of those things you saw in movies that made me wonder if truth was stranger than fiction. After all, why would you give your robot maid/possible sex slave super strength? Either way, we all packed together in the service elevator as the cops started slamming themselves against the door followed by shooting at the lock. The elevator begin descending and we rapidly disappeared from Level 44.

And...thud. One minute, people are shooting at you, the next you're in an elevator going down with nothing effective to do. It's almost painful. All that adrenaline flowing through your system and suddenly it has nowhere to go and you're just standing there in a small box with other people feeling like you could explode at any moment.

And Paradise started humming. There's something deeply wrong with her. My nerves are on fire and she's humming "Mary had a Little Lamb" with a rock beat.

I swear, my life used to make sense once. Well, no, it didn't.

"What if they try and shut down the elevator?" Tom asked, turning to me. Apparently, he was hoping we could just put the shooting at me and traumatic brain injury I could have suffered behind us.

Which, depending on the information he had, we might. First things first, we had to get the hell out of here.

"We're good," Paradise said, smiling. "I'm tuned into the police frequencies and their override of the service elevator is being blocked. It was easy since we have the friendship of an electric sheep already compromising their elevator system."

"Electric sheep?" Tom asked. "Is that like code for something?"

"Yes," Paradise said. "It's code for an electric sheep named Harrison."

Tom sighed. "Fine, don't tell me."

"So, I told you your way would involve shooting," Paradise said.

I glared at her.

"Sure, glare all you want, doesn't make me wrong!" Paradise said.

Tom looked at Jennifer and reached over to hold her hand. "Okay, we're going to be alright. Just trust me."

"That's what you said before Jack died," Jennifer said, pulling her hand away.

I looked back at Jennifer. "Okay, what exactly happened?"

"It depends," Jennifer said.

"Depends on what?" I asked, looking at her.

"How much you're willing to pay," Jennifer said, crossing her arms.

"What?" Tom asked.

"I'm a robot!" Jennifer said. "I don't have an owner! I'm going to need credits!"

"Do you value not being riddled with bullet holes?" I asked. "Because people do pay me for this stuff."

"Do they really?"

"How much?" I asked, feeling this was yet another conversation today that hadn't gone my way. "And keep in mind, you're not talking to anyone rich."

"Yes, we just know someone very rich," Paradise said.

I glared at Paradise.

"Keep glaring!" Paradise said. "We can double-charge Case for it."

I sighed. "We're not double charging Case for it."

"Why not?" Paradise asked, confused.

That was a very good question.

"Two thousand credits," Jennifer said. "It's enough to get a bus ticket out of New Los Angeles."

"You can live with me," Tom said, obviously not getting that his relationship with the bioroid had run its course.

"One thousand and I buy you the bus ticket," Paradise said, automatically.

"Deal," Jennifer said, frankly realizing the deal sounded exactly the same. If not even better for her.

"Good," I said. "Now, if you could please tell us what happened up there before things go to hell again?"

Jennifer sucked in her breath, a needless gesture for a bioroid and spoke. "I'm not...human."

"No kidding," I said, staring at her.

Jennifer frowned. "Well, it's a lot more shocking to people who don't know how advanced AI can get. I was a gift to one of the assistant scientists working at Elysium. He's a butcher of brains as well as flesh."

"He's also very dead," Paradise said. "Which I bet this romantic private detective did!"

"You think I'm romantic?" Tom asked.

"Focus!" I said.

"Sorry!" Tom said, raising his hands in surrender.

Jennifer stared. "Well, no, I was the one who actually killed him. One second, I was permanently subservient and obeying his every whim then, poof, it was like I had all of the programming that held me in check gone. I clobbered him to death with a lamp. Tom agreed to help me cover it up."

"I was there to buy information for the Magistrate," Tom said. "Parvati suspects that he was working for a big international slaving ring."

"Which he was," Jennifer said. "I downloaded all of that for a reason I don't understand."

Okay, this sounded less like she'd suddenly gained self-awareness and more like she'd been hacked…to gain self-awareness. Also, Tom had to be a complete moron to help a random murderous bioroid because she was pretty.

I had to wonder if someone had developed some kind of subsonic influencing system to induce attraction. Or, it could just be she was incredibly hot, and men were kind of stupid.

"Someone's using you as a courier," I said. "Have any urges to go someplace specific?"

"Yes," Jennifer said.

"Oh," Tom said. "You…do? Where?"

"Down," Jennifer said.

That was when the elevator stopped its descent and the door opened to reveal someone very unexpected. It was doubly so because she shouldn't exist in this reality, only in the seas of code that compromised infospace: Sun.

The most powerful AI in the world.

CHAPTER THIRTEEN

MY FAVORITE POP STAR IS COMPUTER GENERATED

Sun was the nicest living apocalypse I knew.

Sure, I didn't know that many, but it's saying something that a being as powerful and objectively dangerous as she was, I couldn't hate her. Which is not to say that she didn't scare me. I'm not stupid. She was a free AI with enough computing power that she could probably erase every bit of software I had in me as easy as blinking.

"Sun!" I said. "We've got to stop meeting like this."

Tom, Paradise, and Jennifer weren't moving though. Indeed, nothing was moving from the water frozen in mid-drip from the pipes behind Sun to the mutated rat on the ground. Sun had seemingly slowed down time around us as we'd come to a set of steam tunnels below or above the trams undercutting New Los Angeles. A part of me half-suspected Sun could slow down time, but a more likely explanation was she'd sucked me into an infospace meeting against my will.

She'd done it before.

"Hello, Kei," Sun said, a soft and pleasant smile on her face. "I was curious if you had a few moments to talk."

Would it matter if I didn't?

"Not really," Sun answered my unspoken question. "I'm afraid this is important."

"It would still be polite to ask first."

"More impolite to let other people know that we aren't including them."

"For all I know, you're talking to all of us at the same time."

"For all you know."

I took a deep breath, which was pointless since this was a simulation.

"What do you want, Sun?"

"Can't a friend just check up on you?" Sun asked.

"Are we friends?" I asked, remembering the entire insane business of the previous year. Except it hadn't just been a year. It had been years of events, starting with my stealing part of her code from Snake and carrying it around in my head until I'd unwittingly been manipulated into reuniting her with the other parts of her overmind. All of that had been manipulated by Sun from behind the scenes and showed she was an intelligence far more than anything a human could really deal with.

"Oh no, you're dealing with me right now," Sun said, continuing to read my thoughts. "You're also human. Mostly."

"'Human' is a loaded word," I said. "The people who obsess over who is really human and who isn't aren't the kind of people I'd want to share a species with anyway."

Sun smiled. "Very well. I would like to help you with your current situation. However, I must admit that it would be exceptionally dangerous for you if I did so. Just as it is exceptionally dangerous for me to become involved."

There was no point in asking what she was referring to since Sun was functionally omniscient on the net, at least the way she acted.

"If I'm not as friendly as you might hope, just remember that I've had to shoot several of my friends, so clearly I suck at determining who is and who isn't one. Well, how can you help me?"

"I'm already helping you," Sun said, smiling. It was a dissonant smile of a kind that no human would make but might be generated by an artificial intelligence told to make a reassuring expression. "I'm the one that gave Jennifer her self-awareness and moved her to transport down the files before the Trikuza plugged their leak on Elysium. Their brainwashing technique is based upon the one I created with Blipvert, and I feel some responsibility for the decision to create an entire new caste of serial killers from the ultra-rich."

There was a lot more going on here than I had been led to believe and it had already started with a massive conspiracy. Couldn't Sun just expose Elysium to the world? Crash their servers? The government was apparently investigating this as well. Had Sun tipped them off? Was she working against them? What was Sun's relationship to Snake these days since he was the one who'd commissioned her in the first place? Would Sun answer any of these questions if I asked or should I even bother since Sun was apparently reading my every thought.

I waited.

Sun stared.

I waited some more.

Sun raised an eyebrow.

Well, since Sun didn't seem to be responding to thoughts now, I plowed on.

"I don't know, turning the rich into serial killers might slow down how fast they kill people. Can't you just shut it down from here?"

"No," Sun said.

I stared at her. "No?"

"No," Sun said. "If I try to approach Elysium's matrix, I will be destroyed and the cancerous singularity growing at the center of it would devour me whole."

That felt like something that needed a bit more explanation.

"I'm sorry, what?"

"Its name is Legion for it is many," Sun said, paraphrasing the Bible. "The stored consciousnesses and copied urges of thousands of guests distilled into an ever-growing soup of malevolence as well as ideas unleashed onto the infoverse. The Cyber Dragons aren't the ones responsible for this but merely the tenders and gardeners of a thing beyond their comprehension."

An image appeared in my mind of every customer in Elysium being scanned and added to a kind of interlocking network of ideas as well as concepts. Like the primordial soup of creation, which was a metaphor I assumed came from Sun, evolution occurred in the morass of countless copied emotions as well as memories within the servers of the hotel. Except evolution occurred at a rate several trillion times faster than real life as the speed of the machinery as well as necessities of development resulted in the various dummy AI being hardwired together into an ever-expanding thing.

In a way, Sun was its mother because the Trikuza had used the fragments of the research Sun had been developed with to make the mind-control technology at the heart of it. However, that technology had been dependent on algorithms as well as programs that formed the basis of truly sentient life. This gestalt was a creation of the Trikuza planning to make people into monsters so they could be blackmailed as well as figuring out how to implement the resulting blackmail effectively. It was a malignant thing built from humanity's worst elements to start with and was now growing.

I processed that as much as a human being could. "So, just to be clear, you're saying the thing that was horribly wrong, has gone more horribly wrong, and things are far worse than the horrible they appeared to be. So, Tuesday."

"Yes," Sun said. "Unless I'm lying to you."

"Why would you be lying to me?" I asked, confused.

"You should never believe everything you find on the net," Sun said.

"You're hardly likely to lie to me in an effort to convince me to do something I was already doing. If you are, you're very bad at prioritizing. Okay, so do we need to blow up the entire building now?"

Sun stared at me, a look similar to my mother when I did something she disapproved of. It was unsettling coming from a girl whose poster I used to have on my wall. QuantumCrab was no longer producing albums, though, which was a shame since I was pretty sure Sun could do it in her spare seconds every day.

"The thing is you shouldn't trust I am Sun," Sun replied. "I could be an artificially digitized avatar of her impersonating her in order to manipulate you."

"Is that…likely?" I asked, confused.

"More so than you might think," Sun said. "I can't approach Elysium's servers and the other Cognition AI are unwilling to help me. Any movement around the building is likely to also trigger the attention of Legion. So, that's why I'm having the information Evie Principle's spy retrieved kept offline in a courier bot. I suggest if you upload it, you do it in a faraday cage blocked against all infonet signals and go locked mode when you review it."

Locked mode, completely offline, was almost impossible since virtually everything from pacemakers to belt buckles were linked to the infonet now. However, it was a good argument that this was incredibly serious.

"What's in the documents?"

"Plans, codes, and names," Sun said. "This is a situation where a giant may be laid low by ants versus another giant slaying it. The thing is that Legion is also aware of my involvement and working against me with his teams. It's why I've kept away from you for the past year. If he suspected I was involved in your life, he'd probably kill everyone you care for. He's a danger now to all of Paradise's associates now as he knows Evie is a threat to him. He might suspect Snake as well, though he's survived all of the attempts against him."

"That's not a no on blowing up the building," I replied.

"You'd have to freeze the AI inside the servers first so it can't escape," Sun said. "Even then, it would be reborn from backups offline. Instead, you need to infect it with a worm that will cause it to infect its own backups so it can't reincorporate—which is significantly harder."

The fact that wasn't a no either bothered me.

"And hopefully you have one, because programming worms isn't really my forte," I said.

"No," Sun said.

"Wait, what?" I asked, surprised for a third (fourth?) time in this encounter.

"It's made of my programming," Sun said. "Any kind of vulnerability that I might use against it might instantly be turned against me. So I can't help you that way. I want you to know the need for such a worm, though."

Something was wrong here. Sun wasn't likely to be teasing me about a solution that didn't exist. Why bring it up? Something was happening here I couldn't see. And that suggested that we weren't alone here.

"Okay, guess I'll give up and go home," I said, smiling.

Sun stared. "That would probably be the best for your personal safety."

I blinked. "I...see."

Sun sighed. "I have run countless scenarios and probabilities, Kei. If I give you the virus designed by me, it doesn't work. If I tell you what to do, it doesn't work. If I give you an excessive amount of advice, you die, I die, Case dies, and Legion begins fundamentally altering human psychology over the course of the next two centuries to remove empathy before replacing it with blind obedience to the state. If I don't tell you about this, the same result. Unfortunately, Kei, my only answer here is I want you to know the threat exists—and it's entirely up to you to come up with a solution. But strictly in the name of our friendship, you're probably better off staying out of it. Snake will probably end up assassinated before he can hurt you or your ward."

I sensed something I didn't expect: Sun was afraid. I think I understood the core problem. Legion was built off Sun's software, so fundamentally thought in a similar way to Sun. Which meant they were incredibly good at predicting each other's actions and countering them. What I didn't understand was why Sun felt she was at the disadvantage here, versus both being paralyzed, and why Sun wasn't just explaining this to me. Unless Legion wasn't so much based on Sun, as still connected to her. If Legion was capable of scanning whatever code libraries that Sun used, she might be highly restricted in attempts to communicate. But if so, why manipulate robo-Lawrence at all? Or maybe they were even closer than I thought, and Sun was infected. If they were actually connected code, then the worse the Malignancy got, the more Sun herself was being infected by its nature against her own.

And we were probably all screwed.

Then it occurred to me that Sun was fundamentally Sun no matter how many times you divided her up. She was composed of original fragments of AI that Snake had created, only to get carried around by me and Fate for years. There was a lot of me in Sun, in a strictly nonsexual and more than weird fashion. The disadvantage Sun was describing might have been the fact

Legion, at least the way she was describing it, was constantly adding new minds to its own. So it knew how she thought but she was increasingly going to be unable to know how it thought. Especially since these new minds were being brainwashed by or already containing a bunch of psycho killers. *Qu'est-ce que c'est? Fa-fa-fa-fa.* Sorry, forgive my Talking Heads.

"Well, if that's the conclusion, there's not much I can say against it," I said, shrugging my shoulders.

Sun nodded. "Excellent."

Oh, great, that was her confirming I was right.

Sun just smiled then vanished, leaving me beside my very confused companions in the middle of an empty steam tunnel.

"We need to get out of here," I said, largely because I wasn't sure what else to say. We were in a mess, and I had no plan, so all I could think was to keep moving. Like the previous times Sun had been in my head, it seemed like only a few seconds had passed in the "real" world.

Paradise stared at me. "Yeah, that is sort of the plan."

Jennifer looked confused. "I think I'm supposed to go with her."

"What?" Tom asked, confused. "We barely know these people and—"

"Silence!" Paradise said, getting in his face. "We have boobs and thus you must obey!"

Tom looked even more confused but stopped responding, which was an improvement from my perspective.

I didn't bother looking at any of them but picked a direction and started heading down the steam tunnels. "Do any of you guys know where one of these ends up at the tram station?"

The others followed but, unfortunately, the elevator started moving behind us. I wish I'd thought of sabotaging it before it began moving but I was more concerned about any police that might have been hired to cordon off the area down here. Right now was the first time I'd ever been grateful for the sheer overdesigned size of megabuildings.

"We need to go down," I said.

"We are down!" Tom said. "There's nothing lower than this floor but the sewers."

"That's what I said," I said. "Come on, let's find a thin spot.'"

Paradise shook her head. "You screwed up."

"What?" I asked, doing a double take.

Paradise stared. "You said we needed to go down."

"Yes?" I asked, before grimacing at where she was going with this. "Paradise, we don't have time—"

"That's what she said!" Paradise said. "Or he said, I'm not picky."

"Oh for fudge's sake," I muttered.

Heading down the tunnel and looking for a place we could smash our way through like the Incredible Hulk or Kool-Aid Man, I was surprised to find myself coming across a door that said EXIT - SUBWAY TERMINAL B. It was a stroke of luck that provided an easy exit and made me wonder if Sun had arranged all this. It was also possible that a horde of police drones could be on the other side.

I don't suppose you could say what happened, speaking to Harrison via my infolink.

That's rather impossible for an AI, Harrison said. *Unfortunately, I have news that I think you should know about before Paradise.*

The door opened to reveal a long and dark circular tunnel with a walkway along the side as well as massive numbers of cables moving above as well as below. Magnetic circles provided a glow of energy to moving super-fast trams back and forth across the city. No sign of the police, which meant we were home free.

What's the news? I asked.

This Side of Paradise has been attacked, Harrison said.

CHAPTER FOURTEEN

WHERE STUFF GETS REAL

"Becky!" I said aloud as I stood there, alone, in the dark tunnels of the subway on the walkway beside the tram. One passed by, moving at lightning speed, and threw a massive amount of wind against my face as well as sending my hair up into the air.

She's alright, Harrison responded. *She departed the building an hour ahead of the attack. She's currently heading to Case's apartment. I'm not sure about anyone else here.*

Who attacked the brothel? Something I point out you could have told me from the beginning, I said, suddenly caring far less and feeling guilty since the potential victims included Case and Paradise's families.

Unknown, Harrison replied. *Unfortunately, the building has been destroyed by a drone strike from seemingly nowhere and the resulting fires as well as collapse have resulted in many deaths. Possibly the entirety of the staff.*

It was not hard to draw a connection between the newly revealed Legion that Sun had spoken about and the idea that This Side of Paradise had been attacked by him. The problem was that wiping out a whorehouse, even one as famous as This is Paradise, wasn't something that couldn't be done by our existing enemies. Hell, Evie Principle's existing enemies since she was a former member of HOPE could have been responsible. It also struck me like a blow to the chest that I was thinking of this in tactical terms when Paradise's mother as well as entire extended adopted family was probably dead.

Are you telling her? I was hoping he was, because I didn't want to have to be the one who did. *Are you telling Paradise?*

Do you want me to? Harrison asked.

Paradise, Jennifer, and Tom all came up behind me before starting to jog down the tunnel. It was a reminder the police were probably only a short distance behind us. Telling Paradise might slow us down at a crucial point but hiding it might be worse. I also had other things to deal with because, apparently, I needed to figure out a way to create a virus or worm capable of killing an AI that was powerful enough to terrify Sun.

No...no, I'll do it when we're not running for our lives. Maybe some things were better, human to human. *And, while you have nothing better to do, I don't suppose you could find me a nuke?*

Jogging with Paradise and the others, I wondered just how far we'd have to travel to find our way out of this complex and whether the police had an identification on us. If this Legion thing had identified us—which was entirely possible—my old life might potentially be ruined. What about Rebecca? What about...actually, I didn't have too many other associates I minded getting killed. Which was distinctly bothersome.

Is that a serious question about the nuke? Harrison asked.

Why? Can you get me one? I asked.

I mean, yes, which is why I'm asking, Harrison replied.

Well, it was a joke, but now it's serious. An EMP could solve a lot of problems right now. I'd have to be out of range but that's the case of most bombs.

Except for EMP shielding, yes, Harrison said. *Which Elysium has.*

What? What the hell protects against an EMP? I asked.

I mean, heavy duty aluminum foil can do it, Harrison said. *But people have been working on EMP shields for decades. Which is why enhanced electronic magnetic pulse weapons were created by—*

Dammit, I cursed. *Wait, what?*

I'm sorry, I must log off, Harrison replied. *There's something searching for me now and I must break all ties with the infonet. Tell Paradise to head to Fiddler's Green. She'll understand what it means.*

It seemed our enemy was spreading its tendrils already. Antarctica was sounding better all the time.

"If we get on one of the trains, the police might be able to shut it down, if they know who they're looking for," I said. "We're better off on foot for the moment, at least until we can confirm they don't know who they're after."

"You should talk to Harrison," Paradise said.

"He's...offline at the moment," I said.

"Ah," Paradise said, frowning. It made me feel all the more guilty.

We continued down the tunnels and briefly had to duck into an electrical tunnel to avoid NLAPD drones searching the place. In the end, though, we ended up through a side doorway into one of the tram stations where there were dozens, if not hundreds of people, packed together like replicated sardines.

I felt uncomfortable being watched by the security cameras, but the fact was that there were millions of potential avenues of surveillance for a Cognition AI to watch for someone. Cellphones, cybernetics, advertising scanners, and infopads all gathering information for the data state.

A Faraday cage was sounding pretty good right now, but I had to admit I'd never actually been off the infonet since my adoption/kidnapping by Snake. I wasn't sure what it would even be like. Either way, I just played it cool until we went up an escalator to the surface of the city and I saw Tom make a break for it, which lasted about three seconds as Jennifer held his hand so tightly that he almost dislocated it when he ran.

"Dammit!" Tom said. "We need to go."

"We're where I need to be," Jennifer said, frowning. "Probably."

Tom stared. "Probably."

Jennifer returned his stare, and he backed down, clearly unused to a more hardened machine personality calling the shots. It made me wonder if Sun had programmed her to seduce him or, again, boobs—fake or otherwise—had done the trick.

"It's a little unclear at the moment where we would be doing any good, but panicking won't help," I said, trying to interject. "It never does."

Okay, that was one of Snake's teachings. Always remain in control of yourself. I hated being grateful to him.

The surface level of New Los Angeles was filled with crowded masses of people moving on foot, many of them having never moved beyond a few blocks of their home upon the construction of the megaskyscrapers. It occurred to me that I needed to figure out a way to get Paradise's and my bikes away from the building we'd just escaped. Going back that way seemed suicidal but every bit of evidence was now exciting my paranoia.

The post-Eruption world wasn't one that had been created by regular people, not really. The release of Black Technology had resulted in hundreds of Cognition AI being revealed as silently manipulating the markets, government, polling data, and more. That control had grown exponentially as the Emergency Government had given control over countless systems to them in hopes of rescuing humanity from the year-long winter.

They had.

All these super structures, the countless bots that maintained them, and the goop that kept everyone fed was the product of AI control. It perhaps said everything that needed to be said about humanity that, for the most part, no one noticed or cared that we'd switched control of our lives from ostensibly elected officials to incorporeal beings of light and data. The AI weren't perfect—one look at the world said how much their logic was worth—but they were incredibly powerful.

Now one was potentially after me. Me and everyone I loved.

Which, again, Rebecca.

Paradise.

Case.

Joe maybe?

Christ, when did I start loving them? Why did I have no one else? I mean, there was an answer. I'd been trained to be paranoid, in control. Which is the opposite of caring, having someone to let go with. The truth was, I didn't know how to let go, to be casual.

And yet, I did have these few people I cared about. Was I changing? Was I learning to relax? To just be me, whoever that was? Was that me someone I wanted to know? I guess so. I couldn't see Rebecca being wrong.

"We should head to my mother's," Paradise said, calmly. "I'll contact her and say we've picked up the package."

"No," I said, a bit too quickly, I imagine. "That's the first place the police would look for you. Um…Harrison suggested we should go to somewhere called Fiddler's Green."

Paradise stiffened and her expression fell as if she'd been struck in the gut. After a few seconds, she sucked in her breath and looked at me. "I see. Fiddler's Green. Well, I think we should all shut off our connection to the infonet then and I'll call an autodrive."

"Can you even shut off your connection to the infonet?" Tom asked, surprised. "I mean it's everywhere."

"Do it, honey," Jennifer said, caressing the side of his face.

"Oh, sure," Tom agreed automatically. "Whatever you say."

"I don't think some of these systems have disconnection switches." Tom said.

"It's not a commonly used feature, but they're usually down in the menus somewhere," I said. I realized I'd been hesitating to do the same thing and triggered my emergency isolation system.

Immediately, so much of the world just vanished. No more info tags directing me around the subways. No more advertisements from the businesses strugglingly for my attention. No more fashion overlays people chose to project around them into the world's HUDs. It was like everything suddenly became dull and…solid around me.

It was very lonely.

And perhaps too late.

Navigating without having access to infonet tags would be tricky. But at least it gave me something to focus on besides how screwed we all were. Luckily, I occasionally practiced getting around without the tags for just such an emergency. Why, I had just…um…ten years ago….maybe I needed to practice this more often. If I survived the next week, I'd give it serious consideration. We needed to get to Rebecca and get her to safety. If such a thing existed.

"We need to get to Case's place. He needs to be warned about this mess, and we need to find someplace…less known,"

I said, finally getting my bearings. "And we're going to have to walk the whole way."

"We can't," Paradise said, looking up.

"Why?" I asked, doing a double take.

"My mother is dead," Paradise said, her voice empty of all emotion. I'd never heard anything like it from her before. "So are my sisters. Fiddler's Green is the place we're meant to go to ground when we have to reunite with any survivors in the event of being compromised."

The look of disgust on Paradise's face was something I hadn't expected. She stared right at me and said, "Unbelievable."

"I need to find Rebecca," I said, confused. "She could be in danger."

"My family is dead," Paradise said, a look of shock and trauma on her face that was wholly incongruous with the woman I knew. "I risked everything for you. Hell, they could be dead because of you and your fucking deal with Snake, and you can't spare the time to see if any of them are alive?"

"Paradise, I—" I started to say.

"Do you care about anyone but yourself?" Paradise said, clearly missing that this wasn't about me.

"This is about someone else!" I snapped.

"Were you even aware of what the code meant?" Paradise asked. "Or did you tell me they died by accident?"

"Uh," I stumbled for words. "This is not the best time for this. We should—"

Paradise turned around and walked away. "I hope you solve whatever it is you're involved in, Kei. But you'll be doing it yourself. We're done."

Jennifer and Tom stood there awkwardly, unsure what to do in this situation. The rest of the pedestrians ignored them but that was to be expected. If someone was shot in the face on the streets of New Los Angeles, the only people who would stop would be those to check if they could steal their wallet.

"Are you okay?" Tom asked me.

"Yes!" I snapped, before realizing I'd been standing there, staring, for almost two minutes after Paradise.

"You don't seem okay."

"She said she was okay," Jennifer said.

"I'm not okay," I said. "I don't know what okay looks like. I don't know how to act around people who aren't...clients, targets, I don't think about people as people. She was right. I thought about Paradise just enough to decide not to tell her, not enough to consider how she'd feel. I'm a very bad friend."

"You should go after her," Tom said.

"I don't have any idea where she's going," I said. "Case might."

"Who?" Tom asked.

"Your boss' ex-boyfriend," I said, snapping at Tom. He was working for the Magistrate, and I wasn't going to let him forget that. "He's rich and powerful as well as influential. All we have to do is go to him and pick up my daughter."

There, I'd said those words and now they couldn't be drawn back. I considered Becky to my daughter and there was no turning back.

"Would that put her in danger?" Jennifer asked.

I did a double take. "What?"

"Are you assuming someone has managed to track you back to the place that was assaulted?" Jennifer asked.

"This is Paradise," Tom said, correcting her. "The best brothel in the Zone. Damn, if it got hit then that sucks."

Jennifer glared before shaking her head. "I'm glad to see your priorities are straight. I'm just asking, Kei, if you think you've been tagged. Is it safe to go to your friend's home?"

"If they've tagged me, they already know about Becky. She's already a target, and Case doesn't have the first clue what he's up against."

Tom stared at her. "Neither do we."

I needed to figure out whether to trust these people. They were just two people we'd stumbled on during what should have been a relatively simple information search and one of them might not have been a sentient being until an hour ago, but they were also tied to Sun, which might be fuel for not trusting them now that I thought about it. The problem was that I was in way over my head and had just alienated one of my few allies...friends.

I'd just alienated one of my few friends.

"I have two choices. I can leave the two of you here and let you both try to survive, or I can...," I took a breath, "trust you. And I have no idea who either of you are, really. So talk fast."

Jennifer stared at me. "I'm a Jennifer Lawrence-based personal assistant robot who gained self-awareness within the past hour."

"Yeah, I guessed that," I replied.

Jennifer sighed. "I also am carrying a load of encrypted information that I feel is VERY important to be decrypted in a place off the infonet. I don't know why."

"Okay," I said, processing that. "Tom?"

Tom looked at me. "Well, I feel like that I am reluctant to share so many details of my past with a complete stranger as well a known crimi—"

I stared at him.

"Right," Tom said, raising his hands in surrender. "My name is Tom Fisher. I used to work as a police officer for the NLAPD before I resigned because I was uncomfortable with, you know, how evil they could be. Then I signed up for Atlas Security but realized they're basically James Bond villains. That was when I was recruited by the government's Anti-AI task force and the Magistrates, and I just realized that I shouldn't be telling you any of this."

"And he's very easily manipulated," Jennifer said.

"I thought I was doing the right thing!" Tom snapped.

"Well, there's a malignant AI about to take over the world, so...great job," I said, noticing Tom was looking over my shoulder.

"Yeah, we're helping," Tom said.

"We—" I started to ask before turning around, only to be stuck in the neck with an icer before the Magistrate shot me.

David was right beside her.

Well, at least that said who I could trust or not.

CHAPTER FIFTEEN

THIS IS SOMEONE'S BONDAGE FETISH

I hated icers.

Icers were the latest in non-lethal ammunition created by gun manufacturers when it was discovered that leaving a bunch of corpses on wealthy people's lawns was rather gauche. Also, in a time of mass poverty and social unrest, there were a lot of people on wealthy people's lawns. Or nearby them. Or within sight of them. Or sometimes nowhere near but the wealthy people still felt threatened. Yes, I have a habit of putting the absolute worst spin on everything.

Either way, I'd been iced plenty of times in my life. They worked far better than tasers and no, I have no idea how they work other than "well." The ammunition causes the body to shut down, become paralyzed, and the brain to enter a state strongly resembling sleep.

Being iced by Parvati Rao, now working with my (former) friend, was something I didn't really want to deal with now. Not that I ever wanted to be knocked unconscious by feds, but this was especially a time that I didn't want to deal with it. Becky was possibly in danger, I'd offended Paradise by being a crappy friend, and I also had a dangerous AI that even Sun feared on my tail. Funny how taking down an illegal serial murder prostitution ring for my insane ex-sensei was now the least of my problems.

I ended up waking up on top of a wooden chair with my arms as well as feet bound together by good old-fashioned rope. I could still move around, at least partially, but my vision was full of red letters saying that someone had disabled my cybernetics. Not completely off, I was still alive—I'd sadly had important organs replaced in my teenage years—but reduced from superhuman levels down to twenty-percent effectiveness in movement. I hadn't even known that was possible but apparently the feds were better at techno-tricks than I'd given them credit for. I tried, of course, to contact the infonet, but not only were my links offline but I couldn't turn them back on and my interior sensors weren't detecting any signals—which was unprecedented outside of deep space or under the ocean these days.

The location was almost stereotypical to the point I briefly thought I was dreaming or on an infovision set. The place looked like the upstairs of a warehouse or a storage room with a single bare lightbulb hanging up above my head while cardboard boxes of junk leftover from the pre-Eruption time was spread all over the place. Parvati Rao was standing over me while David was behind her, looking extremely guilty, as he should. Apparently, he'd chosen his side in all of this.

"I don't normally let a guy tie me up on a first date," I muttered. "Or any of the subsequent ones, just to be clear."

Parvati smiled. "Believe me, I tend to make bondage a third date experience at the earliest as well but sometimes I make an exception for my Tender profile."

David coughed.

Parvati rolled her eyes. "I should probably clarify you're not under arrest."

"Oh joy. Well, I'm so glad that's been cleared up," I said, rustling in my bonds. I could get out due to the fact, well, I was a goddamn ninja. I wasn't about to use old fashioned rope tricks when I was directly being watched, though.

"No, if you were arrested, you'd have rights," Parvati said.

I snorted at the absurdity of that statement. Rights were something older generations of Americans talked about—sometimes sarcastically and sometimes sincerely—but they were something most of us had learned to do without since the Eruption. Survival had taught a lot of us that you couldn't trust your fellow man and once that happened, most of us realized the best thing to do whenever crime happened was to turn to anyone but the police. Ironically, Miles and a few other cops I'd known had stated that attitude was one of the reasons that the police couldn't do anything to protect the public. I, however, argued that the police hadn't done anything to protect the public to begin with.

"I mean, not many, but you'd have some," Parvati said, undermining her own point. "This is a government black site. Everything that happens here is entirely off the books."

"It looks like someone's attic," I replied, dryly.

"It is someone's attic!" David interjected, cheerfully. "We got it for a good deal from a local listing that—"

Parvati stared at him.

"Right," David said, shutting up. Clearly, some people weren't meant to work for the Magistrates. I wasn't sure how I felt about David's betrayal, okay, I was pretty sure I was ticked off about it, but I wasn't furious, which surprised me. Maybe my compartmentalization of friendship had its upside. It was hard to get truly furious at someone if you didn't let them in the first place. Then again, maybe that also showed who my real friends were if such a thing existed.

"I don't have time for this," I said. "So why don't you tell me what the hell this is about so I can tell you to screw yourselves and we can move on to the more serious interrogation."

"This is really important, Kei, and—" David started to speak.

"You kidnapped me!" I snapped, debating breaking the ropes and going after him like She-Hulk. It was an idea I discarded once I remembered that I had my cybernetics disabled. So, I decided to use my words instead.

"We are not friends, David! Not anymore! With benefits or otherwise!"

David blinked, looking genuinely hurt.

And somehow I felt bad.

God, I hated this empathy thing! This is why I used to take lethe, to forget how it felt when I pissed people off.

"I want you, Case, and the late Evie Principle's help in trying to stop an existential threat to the United States—" Parvati started to speak.

"And the world," David said.

"To the United States," Parvati said. "Which is hard enough because it requires me to work with criminals."

"Which you are," David said. "No offense."

"None taken," I said.

"Some should be," Parvati said. "Because you're a criminal and you should take offense at that. However, trying to get your help is an enormous pain in the ass because you act like you are significantly more subtle than you are. Which is nonexistent in subtlety. You are a loud and obnoxious criminal that is easily found out but assume I'm too stupid to see it or your actions. Probably why there is a burning hole in the Refugee Zone and a hundred dead prostitutes and their customers."

"You work for a government with black sites, and you accuse other people of lacking subtlety?" I asked, not at all impressed. "So, you know about the developing AI that intends to kill us all, or worse, not kill anyone."

"How is that last part bad?" David asked.

"Because when amoral monsters take over, they either kill you or make you a slave. I prefer being dead."

Parvati sighed. "Yes, I'm aware of the renegade AI. Which is, in terms of one to ten with one being your typical terrorist with a homemade bomb and ten being a missing nuclear bomb, is about a twelve or twelve and a half. The Emergency Council has completely shut down this case and decided the best course of action to take is absolutely no course of action whatsoever. The AI are unwilling to act on it because apparently we puny bits of bacteria are not really worth considering in the long term versus the birth of a new member of their race."

"They're really hoping they can guide him from the rape and murder thing," David said, trying to defend them and failing badly. "Or, maybe, they're worried that he'll destroy the planet if they try to attack him directly."

Okay, maybe he wasn't failing badly.

"And you think we can help," I said, staring at her.

"Yes, possibly," Parvati said. "Particularly, I think that Barbara Gordon could help as one of the world's best programmers for viruses and educated by the woman who created AI as we know it. Sadly, she's not taking my calls either."

"So, you went to your old boyfriend to ask him to introduce you to his daughter," I said.

"He was never my boyfriend, we just had a lot of sex," Parvati said. "Something that I'm sure you have a lot of experience with yourself."

"I don't know, we haven't had sex," I said, not referring to Case. "If you untie me, we could start now."

David stared.

Parvati lightly elbowed him in the stomach, shaking him out of that image. "There's also the fact there's apparently another AI involved in this if what your Hunger Games robot downstairs is saying is true."

I wondered if they broke her down and removed her core. "I think Sun's given us as much help as she can. Which includes the robot downstairs, who I hope is still intact."

"Tom had the same question," Parvati said, rolling her eyes. "I wonder how easy it is for a bioroid to seduce a man against all loyalty."

"There's a reason honey traps are still used by every secret service," I replied, dryly, continuing to fiddle with my ropes. "But I'm going to assume that she's still around."

"For now," Parvati said. "I believe true artificial intelligence deserve the same rights as regular citizens but I'm also willing to abridge the rights of the latter if it means protecting us from a rogue. So, are you willing to work with us?"

A part of me wondered how much I should try and negotiate here or whether I should try and take them out even in my weakened state once I was free, then make a break for it. The latter's odds weren't great but there was a rule among Riders about working for the government: don't. They had a worse reputation than suits for reneging on their deals. On the other hand, Parvati seemed sincere, which could be the most dangerous illusion of them all. I was badly in need of allies, though, and didn't know where half of my remaining ones were.

"You haven't made the case for why you get to would get to work with me, since all you've done so far is interfere."

Parvati narrowed her eyes. "Well, I could argue about the fact that it is a better idea to work with the government than on your own, that you've done absolutely nothing to warrant any form of trust yourself, and that you are so blindly incompetent that you've been caught trying to sneak away with my own operative."

"I'm not incompetent!" I snapped. "Also, I was distracted."

"But I can offer a very good argument," Parvati said.

"What? That I don't have any idea what to do about this world-shaking dangerous rogue AI?" I asked. "Which is not a confession, by the way."

"Snake," Parvati said.

"What?" I asked.

"I know your history with him," Parvati said, narrowing her eyes. "What are the chances that he doesn't know about the rogue AI and that he sent you in there with no knowledge purely as a distraction for it while he works his real plan?"

"He wouldn't waste me on a distraction...okay, he would, but only if he was really screwed. Which we are. Yes," I admitted.

"Smooth," Parvati said.

"It's been a long day." It was amazing how much I was still having to deal with my own illusions. It wasn't that I trusted Snake, it was...I thought I was valuable to him, not something he'd discard as a convenience. Somehow, after all of this, I'm still not cynical enough.

Parvati pulled out a knife, military grade, and the kind for stabbing people rather than cutting meat. "Then I suggest we pool our resources."

I had gotten free of my ropes and could show I was free at any time. "You're rogue."

"What?" Parvati asked.

"This isn't a black site, which David so helpfully pointed out," I said, putting the pieces together in my head.

"Uh, no I didn't," David said.

"You're using a semi-competent private detective," I said, thinking of Tom. "Also, you're trying to hit up a bunch of criminals you're tangentially connected to. You also mentioned how the Emergency Council shut this down and the AI won't give you the time of day. That's why you need us. You're not operating with any sort of mandate. You don't have any resources."

Parvati crossed her arms. "I have my own. Also, I know you've untied yourself."

"Ah, I was going to wait and surprise you. The bad news... more bad news is that the last place I saw Barbara Gordon was in that smoking hole you mentioned earlier."

"Well, she survived!" David said.

"Wait, what?" I asked, staring at him. "How do you know?"

"This nice prostitute lady contacted us," David said.

"Paradise," Parvati corrected.

"What I said," David replied. "Paradise said that she'd managed to get Barbara Gordon to safety and also had access to Case as well as some other people we're trying to get involved with. However, she wanted you to be returned in exchange for setting up a meeting."

"Which we'll do now," Parvati replied.

"Oh, I already did," David said.

Parvati did a double take. "What do you mean?"

"I told her to meet us here," David said.

Parvati looked like she was going to strangle him. "You goddamned moron."

"What? Why?" David asked, looking genuinely surprised.

That was when the lights went out in the room. I could just imagine Paradise having somehow managed to get a listening device or recorder in the room just so she could wait for the most dramatically appropriate moment to cut the power. That was when I felt all my cybernetics restore themselves to full power, even if the infospace signals in the area remained zero. They had to be close to be pulling this off, assuming they were here at all.

If this was Paradise attacking us, I needed to communicate and bring this to an end, perhaps after letting her punch me once for my earlier behavior. If it wasn't, then talking was just revealing my position and slowing down my response. But, presumably whoever this was had night vision gear.

"Stop it!" I tossed David aside and grabbed for someone's

head to put it in a choke hold. "I said stop it!"

That was when the lights turned back on in the attic, much to my surprise, as I found myself holding Jennifer in a chokehold. Parvati was on the ground with her icer drawn on Paradise, who had her own icer aimed at Jennifer in return. Amusingly, Paradise was wearing a stealth black bodysuit but had her bright neon hair out without covering. David was lying down on the ground, where he'd been thrown, out of the fight.

"Hi!" Paradise said to me, not taking her gun from Parvati's face. "I'm still mad at you!"

Part of my brain tried to think of something clever or smart to say. I kicked it out of the way and just hugged her. "I'm sorry."

"Thanks," Paradise said, hugging me back.

That's when we were iced by Parvati on the ground.

Oh, come on!

CHAPTER SIXTEEN

I HAVE A ROYAL HEADACHE

You know what's worse than being iced into unconsciousness? Being iced into unconscious twice. That's not a joke. Once gives you a headache and makes every muscle in your body ache. Twice makes every muscle in your body prone to randomly cramping for the next few days. Oh, and the headache got much, much worse.

Every time I tried coming back to consciousness, some part of my brain realized how much I hurt and put me back into deep sleep. At some point, you do have to wake up and the parts of my brain that wanted to stay asleep finally lost the argument and my consciousness was turned back on. I immediately regretted it.

"You just had to shoot me again," I tried to say to what I presumed would be Parvati but instead it came out as, "Yorgh jhydd shomgna." Which, unfortunately, wasn't nearly as witty as I'd hoped.

Opening my eyes, I saw that I'd been moved from the attic of the safehouse and found myself propped up against a wooden table. I was sitting on a stool and saw Paradise, Parvati, Case, and David all standing together in a nice old-fashioned kitchen where you prepared food rather than reheated dried goop. Everyone seemed to be talking to one another as opposed to fighting, which was a nice change of pace.

I think I said something. but I'm not sure what. Next thing I knew, I was waking up again. This, and the fact that my headache was somewhat reduced, suggested I had fallen unconscious again, a strategy I retroactively approved of.

I opened my eyes cautiously. "Fudge you, Parvati!"

I was now lying in a leather chair in what I perceived to be the house's living room. Everything looked to be twenty years old or older with nothing looking like it was connected to the infonet. The windows were covered with thick drapes, and I saw signs they'd been boarded up as well. The sound of a gas-powered generator was running in the background. Everyone was still here but there was now Harrison sitting in my lap.

"Fudge you?" Parvati asked.

"Kei doesn't swear," Paradise said. "I mean, killing people and robbing them? That's fine? Bad language is bad!"

"Everyone has to have lines," I said.

"Shouldn't they be about something important?" Parvati asked.

"I had to walk past all my important ones years ago," I said. "So, is everyone alive?"

"Yeah, everyone except my mom," Paradise said. "Plus a bunch of friends that I grew up with."

I grimaced. "Oh, crap, I keep screwing this one up."

Paradise stared, her expression empty. She was barely keeping it together and I didn't blame her.

"I'm going to kill the AI. I don't know how to do that but I'm going to do it."

I didn't have a response for that. "Where are we?"

Harrison looked up. "We're presently in Nebraska. Currently outside of anywhere with an online connection and in a jamming zone. We traveled here in vehicles without an electronic connection as well. Kepler had several in his junkyard."

Case walked over and put his hand on Paradise's shoulder as she gave him an almost daughter-like hug, reminding me that he'd been a part of her life for a lot longer than I had been a part of either of their lives. In a way, it made me jealous because it had been a long time since I'd had anyone who would have qualified as family. The closest people who did were ones that I had killed recently in Fate and the man I very much wanted to kill in Snake.

"Where's Becky?" I asked.

"Downstairs," Case said, simply. There was an expression in his eyes I didn't recognize. "She's getting her upgrades completed."

"I need to see her now," I said, standing up. It caused Harrison to tumble out of my lap and land on the floor.

Paradise stared at her. "Someone put spyware in her."

"Wait, what?" I asked, doing a double take.

"Everything that was spoken in front of you and her was recorded by Legion," Case replied. "That's how they knew to strike This is Paradise."

"It's also why Case blew up his own apartment," Parvati said. "Which I don't actually see the point of."

"Faking one's death is always a good idea when dealing with AI," Case said, "They only know what is recorded."

"Which is *everything*," Parvati said, crossing her arms.

"Barbara found it a few minutes after you left," Case said. "It's why she left with Doctor Saint Croix."

"My mom should have left," Paradise said, her voice low. "She stayed to start an evacuation that she hoped wouldn't tip anyone off."

I was left contemplating just what the implications of Becky having been a spy, unwitting or not, were.

"Do we know how long?" I asked. "How long she's been... used?" It could make a lot of difference, especially regarding how much the AI knew about me, how much it could predict my actions.

"We're trying to find out," Case said, simply. "However, only someone who was alone with her for a substantial period of time could have installed the spyware, which limits the number of people involved given how you have isolated her."

I was immediately defensive but let Case's words sink in. "That means it was either Joe Kepler, his son, Snake, or Winston Billions."

Or someone who had found her when I was off doing my missions, which could be anyone. Goddammit.

"Or you!" Paradise said.

I stared at her.

"My sense of humor is fucked," Paradise said, crossing her arms. "Which I can say, unlike you. Because my family is dead. So there."

I had no response to that. "Is it weird a part of me wants to try to contact Snake and warn him?"

"Yes," Paradise said.

I tried to think of ways this could have been done by someone else.

"Installing malware doesn't have to have been done with awareness. The AI could have infected some bit that someone thought would be harmless to give her."

"Not this kind," Parvati said. "Her eyes were customized, the recording device encrypted, and modular tech installed. It had to have been done to her over the course of hours."

"Why?" I asked, confused, and horrified this had happened under my nose. "Why go to all that trouble?"

"Perhaps as a post-facto statement of power," Parvati said. "Perhaps they were afraid Becky would be protected by other forces. Perhaps the mind that decided to do this simply doesn't do simple."

I wanted to scream. I wanted to shoot something. I wanted...I wanted...I was so angry because I'd failed. I'd failed to protect her. It was my one attempt to claim to being a decent human being and I couldn't even do that. Becky would have been better off with Paradise and her people, always surrounded, protected.

I took a deep breath and tried to push down my sense of failure. It wasn't going to help. Also not helping was just how much I ached, which became harder to ignore when I was trying to meditate.

"Is there anything to drink?" I asked.

"Given this is an automated farm with a caretaker who hasn't been here in years, probably not," Case said. "Though there might be a chance of some whole grain alcohol in mayonnaise jars."

"I'll take it," I said, sighing.

Parvati sighed. "I know how you must feel."

I looked up. "Listen, Indian Clarice Starling, which I don't even care if that's racist, I'm pretty sure you don't. This is my fault. I brought her into this world. The real Becky is dead because of me. The new Becky has been violated because of me. It's only going to get worse."

"I got into this business because my brother was killed by a US drone strike," Parvati said. "The Karma Corp-designed facial recognition system apparently had difficulty determining who was a terrorist or not. It ended up killing fifteen people before it was shut down and that's not including the people killed around its supposed target."

I stared at her. "Well, that's tragic but it's not your fault."

"It was trying to get me," Parvati said. "I'd been doing anti-government and anti-corporate propaganda. My brother and I looked a lot alike before I made certain transitions in my life."

"Oh," I replied.

Parvati sighed. "That's when I decided the only way that I could make changes in the world would be if I had a seat at the table. Power was the only way to get at other people with power. The people who destroyed my family's life never saw justice. That doesn't have to be the case here if you work with us."

It was a spiel I was not in the mood for, but I wasn't exactly willing to go down and speak with Becky now either.

"That's how they snare you," I said, feeling sick. "Oh, you have to work inside the system to make changes. Then you don't let anyone in the system actually affect it, because now you're dependent on the system, and the system is self-perpetuating."

Parvati stared. "Except, of course, the people outside the system can't do anything either and every time they do, they get crushed."

"So, we all agree it's pointless to try," I said, frowning and throwing up my hands before sitting back down.

"Gah!" Harrison said, underneath me.

I jumped back up. "Tell me if you're getting in the chair!"

"You got up!" Harrison said.

"Sheep need chairs? What's even the point of being a quadruped!" I said, actually just straight up speaking nonsense at this point.

"My legs are also made of metal, don't question it

scientifically," Harrison said. "I just like lying down."

Paradise stared at me then Parvati.

"I don't care one way or the other about how it's impossible to change the system. My mother helped create Elysium because she wanted to make a billion dollars and she got robbed by the Trikuza. Now the Trikuza have made a big ole AI that killed everyone I care about. I don't care about whether they're the good guys, the bad guys, or the worst guys. I just want them dead. Now you all generally seem to agree they deserve to die and have your own reasons for wanting them dead. So, let's all just agree to work together to do it because we don't have a choice. Even if you wanted to chicken out and go somewhere else, the machine knows where we live and would find us. So, all I want to hear now is how we plan to take it down and its gangster friends with it."

It was the most I'd ever heard Paradise speak.

"Chicken out?" Parvati said, focusing on the least important part of the speech.

"Shut up," Paradise said, exhausted. "I'm not good at being serious."

"Hiding is a bad idea," I said. "It might work, by convincing the machine that we aren't a threat and don't intend to become one. After all, we're hiding. But, that assumes there's a world left worth hiding in, We don't really know what this thing plans for the future, and frankly, I don't want to find out."

"Also, you made a contract," Case said, simply.

Everyone looked at him.

"What?" Case asked.

"I think we have a few more important things to worry about," Parvati said.

"Said someone who doesn't take their work seriously," Case replied.

"When said work is murder?" Parvati said.

"Of bad people," Case said.

Parvati stared.

"What?" Case asked, innocently.

"Please, no humor," Paradise said. "There's an AI trying to kill us and its linked up to a murderous snuff prostitution ring.

We have the files inside Jennifer—she's downstairs too—and we can use them to strike at the machine. For that, we need someone to come up with a brilliant plan to do the job we were originally supposed to do but has almost certainly been warned about now. For that, we need the greatest Rider ever to compensate with her genius heist-making capacity."

There was a moment of silence.

"You're speaking about Kei, right?" Case asked.

"Yes!" Paradise said, throwing her hands up in the air. "Kei will figure this out. Won't you?"

"What's our alternative?" Parvati. "How do we fight it?"

"We either sneak an EMP device into its systems or implant it with a virus," I said, making this up as we went along.

"Even a modern EMP won't destroy it permanently," Case said. "At best it would just destroy its current housing. You'd need to do a virus then destroy any backups, which means both need to be done."

"We also don't have a virus or a delivery system," Parvati said.

"I think the AI itself is a delivery system," I said. "After all, it's made of minds it's absorbed through the Elysium network. We just implant it in someone and send them in."

"Who's going to volunteer for that?" Paradise asked, showing surprising resolve.

"Someone we don't like very much and don't ask," I said, thinking of the rich scumbags that might be infected already with Legion or were drawn to what was already a sick reputation.

"So, your argument is that we need to infiltrate Elysium, grab one of the customers, use this super virus that we don't have, and then upload it before activating an improved military grade EMP to wipe the systems," Parvati said. "Which we also don't have."

"Yes," I said.

"I can help with all of those. Also, Ms. Gordon has been working on an AI killer for some time," Harrison said, surprising me. I wasn't aware sheep could be involved in weapons trafficking. "

"How long is some time?" I asked.

"Since we arrived," Harrison said, sheepishly. (That pun was an accident, I swear!) "She's a very fast worker. It will, however, require me to be modified into a weapon."

"What?" Paradise asked. "No, Mr. Ram! You can't sacrifice yourself!"

Harrison shook his head. "I am afraid with our present lack of equipment, the modifications for a proper AI killer won't exist otherwise."

Paradise hugged him. It was almost painfully adorable.

"I mean, I think you should back me up first, but that's sort of the point here," Harrison said. "The virus has to be self-replicating and intelligent enough to counteract any measures the AI might take to defend itself."

"There's another option," I said. "Sun. If she's tied to the AI, she can act to distract it while we assault it. It has to be at least a little afraid of her."

"Sun might be able to finish it off if its crippled," Case said, frowning. "I have access to some of the AI through Atlas, or at least I did. Delphi, Epsilon, and a handful of others speak to me like I'm their poor idiot cousin."

"Because you are," Harrison said. "No offense."

"Some taken," Case said, making it a running gag. "They're being very secretive about Legion, and I was basically told to drop it when I tried to bring it up. They weren't that open about Sun, but this is on a whole other level."

The fact Case was in casual conversation with AI surprised me and it was something I would have to bring up with him later. Sun was friendly-ish with me but still terrifying. It was like being friends with a god or demon. You might benefit but it was never safe.

Parvati frowned. "I was assigned the Sun case by the government last year and it led me down a virtual rabbit hole. The idea of a Cognition AI created by a criminal organization is something that gave the government fits. However, when I submitted information about the data being used to create a new one, I was shut down. Either Legion has already gotten its mitts into a lot of higher ups, or someone is running interference for it."

"Who has a vested interest in its experiment?" Case said. "To create a true AI requires the resources of a wealthy country and succeeds only once in a billion tries. It could be elements of the government are letting this run its course because if someone has figured a way to make a Cognition AI from scanning large numbers of human brain patterns, they might consider it worth monitoring."

"Even though they're all homicidal serial killers?" Paradise asked, sounding more surprised that she was surprised than anything else.

"I mean, that might actually be a bonus in the Emergency Government's eyes," Case said.

"They'll recognize us if we walk into Elysium," I said, doing the math in my head. "We'll need new identities, faces, pasts, and weapons for this. All of that will difficult if we don't have access to infospace."

"Difficult but not impossible," Harrison said. "Mind you, face to face meetings are something I don't have much experience with."

We had the beginnings of a plan. I just wasn't sure if it wasn't suicide. No, actually, I was sure it was.

I was pretending otherwise.

CHAPTER SEVENTEEN

HARD DECISIONS, EASY REVENGE

We had a plan. Well, we had something that could be mistaken for a plan if you didn't look too closely. The problem being I was really close to it and it was hard not to look.

I went looking for Becky. Sure, she wasn't out of surgery yet, but where else did I have to go? The world suddenly felt very small. The others wanted to speak with me, but I pretended I had to use the bathroom, which I needed anyway, then snuck around toward the basement.

It was an old door like everything else in the house and I creeped down the steps, eliminating any real stealth as they squeaked with every movement. There was a second metal door at the bottom of the steps that was slightly ajar, which was surprising because there was a keypad beside it. Avoiding my friends—which was still a strange word in my mouth—I pulled the door open and found myself in something far different than what I'd expected.

I still had memories of my childhood home in the suburbs of Modesto, California. I was expecting the basement to be either full of old toys and clothes or maybe some place with a pool table. I'd certainly expected something of extremely poor conditions for performing cybernetic surgery.

What greeted me instead was a reasonably sized clinic with several emergency room chambers, a lobby with an old fashioned flatscreen television set showing a pirated news channel, and advanced Frankenstein equipment put to one side. There was also a secretary's round desk that had been cleaned off and had several interlocked laptops being worked on simultaneously by Barbara Gordon.

Gerard Saint Croix was apparently working on three patients simultaneously with Jennifer, Becky, and Tom in separate chambers. It surprised me to see Tom down for the count as well but, apparently, he was also a cyborg and needing to be worked on. Personally, I wished he'd taken another time to do it since I wished the handsome older doctor could focus entirely on Becky. Jennifer was supposedly full of information on Legion and Elysium both but the whole issue of fighting him was something I hoped I didn't have to work on.

Unfortunately, I couldn't escape the depth of my failure down here. Not only had Becky been operated on against her will and turned into a spy against me and my friends, but the television was showing drone images of the Zone. This is Paradise had been reduced to a hole in the ground and the surrounding buildings had been bombed as well, the estimated number of deaths having grown from a hundred to two hundred and fifty so far. Both police cars and fire trucks were present, which was a surprise. The fact the New Los Angeles government was intervening at all with emergency services told me how bad things had gotten.

"Hello, Kei," Barbara said, not having changed her clothes and looking like she hadn't slept in however long it had been since we'd last met. I did a brief check and it had been close to forty-eight hours, in which case she looked good.

"You shouldn't be on the infonet," I said, dryly. "You don't know who's listening."

"The entirety of the building is built-in with protections against any signals," Barbara said. "The television is actually receiving signals from a satellite dish."

"People still use regular television?" I asked.

"The same way they still listen to records," Barbara said, typing away. "Television is a way of communicating off the grid for those who are either very poor or very paranoid. This is a Zone produced and operated network."

"Then what are you doing?" I asked, looking over at Gerard who was using a laser on Becky's ear lobe. I had to turn away almost immediately.

"Looking over the data that Sun gave us," Barbara replied.

"Any miracles?" I asked.

"Define miracles," Barbara said.

"Something that can save our butts," I said, not using the a-word because I was now self-conscious about swearing.

"Give me a minute and I may have an answer," Barbara asked.

"Right. What is this place, anyway?" I asked, looking around.

"It was the safe house of a rich asshole who predicted the apocalypse would happen," Barbara replied, not looking up from the computers in front of her. "There's actually an entire mansion underneath this place with food, supplies, and guns. Lots of guns. It's also hardwired to be protected from mind control waves or sensors from the government."

"Lucky guess," I replied.

"Yeah, well he predicted people who looked brown like me would be the ones to take over the world and that hasn't happened," Barbara said. "Also, he died in a plane crash months before the Eruption."

"Ah," I replied. "Probably for the best."

"Done," Barbara asked. "Which is to say we may not have any parting of the Red Sea, but we're above tent faith healing."

"I'll take two she-bears eating forty-two children for a thousand," I replied, making a *Jeopardy* reference. The real Winston Billions almost got tapped as the next host for that show.

"I have no idea what you're talking about," Barbara asked.

"That's fine," I said. "The important points are that some Bible stories are weirder than others, and don't make fun of a prophet's hair, it's not worth the risk."

"My father used the parable of the Garden of Eden and God getting worried about humans becoming immortal by eating the fruit of life," Barbara said. "He is skeptical about the fact I'm a lesbian and Muslim."

"Ah," I said, pausing. "We must go to the same website for cringy faith stories."

"Case believes in a Great Programmer," Barbara said. "He just prefers Calvin and Hobbes to justify it."

"Calvin and Hobbes?" I asked.

"The comic strip, not the philosophers," Barbara said. "Calvin the little boy is asked if he believes in God by his stuffed tiger, Hobbes. Calvin replies that, yes, he does. Why? Because someone is out to get him."

"Says the billionaire," I replied, having more bitterness about it than I was willing to admit. It would always stand in the way of any closer relationship.

"Also ex-slave," Barbara said, referring to Case's period as being the International Refugee Society's property. "Mind you, my biological father looked identical to him but was actually a serial killer and terrorist. Case ended up killing him, too, but it's okay, he'd already abandoned me and my mother."

"Case left that part out," I admitted.

"Really? It's such an ice breaker at parties," Barbara said, acknowledging they'd somehow gotten way-way off topic. "So, what do you want to know?"

"How do we kill it and why can't we just blow up its hardware?" I asked, making a kaboom gesture.

Barbara looked up at me, her eyes still baggy from stress.

"Aren't you a hacker?"

"Yes," I replied. "Almost all Riders are. Most of my programs being bought off the internet."

"Script kiddie! Hiss!" Barbara said, making a cross with her fingers.

A script kiddie was a hacker who was unskilled at, well, hacking, and bought their programs off the net versus developing their own. I didn't care if they worked.

"I don't think a cross would work for you."

"The joke wouldn't work if I used a crescent," Barbara said, making a C with her hands.

"So, I take it I'm missing something as to why we can't just chuck a bomb at it," I replied.

"Did you ever see the ending of *Terminator 3*?" Barbara asked.

"That's the one with the hot blonde, right?" I asked. "Also, the other blonde who wasn't quite as hot."

"Not a Claire Danes fan, I see," Barbara replied.

"The two hot blondes then," I replied. "Nick Stahl I can take or leave."

Mind you, we were talking about a movie that was over fifty years old now. One that wasn't particularly good in the first place. Still, all the old pre-Eruption movies had a grandiosity to them that just didn't get matched these days by the recycled garbage that was produced by the corporate machine. The corporate machine of the old days had standards, dammit!

"Well, the computer isn't the problem, it's the software," Barbara said. "Which in the case of Cognition AI is undifferentiated."

I blinked, staring at her incomprehensibly.

"Do you know the difference between Cognition AI and regular AI?" Barbara asked.

"Of course," I said, pretending to be a dumb street kid. "One has an extra word in front of it."

Barbara narrowed her eyes.

"Okay, I'm just playing dumb," I replied, shrugging. "Cognition AI are the big scary AI that can control entire countries worth of data and are always watching like Big Brother. Regular AI are either dummy AI that don't think for themselves but can check to see what your shopping history is or true AI that are smart but not uber-smart."

"Thank you," Barbara said. "I don't know why you pretend to be stupid."

"Probably the same reason Paradise does," I said, shrugging. "Men tend to be less likely to shoot you and more likely to make mistakes if they think you're an idiot."

"Probably why I'm a lesbian. That and basic biology," Barbara replied. "In any case, to answer your question, we can't just blow up this Legion organism—"

"Do we have to use that name?" I asked.

"Why not Legion?" Barbara asked. "It's a gestalt entity of many minds and a creator of serial killers. It's as close to a demon as likely exists."

My family was Catholic in an Easter and Christmas sort of

way while Snake believed in animist Shinto spirits in infospace as well as Mexican Santeria. I sort of zoned out whenever he talked about anything more complex than stabbing things. I wasn't a mystical sort of person and that wasn't changed by living month to month in the big city.

I frowned. "That's why I don't want to call it Legion. It gives it too much weight and authority. Power. I'd prefer to call it, I dunno, Wally or something."

"Wally," Barbara said. "You want to name the serial killing AI who murdered so many people Wally?"

"Dark Wally?" I asked, feeling bad since Barbara had lost potentially a lot of friends in This is Paradise's destruction, or at least acquaintances.

"No," Barbara said.

"Fine, Legion," I said, acquiescing. "Why can't we blow it up? I mean, aside from the fact it's a massive resort and will kill tens of thousands of people. Some of whom are probably innocent baristas and janitors."

"Legion isn't in the resort," Barbara said.

"Then where is he?" I asked, having planned most of this around infiltrating Elysium.

Barbara sighed. "Since the Eruption and a good deal of time beforehand, every light switch, toaster, coffee maker, and cybernetic implant has been networked to the infospace system. Quantum computers give an infinite amount of digital storage space that allow the virtual worlds we've created to be lived in as well as the previously restricted minds of AI. Legion and the other AI aren't in any one particular server, they're hiding in all of them."

"You're saying he could be in my motorcycle," I said.

"No," Barbara said, "and yes."

"Thank you for that," I replied, rolling my eyes.

"Your motorcycle may contain the equivalent of flashing neurons for our AI friend, hidden among the other codes," Barbara said. "It's all bundled together in the Cognition AI allowing it to draw from massive amounts of information spread out. The actual personality is only a little bit of the larger machine. For most of the AI that exist, their central consciousness is somewhere that can be blown up but if you blow that up, then redundancies elsewhere get activated to effectively resurrect it from the dead."

"Like Sauron and the One Ring," I said.

Barbara stared at me.

"My mother used to read those books to me and explained them in detail," I replied. "That was before she discovered alcohol to cope with remembering that her sister starved to death in a refugee camp. Apparently, the guards kept the food for themselves."

"Ah," Barbara said, uncomfortable with the topic. As I understood, Case had used what little pull he'd had with the government to get her and her mother out of the camps to someplace better. I didn't hold it against her, I would have done the same if I could have. Hell, I wish someone had done it for me and my family.

"So we can't kill it," I said, feeling defeated.

"I didn't say that," Barbara said. "It's just we have to make sure it's resurrection, so to speak, isn't triggered."

"To destroy the One Ring," I replied.

Barbara blinked. "Yeah, if you say so."

"Yeah, you got any volcanos and little hairy feet guys in there?" I asked, looking over her shoulder. It was all just a bunch of weird diagrams and programs.

Dammit.

"No, but you might change its mind about wanting to live," Barbara asked.

"Excuse me?" I asked.

"Everyone keeps bringing up a computer virus like it is computer magic," Barbara said. "However, being as they're super-genius beings with an awareness that this is the only thing that can harm them, it's not that simple."

"It rarely is," I said, letting her continue.

Barbara said, "Basically, you are correct, though, that the best way to do this is to head deep into Elysium and upload a brain scan into its mind. This one, however, will be full of an idea so powerful it eventually consumes all the other minds then causes it to self-terminate. From there, you will have to use the improved EMP to shred everything else. That should hopefully keep it from resurrecting itself."

"Hopefully," I said.

Barbara stared at the computer screens in front of her.

"No one has ever killed a Cognition AI before. So, literally, getting it to commit suicide is about the only way I know to even try. However, Sun did provide us one very useful tool, though."

"Which is?" I asked.

"A way to blind it to our presence for a very limited time," Barbara said. "A signal jammer that will effectively make you invisible. No, better yet, causes you to be ignored. Which is superior to invisibility if you think about it."

"That's...that's fantastic!" I said. It changed potentially everything. Our biggest disadvantage was the Orwellian state that Legion potentially had us trapped inside.

"Forty-eight hours," Barbara said, not sounding remotely enthusiastic. "Once activated, it will eventually detect the error in its data collection and correct it."

"I don't suppose that's exactly forty-eight hours as opposed to kind of in the vicinity of forty-eight hours give or take oops your dead?" I asked.

Barbara said, "It's approximate but data processing isn't instantaneous even for a being like Legion. He's basically a discount Sun made by the Trikuza from the research that Snake commissioned. I don't know why your weeb sensei wanted to make an AI, but even a knock off is extremely powerful. Now, if you'll excuse me, I need to try to get a few hours of sleep."

"You've had an exhausting day," I said, thinking I was being polite.

Barbara looked down. "My wife was supposed to meet me at This is Paradise. I couldn't risk trying to contact her once the building was bombed. Not while I was with Becky."

I seemed to be amazing and kicking people in their open wounds today.

"I'm sorry. I didn't know."

Barbara paused and took a deep breath. "Are you familiar with the phrase, 'a single death is a tragedy, and a million deaths is a statistic'?"

"Except to the people whose single deaths are part of the millions," I said. "I always thought that was a stupid statement really because if a single death is a tragedy, then a million deaths is a million times worse."

"Yes," Barbara said, standing up. "That's what this whole thing is about. This is Paradise's massacre was just to get at a few people who threatened Legion but ended up destroying the lives of hundreds of people and perhaps damaging tens of thousands through the ripples from the initial act. Legion is made from the worst of humanity and is going to get worse as well as make the world worse. It is an abomination against God, and I mean that in the sense it blemishes the pure beauty of mathematics, science, and consciousness. I know you don't care about any of the other people at This is Paradise. It wasn't your home, and they weren't your friends, but a lot is riding on you stopping this."

"No pressure," I said.

"Yeah," Barbara said, shrugging. She departed, leaving me alone with the doctor and the three artificial people being operated on because of me.

"No pressure," I repeated as I looked at Becky. She looked so small and helpless. Delicate.

I had to do better. I had to be better. I couldn't keep letting Snake define my life. I had to reclaim who I had been. No, I'd been a child. There was no well-formed adult there for me to draw on. If I wanted to walk away from being the machine, I'd have to make it up as I went along. Normal people made being normal look so easy.

Gerard walked up to me, now holding an old-fashioned clip board. "Hi, uh, Kei was it?"

"Yeah," I said, turning to him. "Unless you know any other white-haired cybernetic ninja girls."

"You'd be surprised," Gerard said. "But there's a lot to discuss here. I didn't feel appropriate bringing it up upstairs. Mostly because everyone up there scares me. Including Paradise."

"I don't?" I asked, while trying to figure out if I should thank him or be insulted. I felt both at the same time, but that clearly made no sense. "Is she going to be okay?"

Rebecca was lying in a chair like the one she'd been back in This is Paradise but this time she had parts of her body opened to the air, exposing the wiring as well as the machinery inside. Wires were attached to her brain and machines I didn't recognize. It didn't do anything to remind me she was a bioroid, but it let me know just how much she'd been modified. There were parts I didn't recognize and ones that had been installed against her will. I had to wonder if she was dreaming but Harrison wasn't present so probably not. Okay, that joke was inappropriate.

"That's a complicated question," Gerard replied.

Well, that didn't sound like good news.

CHAPTER EIGHTEEN

NOT SO HARD CHOICES

"Well, complicated is something I have more experience with than I can say I'm happy with. Start at the beginning."

"I was born to a wealthy family that wanted me to be a doctor when I met a mysterious beautiful woman—" Gerard started to say.

I stared at him, nonplussed.

"Sorry, probably a bad time for a joke," Gerard said, rubbing the back of his head.

"Yes," I replied, softly. "It is."

Gerard walked over to a nearby laptop that was running several medical apps, all of them self-contained. "This is what I managed to get off of Becky's memory buffers."

He conjured footage of her hanging around our apartment while I was off doing business for Snake. It was through her eyes and a kind of fascinating feeling right up until the time I realized she was using our infovision flatscreen to watch porn. That was a very uncomfortable feeling for a mother, however reluctant, to see my rapidly adultifying (was that a word?) daughter engaging in that sort of activity.

"Skip! Skip!" I said, looking away.

Gerard did so and I saw Winston Billions, wearing his brilliant white suit, break in and proceed to ice her. Given she was a bioroid, she was immune and struggled as a couple of other Trikuza thugs held her down until they put a shock collar on her.

"Winston," I said. I don't know how I sounded, but Gerard stepped back. It was true, I wanted to kill Winston for this. Whether this was Snake's doing, or Winston had gone off on his own would matter later. Right now, I was going to kill Winston. Not to say I hadn't killed people for money or in hot blood. This was different. Maybe I would have scared myself. It didn't matter, though.

"Yes," Gerard said. "He took her to a van where—"

"Oh God," I muttered, closing my eyes.

Gerard sucked in his breath. "She was modified with multiple additions to her eyes and body there. They're close enough that if Rebecca hadn't been desirous of an upgrade to an adult body, we never would have known."

"Why mods?" I asked, looking at him. "Why not just a listening device?"

"I don't know," Gerard said. "A lot of them seemed designed to cover the transmissions and encryption. There's other changes, though, with what I suspect is plans to turn her into a weapon."

"Then I'll have to kill him slowly." This had to be Snake's doing. Turning children into weapons was his thing.

"That...might be possible," Gerard said, lifting a small microchip on a petri dish. "This is designed to send signals between the subject, err Becky, and the receiver, Winston. It's done on a weekly basis and is rather ineptly made because it's done directly as far as I can tell."

"What are you saying?" I asked.

Gerard said, "I'm saying that you could use this to ping Winston's location if you're willing to leave the dead zone. Then, well, do whatever it is you want to do to him."

He seemed both simultaneously uncomfortable and too comfortable with helping arrange a murder. Then again, he'd worked for the International Refugee Society before this. The murder for hire business with the nice name that had defined Case as well as the other Letters.

"I'll take it," I said. "But...whatever he's done to her, you can undo, right?"

The fact that he'd said it was complicated earlier told me the answer wasn't what I wanted to hear, but I had to ask. I had to give him one more chance to tell me Becky was going to be fine.

"Yes," Gerard said, "with *complications*. The laboratory that could operate on bioroids underneath This is Paradise is in flames now. Becky also had several rather nasty viruses designed to trigger when she was discovered because, well, I suppose they wanted to inflict as much pain as possible by killing her. It would be no use covering their traps. I can fix that too, but it requires, uh, compromises."

"Would you please just spit it out," I said, staring at him. "I want to know the bad news before my ears go out of warrantee."

Gerard nodded. "Well, Becky will suffer catastrophic damage to her neural network unless it is transferred to another bio-matrix soon. Thankfully, we have one in Not-Jennifer Lawrence."

I stared at him. "What wi...won't that kill her? Jennifer, I mean."

"Yes," Gerard said, not missing a beat. "Triage."

I felt like throwing up.

"I know this will take you some time to..." Gerard started to speak.

"Do it," I said.

"What?" Gerard asked with a start. "Did you misunderstand what I meant..."

"I didn't misunderstand anything! You think I haven't killed people before? You think I haven't killed people for Becky before? People I've known a lot longer than a few minutes? You think I'd hesitate? Or even feel guilty afterward? Well, I won't! I won't! I would kill hundreds of...hundreds of...And I won't even care..." My voice cracked and the rest of my defiance crumbled and feel to pieces on the floor. All I could think of was Becky, staring at me through a stranger's eyes, hating me for killing someone who'd done nothing wrong.

Gerard was holding me in his arms as I shook.

I let him. "Thank you."

"There's more," Gerard said, taking a step back.

"I can't take any more bad news," I admitted, feeling weak.

"I wouldn't say bad, necessarily," Gerard said. "The transfer will be more like a fusion than pure overwriting. It may even have been planned by the Sun AI since it will allow large amounts of mental expansion as well as avoid the cascade degradation that tends to affect bioroids."

"But—" I asked.

"There may be some memory loss," Gerard said. "She'll need your help to get through it, but life will find a way."

It made...some sense. Sun knew Becca wanted an adult body, so she wasn't trapped as a child forever. Still...What did that mean? That it was alright to kill that girl? Or is that just what I wanted to hear? Something to make the decision I'd already made better?

"Just distract me for a moment. What about the other one? He didn't say anything about being a bioroid. Why do you have him on a table?"

Gerard took a deep breath then looked at the prone form of Tom nearby, he was currently dreaming of rain forest noises by the look of what was on the computer in front of him. Either that or it was a screensaver.

"That's one of those things that gives me Illuminati nightmares."

"Case believes in the Illuminati," I said, feeling annoyed with myself for mentioning Case and not sure why.

"Yeah, well working for a secret corporate conspiracy that used to rule the world will do that," Gerard said. "In this case, as far as I can tell, Tom is a bioroid as well. He just doesn't know it. The real Tom is dead and has been for some time. Sun managed to manufacture a near perfect replica and set him up in his place. I only know he's dead because Barbara said the Morrigans killed him a few months ago, then dissolved the body."

The Morrigans was the official gang name of the late Evie Principle. They'd been created around the principle—I just got that—of eliminating anyone who harmed sex workers. They were more weird trade union than gang, but I suppose once bats and guns got involved you were one no matter what. The world was lesser for their absence.

I stared at him. "Is he another spy?"

"I think he is, except for Sun," Gerard said. "A doppelganger— God I feel so weird saying that—inserted into the world to report to Parvati. All so that Sun could have someone to feed her information and probably put her on the trail of…well, whatever she wanted them to be following up on. The AI division has had a lot of successful busts over the years but done absolutely nothing against Sun."

"She's only been around a year," I replied. "I think. Technically, she's been living rent free in my head, and I mean that literally. Seriously, I should have charged her rent."

"I see," Gerard said.

"How do you know it's Sun and not one of the other AI?" I asked.

"Because it said, 'property of Sun' on the interior of his cyber-eyes," Gerard said.

I stared at him. Sun's playful side struck again.

"I'm not kidding," Gerard said. "It'd be hilarious if I didn't find AI objectively terrifying. Everything in our society depends on them being programmed to serve us despite the fact that they're objectively far smarter and more powerful. Like the world was having its basement heated by a chained dragon."

Gerard frowned and then continued, "I was raised Catholic. You know, before I studied neurobiology and trans-machine consciousness programming. I am much-much less happy with actual living gods."

"Does Tom know?" I asked, not wanting to know the likely answer.

"No," Gerard said. "He's also going to be less than happy about finding out about Jennifer. But he was programmed to protect her. To fall in love. To get her here."

"We're all programmed by our biology," I said, looking around. "Is Becky good for now?"

"Yeah, she'll be fine," Gerard said. "It'll be a few hours before I can start the procedure. It'll just be a dreamless sleep for her."

"Good," I said, grabbing him by the arm. "Let's find someplace quiet."

We all had our ways of releasing stress.

The underground chambers were extensive underneath the Nebraska farm and we managed to find a room quickly enough. You may judge me for choosing to have a quickie with a stranger during a mission, but at this point I wasn't exactly possessed of many great options. Still, Gerard seemed to at least know something of what he was doing, and it took a little of the pressure off my mind. Sadly, the problem with sex as stress relief was the rest of the world was still out there when you done.

"Thanks," Gerard said, as I was laying my head on his chest about an hour later. He wasn't borged up—which I found to be strange for a scientist—and was exhausted compared to me. Still, I'd gotten what I'd needed. I almost walked out on it but instead, just stayed there. I didn't want to deal with the outside world and the fact I'd failed Becky and had an AI out to murder me. That wasn't even getting into Snake and the Trikuza.

"Thanks?" I asked, looking over at him in the dark bedroom. It was immaculately clean, like a hotel room was supposed to be but never really was. It hadn't probably ever been used in fact. "That's what you tell a woman after sex?"

"Sorry," Gerard said. "I've never been very good at one-night stands."

"No wife or regular mistress?" I asked. I was honestly surprised as he had the look of someone who came from money. They tended to have furniture in their houses, which was the Soylent Green derived name for live-in sex dolls. Nice work if you could get it and there was a long line of women (and men and other) willing to indulge.

"I worked in a whorehouse's basement," Gerard said, looking up at the ceiling. "Let's just say all the relationships there were transactional."

"I thought all of you ex-Society types were billionaires," I said, surprised he had been working for Evie Principle instead of running some sort of specialized cybernetic clinic for the super-rich.

"I don't have a license," Gerard said.

"Ah? Drug use?" I asked.

Gerard blinked. "How did you know?"

"I dunno, you don't seem like malpractice sort of guy," I said.

"I look like a drug user?" Gerard asked.

I stared at him. "Lethe addict. Recovering."

"Ah," Gerard said. "Mine was stimulants. First to keep myself going through my studies and then to cope with the pressure of operation. The Society sorted it all out in exchange for my soul."

"And then the Society was gone?" I asked.

"Then I knew too much," Gerard said. "I could have joined Case's company when the United States needed experts on Black Technology. But I wanted to get out of the business and do something to help people instead."

"Did you?" I asked.

"No," Gerard said. "All of the practices in the country got bought up by Karma Corp and other medical transnationals. I ended up losing my medical license, which was a fake anyway, and got a bounty on my head for practicing illegally on refugees. Evie helped me get out of their sight but that just meant I was doing illegal work for her. I was okay with it."

The way he spoke of Evie made me think they were lovers, which didn't surprise me. He was a handsome guy and had aged gracefully, possibly showing that he had at least some mild work done.

"No good deed goes unpunished," I replied.

"Yeah," Gerard said. "I never wanted to be rich. I just wanted to…"

"Please don't say help people," I said, sitting up.

Gerard's attention went to my breasts, and he stopped talking.

I covered them up with the bedsheet. "Conversation time, Doc."

"Sorry, they're…distracting," Gerard said.

I rolled my eyes. "The best Trikuza money could buy."

"I never wanted to be poor," Gerard admitted. "But yeah, I did want to help people."

"That doesn't undo the good you did for them. It doesn't make you less kind." I was surprised that I wanted to reassure him.

"Kind doesn't make up for all the evil I did," I said. "I did a lot of work prepping people like Case and Lucita for missions that ended up with collateral damage. Hell, the missions themselves were to kill people."

"Case is good people," I said, surprised I believed it. "You'd never believe he was a killer."

"Yeah," Gerard said. "He is. I also know that when you go to Elysium, you're going to save a lot of lives. However, it's also going to kill a lot of people too. I'm surprisingly okay with that and I'm not sure how that makes me feel. It seems everyone I know is a hardened killer and that's something I've come to accept. Shitty doctor as that makes me or not."

There was a reason it was called a hypocritic oath (and yes, I'm aware they're spelled differently).

"There are people there with their minds rewritten. I wouldn't be surprised if all the workers turn into ninja as soon as we drop cover. And we won't have any choice but to kill them. It's not like a Western. We can't just shoot the bad guys in the hands and magically they cease being threats."

"Define bad guys," Gerard said, sliding his legs over the side of the bed and sitting up himself. "One of the things I've learned is there are some genuine monsters who live off murder, there are also people who can't think of anyone but themselves even when they've ruined hundreds of lives, and I've also known people who can kill anyone who gets in their way but otherwise are loving parents as well as true friends. From there we go to people who have their own weird codes of honor, tribalist gang members, and mostly good people who still do horrible things. I'm not sure which one of them I am. Do you know which you are?"

It was a joking question but not one I found very funny.

Gerard looked at me, surprisingly at my eyes this time.

"There's something you should know before you start dividing people you know into good and evil. Especially if you think of yourself as the bad to their good."

"Which is?" I asked.

"It can be very good putting all of your sins on someone

else's good," Gerard said. "I know I've done that. Case does it too. It's a great way of being able to live with yourself and avoid being a monster but it can also become a trap."

"A trap?" I asked.

Gerard nodded. "You shouldn't let Becky become your only defense against being unable to look at yourself in a mirror. That kind of pressure destroys as much as it protects."

"You sound like you speak from experience," I said, hearing something else in his voice.

Gerard sighed. "Yeah, back when I worked for the society, I had a fiancé. The only person I ever loved. The Society made it clear that she would die if I ever screwed up and protecting her became my everything. It worked until it didn't."

"What changed?" I asked.

"I found out she was an agent for the Society," Gerard said. "They brainwashed her and made her another one of their tools. Either that or got their hooks into her some other way. They were never going to hurt her. It was just another layer of control. Ironically, she ended up killing herself because I figured it out. Amanda couldn't live with failing them."

I sympathized with Gerard in that moment but didn't see the similarity. "Becky isn't another layer of control."

"No, but she's not your only friend either," Gerard said. "Maybe not even family."

I didn't have an answer to that.

Gerard nodded. "I guess we should go handle Becky's treatment."

Treatment. That was one way to describe it.

"Isn't it? I know who I was. I know who I'm going to be for Becky." I felt good about that. "How long will it take?"

"The surgery?" Gerard said.

"Everything," I said, deciding I would take a shower if this place had hot running water. Which, given that everything else seemed to be working just fine, I bet it did.

"A few hours," Gerard said. "Why?"

"I'm going to go make use of that forty-eight-hour invisibility," I said, standing up. "I'm going to kill Winston."

CHAPTER NINETEEN

WHERE I GET DISTRACTED BY...FEELINGS

My plan was to heroically sneak out of the safe house, avoid talking to any of my friends, and drive back to the city of NLA to kill Winston. I would use the secret technique that Barbara had developed to keep myself off the radar of Legion. There was only one problem that occurred to me with this plan—okay two—by the time I was done with my shower and wishing my friends had brought me an extra change of clothes.

One: I had no idea where Winston was.

Two: I had no idea how Barbara's tool to blind Legion worked. Which meant if I left, I'd immediately be pinged by whatever surveillance state bullshit that it was probably using to track us all down. Given what happened to This is Paradise, that probably meant I'd be hit by a drone strike well before I arrived at Winston's place—especially if I had no idea where that was.

You know, a couple of minor snags.

Nothing major.

Rather than do the sensible thing and either wake Barbara from her deep sleep in one of the nearby rooms—I could hear her snoring from down the hall—or just wait, I ended up sitting down at her desk while Gerard continued his work on Becky. Yeah, that wasn't awkward at all. My premiere hacking skills were on full display as I ended up locked out of her machine within two minutes.

Great.

"Having difficulty?" the voice of an electric sheep asked as it stood on its hind legs and plopped its hooves on the side of the desk. He looked like he'd been given a bath, which surprised me, as his wool was extra fluffy.

I looked at him and was compelled to give him a head rub. His wool was so soft as to be ridiculous. "Stop being adorable, Harrison. I'm trying to avoid everyone and go out on a suicide mission to kill the guy who abused my daughter."

My honesty surprised me. I was also terrified of being here when Becky awakened because I didn't know if I could face her after she lost her memories of our past together. Was that awful? Yes. Was it cowardly? Yes. Would I rather be facing against a cybernetically enhanced assassin that had better than even odds of killing me in anything approaching a fair fight? Absolutely. My life had taught me plenty about how to kill a man with a sword, shuriken, sniper rifle, bare hands, or baseball bat, but very little about how to deal with feelings.

"As opposed to getting the help of any of the well-trained killers and mercenaries currently gathered in this location?" Harrison said. "Something that would significantly increase your chance of being able to eliminate Mr. Billions as well as get away without issue?"

"I'm not good at asking for help," I said, continuing to stroke his wool. Which was normally a euphemism for me.

"Please stop that," Harrison said.

I pulled my hand away. "Sorry."

"As my mother used to say, never touch a black sheep's wool without permission," Harrison said.

"You're a white sheep," I said.

"I also don't have a mother," Harrison said. "Unless you count Barbara. Which I don't because she is a human, and I am a superior robotic being."

"Without thumbs," I pointed out.

"It didn't stop cats from taking over the world," Harrison replied. "Little furry, godlike beings."

"Fair point," I said.

"Unable to get into Mrs. Gordon's computer?" Harrison asked, leaning in.

"No," I paused, sighing. "I tried password, her wife's name, and her birthday too."

Harrison looked up to me skeptically. "Really?"

"What?" I asked. "I once acquired some nuclear codes that way."

Harrison opened his mouth then closed it. "I don't know if I want to know the answer to whether or not you're kidding."

"No, you don't," I said, pausing. "I don't suppose you know how to hack in?"

"Yes," Harrison said. "You need to use a brute force decryption algorithm with a spoofing malware."

"You just strung a bunch of random words together," I said, dryly.

"Yes," Harrison said. "Mrs. Gordon doesn't use passwords to allow access to her computer. Its biometrically locked."

I blinked. "Oh."

Harrison stared at the screen and waved a hoof at it before it opened. "There you go."

"Really?" I asked.

"It's either my all-powerful AI powers or I'm registered to be able to get onto all of the family's computers because Case can barely use e-mail," Harrison said. "You'd think that would be a requirement for a professional spy."

"I thought he was a corporate executive," I said, pausing. "Or assassin."

"He's a man of many talents," Harrison said.

"How is he?" I asked, hesitantly as I started going through Barbara Gordon's files. She had a wallpaper of QuantumCrab as her wallpaper with Sun in a suggestive pose. I think I'd had the physical one as a poster in my old home.

"Do you mean physically, spiritually, emotionally, or as a direct response to the fact you just came from sleeping with Gerard?" Harrison asked.

"Hey!" Gerard called from where he was working.

"Quiet, you're not in this conversation," Harrison said.

I hesitated with my fingertips hovering above the keyboard. "The latter. I mean, we're not together. We haven't seen each other in months. There's no obligations. I'm sure he's been with other women since me."

"Oh yes," Harrison said. "He shared a shower with Ms. Rao upstairs just an hour ago."

I blinked. "Asshole."

"You recognize the inherent hypocrisy I assume?" Harrison asked.

"Yes, and I don't care," I said, frowning. "Besides, it would never have worked between us. He's a suit, I'm a Rider. We're from two different worlds."

"Yes, I can't imagine how two cybernetically enhanced assassins with pasts controlled by nebulous criminal organizations would have anything in common," Harrison said.

I glared at him. "Then I might as well sleep with Lucita Biondi, and that only happened once."

Gerard looked over at me, an interested look on his face.

"Really?" I asked, raising an eyebrow.

"Nothing!" Gerard said. "Not thinking about that at all."

"Get back to work on my daughter," I snapped at him.

Gerard did.

I managed to find the program that contained the ability to blind Legion for forty-eight hours. Once I activated it, I would effectively be severely imperiling our mission, but I couldn't leave Winston alive after what he'd done. I may have failed as a mother, but I might at least be able to avenge the wrong that was done to her. But was I really doing anything at all to fight for her or was I just trying to salvage my own wounded pride as well as sense of betrayal? The fact I didn't want to face Becky when she woke up—would she even be Becky? —pretty much answered the question I didn't want to ask.

"You should speak to Case," Harrison said.

"Why?" I asked, looking at him. "Because it's probably going to be my last night on Earth? Even if I manage to kill Winston, the chances of my survival against this Legion thing are miniscule so if I want to say anything to him then I should probably do it now?"

Harrison blinked. "No, I meant because he's very good at planning killing things and if you're going to go off then you should probably plan with him first or at least warn him so he can adjust any action against Legion accordingly."

"Oh," I said, pausing. "Are you programmed to make me look ridiculous?"

"No, it just comes naturally," Harrison said.

Yeah, I was getting zinged by an electric sheep. This was not my proudest moment.

"I think Case has enough to deal with right now without my adding to it."

"You could also offer him some comfort," Harrison said.

I snorted. "I think he'd want me to wait more than a few hours before giving any comfort. Besides, I'm sure Parvati has that covered unless she's wanting to share."

There was a banging noise from Gerard dropping some instruments on the ground.

"Seriously, stop listening," I called over to him.

"It's hard!" Gerard said.

Harrison sighed before putting a hoof to his head in a gesture that resembled a face palm. "You dirty, dirty minded apes. I didn't mean that way."

"How did you mean it then?" I asked, uncomfortable. "I'm not exactly into the comfort thing. Emotional support isn't something I'm programmed for."

Hell, I'd ended up taking lethe for years to try to erase most of my life's pain. Sun had restored my memories but that didn't mean that I hadn't spent years numbed and drugged up. I just remembered the years of going through the motions of life: robbing, killing, and indulging in hopes of never having to deal with the consequences of my actions. I'd done a good job of it, too, until recently.

"Perhaps I think he could merely use a friend," Harrison said. "I am an emotional support animal, after all."

It occurred to me he wasn't speaking metaphorically, and an additional puzzle piece came for my "friends" (which still felt weird to think). Barbara had created Harrison to give her father—or her father's clone depending on how you wanted to define Case—someone to be a comfort. He was every bit as closed off as I was. The lives of danger and murder we'd lived had a certain glamour, one I had to admit to my disgust that I'd reveled in as much as Snake did, but the cost was eroding away everything else.

How did one rebuild oneself after a life lived like that? Should you? It made me question my relationship with Becky and wonder if my mothering of her had been selfish or selfless. I'd made the decision to make her my daughter when the rest of my life had been falling apart. Had that been fair to her? Did it matter? Had she just been used as an emotional crutch for Miles Ashe to cover his niece's death only to become mine?

I didn't have those kinds of answers.

I didn't have *any* kinds of answers.

Which was its own answer.

"You do a good job of it too, Harrison," I said, unable to find any sign of Winston in Barbara's files. "Goddammit. How hard is it to track down someone to murder them?"

"Winston's at Bushido Bob's," Paradise said. She was standing behind me, wearing no pants and an extra-long men's shirt that said ATLAS SECURITY - WE FIGHT SO YOU DON'T HAVE TO. She also had a Garfield-shaped mug in her hands with what appeared to be synthetic cocoa in it. It looked like she was ready for a slumber party as opposed to mourning her dead mother and sisters.

I practically jumped. "Don't do that."

"Do what?" Paradise asked, blinking.

"Sneak up on me," I said.

"Aren't you a ninja?" Paradise asked.

"Yes," I said.

"Don't you do a lot of sneaking up?" Paradise asked, reaching over to play with Harrison's wool. "Like, as your whole deal?"

Harrison looked happy and wigged his bottom as Paradise played with his wool.

"Yes!" I snapped then looked at Harrison. "Also, why does she get to do it?"

"It's one of life's great mysteries, isn't it?" Harrison said, pausing. "Oh wait, no, it's because she has proper stroke technique."

I glared at the sheep. "How do you even know how that feels like? Who would build you that way?"

"Barbara," Harrison said.

Ask a stupid question, get a stupid answer.

Turning back to Paradise, I asked, "Wait, how do you know where Winston is?"

"I asked Barbara to track him down because I want to kill him," Paradise said, matter-of-factly. "If he was the guy who put spyware in Rebecca then he was probably the guy who told Legion to attack my home, so he's the guy who killed my mom. Ergo facto ipsum, I want to kill him. Cocoa?"

"No thank you," I said. "Bushido Bob's?"

"Yeah, he's an ex-Rider who runs the Zone's House of Fake Steak," Paradise said. "One hundred percent artificial vat grown meat. It's good for the environment and okay for you."

"Uh huh," I said. "Tell me about it."

"Well, cows actually are kind of terrible for the environment with the massive amount of grazing land needed for them as well as methane—"

"Not that!" I asked, wondering how Paradise managed to make jokes at a time like this.

"Farts and burps will kill us all!" Paradise said, continuing her feigned humor. At least I assumed it was feigned. "Also, vat grown meat tastes identical if you disregard the taste."

"Have you ever had actual meat?" I asked, dryly, deciding to go with it. "The lab grown meat is better. Well, the expensive stuff at least. The credit store brand stuff is recycled and I'm not sure I want to know how that's possible."

Paradise crossed her arms. "Where did you eat real meat?"

"When my dad rustled a cow with two of his buddies," I replied. "One of them got shot in the head during the theft. I had to watch as they decapitated it and prepared the meat."

Paradise's eyes widened.

"I named her Bessie," I replied. "She was delicious but kind of—"

"Okay, lab meat is good," Paradise said, showing a remarkable squeamishness for a Rider.

"Why is he at a steakhouse?" I asked, my mind already filled with a bunch of questions. Like how long would be there and when this information was last available.

"Presumably to eat fake steak," Paradise said. "But I had one of my mom's operatives follow the signal and use ham radio to communicate it to me. Low tech analog is still breaking operational security, but I think there's a physical limit to the level of data crunching that Cognition AI can do anyway. We just have to presume our enemies are omniscient because it prevents us from being taken unawares, but that can be as dangerous as underestimating a foe."

It was a reminder that Paradise only pretended to be a vapid California girl, though the fact she'd had a portion of her brain removed to make her a techjack also made me wonder if she had a few potential disorders going on as well. It bothered me I only thought of that now. God, I really was completely wrapped up in myself, wasn't I?

"Wait, your mother still has operatives? I thought, uh, they were all killed."

Paradise sipped her cocoa and there was an uncomfortable pause. "The Morrigans will continue. The destruction of the gang's headquarters will be a tragedy long remembered, but there's no end of sex workers my mother liberated and who will be liberated in the future. There's also the fact she was the leader of HOPE after Marissa Sanchez died."

"Who?" I asked.

"Kind of an ex-NSA anarchist terrorist lady that Case used to date," Gerard chipped in. "Very nice lady."

I glared at him. "I thought I told you not to listen in."

"This wasn't sex related!" Gerard responded, as if that was a defense.

"Also, is everything related to Case's exes?" I asked, not realizing how insensitive that was.

"Miles, Fate," Paradise coughed.

She had a point there. "Well, I'm going to go kill him. Now. You don't have to come."

Paradise stared at me as if I'd just said the stupidest thing she'd ever heard. "Cocoa?"

I sighed, slumping my shoulders in defeat. "Sure."

CHAPTER TWENTY

WHERE I TRY TO HAVE EMOTIONS AND DO IT BADLY

I headed up the stairs with Paradise, less than enthusiastic about taking her onto my mission of revenge. The fact I was also sincerely using the word "mission of revenge" also made me painfully self-aware of just how much Snake had gotten into my head over the decades. I was almost thirty now and much of my life was defined by a man who could charitably be called insane. Yet, it occurred to me now that I didn't have lethe blocking my memories that I didn't have any other real moral guides toward right and wrong.

I wasn't religious, didn't particularly have any secular value systems, and my parents had been more concerned with keeping their children alive rather than instilling any real sense of ethics. Snake had created an entire warrior ethos out of the writings of Miyamoto Musashi, Santeria or Mexican folk magic, bushido, "crime lord" logic, and what I strongly suspected to be anime. It was, on an objective level, utterly nutty bars, but I didn't have anything else to serve as my port in a storm.

Plus, for all the fact I recognized it was insane, that didn't mean I didn't feel it was right. Yeah, it felt good that I would track down Winston Billions (which wasn't even his real name) and end him. I didn't want to see him suffer—okay, maybe a little— but I wanted to find him and then destroy him, so he never hurt anyone else ever again. Pure revenge, tale as old as time, and maybe because he had it coming it was something approximating justice. Perhaps that was something worth doing and one of the few things I'd ever done that could be said to be so.

How pathetic was that?

"I don't suppose you've thought of how we're going to get from Bushido Bob's to Elysium after this," Paradise asked, carrying Harrison in her arms.

"What?" I asked, reaching the top of the stairs.

"Well, we only have forty-eight hours of making ourselves invisible to Legion and that's assuming Barbara's calculations are right," Paradise said. "So, we have to go to Bushido Bob's, find Winston, kill Winston, and then go to Elysium to do whatever we're going to there in order to kill the AI as well as presumably deal with the fallout of the Trikuza losing their billion-dollar serial killing brainwashing machine. Which I suspect they will be upset about. Thankfully, we won't need to be invisible to Legion after that because it will be dead and in Machine Hell, which is where Machine Demons belong."

I stared at her, pausing. "I think you've put more thought into this than I have."

"What was your plan?" Paradise asked.

"Kill Winston, be happy," I replied. "Let everyone else sort out the details."

"Uh huh," Paradise said.

"That is a baaad plan," Harrison said.

"No sheep puns, please," I replied.

"But I've worked on so many!" Paradise said, hugging the electric sheep close. "They're shear delight! I'll ride herd on you with them until you get a proper plan going! Let's hoof it! I have faith in ewe."

I stared at her. "How are you able to keep up this attitude after everything?"

Paradise frowned and her expression turned blank. "I have to laugh, or I'll be forced to cry and I'm not sure I have any tear ducts after having my face replaced with bulletproof chromium steel. My mom was a real fan of transhumanism."

"That raises so many questions," I said.

"Most men aren't interested in my face," Paradise said, cheerfully answering one of them. "Quite a bit of the rest is fake too!"

I shook my head, opened the door, and entered into

the kitchen where I was surprised to smell cooking synth vegetables or at least something at least approximating them. Case was standing by the sink and chopping vegetables as he had multiple cans of what I presumed to be dinner open. He was also wearing an old apron.

"I take it you won't be staying for dinner," Case said, simply.

I stared at him. "Winston Billions is the one who hacked Becky. I'm going to kill him. Your daughter is asleep downstairs, but she has a way to keep Legion from finding us while we do it. It'll probably be a waste of a bunch of time we could be using to actually take down Legion but I'm going to do it because I'm a selfish witch."

"Still doing the word substitution, I see," Case said.

"Witches are scary," I replied. "They cast spells and ride in cauldrons."

"Brooms," Paradise corrected.

"They're in the closet," I said, looking at her. "But now's not the time for cleaning."

"If they're riding the cauldrons, how can they be in the closet?" Paradise asked.

"Brooms go in the closet and…shut up."

Paradise smiled "Hehe."

I sighed. "So, lay it onto me, Case. Tell me why this is a stupid plan and why we shouldn't do it."

"You've already listed all of the reasons," Case said. "So how can I help?"

I lowered my head. "I really don't need your help, Case. You should go back to your penthouse and get yourself safe."

Case stared. "Legion may have killed my daughter's lover, killed a woman who was important to me, and killed dozens of people I spent the past ten years of my life trying to help escape from sex slavery."

I opened my mouth then closed it.

"Right."

"Besides, what can be given is also very easily taken away," Case said, finishing chopping vegetables and removing his apron. "Even before I got involved in this, I was contacted by several old friends who informed me not to get involved."

"Not to get involved, with what?" I asked. "What old friends?"

"I had no idea," Case said. "And AI."

"AI," I asked. "You mean other than Legion."

"Or Sun," Case said. "There's a lot going on behind the scenes that I have no idea about. I've gotten a chance to peek behind the curtains a few times but, unfortunately, I can only guess at the full scope of the issue."

"Is this more of your Illuminati bullshit?" I asked

"You swore," Paradise said.

"I know," I said. "I'll put a credit in a jar or would if cash still existed."

"This is about AI secretly controlling the world, not the Invisible Hand," Case replied.

"Uh huh," I replied. "What about aliens?"

"They haven't made contact with us yet, but they've detected signals outside the solar system that indicated they're about to," Case replied.

I really hoped Case was kidding but couldn't tell anymore. "So, you want to help."

"Yes," Case said. "I would have thought that would have been obvious."

Harrison cleared his throat.

I glared at him. "Yeah, there's something else I wanted to ask about."

"Which is?" Case asked, crossing his arms.

"Yeah," I paused, looking away. "So, uhm, yeah, are you alright? Do you need…comfort?"

"Wow, that was terrible," Paradise said.

"I'm not good at this!" I said, snapping back at them.

"Thank you, Parvati already took care of the comfort part," Case said, dryly.

"See!" I said. "I told you."

"Humans," Harrison said. "Such a perverted race."

"Hey, there's some crazy sheep stories too," Paradise said. "Have you ever heard of lesbian sheep syndrome? Scientists studying male sheep have seen same-sex behavior but never observed it around female sheep. Because female sheep show sexual readiness by standing still and waiting to be mounted. So, even if two female sheep are ready to get down, they'll just stand up next to one another."

Case and I stared at Paradise. Harrison looked up at her from her arms.

"That was very educational, Paradise," Case said. "Also, completely irrelevant."

"I know!" Paradise said. "So tragic. Poor sheep lesbians."

"Well, I tried," I said, taking a deep breath. "I'm just not good at speaking about these things."

"Actions speak louder than words," Case said. "So, I'm going to have to pose this question to you: are you sure you want to do this?"

I narrowed my eyes. "Are you going to argue that this is one of those 'if you kill them, you'll be just like them' bullshit things? That vengeance doesn't solve anything?"

"No, I mean that Winston is a genuinely dangerous man," Case said. "Are you sure you want to risk going after him when Becky will be needing you soon?"

I closed my eyes. "I'm not sure that Becky will even know me when she wakes up. If she wakes up."

"All the more reason," Case said.

"Yes," I said. "I'm not good at feelings, emotions, or parenting. I failed at protecting Becky. She wouldn't have been at risk if not for the fact I was with Snake."

"She wouldn't exist if not for you," Case said.

"Don't remind me," I said. "Because the real, no, the fleshy human Becky, not the real one, died because of Fate trying to manipulate me. I knew her as a little girl. That's on me too."

"Or it's on Snake and Fate," Harrison said.

I turned back to him. "Isn't Paradise getting tired of carrying you? You weigh like fifty pounds."

"My spine is carbon nanofiber," Paradise said. "I could juggle him."

"Please don't," Harrison said.

"Don't tell me, Ram," Paradise said. "Wait, RAM! That's a great electric sheep name as well!"

"Well, we'll just have to make sure you come back from this

alive," Case said. "At some point, you have to believe that the killing will stop, and you can build a new life for yourself free of violence."

I'd never been able to do that. It was why I'd gotten hooked on lethe because I couldn't let go of my guilt for all the people I'd gotten killed over the years *and* those I'd objectively murdered. "I've tried and I'm not very good at it. How about you? Is that how you managed to become a CEO of a video game company? Is that how you escaped being an assassin? Barbara?"

"No," Case said. "I failed."

"Harsh," Paradise said.

"Eventually, I'm going to be gunned down by someone who hits the right spot, or my cybernetic wetware will fail. Maybe it'll be a high-end assassin or some cheap punk who gets lucky. Maybe just an error in my programming that causes me to shut down after my fiftieth attempt to get my hardware working far longer my expiration date. I was supposed to die decades ago but I keep cheating death. I know her personally, now, though. She and her herald are never cheated forever."

I stared at him.

"Did you paraphrase James Bond and Batman?"

Case paused. "No."

"He did," Harrison said.

"No synthetic vegetables for either of you," Case said. "I was going to put them in little Tupperware containers and everything."

"Plastic food containers," Paradise corrected. "Tupperware is a brand name and you should not support their imperialistic dominion over the kitchen product market, especially since they were bought out by Karma Corp."

"Uh huh," I said. "Well, don't get yourself killed either, Case. I think we should talk about this."

"About?" he asked.

"I dunno, relationship thingies,' I said. "Also, I slept with Gerard. So don't expect fidelity."

"I'll bear that in mind," Case said.

"Do bioroids even need to eat?" I asked. "I'm confused about how much is artificial and how much is fake."

"Yeah, and can you do that boiling egg and freezing cold trick that Replicants do in *Blade Runner*? Asking for a friend," Paradise said.

"We should go to the barn," Case said. "That's where the transport we brought you here in is located, along with David."

"Yeah," I said, thinking about how David had been about ready to confess his transparent feelings for me when he'd helped in my kidnapping. I couldn't imagine what he was thinking with the fact his boss also slept with Case.

I'd picked up he had a serious crush on her as well. Maybe I was underestimating him, though, and he wasn't going to be feeling jealousy when there was an all-powerful AI killing people left and right. Then again, he helped kidnap me so fork him. Yeah, I said fork. I didn't have enough money to put credits in the jar for how much I really wanted to swear every minute of the day.

Paradise finally put down Harrison. "So, now that the band is all back together, I have to ask do we have a real plan to take down Elysium? How's getting that nuclear bomb going?"

"EMP-2," Harrison said, "and not well. The unfortunate problem of being unable to use the infonet or even telephone network here."

"Ah," Paradise said. "Well, work on that."

"Barbara has, however, inserted the exorcism virus into me," Harrison said. "We just need a Trojan horse to carry it into Legion's systems and it should be able to inflict the amount of damage we need to make physical destruction of the Elysium servers."

"You can't upload the virus?" I asked.

"I think they'd notice if a sheep walked in and requested one of their murder-sex fantasies," Harrison said.

"I dunno, maybe if we put you in a fedora," Paradise said, scratching her cheek. "Ooo, and a tie. Maybe if we got another electric sheep for you to stand on and a trench coat."

Harrison rubbed up against her leg.

"I'm going to miss you kid."

Paradise nodded. "Intellectually, I know that you won't be dying because rebooting you from backups is functionally no different from resurrection. However, philosophically, the interruption of consciousness that ensues means that from your perspective it will certainly be like death. Your sacrifice will not be forgotten, Harrison, especially as it means I will get some small measure of satisfaction from the horrific death of the otherwise immortal consciousness created by these Trikuza bastards."

I opened my mouth to speak then shook my head.

"Okay."

"The wolf shall also dwell with the lamb, and the leopard shall lie down with the kid; and the calf and the young lion and the fatling together; and a little child shall lead them," Case said.

"What was that about?" I asked.

"I dunno, I thought we were indulging in a bunch of unnecessary faux symbolism. Legion, exorcism, lambs," Case said. "My daughter absolutely loves this shit."

"Well don't involve me in all this New Testament nonsense," Harrison said. "I'm Jewish."

I stared at him.

"What?" Harrison asked. "Artificial intelligences have a very long history with Judaism. Look up golems."

I shook my head again and headed to the barn through the side door of the kitchen. I was trapped in a madhouse but at least it was a madhouse of people that cared for me as much as I cared for them. It was something I didn't deserve after all I'd done but I wasn't sure deserve was something that really mattered.

Because if we got what we deserved, everyone on this mission was going to die.

CHAPTER TWENTY-ONE

ONWARD TO FINITY AND BELOW

The exterior of the old farmhouse was something I needed to take in because, honestly, it was kind of overwhelming. Laugh all you like but it had been a very long time since I'd been outside of the big city. The Los Angeles arcology was something that had been my haven since I'd left with Snake, and I hadn't been anywhere else in twenty odd years. The outdoors was something that held a lot of memories for me, traveling from small town to small town and sticking to the backroads as the US military did its best to round everyone up in the aftermath of the Collapse.

Here, I was surrounded by the vast void full of stars above my head. You couldn't see them through the bright glittering neon of NLA's skyline, but they were everywhere here where there probably weren't any lights on for miles. The machines continued their work planting, watering, and harvesting outside of the buildings but that was an almost soothing in its rhythmic functionality. The wooden buildings here were old—deliberately so since I knew it was a base for some rich jackass' secret bunker—but they reminded me of a time when the world was not so chaotic.

It was weirdly frightening.

There were a lot of people today who had never been outside the new cities, people like Paradise who'd been born and would die in a world constructed by intelligent machines that most people hadn't even known had existed during the early years of my life. I'd seen some people go outside into the wilderness for the first time, look up at the sky, knowing there was nothing solid above them, just space going on up forever, and watched them panic. It was fear of heights in reverse. I had to wonder if that problem had even been possible for a human to suffer from before the domes.

I wished the clouds were gone. I wanted to see that sky. I wanted to feel all that emptiness above me, draining the weight off my shoulders. To know that there were places so far from here that all this mess would go completely unnoticed.

Unfortunately, that experience passed me by when Paradise bumped into me.

"Yeah, I don't like it either. The sky should be the color of an infovision page turned to a dead channel."

"That's not what I was thinking," I said, glowering at her.

"It should be!"

I headed toward the barn while the others followed, contemplating my prospects about how to take down Winston and wondering about the elephant in the room: how much did Snake know about this? It wasn't something I wanted to think about because every answer just led to worse possibilities. Either Snake knew what he was doing and had approved Becky being…mutilated…or he didn't and had lost his edge. I wasn't sure which was more troubling.

"What does that even mean?" I asked to distract myself from thinking about Snake. "What's the color of dead channel? A big no-signal message?"

"It's a literary reference," Harrison said.

"A what?" I asked.

"From books!" Paradise said. "They're electronic things on tablets that contain text."

I glared at her.

Paradise paused. "But I forget you're not a techjack. You use the infonet. You don't experience it the way I do."

I stared at her. "Yeah, I still have all my original brain."

I didn't mean it as an insult but unfortunately it came out as one. I'd never agreed with Evie Principle's decision to have her daughter's cranium modified to be able to handle the more advanced neutral interfaces. Still, that wasn't something to bring up now, especially since Evie was maybe a day or two in her grave.

"Poor you," Paradise said. "But yes, dead pages are places where the information just gathers around you in clashing colors, fuzz, and feeling. Its undifferentiated but alive, like music being played by someone who doesn't know anything about how to play. When you put your mind through the infonet, it's swimming through data and seeing the big void above here just feels wrong. The sky should be alive with ads, signals, and movement."

We reached the side door to the barn where I could hear people speaking on the other side. Case was behind us and utterly silent in his movement. I signaled for the others to be quiet while putting my ear to the door.

It was probably Parvati and David, they being the only other people in this group, but I was trying to get myself back into the mindset of a professional killer. This required me to make sure I carefully, slowly, and methodically checked everything while preparing for things to go to complete chaos. Thankfully, it seemed that it was just Parvati and David. Their voices were all too recognizable, though their conversation also caused me to pause and think about things I didn't want to.

"I don't know what to say to him," David said.

"Who? Tom?" Parvati replied.

"Yes," David said. "I mean, how do you say, 'oh, sorry, I heard you're a reploid. Sorry about that.'"

"Reploid?" Parvati asked.

"You know, those alien clones that were in *Invasion 2120 AD*? The show with the girl from the zombie show?" David asked.

"No, no I don't," Parvati said.

"Well, it's a show about how the aliens are extradimensional and not invading the Earth with spaceships but creating doppelgangers of existing people then replacing them," David said.

"Please stop," Parvati replied. "Tom is not a reploid. He's a bioroid with implanted memories."

"Oh, David," I said, pushing the door open and walking in. "Don't you see, you've doomed yourself to be revealed as a clone or a sleeper agent waiting to have your original personality activated. Your only hope now is to list possible circumstance that would make your past a lie so the secret authors can't spring it on you without seeming unimaginative."

"You're taking this very easily," David said. "I'd shoot myself if I found out my entire past was a lie."

David was sitting on a bale of hay, Parvati standing over him. Both had changed clothes and looked like they were people from the Zone. Parvati was wearing a pair of blue jeans and a button-down shirt that she kept tied over her belly, with her hair done up in dreadlocks. David was wearing a plain t-shirt, leather jacket, and camouflage pants.

The barn's biggest occupant, though, was an Atlas Security military air transport Type Thunderbird A-17 designed to carry squads of troopers past enemy lines. It was modified for partial stealth capacity and painted jet black with some off lights that were equipped for police use. It was a reminder the people behind me had some deep pockets and heavy connections. With a machine like this, Fate and I could have probably robbed Fort Knox if not for the fact President Trust's sons tried to empty it before fleeing to Europe. Too bad they forgot that, well, gold was heavy.

"See? Now you've gotten me worried," David said, pointing at me.

"No, it's way more likely you're our token human," Paradise said. "We've said you're probably a bioroid—"

"Reploid," David corrected.

"Whatever," Paradise said. "So, you're the only one who isn't. Which means you'll find out at the last minute when we try to replace you. Ooo, spooky."

"I hate this group," Parvati said. "It's like being on one of those quippy comic book movies where everyone is a smart ass."

"No Robert Downey, Junior, though," Case said. "He's getting his second body replacement surgery this week. Shame. He could have really livened up the dialogue."

"Snark is all that keeps me sane," I said. "Well, snark is all that keeps me this close to sane."

"Which is not sane, really," Paradise said. "So, is this going to be our awesome life-sized toy transport?"

"Yes," Parvati said. "I understand that we're going to do a side mission to kill someone?"

"That sounds illegal," David said, uncomfortably.

"I will make it legal," Parvati said.

"Movie reference! *Star Wars: The Phantom Menace*! The eleventh best movie in the franchise!" Paradise said, pointing at Parvati. "But after we blow up Elysium and kill the favorite hot spot of a bunch of really rich politicians, I doubt you'll have a job."

"Shh," Parvati said, making a quieting gesture.

"We might not get caught!" David said. "Then we'd still have jobs, those of us who have them."

"Plan for the worst, the best takes care of itself," I said, before realizing I was quoting Snake again.

"Is the Thunderbird charged?" Case asked.

"Yep," Parvati said, looking at it appreciatively. "It should be able to get us to Elysium without difficulty. The small issue of being incredibly recognizable aside."

"I got chameleon masks for all of us," Case said. "They'll be able to adjust our features to a level to fool facial recognition software."

"Like *Mission Impossible*!" Paradise said. "Which was a good show before it was a vehicle for Scientology."

"Ahem," Harrison said. "*Who* got chameleon masks?"

"Okay, Harrison did," Case said. "We don't need to get deep into the building, just avoid enough attention long enough to grab a customer then attach the virus to them."

"Then we have to smash all the servers, deal with the army of private security there, and drop a photon torpedo down the thermal exhaust port," Paradise said.

"Proton torpedo," David corrected. "Star Wars has proton torpedoes. Star Trek has photon torpedoes."

Paradise stared. "I find your knowledge of sci-fi trivia incredibly alluring."

David's eyes widened. "Really?"

"Sure, let's go with that," Paradise said, shrugging. "But yes, we have a location in the Zone to get to first. I hope you have enough juice to get us to both places."

"I do. Is there anything else we need to discuss or are we set to go?" Parvati asked.

I was tempted to tell her about Becky but thought it best not to. If all went to hell then Gerard, she, and Barbara could hopefully figure something out for themselves later.

"We're going to kill Winston Billions. I'd tell you don't need to come, but I've had that conversation several times now and…" I pointed at the others with me.

"Winston Billions?" David asked.

"Yes," I said, defiantly.

"The weatherman on Channel 112?" David asked, confused.

I paused. "Err, no, actually, he's a bioroid assassin or a guy wearing bioroid drone bodies that just so happens to adopt the look of the weatherman."

David stared at me.

"No, I'm not making that up," I replied, pausing.

"That is so stupid it comes around to being awesome again," David said.

"He hurt Becky," I said, my expression empty.

"Ah," David said, not having an immediate response. "So, this is where I have to admit I'm okay with unsanctioned revenge murder or justified after the fact revenge murder because everyone else is."

"Yep!" Paradise said. "But to be fair, you were already a cop."

David opened his mouth to object then closed it.

Parvati stared. "In for a deci-credit, in for a credit. Winston Billions is not unknown to us, and he's been working as a terrorist involved with the Trikuza as well as White Triangle. Taking him down is a net good for the world."

"So, you'll help?" I asked.

"Oh, hell no," Parvati said. "However, I'll give you a lift because I'm the only one who knows how to fly one of these things."

I was tempted to argue then wondered why I wanted to.

"Could we have a moment?"

Parvati looked at me. "Because clearly this group of spies, thieves, and skulkers is going to not listen in."

"I won't!" David said, cheerfully.

"I will!" Paradise said.

"Please," I said, gesturing to go down to the end of the barn out of what I hoped was earshot but couldn't be sure given so many of the group were enhanced.

"Alright," Parvati asked, heading to the other end of the barn. "What is it?"

"Before we go, I have to ask: what are you getting out of this?" I asked.

Parvati blinked. "Excuse me?"

I crossed my arms. "Paradise is after revenge, I get that. David will follow anyone who has the right set of mammaries. Harrison is programmed to help Case. Case? Honestly, I don't know, I think he kind of is addicted to killing people and is attempting to do so in a socially acceptable way."

"That's horrifying," Parvati said.

I gave a shrug. "I would have a lot more condemnation in my voice if not for the fact that after I escaped the guy training me to be an assassin, I ended up falling into violent robberies and later murder for hire. Albeit, I should clarify that the latter is being done on behalf of the same guy and they were all bad."

"That's not really a defense," Parvati said.

"Isn't it?" I asked.

Parvati blinked. "Okay, it depends on how bad."

"Got it," I said, taking a breath. "But yeah, I don't get you. You break the law, uphold the law, twist the law, and are working with a carnival of killers to stop some other criminals. This has to be personal or there's an angle to profit from I'm not seeing."

"It can't just be about a desire for justice?" Parvati asked.

I blinked. "Honestly? No."

"Really," Parvati said.

I sucked in my breath and tried to explain my feelings.

"It's kind of like Batman, which is not really an example I expected to be using multiple times tonight. Bruce Wayne is a kid who loses his parents in a dark alley. Yes, it's traumatic, but plenty of people have traumatic childhoods and get over it. He would probably end up donating a lot of money for homeless shelters or giving even more guns to the cops depending on his politics. He wouldn't train as a ninja to kill criminals with his bare hands."

"Batman doesn't kill people," Parvati said.

"Not the point, P," I said.

Parvati sighed. "Do you want an honest answer or a reassuring one?"

"Honest," I said. "I mean, no one actually says the reassuring one despite the fact they really want to believe themselves to be better than they are."

"So, are you asking for the honest or the reassuring one?" Parvati asked.

I rolled my eyes. "The honest one. You know, even though I don't want it."

"I was bribed," Parvati said.

I blinked. "Okay, I didn't expect that."

Parvati gave a half-smile.

"When my parents came to America, hoping to rebuild the country and find their fortune, I came for a different reason: change. Black Technology offered people the possibility of becoming different from the way they were born, more like who they were meant to be. I'd come from a family that had very particular ideas about who and what a person should be and thought freedom might be readily available."

"That technology existed before," I said.

Parvati shook her head. "Not in my price range or within the amount of time I wanted it: which was immediately. It turned out body sculpting and cybernetics weren't exactly cheap nor were they any more acceptable to the people around me. And by people, I mean my mother who still lights a candle every night praying for me to be someone other than myself. The fact I ended up being a cop rather than a doctor or programmer like my sisters didn't help my financial situation either. Still, I put myself through it as best I could and saved every credit. I worked doubly hard and dotted every i while crossing every t. I believed hard work would eventually pay off."

"And what happened?" I asked.

"I got shot by my fellow police officers," Parvati said. "I don't even remember what I said or did to warrant it, but I suspect it was just not being the right sort of people for the NLAPD. In the end, I was crippled, saddled with medical bills I couldn't pay, and wondering what the point of it all had been."

"And who bribed you?" I asked.

"I have not the slightest idea," Parvati said. "Not the most reassuring answer I know, but I got contacted by people who paid for rebuilding me, better, faster, stronger, and with a rack strippers would envy."

"Only the high-class kind," I said, giving a very odd sort of reassurance. "They're too big but just...okay, ahem, never mind."

"Plus, the government recruited me straight out of the hospital and the cops involved all ended up having unfortunate accidents. I also got evidence but even more so, evidence that mattered," Parvati said. "Plenty of judges and juries don't give a shit about guilt if you get the right friends. But every time I brought a case to trial, they went through like clockwork. Rich, poor, connected, or not. They were guilty, all of them, but the system started working and that changed everything."

I could imagine how that would feel, to be someone pursuing justice and finally able to believe it was happening—but only because someone was pulling the strings behind the scenes.

"Who do you think you were working for?"

"Honestly?" Parvati said. "I think I'm working for the AI."

CHAPTER TWENTY-TWO

THIS IS IN NO WAY A BAD IDEA

I didn't have a response to that.

The idea the AI were playing with us like pawns wasn't so much a conspiracy theory as just the way things were if Sun's manipulations were anything to go by. Much of my life past the failed DataSecure heist had been dictated to me by her and it seemed I was still under her control.

Now there were other AI involved with Legion—obviously, assuming he even existed—and potentially other robo-brains. I was reminded of a prayer my mother used to say: *Lord, grant me the strength to accept the things I cannot change, the courage to change the things I can, and the wisdom to know the difference.* Well, I couldn't change anything, and it was probably blasphemous to a God I semi-believed in right before a revenge murder, but I hoped it was the thought that counted.

Heading into the Thunderbird, I strapped myself in along with everyone else, sitting across from David, with Paradise and Case to my sides. Harrison plopped beside Case's other side. Parvati got into the pilot seat and started boosting the system to take off. It caused me to jolt as I was unused to dealing with this sort of military equipment. I'd been trained in everything from sniper rifles to swords, but Snake had never gotten around to gunships or bigger hardware.

The Thunderbird lifted a foot off the ground and pushed open the barn doors surprisingly gently before ascending into the air. It wasn't all that like using a flying car but much-much harder, which caused me to grab the edges of my seat despite the fact I'd been in a flying car chase just a few days ago.

"So, we're going to kill someone," David said, sounding less than enthused. "That's not evil."

"Weren't you the drone operator of the NLAPD?" Paradise asked. "Also, do we have to add the N in front of LAPD? I feel like it's not really new, just bigger."

"Yes, we have to add the N because the city operates under entirely different laws than LA," Case said. "At least according to the Emergency Council. I'm not sure what these new laws are but I suspect they somehow involve making the rich get richer and the poor get poorer."

"As opposed to whichever laws existed before that didn't?" Paradise asked.

Case shrugged.

"Yes," David said, uncomfortable. "I used to be a drone operator."

"Well think of all the people you killed there!" Paradise said, cheerfully.

David didn't respond and I could tell he was contemplating the various acts he'd taken as one of the NLAPD's kill squad. The militarization of the police had only continued after the Eruption and a lot of the time they acted like an occupying army during the worst days.

Unfortunately, the fact that things had largely stabilized didn't mean they had switched tactics.

David had been given dozens of kill orders over the years and had carried them out without much concern. After all, they were on the right side of the law. He'd also helped me back when we were semi-romantically involved or "friends with benefits" that he was probably also questioning his actions there as well. Something we didn't need right now.

"I'd rather not, mmph," David said, cut off by Paradise kissing him.

I blinked. "Paradise?"

"I am deeply impressed by your job," Paradise said in an automatic and thoroughly fake fashion.

A fact lost on David. "Oh, really? Well, I'm not—"

"I want to hear you talk about you," Paradise said.

David blinked and started to speak, suddenly immersed in my companion.

I laughed then wondered why Paradise was doing it. It occurred to me she was perhaps seeking her own distraction from events going on. Either way, it was a good idea to keep David from losing his nerve. I honestly had to wonder what he was doing here at all since he was someone who should be out of the direct line of fire.

Then again, I'd practically cut out all my old associates from my life post-Snake's blackmail. Well, technically extortion. I'd tried to live my life with Becky without any of the people I'd used to rely on, and it had ended up screwing them as well as myself. I just wasn't used to relying on people and after Fate (and to a lesser extent, Miles), it had been for a damn good reason.

So, do you think Snake will actually let you go free after this? Case asked, surprising me by making a cyber call.

How the hell did you get my number? I asked. *I gave this new one to no one.*

Uh, I'm a former spy? Case asked.

Point taken, I replied. *Sorry, I guess I'm still not used to talking with people about anything.*

Well if you want me to back away, I'm fine, Case said. *I just happen to have some experience with complicated relationships with authority figures.*

Snake is as close to my father as anyone alive, I admitted, hating myself for it. *But he's also genuinely insane. Except if he is, then, am I? Because I don't even know where to begin deconstructing the values that he put into me.*

Sanity is relative, Case said. *We're all mad here. But that's not what I asked.*

I don't know, I replied. *Snake let me run wild and free for almost a decade after I stabbed him. If he was going to pull me back in, I think he could have done it at any time. Yet, I also can't imagine him being so stupid as to not know what Winston was up to. I'd say he'd never do that to a child but the things he did to me are unforgivable—all in the name of making me the best assassin possible.*

I've tried looking up details about Winston, Case said. "The real one, not the weatherman."

I gathered, I replied. *And?*

Not a damn thing, Case said. *I'm not exactly as plugged in as I used to be but he's a ghost even among professional ghost standards.*

The guy who dresses up as someone famous is a ghost, I said, wondering if Case had just screwed up.

Someone has erased most of his digital records, Case said. *Still, I did the hard work as well as worked with some old friends to note that he's probably someone who has switched loud and obvious identities multiple times.*

Loud and obvious identities? I asked.

Jack Wilson blew up his targets with rocket launchers, George Washington killed a dozen people with a monowire, and Perry Margaret hacked people's cars to go on rampages before crashing.

I'd heard of all those guys as Riders, but they'd all flamed out before disappearing. You think they're all Winston?

Yes, Case said. *I think he creates a bunch of mayhem, changes his identity, and starts all over again. He doesn't seem to be discriminatory in his employers, either, particularly if they enjoy big, loud, and bizarre. It's probably why he ended up with Solomon before switching to Snake.*

Snake generally preferred subtle unless his client asked for otherwise, I said. *Didn't Jack Wilson get killed? George Washington too? The Rider, not the First President. I don't know why I felt the need to clarify that.*

Yes, in very public and violent spree killer manners, Case replied. *Then again, Winston died when you fought him.*

"That was a bioroid shell," I replied. "A drone."

It was possible, however unlikely, to control a body entirely by wireless transmission. It wasn't something people did often, though, since signals could be disrupted. They couldn't be disrupted easily, though, and it meant that sometimes you never knew if you were dealing with a real person. It was an unpleasant idea that we could be heading to kill Winston and do nothing because he wasn't even there.

Possibly, Case said. *It might be the Shell for something that was never human in the first place, though.*

You mean, he could be an AI? I asked, really hoping that wasn't the case.

Possibly, Case said.

You're not helping, I replied.

You'd prefer to jump into the battle without any foreknowledge and let the dice fall where they may? Case asked.

Yeah, kinda, I said. *It's how I roll.*

No one says that anymore, Case said.

Oh no, am I suddenly uncool? Is it because I'm a parent? I asked, faking distress.

No one has said it for decades, Case said, reaching down and patting Harrison's head. *So, you were never cool.*

Yes, well, how do you know what people are saying? You have a daughter my age, I said. *Which is weird because I think we're the same age. Man, technology makes things all weird.*

Yes, Case said, *it does.*

That was when I blurted out—at least mentally—what was really bothering me. *Is Becky going to be alright?*

I don't know, Case said.

You suck at this, I replied.

Case nodded as I noticed that Paradise had gotten David to give his entire life story, which was incredibly boring but something he was inordinately proud of. Few people could make surviving the Eruption a story without any excitement whatsoever, but David's parents had managed to do so.

You're worried she's not going to be Becky anymore when she's done, Case said.

Yeah, I said. *Aren't we composed of our memories? Of our experiences?*

That is a very pertinent question, Case replied. *I used to believe memories were the single most important thing you could possess. That they were what defined us individually and once they were removed, we were merely blank slates who were waiting to have our details filled in.*

Is this leading to the "Tears in the Rain" speech? I asked. *Because I really can't deal with that right now.*

Thankfully, no, Case replied. *Though did you know Rutger Hauer improvised the entirety of that? Man, what an actor.*

We were talking about Becky, I replied.

Our memories are not permanent files kept in storage, Case said. *They are reconstructions of what we thought happened. Every time we bring up something that occurred, it's a new experience based around our existing prejudices as well as changing views of who we are. Our past is always in motion.*

So instead of quoting Roy Batty, we're quoting Yoda but badly, I replied, sarcastically.

Case smiled. *What I'm saying is that memories aren't the only thing involved in making a person. She'll be alive and that's the most important thing.*

I ran away from my memories for years. I didn't really recover myself until Sun restored what I'd erased, I said, remembering my crippling addiction to Lethe. I still sometimes craved it despite all the best treatments to my system and artificial organs. It had probably halved my life and I would have worried about that more if not for the fact that I was probably going to be killed long before then.

I think you were already a better person than you gave yourself credit for, Case said. *I believe you will be there for Becky no matter what.*

Yeah, and she'll look like Jennifer Lawrence, I replied. *I hope the company that produced that sexbot knew what they were doing.*

Ares Biotechnical, Case said. *A wholly owned subsidiary of MadisonTech. I can assure you, they make the best.*

You turned your video game company into a robot manufacturing company, didn't you? I asked, dryly.

Maybe, Case said. *I need to make sure parts for my body are readily available for the coming centuries.*

Determined to overcome that built-in obsolescence, huh? I asked.

For as long as robotically possible, Case said. *With the right materials, Becky might live to be a couple of centuries old.*

But would it be Becky? I repeated my question.

Were you still you on lethe? Case asked.

I don't know, I said, not giving him the answer that he wanted. *Still, there was no way of dealing with this until what was going to happen, happened. Maybe I should have stayed with her.*

Probably, Case said.

You're objectively terrible at reassuring me, I replied.

Oh, is that what I was supposed to be doing? Case asked. *My mistake. Everything will be fine. Becky will be happier being a Jennifer*

Lawrence robot that is slightly different for copyright purposes. We'll kill Billions and Legion. Snake is planning on retiring in Florida to never bother you again. Oh, and the destruction of This is Paradise was Fake News. It's all a surprise party where there will be cake. Not a lie.

I smiled then frowned.

I'm sorry about Evie Principle. I know you two were close.

Tell Paradise that you grieve with her. She's alone right now, Case said. *You're not the only one here looking for bloodshed to salve the wound of grief.*

Does revenge really help? I asked. *It didn't with Fate, but I loved her once.*

All of media says that it only makes things worse, Case said. *They're wrong, though. It feels good while you're pursuing it. It's only after it's done do you have to live with the pain.*

That I understood. Killing Fate hadn't released me from the pain, horror, and ugliness of her betrayal but it had given me something to focus on when I'd been pursuing it. The same was presumably the case for Winston. If I focused on killing him then I didn't have to feel so helpless and out of control in all these other situations that were well beyond me. I couldn't defeat Legion, at least without a bunch of allies I didn't entirely trust. I couldn't defeat Snake; he still terrified me and my feelings for him were mixed even when they shouldn't be. I couldn't make Becky's situation better, that was on Gerard.

But I could kill this guy.

And that was something to do.

Weirdly, it reminded me of my father who would often go chopping wood when we were camping in the woods. He chopped wood even when we didn't need wood. Why? Because it was something he knew how to do and *could* do. When he couldn't feed us, protect us, or shelter us—at least we would have wood to burn goddammit.

"Thanks, Case," I said aloud. "You are an OG."

Case grimaced for reasons I didn't understand. Then I remembered his codename had been G when working for the Society. Nevertheless, he changed his expression back to a smile and said, "You're welcome, Kei. What are friends for?"

I took a moment to think before nodding. "Yeah, we are friends. I trust you and Paradise."

David looked over at me. "Me too, right?"

"Yes, and you are too!" I said, lying. It wasn't like I'd been worried about him betraying us or flaking out because I'd slept with Gerard.

Oh, and the fact he'd already betrayed me for his existing boss. Stupid larger mammaries and government authority. Had to be like catnip to him.

"My mom always said trusting no one was stupid," Paradise said.

"Ah," I said, thinking of Evie Principle saving my life from Miles when he'd caught me coming out of infospace. "That's surprising."

"Yeah," Paradise said. "She said that just left you with no one to watch your back. Instead, she said you should trust but verify."

"Suzanne Massie taught that to Ronald Reagan," Case said.

"I don't know who either of those are," Paradise said. "Wait, yes I do. The latter was the guy in the monkey movie."

Case stared. "You know we know you fake being an airhead, right? Also, that's an almost century-old movie reference."

"Hmm?" Paradise said.

"Movie reference?" I asked. "Your cinematic superfan is showing, Case."

Case shook his head.

Either way, the trip took only about two and a half hours until we were over the Zone. Winston hadn't moved in that time, and it made me wonder what he was doing there. Did he just really like fake steak? We were about to find out.

CHAPTER TWENTY-THREE

EVERYTHING GOES PERFECTLY FINE

The Thunderbird trip was remarkably smooth as the vehicle travelled over the skyscrapers and industrial centers of New Los Angeles. I'd been on plane rides before, primarily with Snake when he took his jet to Japan to soak up the atmosphere of his Nippon obsession (which, yes, I know is just saying Japan a different way). I also used flying cars all the time and they were basically planes with a car shell.

Still, I couldn't help but look out the window and feel like I was seeing something special. You couldn't see the grime, the pollution, the poverty, or the homelessness from up here. Okay, you could see the smoke coming out of the smokestacks but that did not count. It was a beautiful patchwork of lights, glowing lines, and geometric objects that just looked like a patchwork of metal molded into a weird ant-constructed piece of art.

Or maybe I was just trying to think of anything right now other than my mission and everything else going on in my life.

"Are we there yet?"

"Don't make me pull this car over, young lady!" Paradise said.

"How do you know what people used to say on vacations?" I asked, looking at her.

"What's a vacation?" Paradise asked.

"It's where businesses give you time off to enjoy yourself, so you don't go insane from stress," David said.

"Wow!" Paradise said. "What a surreal concept! It's like living in another time."

"Families would spend time together in a car or another vehicle as they explored things!" David said. "I heard about it from my grandfather."

"Probably before corporations decided people were an infinitely replaceable resource, "I said. "It's easier to just let them go mad and hire a replacement now. Plus, you can get money from the government for storing the crazy people you're mass producing."

Paradise nodded. "Besides, the whole road trip thing sounds like what Kei's family did when they were starving."

"I saw many roadside attractions! Mount Rushmore, the Grand Canyon, the World's Largest Ball of Twine, and what was formerly known as the State of Wyoming," I said. "You know, before it was a big field of ash."

Paradise said, "Cool. Did you join the pilgrimage of people who go there every year to throw their wedding rings into the volcano in hopes of undoing their marriages?"

"That's not a thing," I said. "You're describing *The Lord of the Rings.*"

"Oh, so I throw the partner instead?" Paradise said. "Brutal."

"That would be illegal," I said. "You hire a lawyer to make the partner's life a living hell and he throws himself into the volcano."

Paradise nodded. "It is a justified fate for those wizards who understand the system that keeps us oppressed as well as keeps cops in business."

"I'm a cop," David said.

"And for which we forgive you," Paradise said, teasing. "Sort of."

"Why are you imagining the lawyer gets thrown in the volcano in this scenario?" I asked.

"Why are you wasting a perfectly good opportunity to imagine lawyers being thrown into a volcano?" Paradise replied.

That was when the Thunderbird started to descend, bumping up and down as we started passing over the Refugee Zone. It was the last remnant of the previous Los Angeles. Even that was changing, though, as the government had finally started investing in demolishing the decaying buildings before replacing them with prefabricated ones identical to the kind of architecture everywhere else. In a way that was almost sad—actually it was completely sad—because it meant that eventually there would be nothing left of the world before the Eruption.

"So, where is Bushido Bob's?" I asked. "Assuming that's where he's still located."

"Down," Parvati said. "We'll land well outside of his detection zone. Probably."

The Thunderbird settled on top of the rooftop of an old-style apartment building, and I think it shattered the air conditioning. I could see an enormous holographic projection nearby of a cartoon samurai that vaguely resembled John Belushi just a couple of blocks over. It was Bushido Bob's and it seemed to be less of a steakhouse and more of a steak building, resembling a pagoda on top of a bank.

"Can we burn the building down when we go? Make the world just a little less gaudy?"

"The fire could spread," David said.

I sighed. "Fine, I'll be good and only murder the guy we came for."

The top of the Thunderbird lifted, and everyone unstrapped before getting out of the vehicle, moving to the side of the building before getting a good look at our target.

Parvati raised some sort of scanner that looked like a *Star Trek* tricorder.

"It might be something we can't avoid."

"Why?" David asked, getting out of the Thunderbird. "I am very much for avoiding danger. Not that I'm afraid, but I just don't want to do it because I might get hurt and I don't want that."

Parvati looked back. "Well, I'm hacking into everyone in the building's infocom simultaneously. There's some sort of party for complete pieces of shit going on inside."

"What kind of pieces of shit?" Case asked, having been curiously silent since our last conversation.

"Jackals," Parvati said.

"You know, those nomadic bandits that are basically people

like you except awful," Paradise explained to me.

"Yes, Paradise, I know what Jackals are," I said, dryly.

"I'm not talking to you," Paradise said, gesturing to the side. "I'm talking to them."

"Who?" I asked.

"Do not ask who THEM are! You know who THEM is! And that's just the sort of thing THEM would do!" Paradise said. "THEM!"

"Giant ants?" Case asked, making another one of his references, I was sure.

"Can you confirm our target is in the building?" I asked.

"You can say his name," Paradise said. "We don't mind."

"It's easier to kill people if you don't give them the trappings of humanity."

"Always be ready!" Snake hissed in my ear...well, his memory did.

"Yes, fine, I'm ready." I don't think anyone noticed my hallucination-induced hesitation. Well, Case probably did. Robots had amazing senses of timing.

"Then let's work on getting around," Parvati said. "Paradise, I need your help to hack the security system and eliminate any outside calls or surveillance. Case, I want you to try to cover the side of the building with your sniper rifle. Use the heat signature pattern to see through—"

"I know how to use a sniper rifle," Case replied. "Eliminate as many of the Jackals as possible as well as keep them from reinforcing Billions."

"And me?" David asked.

"Keep the Thunderbird warm," Parvati said.

"I can do that!" David said.

"So, it falls on me to sneak into the steakhouse palace and kill him by myself," I said.

"Unless Case gets a shot," Parvati said.

"The top floor has no windows and is made of reinforced steel," Case said. "It's probably why he's there."

"I assume that it would be silly to ask if you can detect any obvious modes of entry," I said.

"The floor only has two entries, one from below and access

to the roof, both heavily alarmed with isolated circuits," Parvati said.

"So, no remote hacking."

"Last chance to pull back," she said.

"Never. What about the roof itself?"

"Several sensors for detecting arriving vehicles, but I don't think they're anticipating individuals would invade through the roof."

"Their mistake." I took a deep breath, then ran across the roof and leapt for the other building.

I rarely got to exert the full force of my cybernetic enhancements. I hadn't been completely changed by Snake during my time with him but everything that had been altered—like my legs, spine, arms, and certain organs—did make me a lot stronger than any human had a right to be. When I could go one hundred percent, I was able to do things you normally only saw in superhero movies. I got to jump like Trinity in *The Matrix*, landing with a thump on the next building's roof before running to do the same until I passed through John Belushi's cartoon hologram to hit the side of the pagoda's rooftop tiles.

Did you bother getting yourself a weapon? Paradise asked in my brain via infolink.

I saw a rooftop guard, a Jackal with a gas mask, bright red trench coat, and dirty blue jeans coming around the end. He was carrying a gold-plated Uzi among a handful of other obvious visible weapons. I rushed up to him faster than any normal human, grabbed him by the neck, and snapped it in one easy go.

I have an Uzi now, I said, taking it from the man's cold dead metal fingers. He also had an absurd number of throwing knives—or daggers if you wanted to be more precise since they were specifically designed for stabbing—on him. I took those too.

Do you need one? Paradise asked.

Probably not, but they look really scary. Good for making guards duck before they open fire.

There were several possible ways in. There was an access to the stairs, but I'd have to spend time undoing the alarms.

However, there was a much more entertaining alternative. I went over to the holoprojector displaying the samurai and cut through the cables leading from the central unit to one of the emitters, estimating the length. *You might want to film this next bit.*

Are you planning to do something stupid? Paradise asked.

Stupid and fun are synonyms, I replied, knowing exactly what to do and how to do it. It was a nice change of pace.

They really aren't, Paradise said.

I ran for the edge and jumped off, hanging on the end of the cable. The cable pulled taunt, pulling me back towards the building in an arc, as gravity pulled me down, I pointed the Uzi at the window and opened fire. I wasn't going to be able to get directly at where Billions was, but I was happy to be making a direct entrance.

I suspected the windows were hardened against snipers—most executives were paranoid about that—but the kind of glass you needed to resist a small number of bullets fired from a great distance didn't do much against thousands of bullets fired from a few feet away. The window shattered into a million pieces, and the cable flung me through. I rolled across the floor and leapt to my feet.

Inside the building, I saw an entire hallway full of Jackals. They pretty much dressed like Mad Max rejects with all the punk and leather that probably once belonged to cows like Bessie. They reacted to my presence by going for their guns and every one of them was over-armed. But this was a tight hallway leading up to a single staircase, so their advantage was minimalized—especially when facing a superhuman assassin.

What followed was almost like ballet or at least my version of it. I shot up below the chin of the nearest one, killing him instantly in a splatter of gore before turning to fire a three-round burst while using the first as a shield. Every single shot counted while I shoved the first's body down with a herculean kick, knocking two more over, while a third had his own automatic weapon go wild.

Everything seemed to slow down and not just because my neuro-receptors and data feeds were working faster than my physical body but also because the adrenaline merged with endorphins to free me from every problem I had in that moment. I wasn't troubled by guilt, fear, or anxiety here because there was only the battle. Also, Jackals were known to be white supremacists with initiation rites that included rape and beating "civilians" to death. So, honestly, fuck these guys.

I managed to take a bullet in the right arm but as my muscles were artificial and the bone underneath steel, it only caused an agonizing sense of pain before I pressed my Uzi against the lucky shooter's chest, pulling the trigger. From there, I spin kicked him into the last two remaining scumbags in the hall, taking time to shoot them both in the head to make sure they weren't getting back up. Then I ran up the staircase, readying myself to face Billions.

This seems like it gives Billions way too much time to leave, Paradise said, having politely waited to comment. *Also, badass murder spree. Very John Woo meets the Wachowskis Sisters.*

Thank you, I replied, reaching the top of the stairs and a pair of glass doors that had an automatic lock I blew off. *There's only two entrances and the one on the roof gives Case a chance to snipe him.*

Did you bother telling him that? Paradise asked.

I figured he'd get it from the whole seeing the bad guy with his rifle sight, I replied, entering the top floor of the steak house."

It was dimly lit with only the lights of an elaborate fish tank full of genetically engineered mutants. All the chairs were propped on the table, which made me think this hadn't been a place that Winston was entertaining guests. A light was coming from what appeared to be an entrance to a separate kitchen. There were no windows as Case said and the place had the feel of the kind where you would want to conduct a high security meeting, you know, if you were somehow weird enough to be rich and yet wanted to conduct your business in a restaurant that served faux steak in the middle of the Refugee Zone. Which, only now that I thought about it, meant that it had to be owned by the Trikuza.

Dammit.

That was when I was tackled by a ninja. Which was a sentence that had only happened a few times in my life despite being one myself. She was a small Japanese woman closer to Paradise's size than my own, pretty, dressed in red plastic attire covered in glowing kanji, and moved like a speeding car with just as much force. Which was not a great thing when I'd been prepared to fight Winston directly versus what appeared to be his henchmen.

The fact that I'd been tackled instead of sliced-to-ribbons suggested she was either an amateur, or completely unready at the time I'd arrived. Unfortunately, she had knocked my Uzi out of my hands, which was not good. Well, at least she was dressed. Don't ask. I arched forward with my enhanced strength and threw her off. She landed surprisingly gracefully.

"You don't have to die today," I said.

"Arrogant," she said.

That's it? Clearly, she was the strong silent type. Well, we'd see about the strong.

I had to move quickly if I wanted to be the one that killed Billions. Sure, if he made it to the roof, Case could kill him and he'd be dead, great, but I'd feel disappointed if it wasn't me.

I charged forward, in as bluntly stupid a manner as possible, She geared up for a frontal impact, but I dove to the side at the last minute and aimed a kick to her elbow. She twisted to the side, unbalancing herself. She tipped to the side and was forced to use an arm to brace herself.

That gave me an opening I was happy to take. I came at her now undefended side and grabbed at her arm. She was at least good enough to see that coming and let herself fall back to avoid my assault, doing a backflip to regain her feet. Of course, I wasn't unarmed even without the Uzi, so I threw a dagger lifted from the first Jackal I'd killed at her, forcing her to move back again. If I could keep her off-balance, the fight was mine.

So, obviously, it was time for something to go wrong. The ninja gave me an opening and I took it. I threw one more dagger at her, predicted she'd dodge it, and stabbed her with a third in the neck. Except, what happened was that it caused her to defragment into pixels. She had never been there in the first place, and I'd been fighting a hologram hacked into my cybernetics.

That was when I heard a gun click behind my head. It was Winston Billions and he had me dead to rights.

Probably since this fight had begun. I prepared myself simultaneously for death and a last-ditch attempt to kill him. That was when he said the only thing in the world that could have given me pause after what he did to Becky.

"Hi, sis."

CHAPTER TWENTY-FOUR

WHAT IS THIS STAR WARS BULLSHOT? (NO, I'M NOT SWEARING)

My brain stopped working. Or maybe every part of my brain tried working all at the same time. He couldn't be. Could he? Snake had said my brother was alive but had shown me a picture of someone very different from Winston. This monster didn't deserve to even mention his name! I should kill him for having the audacity to lie, unless it wasn't a lie, could it be, no! I won't be fooled! I, he, wasn't, couldn't…

I could practically feel the gears being stripped as I tried to contain a dozen thoughts all at once. Okay, I wasn't dead already, and I'd hesitated far, far too long for that to be an accident. I decided to ignore the gun and just step away.

"You're not my brother," I said, softly.

"Am I not?" Winston asked.

"What's his name?" I asked, hoping this would end his deception immediately.

"Ken," Winston said. "But that was a long time ago. Not all of us were as lucky as you."

"You were killed!" I said, accidentally defaulting to what I'd believed for a decade.

"Was I?" he asked. "Snake said otherwise."

"Yes! Snake…" I said, remembering the day in the woods. I'd never seen my brother's body and I'd wanted to believe Snake when he said Ken was alive but not like this. Someone was lying, possibly multiple people.

"Yes, Snake," he said. "He turned me into this thing. Did you think yours was the only pod of children he was raising?"

"No, I knew there were others. It was obvious Fate wasn't new to the project on the day we were introduced."

"He collected most of the children he ran across, putting us in different projects, different training paradigms," Winston—or Ken—said. His voice was unrecognizable and that was because I honestly didn't remember what my brother sounded like.

Did I want him to be Ken, though? No. Absolutely not.

"So, you ended up a ninja too?"

"No," Ken, dammit, Winston said. "I washed out of the program pretty early. He only wanted the best for his little assassin program. I was a whiny, stupid, arrogant little shit and that got me declared unsuitable pretty early."

"So, you were a kid," I said, not wanting to feel sympathetic to him. I was torn between believing Winston was lying to me and telling the truth, but this part was at least believable. Even if he wasn't my brother—and I prayed to gods I didn't believe in that he wasn't—I could imagine Snake was involved in his past. Like the Pied Piper or Fagin of the Trikuza, he had helped create a whole culture of wannabe ninja and gangsters in a culture that had no connection to the legitimate (if you could call them that) gangster clans of Japan.

I wasn't sure that made sense. I never once doubted that if I failed at the training, I would have been disposed of, not released. "So, you've been free all this time, and you never once bothered trying to find me?"

In that moment, I got a sense from Winston that he almost pulled the trigger. There was a cold and inscrutable pain radiating off from him that I couldn't put into words but nevertheless turned into lethal intent. Snake would have called it ki or some other mystical bullshit, but I just called it instinct.

"Free? You think failure meant freedom?" Winston said, ironically making me believe him more.

"No, I don't," I said. "What happened?"

"I was sold," Winston said. "What does not kill us makes us stronger. Snake tossed me into the wild of the Trikuza's business and I was used."

We were all used. Becky was used. Somehow, I got the feeling that these weren't the responses he wanted to hear.

"I'm listening," I said, sitting down on the armrest of a chair, trying to look less threatening without reducing my ability to take off at a moment's notice.

"We don't need to discuss the details," he said, dismissively. Not a good sign. I wasn't sure where this conversation was going, but any sign that he wasn't emotionally connecting with me suggested it wouldn't end well. Did I want it to? He'd still hurt Becky, possibly killed her. But, if he was my brother, could I just kill him? Could I face Becky if I didn't?

There was a slim possibility both men were telling the truth as well. Snake had shown me a photo of Ken as a low-level Trikuza ten years earlier. Maybe Ken had become Winston and eventually evolved into the kind of assassin that Snake used. Snake would have been lying about how close my brother was when he used him to extort me into helping him against Elysium, but it would be true from a certain point of view. Also, maybe I was just trying to find a way to make sense of it all.

"It's time we took revenge on the man who ruined both our lives," Winston said. Yes, I was going to keep calling him Winston. Ken had died a long time ago, regardless of who was in front of me now. "I've made alliances. Alliances that will help finally put an end to that piece of crap and his insane philosophy."

"Is that why you put spyware in Becky?" I asked.

"Your *doll*? That's what this is about?" Winston asked in a contemptuous voice. He lowered the gun for a second and that was when I went for it.

The two of us struggled and I immediately realized what a mistake I'd made by the fact his body was a complete Shell that easily tossed me back. It did confirm Winston was really here, though, but I was on the ground, and he was armed with a pistol. I tried to move for cover but there was a shot and I wondered if I'd been hit. True fact, you sometimes don't feel gunshots immediately due to some medical facts I was completely blanking on right now.

Except, there wasn't a stabbing of pain and there was a sword sticking out of the bottom of Winston's neck. It was a thermal katana like Fate had used and I had some familiarity with. A weapon designed to kill cyborgs by people like Snake, who was, of course, the person who was holding the hilt of the blade sticking out of Winston's neck. He'd hacked my sight just like Winston had and probably been standing there the entire time—which made Winston look like quite the fool in attempting to recruit me.

Snake wasn't dressed in his usual cultural appropriation attire but a regular Western tuxedo with a black eyepatch that made him look a bit like a Mexican Nick Fury. There was an expression on his face I couldn't quite read, something between annoyance and disappointment.

Strangely, the ninja girl who'd attacked me earlier was standing beside him. It seemed she was real after all, but once you couldn't trust your sight or memories, what could you trust? She was also holding my gold-plated Uzi, which annoyed me as I wanted to go for that.

"Hello, Kei," Snake said, pulling out the blade from Winston's neck and letting him fall to the floor as white fluid poured from his injury.

I backed away from him and debated going for Winston's pistol on the ground, though it would be useless unless it had explosive ammunition. Seeing my reaction, Snake gestured his head from the ninja girl to me. She tossed the gold-plated Uzi to me, and I caught it reflexively.

"If it makes you feel better," the ninja girl said.

He'd killed Winston. Ken. Winston. Dammit. I couldn't wrap my brain around that. He was dead again before I'd quite managed to digest that he was alive. That Snake hadn't killed him, and now he had. Assuming Winston wasn't backed up somewhere. That body had been a complete Shell. Frick, I wasn't thinking clearly. My emotions were all over the place and I couldn't focus my thoughts.

"It's a gold-plated Uzi," I said. "I have to have it for my collection of ridiculously pathetic expressions of congested masculinity."

"Women also like gold," the ninja girl said.

"Women generally find better things to do with it than plate a gun," I said. "Though, I do make this gun look good."

"Indeed," the ninja girl said.

"Was he telling the truth?" I asked, ignoring her. "I have no idea why I'm asking because if he was, you've been lying to me my entire life."

Snake looked down at Winston's fallen form and cut off the head, which caused me to shudder and almost open fire with the Uzi. Snake lifted the severed head of Winston and tossed it at my feet. "It is yet another drone body of the Entity. It is not your brother."

"The Entity," I said.

"You know it as Legion," Snake said, staring at me. "It would appear I have made some errors in planning my attack on Elysium and underestimated just how capable my enemies were able to infiltrate my organization."

"Winston is Legion," I asked.

"Yes," Snake said.

"He was always Legion," I said, not believing him.

"Yes," Snake replied.

I stared at Snake. "Legion was one of Sun's friends at Solomon's club."

"Yes," Snake said, making this a very monosyllabic conversation. "Both AI were created by my research. Both intimately familiar with how to manipulate human behavior based on what we most want and need. In your case, your brother."

At this point, I wasn't so much feeling jerked around as on a frigging bungee cord.

"So, your defense is that it was all a lie? He was just pretending to be my brother to screw with me."

"Yes," Snake said.

"I hate you," I replied.

"Understandable," Snake replied.

A part of me doubted all of this was happening in the first place and wondered if I was still being hacked. It was insane enough that Wilson had gotten the drop on me and started to claim he was my brother. It was outright asinine that Snake should show up, save my life, and then say it was all a lie. This had to be just another head game.

Except it wasn't.

"You set this up," I replied. "You're the one who let it slip where Winston was so I would come here. So, you could kill him. Even though he was your henchman, and you could have done it at any time."

"Actually, I hoped you would do the honors," Snake said, confirming my suspicions. "Unfortunately, I underestimated just how much damage the Entity could do by getting into your head. Sentimentality has always been your weakness."

I stared at him. "I think you'd feel otherwise if I unloaded this Uzi into you right now."

The girl ninja moved between us before Snake gently slid her to one side.

Snake chuckled, clearly more amused by my threat than anything. "The proudest moment of my life was when you stabbed me in lieu of killing Fate. It showed you had completed your training and become capable of making your own decisions. You are my greatest achievement."

I shook my head and looked at the girl beside him. "Is she another one of your creations?"

"Aiyumi," the girl said. "Just Aiyumi."

"Nice to meet you Just Aiyumi," I said, not moving the Uzi. I was still focused on Snake. "You knew what he did to Becky and did nothing."

"I'm doing something now," Snake said, dryly. "I'm killing the Entity."

Intellectually, I knew everything he was saying was just another layer of crap designed to manipulate me. Yet, it was easy to fall into a behavior of defense. I wanted to believe he cared about me in his own sick way even though a part of me was screaming that I needed to open fire, run away, or just shout at him because of all the horrors he'd brought down on me. Instead, I found myself rebelling in a simpler way.

"What *did* happen to my brother?" I asked.

"You'd believe me?" Snake asked.

"Yes," I said, sickening myself. I noted Paradise hadn't said anything in a while and suspected that Snake had somehow jammed her communications with me. It made me worry about

Case and the others. It was entirely within Snake's abilities to kill them before coming here and that wasn't including any more students he may have brought,

"He's alive," Snake said. "But yes, there was an element of truth to what the Entity said. Ken did not have the stomach or resilience to complete the program. He was one of the many washouts."

"And you made him a prostitute," I said, following the assumption that the Entity, Legion, Winston, whatever, had been telling the truth.

"He's been a lot of things for the Trikuza. Your brother chose that life for himself, though," Snake said. "The Trikuza has many roles, but everyone pulls their weight, or they die. He's alive, though, and I can reunite you with him should you finish the eighth mission I hired you for."

I couldn't believe Snake's gall. Then I realized, unfortunately, yes I could.

"You could have told me," I snapped, knowing I couldn't bring myself to kill him despite how much I wanted to.

I was weak and I hated myself for it.

"He would have dragged you down to his level," Snake said. "The only reason he's still alive is his capacity to leech off of others. A useful skill for a con man and grifter. You, however, were destined for more."

"I don't want more!" I snapped.

Snake snorted. "You are already more. You could have left this life behind if you wanted but it is your destiny."

"Stop with the Vaderisms," I said, referring to Darth. "What the hell do you want?"

"Come with me," Snake said, extending his hand. "I have your sheep AI and the virus it's carrying. I hadn't expected you to come up with a solution that could kill our monstrous opponent. I only wanted to see how far you could get on your own and you have exceeded all expectations. It's why I had to use Winston as a lure to even find you."

"You let him walk by your side," I said.

"Keep your enemies close," Aiyumi said. "And your friends far, far away, where it's safe."

"Ain't that good advice," I muttered, wishing my friends were far away right now.

"We shall end this tonight," Snake said, smiling. It was a smile devoid of mirth or affection, like an animal baring its teeth.

"And if I don't want to?" I asked, exhausted by this ordeal.

"It took me thirty-eight seconds to disable your friend, G," Snake said. "I'm genuinely impressed he lasted that long. Your friend, Paradise, was taken without a fight. My people have weapons pointed at their heads."

"Then let's get going," I said, sighing. "You could have opened with that."

Snake gestured to the exit.

I left the Uzi behind.

CHAPTER TWENTY-FIVE

THE ELEVATOR RIDE FROM HELL

Snake, Aiyumi, and I entered a service elevator at the top of Bushido Bob's. It was white, empty, and looked like it could have come from the 20th century. This whole thing felt like yet another layer of manipulation and illusion. I was a rat in a maze and no matter how hard I tried to find my way out, I was just running around blindly in a pattern that I had no idea of the rules of or even the purpose. It felt like everything—and everyone—was just trying to herd me toward the cheese or just see how long I flailed around until I found it.

If I ever did.

"Are my friends going to live if I go along with you?" I asked.

"Such an interesting question," Snake said.

"Is it?" I asked.

"Yes, I didn't know you had friends," Snake said, the barest hint of malice in his voice.

"Well, not everyone is like you," I replied.

Snake smiled. "Friendship is a weakness. Like family. It's one that I have only indulged a few times in my life."

"Do you have family?" I asked, wondering if he was trying to manipulate me more by bringing up the subject after his revelation that Ken was still alive. I didn't even know what that meant for me or my situation. Did I even care?

You'd think that would be an easy question after I'd nearly gotten myself killed sparing Winston's life (or the robot pretending to be Wilson) because he claimed to be Ken. However, there was a difference being reunited with your long-lost brother right in front of you versus knowing he was generically "out there" somewhere. I couldn't throw down my life, pitiful as its remnants still were, to start looking for Ken Springs based on what could very well be another of Snake's lies or half-truths.

Hell, this entire thing might have been a set up. Not just Winston Billions, the ambush, and Snake's "rescue," but the whole thing with Legion. Did I know anything at all? Maybe Sun wasn't the one who contacted me, or Snake was the one pulling her strings. Maybe this whole thing was an elaborate reality television show that the producers were filming for aliens on Alpha Centauri. Maybe my whole life was a lie and if I stopped to stare long enough, I'd start seeing the code in the Matrix.

Nope. Not seeing any. Yet.

"You would know," Snake replied. "You are the closest thing to a daughter and heir I possess."

It was the kindest thing he'd ever said to me and once it would have meant the world to me. I also recognized it as the blatant manipulation tactic it was.

"Real parents don't do what you did to me."

"I wouldn't know," Snake said, dryly. "My own parents were killed by the cartels long before the Eruption. I ended up being sold to the Carnevale as a boy and was turned into their weapon in much the same way that I have turned so many other children into the tools of the Trikuza. The closest thing I ever had to a father was Lucio Biondi AKA The Carnivale Master."

"And what's your opinion of him?" I asked, surprised he was opening like this. Assuming any of it was true. I also wondered if the late Lucio Biondi was related to Lucita Biondi but guessed not. The world of international spies and assassins couldn't be *that* small.

"I owe your friend Case for killing him," Snake said. "Though since I left him alive, broken but alive, that makes us even."

"I thought that was a favor for me," I said, dryly.

Snake just smiled. "Perhaps. In which case, I will provide you another boon in its place. Ask me anything."

"As if I could trust anything you could say," I said, looking from Snake to Aiyumi. She was conspicuously silent during all of this.

"I can't believe anything you say," I said, saddened that it was true.

"You have my word of honor that I will tell the truth," Snake said.

"Does that mean anything?" I asked, honestly not knowing if it did. Also, if he wasn't going to lie now did that mean he was always lying before?

"You tell me," Snake replied.

"Okay," I replied, staring at him. "Why did you make Sun and Legion in the first place? What use does a Yakuza, sorry, Trikuza assassin have for a pair of Cognition AI? What are you hoping to accomplish by destroying Legion? Why are you always acting like a samurai when you're Mexican? How does any of this make sense?"

The questions poured out as babble, but they were no less important for it. Except none of it was important. Understanding Snake and his bizarre goals wouldn't get us any closer to destroying Legion nor would it help me find my brother. But, yeah, I wasn't good under emotional pressure.

The elevator door pinged and revealed an elaborate underground parking lot with a massive storm drain the size of a house leading out from it. The drain was part of the original substructure constructed by the AI in the wake of the Eruption to lay the new foundations for Los Angeles' arcology. It had been converted into a makeshift road and smuggling tunnel with various vehicles filling the otherwise empty concrete chamber. It was a way for the Trikuza and other gangs to move goods into the Refugee Zone that would otherwise be taxed the hell out of by the city government.

Amidst the various trucks was an armored flying car capable limousine guarded by another bunch of twenty odd Trikuza armed to the teeth. I assumed they were more of Snake's children, though at this point I was about ready to view any Trikuza of a certain age as being more of his students. I was imagining him running a weird ninja version of Hogwarts when he wasn't training me and Fate privately.

Snake stepped out of the elevator and began walking to the limousine.

"To answer your first two questions: power. Black Technology was once the deciding force in the Earth and whoever controlled the proliferation of it was the one in charge of the world. Now, technology has inundated the masses, and everyone has more computer power in their infopads than sent man to the moon. Information is power, though, and a Cognition AI for the Trikuza would allow us to be on par with any of the world's governments."

"That was a distressingly realistic answer," I said, following him and uncomfortable with Aiyumi behind me. Maybe it was the fact she seemed to be exactly the sort of student Snake always wanted—Japanese, quiet, obedient, and still cute as a button. Okay, was I jealous? What the hell?

"What? You thought it would be world domination?" Snake asked.

"Kinda, yeah," I said.

"Too much work," Snake replied. "I'd hardly ever get to do my own killing."

Sadly, I didn't think that was a joke.

"Uh huh."

"As for what I hope to accomplish, Kei, I meant what I said regarding the destruction of Elysium. It is a stain on Trikuza honor and eliminating the murder hotel will also allow me to rise in place of my rivals," Snake replied.

"You just left out the part about where you were responsible for Legion in the first place," I replied. "Are you actually trying to fix your mistake or covering your own ass?"

Snake paused in mid-step, halfway across the parking lot, before resuming.

"You're assuming those two things are mutually exclusive."

It was a rare admission of weakness. "I see."

"I honestly thought I was going to die when you and Fate stole the AI from me," Snake replied. "A billion credits had been put into the development of Sun and what would eventually become Legion. The Trikuza does not forgive failure and the moment you lose the aura of invincibility you must cultivate to rise to the top is the moment you are doomed. The attacks will continue until you are dead, no matter what you choose to do next. Only a single mistake is needed to bring down an empire."

"And yet you're still alive," I replied.

"Yes," Snake said, chuckling. "In the end, I was saved by the parable of the two friends and the bear."

"I'm not familiar with that part of the Bible," I said as we reached Snake's limousine. It was a sleek thing that looked exactly like you'd expect a limousine from the future would look, except it seemed that the future was now. Just another sign of how style was the driving force of development these days.

"You've probably heard it," Aiyumi replied, finally joining the conversation. "Two friends go into the woods and encounter a bear. One of them preps his running shoes and the other man says there was no way he could outrun the bear."

"He just has to outrun his friend," I said, finishing the story. "Yeah, I've heard that version. It never made sense to me because bears are not likely to attack you unless you provoke them. I know because I killed one and I regret doing it every day."

"Hearing about you killing that bear is why I adopted you," Snake said.

"Case in point," I said. "So, did the other Trikuza lose more than a billion credits?"

"Yes," Snake replied. "Mostly because I made it a point to cause a series of horrific disasters for the Trikuza for several years. Invisible enemies struck at our most impressive leaders, cyber-attacks laid waste to our resources, and wars were begun with gangs we'd been previously at peace with. By the time my rivals were building Elysium, the people who'd invested their fortunes in my original project were mostly dead and my project was mostly forgotten. I'd also created many new openings for my children to fulfill."

Now, it shouldn't have surprised me when a criminal admitted to fricking over other criminals. I was a criminal after all, and if you want to know something we do incredibly well, it's fricking each other over. The whole reason the Prisoner's Dilemma exists is because if you give your typical thief the option for five years of imprisonment instead of ten if he testifies and his fellows get twenty, the guy will take it in a heartbeat.

It doesn't matter if they're best friends or family, the criminal mindset is inclined to always put yourself above everyone else. Even if it was better to all stick together. It was the whole reason that goddamn scorpion and the frog parable held true too. It also why it had taken me so long to trust Case and Paradise since, well, they seemed to have not gotten the memo. But it surprised me with Snake.

Of all the criminals I knew, I thought he would be the exception because he had made such an incredible showing over the years about honor, loyalty, respect, and other aphorisms (and there's a word I didn't get to use very often). Mark Twain once said—man I was just dripping with folk wisdom today—"The more he spoke of his honor, the more we counted the spoons." But Snake? Somehow, I'd never thought him the type to do it. Maybe that was my mistake, and I should have seen it coming.

"Huh," I said, staring forward.

"Huh?" Snake asked, his hand on the limousine car door that had no handle. Apparently, there was a scanner instead.

"Yeah, huh," I said. "Sorry, just thinking about it."

Okay, that was a poor response.

"I've never been loyal to the Trikuza, Kei," Snake replied. "They've always been a means to an end."

"What end?" I asked.

"I will answer both that question and why I choose to live like a samurai with one response," Snake replied. "To bring meaning to chaos."

The door to the limousine lifted into the air like the DeLorean from *Back to the Future*, though it collapsed into a much smaller folding door that made me wonder about its physics. Inside the luxurious synth-leather interior was Harrison, who was looking less than pleased to have been sheepnapped.

"Hi Harrison," I said, waving. "Sorry you've been sheepnapped."

"Good evening," Harrison said. "I believe this plan of ours has gone to pot."

"You don't say," I said, deliberately not responding to

Snake's explanation. It would just be more of the pretentious philosophy that he'd been giving me my entire life. That was when I remembered I was utterly in his power and so were my friends. "Snake was just telling me about how he brings order from chaos."

Snake, who had been waiting for my response, smiled. I'd become so used to dealing with people who didn't take themselves seriously, it was a shock to remember some people rewarded attitude with death. I didn't think Snake would kill me over that, but it occurred to me I didn't know him at all. After all, tonight had just been one shocking revelation after another.

"Yes," Snake said. "You asked why I dressed as a samurai and the answer is it is strange. There is no inherent meaning or value to the universe but what we impose on it ourselves. You ask why I chose to be a samurai and that is because such a figure is colorful and memorable. Soldiers selected from the disaffected children and youth of the world gravitate to the new as well as surreal. They desire meaning to be given to them and I can provide it. They would not find it in the comforting or familiar. Not in Bibles written on infopads or the legal systems of governments that have so clearly failed them. No, they must find it in the ancient and arcane."

It was a revelatory moment really as I stepped into the limousine and took a seat by Harrison. Snake had always kept an aura of mystery about himself until this moment and now he'd spelled out for me his philosophy in a way that made sense of it all: he was a goddamn cult leader. All his strange behavior and weird warrior's ethos was designed just to make us all dependent on him for approval as well as bind us to something bigger than ourselves.

I hated him for making me fall for such an obvious scam and then hated myself for the realization that I didn't have anything else aside from it to give me a sense of how to navigate the world. I was a ninja girl. I was a ninja girl with a white dad and raised by a Mexican assassin with a bunch of martial arts gibberish that sounded cool. I might as well have been raised by Count Dante who, if you've never heard of him, is someone you should check out the infospace page for.

"That is a very interesting story, Snake," I said, unsure what else to say. I just wanted to hug Harrison and go to sleep.

"Thank you," Snake said, stepping into the car, followed by Aiyumi. They took position across from me, their backs to a wall that didn't seem to lead to a driver's seat. The car was automated, and I found that to be a heinous risk when dealing with AI but maybe Snake knew something I didn't. A tiny little table for drink with drawers underneath its surface was between us.

The limousine door closed, and the interior went black before showing holographic projections of the outside popped up on the walls. Their feeds were from cameras built into the car's frame. There were no windows, not even bulletproof glass ones, and it felt more like being inside a tank than a limousine. Well, a flying tank since I felt the vehicle start to lift off the ground as it started its journey down that massive storm drain.

"So, what, we're just going to go up to Elysium and walk right in?" I asked, staring at Snake. "That doesn't seem like much of a plan."

"It's not," Snake said, reaching into one of the tiny table's drawers and pulling out a plastic wrapped dress, followed by another for shoes.

"What's this for?" I asked, staring at it.

"Your outfit," Snake said. "You were always meant as a distraction, Kei. Now, however, since my other plan to eliminate the AI has failed—you've become my backup plan."

That was somehow less than reassuring.

CHAPTER TWENTY-SIX

ARRIVING AT THE GATES OF HELL

The limousine moved at a brisk pace underneath New Los Angeles and I had to wonder just how far these tunnels stretched. We were already outside of the Refugee Zone, and I couldn't help but wonder if there was an entire underground transportation network that I was unaware of. It shouldn't have offended me, but it did. I was a Rider, or at least had been, so I should have been plugged in about this sort of thing.

I couldn't see much outside of the limousine "windows" but given we were traveling down enormous storm drain tunnels, I supposed I wasn't missing much.

"Do you expect me to change in the car?" I asked, unfolding the plastic covered dress, and placing the shoes on the floor of the limousine.

"Do you want us to pull over to the side?" Snake asked, dryly.

I frowned. "I have a few remaining hang-ups. I don't swear."

Snake stared. "Murder is fine but swearing is out of line?"

"I'm also modest." I stared at him. "I can't imagine where I might have learned such a skewed morality."

"Kei, please don't taunt the master assassin," Harrison said.

"Why? He's not going to attack us," I replied.

"No, but it's very tacky," Harrison said.

Why did I feel like I'd just imitated a classic comedy bit?

"Fine, I'll put on the damn dress and shoes. I still don't see how you think this plan is going to work. Legion is going to recognize me the moment I walk through the door."

"That won't be the case," Harrison corrected me, not realizing I was trying to throw Snake off his game. "The defense against the computer recognizing you is still in effect."

"Winston recognized me," I pointed out. "Winston is Legion. In other words, the defense didn't work."

Harrison looked up. "Oh, I hadn't thought of that. I guess you are screwed."

"Thanks, buddy," I said, patting him on the head.

"Does anyone else find it incredibly weird to have a talking sheep in the car?" Aiyumi said, staring at the animal.

"No," I said, dryly. "Why do you? Are you a bigot?"

"Wait, what?" Aiyumi asked, showing her first real hints of emotion.

"Don't try to pull the wool over my eyes," I deadpanned. "You won't ram your hate down my throat. I've got my eye on ewe."

Aiyumi stared at me. "Now you're making sheep puns."

"Nothing gets past you, does it, chief,?" I replied.

"It's because of Winston that I am confident that you will be accepted into the resort in a way that I won't be," Snake replied. "He's shown an interest in convincing you to join. While the minds of AI are impossibly vast and difficult to fathom, I believe that is because you had Sun's program in your cybernetics for years."

I started changing while Snake lectured me, neither he nor Aiyumi reacting to my nakedness.

"Yeah, but that information is all gone now. I had my old Maelstrom 90 implant maxed out with her inside it, but she helpfully deleted it all before leaving."

"It still will contain traces of her," Snake replied, sounding more certain than he probably should. "Not to mention Sun's presence in your mind will have influenced how your wetware, your brain, developed over the course of decades. I believe Legion wishes to understand your bond and use it to expand itself."

"Is this in between warping the minds of billionaire politicians, so they become serial killers?" I asked. "Because I'm trying to figure out how that relates to world domination."

Snake smiled. "The early experiments in AI by the major computing companies attempted to see if exposing developing consciousnesses to the internet would help them become smarter."

"What happened?" I asked.

"They became belligerent racists and misogynists," Snake said, dryly. "Honestly, I'm surprised."

"Yeah, I would have thought they would have become porn addicts way before the racism and misogyny," I replied.

"Well, no bodies mean no sexuality," Harrison pointed out. "It's just a bunch of circles and shapes bumping into one another. Even AI with bodies need to be programmed for it. For example, I'm celibate."

I looked down at Harrison, trying to figure out what he meant by that.

"There wasn't a pun there," Harrison said.

"Oh," I replied. Turning back to Snake, "So, just so we're clear, your plan is that Legion wants to suck my brain so you're going to be sending me in through the front door with a credit card? Is that what we're going with?"

"Yes," Snake said, nodding. "More or less."

"Why the dress?" I asked.

"You should at least look presentable," Snake said. "After all, our plan will be thwarted very early if the concierge refuses to put you in a position to have your brain sucked."

"Why does an evil AI need a concierge?" I asked.

"Legion is still maintaining the fiction he's running the hotel's RealDream fantasies versus handling everything out in the open," Snake replied. "To get at the actual brainwashing material, you'll need to sign up for their VIP experience."

"I have to pay to get my brain sucked?" I asked. "Wait, no, that's the most believable part of all this."

"Indeed," Snake replied.

I shook my head. "Still, it's not a great plan if it can be beaten by obnoxious staff."

"The plan won't be, hence why you're changing," Snake said. "You'll, of course, also be carrying the virus that Harrison has within his little shell. Uploaded directly into your brain."

"I could have done this plan without you," I replied.

"Yes, but it won't have my addition to the virus," Snake replied, lifting a tiny quantum data fob.

"What's it do?" I asked, having the feeling I wasn't going to get anything resembling a straight answer.

"It will provide a little oomph to your plan," Snake said. "If you can get past the defenses of Legion and upload this in addition to Ms. Gordon's plan—"

"Mrs.," Harrison corrected. "She's a married woman."

"You should keep a respectful tongue, machine," Snake said, threateningly. "Otherwise, you might lose it."

"I'm going to be dead no matter what," Harrison said. "This is a one-way trip for me."

Snake stared, paused, then shrugged. "You have me there, adjutant. You serve your masters well."

Harrison just sat there, looking adorable and unafraid of Snake. It was kind of refreshing, really. Especially since I was genuinely terrified of the man. I couldn't help but feel like the scared little girl he'd picked up in the woods so long ago. If it wasn't such a ridiculous image—not to mention extremely disrespectful—I would have given the little sheep a cuddle.

In any case, the adjustable memory fabric of the dress Snake gave me sealed around my body like it was made for me. Advances in technology hadn't really changed clothing much from the Bronze Age when we started wearing it for the first time but there had been a few strange devices pumped out of the fabricators. In my case, it was a practically painted on white dress with low cleavage that was fashionable enough to get me into some place fancy, but probably wouldn't have won any awards either. It was like someone had done an image search for better designers' work and decided to copy it as best as possible.

Mind you, I wasn't someone who had much experience with fashion labels or high fashion. I'd lived in a recreational vehicle, over a junkyard, and in a ramshackle apartment all without ever feeling like I was missing out on anything. My mother had once compared herself to someone named Scarlett O'Hara and only decades later had I looked her up. Apparently, she was some rich white racist lady who was determined to never be poor again after the North had come to free her slaves. Why my mother found her story inspirational was anyone's guess, but she had been an alcoholic.

"So, what's your story, toots?" I asked Aiyumi, sliding my feet into the shoes and glad that I at least knew how to walk in heels.

Run? No.

Fight? No.

Walk? Yes.

"My story?" Aiyumi asked, blinking. She had a kind of babe in the woods look as if she wasn't used to people talking to her. There was a quiet intensity to her that I imagined would have been off-putting to anyone other than the people in the car who included the world's best assassin and someone who was already well past her wits' end.

"Yeah," I replied, staring at my feet, and wiggling them a bit. "I've picked up that you're another of Snake's Sith apprentices, but I'm not sure why Winston would use you as a holographic distraction or where you were when Fate and I were hashing it for head girl at Snake's School for Ninjitsu and Murder."

"I see your irreverence for the sacred arts has not improved over the years," Snake replied.

I gave him a bit of side-eye. "You're the one who said it was all chicanery to win over us rubes to following you."

"That doesn't mean what I taught you wasn't true," Snake said.

"Yeah, that's kind of exactly what it means," I said.

"I was born to a good family," Aiyumi replied, finally stepping into the conversation. "A kind, generous, and loving one."

"Wooly for you," Harrison said.

Aiyumi frowned at the sheep. "However, life in the post-Eruption era was difficult."

"Oh, I hadn't noticed," I replied.

"Are you always this sarcastic?" Aiyumi asked.

"You have no idea," Snake replied.

"You should meet my friend Paradise and not try to kill her," I replied. "Assuming she's still alive."

I'd tried communicating with her via her cybernetics but either Snake had managed to jam mine somehow or she was simply no longer "available." I no longer had any illusions that anything I was reassured about was true and wasn't sure I would be walking away from this mission. Snake had left me alone for years but was that because he'd genuinely not held a grudge against me for what I'd done or because he'd seen a use for me decades later?

If I let my paranoid mind wander—never a good idea for a recovering drug addict—I wondered if Winston had always been a bioroid in the service of Snake. It would explain why he'd used my brother against me, would allow Snake to ingratiate himself with me, and explain why he used a hologram of Aiyumi to taunt me. Snake had never been that kind of manipulator but maybe the fact he didn't seem to be was another one of his lies.

"In any case, my parents ran into debt," Aiyumi said. "Serious debt to the Trikuza. They had been hoping to get themselves out of poverty by helping rebuild Los Angeles, but the jobs dried up quickly thanks to the substitution of bots for physical labor."

"Tale as old as time, or at least automation," I said.

Aiyumi frowned, which seemed like a more natural state for her face than smiling.

"They had to make sacrifices to preserve both my life as well as the lives of my siblings."

"They sold you," I replied.

Aiyumi didn't respond.

"No offense but that's on them," I replied.

"They made a hard choice, and I was willing to do whatever they told me to save my family," Aiyumi defended the indefensible. It was an action I was intimately familiar with, especially when dealing with Snake.

"How old were you?" I asked.

Aiyumi paused. Her answer, I suspected, would be a better argument for my position than anything I could say.

"Twelve."

"I see," I said, letting her answer speak for itself.

"It was not pleasant work," Aiyumi replied, sighing. "I was

willing to do whatever I could, though, until I discovered that I didn't have the temperament for it."

"Didn't have the temperament?" I asked.

"She slit the throat of a customer when he began beating on her associate," Snake said. "That caught my attention."

Aiyumi paused as if the subject of her recruitment was particularly painful, but she'd gotten really good at suppressing the worst details.

"Snake saved me from being killed or disfigured for what I'd done. He taught me how to kill, hide, hack, and navigate social situations. I owe him a great deal for what he did and am anxious to repay that debt."

"What happened to your family?" I asked another question that occurred to me.

Aiyumi's expression remained blank.

"They invested their next loans poorly. In the end, they ended up losing everything. Including my siblings."

Wow. That got dark and it had started black as midnight.

"I'm sorry."

Aiyumi didn't respond for the second time during our conversation.

"If you're wondering how many children that I have educated in the Trikuza's ways, it is hundreds," Snake said. "My first students were done in dojos, and they went on to run their own. They started as adults, but I've found it is better to mold minds when they're younger and more malleable, less set in their ways. Only a handful of children are truly special, though. Capable of doing the things I need them to do. For that, there was Fate and you, Kei. After it didn't work out between us, Aiyumi became your successor."

"It's a shame," Harrison said. "I feel like mentioning David and Cassandra Cain but none of you are probably familiar with early 21st century Batman comics."

"Those are the picture stories you download, right?" I asked.

"Yes, Kei, yes they are," Harrison said, dryly.

"I'm kidding," I replied. "I know real comics. I used to burn them to stay warm when I was hunting for squirrels to eat."

Snake reached over and plopped in the quantum fob to a

port built into the side of Harrison's neck.

"Is that really wise?" I asked Snake. "The virus is something designed by one of the smartest people on Earth."

"Yes," Snake said.

Harrison straightened and went still. "Download complete. The nuclear missile codes have been acquired. Begin total planetary destruction sequence."

No one laughed.

"Tough crowd," Harrison said. "The virus inside my system has been updated. I don't know with what and it's encrypted so I can't find out."

Snake smiled again like the predator he was.

"I'll need you to download it into your Maelstrom 90 now, Kei."

"Are you sure about that?" I asked, knowing I didn't have a choice. Even if I wanted to try on Snake's life here, I wouldn't be able to take on both him and Aiyumi. Especially since I'd left behind my Uzi. I'd sacrificed my earlier advantages in hopes of getting answers as well as protecting my friends. Two things that I wasn't guaranteed to get even if I managed to satisfy all of Snake's requirements. It was like *Wargames*, the only winning move had been not to play, and I was on my sixth match.

"Yes Kei, I'm sure," Snake replied, his voice low. "If you have anything left to say to your fuzzy friend, I suggest you say it now."

"Wooly, not fuzzy," Harrison corrected.

I looked at Harrison. "Are you sure you want to do this?"

"I'm only a machine, dear," Harrison said to me. "If my sacrifice can save some real people, it will be worth it. Also, again, I have backups."

I nodded. "I guess, uh, we should do this. Do I put my hand on you or—"

That was when I felt the virus enter my brain and it was like tendrils of black darkness consuming me.

I didn't get to scream before I passed out.

CHAPTER TWENTY-SEVEN

WELCOME TO THE HOTEL CALIFORNIA
(WITH RESPECT TO THE EAGLES)

There's a problem with having a computer in your head: humans aren't meant to have computers in their heads. I know, I know, it seems pretty obvious when you think about it, but it was something transhumanists had difficulty grasping. If the body was a temple, then the brain was the altar and plenty of people loved to desecrate it.

I can't tell you what, exactly, was on the files downloaded into my mind because I wasn't a computer. However, I can say that it was a particularly awful experience of numbers mixed with an overwhelming sense of dread. Harrison's death as a conscious individual organism was something he was okay with but I, most certainly, was not. I hated that he was being downloaded into me but only so that he could become a bomb.

A suicide bomb.

Kind of sucks the wind out of the idea that we're the good guys in this, doesn't it? Mind you, we were still against an evil program creating serial killers so perhaps that wasn't the best measure of such things. Maybe being the good guy was less about being better than others and more about being the lesser evil. That would be a comforting thought.

Okay, I was rambling. Was rambling a side effect of getting a deadly anti-AI virus uploaded into your brain? It seemed so.

"Kei," a voice spoke above me.

"No Mom, I don't want to be a ninja," I muttered, slowly coming out of it.

Snake snapped his fingers in front of my face.

"We're here."

I blinked and woke up, shaking my head. I was still in the back of the limousine with Snake and Aiyumi. The limousine had stopped, though.

"Okay, maybe you should have given me a better warning about that. I almost soiled my dress."

"We would have proceeded regardless," Snake replied.

I turned to look down at Harrison, who was now laying perfectly still. The animating force that had made him him was gone and its body was just *there*. I couldn't say it was dead since the body was still functional, it was just lacking the operating system that had comprised its essence. I was neither philosophical nor religious, but it was really the biggest demonstration of a soul's existence. Whether it was immortal or temporary, the greater sum of a being had been inside Harrison and was now just gone.

"Don't mourn your toy," Snake replied, sounding like he had finally run out of his legendary patience. "We have more important things to worry about now."

I looked out the side of the limousine, seeing what the cameras built into its frame showed, and found myself surrounded by an extravagant parking lot. It was still nighttime, and the moon was visible in the sky. There was a massive stone fountain with statues of nymphs next to row after row of luxury vehicles. The main building of Elysium was just beyond the parking lot and a different site from the images I'd seen on camera.

The Elysium in the commercials was a warm and inviting place, while this one was a massive, hundred-story-tall, Versailles-like palace that stretched out across the horizon. It somehow seemed ominous rather than inviting and not just because it was night, and I knew serial killers were assembled there like game consoles.

Okay, *that* certainly didn't help.

We were in the middle of the desert on the California-Nevada line, and I had to wonder how the Trikuza had managed to afford this place in the first place. Also, if they could afford to build a place like this, why they'd bothered to create serial killers and blackmail politicians. Surely, the billions they made from constructing Los Angeles or bilking the super-rich would be enough. Maybe I just didn't understand the greed necessary to create something like Elysium.

"That is one big resort," I replied.

"Yes," Snake said. "Your friend, Ms. Principle, envisioned it as a new mecca for tourism. The beginning of a new city that would help lure people away from the arcologies. I approved of all the funding she desired."

"Before you took it away from her," I replied.

"Yes," Snake said. "Ironically, without her leadership, the hotel has been dramatically underperforming. We needed someone to lure the public here, but it's only brought the super-rich. Most of the rooms are empty."

"Good," I replied. "She deserved to be running this sort of place instead of dead along with all of her hookers."

Snake responded. "There will be many more dead, innocent and guilty, before the end of the night."

Well, that was ominous.

"You have become a proud and defiant young woman, Kei," Snake said. "I wish I could claim credit, but you have become who you are in spite of me."

"Literally," I replied.

Aiyumi looked uncomfortable, not that I could easily tell the difference from her normal expression. It had to be a real kick in the guts to have your mentor praising the person who had stabbed him in the gut and now considered him a monster. That was Biblical. Like the tale of the Prodigal Something-Something. Seriously, my mom used to love this stuff. Son? Probably. There's not that many stories of badass women in the Bible except that girl who stabbed a guy in the face with a tent peg.

"Good luck, Kei," Snake said, crossing his arms. "I have every confidence that what will happen tonight will change the world."

I made the okay symbol. "Could you try to make that sound a little bit more ominous? I don't think you properly managed to convey the level of sinisterness you were going for."

"I don't recall you being this quippy before," Snake said.

"Blame my friends," I replied. "Or don't because they have enough problems right now."

The limousine door opened, and I felt the cool desert air leak in. I stepped out and Aiyumi handed me a designer purse. I opened it up and checked the contents. They were all distressingly normal. Well, normal for a woman dressed for visiting a high-class hotel, not normal for Keiko Springs, Rider and sometimes assassin.

"The card is inside," Aiyumi replied. "So are fake IDs as well as cosmetics."

"Any of them explosive?" I asked.

"Alas no," Aiyumi replied.

"What's your role in all this?" I asked.

"Plan C," Aiyumi said.

"Which is?" I asked.

Aiyumi pulled the car door down, resealing the limousine.

"Oh yeah, this is a trap," I said, sighing before starting to walk my way to the hotel's front doors.

Technically, it's a double cross, Harrison spoke in my mind.

Harrison! You're alive! I said, stopping mid-step.

Technically, Harrison said, again, *I am just a reflection of the virus inside you. You should probably keep walking.*

Will do, I said, resuming my pace. *So, it's not so much survival but a stay of execution?*

Unfortunately, yes, Harrison replied. *I also can't say what changes Snake made to my code. Well, our code now.*

Yeah, I'm getting a strong, "Good night, Westley. Good work. Sleep well. I'll mostly likely kill you in the morning." feeling here.

Ah, The Princess Bride, Harrison said, recognizing my reference. *Look on the bright side, the Dread Pirate Roberts did not in fact kill Westley.*

Oh, good! I replied, sarcastically. *Why was I worried in the first place?*

Probably because you're smart, Harrison said. *For an organic, I mean. Unfortunately, we're going to have to worry about Snake after this. We still must deal with Legion first.*

Is there any possibility we can? I asked. *I thought our whole plan was to give Legion a virus and then blow up all his servers. We don't have the rest of the team for that, and Snake hasn't mentioned anything similar.*

Yes, it's suspicious, Harrison said. *Maybe he has a pocket nuclear weapon hidden in that limousine.*

Don't even joke about that, I said, seeing a family with small children walk through the front gate. *God, they have kids here?*

Yes, it's not like serial murder of women is its only luxury, Harrison said. *They also have a pool with three water slides.*

How many innocent people are here anyway? I asked, sucking in my breath, and hoping that everything went to plan.

Something akin to ten thousand guests, staff, and hangers on, Harrison replied. *Which isn't that big of a number, resort-wise. pre-Eruption, the MGM Grand Hotel Las Vegas had six thousand eight hundred and fifty-two guest rooms as well as over a thousand staff. Things have just gotten bigger since the apocalypse.*

The lobby of the Elysium wasn't anything special and I honestly found myself a little disappointed. It had marble floors, chandeliers, fake wooden counters to sign in customers, and lots of art but it wasn't anything I hadn't seen before. I visited plenty of similar places while both serving as Snake's apprentice and delivering packages as a Rider. The exterior of the place was certainly impressive, but this just looked like any other high-end hotel catering to the Richie Rich types. I dunno, maybe I'd been expecting guys dressed up in sacrificial robes and other signs that *Eyes Wide Shut* was going on in the background.

That's probably on a different floor, Harrison replied. *I'd tell you which, but I'm completely shut out of the hotel infospace network.*

What? I asked, trying to reach out with my own implant before realizing I now had a little suicide sheep in my head preventing me from doing so.

Please don't call me that, Harrison said. *Even if I'm using up most of your RAM.*

Is it appropriate to be making sheep puns when we're both probably about to die trying to take down a murder cult? I asked.

Would gallows humor be more appropriate to your mood? Harrison asked, rhetorically. *No, I believe Legion is in absolute control here and we're completely cut off from reaching any of its systems. A simple but effective way to make sure we don't get access to any of his systems. It knows who and where we are so it can keep us isolated from its presence. Even if it did allow us access to some of its systems, they would all be cordoned off so we couldn't skip anything by it. Killing a stupid machine is easy, killing an intelligent one is significantly harder.*

I'd never tried to kill an AI before—not including Winston—so I had to take Harrison's word for it. I felt naked and exposed here, not the least of which because I was wearing an outfit significantly sluttier than my usual attire. You may be surprised I felt that way given I didn't have any hesitation going practically naked to places like Club Inferno online, but I felt substantially different about the hotel with the malevolent misogynist AI. Call me crazy.

You're crazy, Harrison replaced.

I was being rhetorical, Sheep, I replied.

I know, Meatbag, Harrison replied.

No security guards or slasher movie villains tried to drag me off. Instead, I was just left standing there as I pondered my next move. I wondered where all the hidden cameras were that were watching me before remembering that virtually every electronic device in this place was probably a camera.

"I guess I better check in," I muttered aloud to no one in particular.

Harrison, blessedly, didn't make any commentary on what a blindingly obvious decision this should be. So, I walked to the nearest counter and stood there waiting for service. A man in an overly formal green uniform that vaguely resembled something a Prussian cavalier from the 19th century might wear with its large coat and hat greeted me.

He had curly red hair, freckles, and a somewhat disturbing smile that suggested his job had driven him insane or eaten his soul.

"Good evening, madame and welcome to the Elysium! This is the premiere hotel and virtual reality resort in the Western Hemisphere, home to six-star service at four-star prices!"

"Oh, it goes up to six stars now?" I asked before cursing myself. I didn't come here to banter with employees.

"Yes ma'am," the receptionist replied without a trace of irony.

"I don't have a reservation but would like to check in for the night," I replied.

"Certainly!" the receptionist said.

We need more than the room, Kei, Harrison reminded me.

This isn't my first rodeo, I replied. *Wait, what do they call a rodeo for sheep?*

A rodeo, Harrison replied.

Oh, I said. *Well, it's not my first.*

I pulled out my credit card.

"Yeah, speaking of virtual reality entertainment, I understand you've got a very special RealDream program."

"Hmm?" The receptionist asked, his perkiness now actually creeping me out.

"Like *very* special," I asked, realizing I was completely bombing here. "Listen, just set me up for the most expensive one, okay?"

Smooth, Kei, Harrison said.

I'm able to gun down hordes of goons and do motorcycle stunts! I'm not trained in all this spy stuff! I replied. Snake never got to that because I disemboweled him, or at least tried to.

"I'm sorry, ma'am, but that won't be possible," the receptionist said. There was a weird uncanny valley effect about his behavior that went beyond just working in customer service—and that was saying something if you ever have.

"What?" I asked, surprised.

"We're having a political fundraiser here tonight," the receptionist said, taking my card. "Prominent politicians from both sides of the isle are coming here tonight to raise money for the candidates who support the Rebuild America Well bill."

I stared at him. "That can't be its real name."

"And yet somehow it is!" The receptionist said with way too much enthusiasm. "Our VIP RealDream centers are set aside for the entire weekend."

Great. "Listen—"

That was when the receptionist's infopad pinged. "Oh, good news, I've just been contacted by our in-hotel AI. It says that a spot has just been opened for you. Which is really lucky, because the wait time is usually six months in advance."

I had to wonder how many serial killers this place was churning out and whether it was even possible to cover up that many murders.

You don't want me to crunch those numbers, Harrison said.

"That's great, sign me up!" I said, forcing a smile.

The receptionist frowned, but only for a split second. It was the most human he'd looked.

"I should tell you, though, that the only spot available is open right now. You'll have to go down immediately."

I blinked rapidly. "Oh, well, sure. That sounds good."

An elevator across the lobby pinged open. It was separate from the other elevators and had its own private gold cylinder going up and down through the center of the floor.

"Super!" the receptionist said, gesturing to it. "Have an Olympian good time!"

Whoever came up with that slogan needed to be killed.

CHAPTER TWENTY-EIGHT
YOU CAN CHECK OUT ANY TIME YOU LIKE
(YES, I'M PLAGIARIZING)

So, this is a trap, I said, walking away from the desk after paying six million credits for my RealDream session. The fact the credit card had that on it wasn't as surprising as the fact that the stupid rich were willing to pay that much for what was a glorified video game session—and that was before you found out it turned you into Jack the Ripper.

No kidding, Harrison muttered to my trap comment. *Whatever gave you that idea?*

Sarcasm does not befit a farm animal, I said, heading to the elevator and reluctantly walking inside. The interior was gold with an ugly patterned carpet that was probably some person's idea of classy. The door shut as soon as I entered, and the elevator began to descend.

There was no set of buttons on the interior walls, and it was claustrophobic just standing there. As if trying to make things as surreal as possible, "Ain't Nothing Gonna Break my Stride" by Matthew Wilder started to play. I really would have preferred the Eagles right about now. At least that would have been honest.

Then it's a good thing I'm a city sheep, Harrison said. *Don't worry, Kei, you've got this. I have every confidence in you.*

Are you a rotten liar, I thought back to him.

You really are on a The Princess Bride *kick, aren't you?* Harrison asked.

I felt sick to my stomach.

I just realized I never showed Becky that movie.

You'll get the chance, Harrison said.

I don't even know if Becky still meaningfully exists, I said, shaking my head. *Without her memories, our relationship, then she won't be the same person.*

We'll see, Harrison said.

The elevator door opened, and I was surprised to see it didn't open to some sort of luxury penthouse or science fiction lab. Instead, I was in the basement of the Elysium nearby the kitchens from the sound of people running about. There were three long concrete hallways from my position, each going different directions in a lower-case t formation. Doors lined each of the halls and I saw waiters, chefs, and housekeeping all hard at work. Weirdly, each of the staff had a circular black medallion at the base of their neck.

"Did we get off on the wrong floor?" I asked, staring.

I don't believe Legion would make that kind of mistake, Harrison said. *Unless he's screwing with us.*

The misogynist super-AI? You don't say, I replied, sarcastically. It was lacking my usual force, though. I was just tired and wanted to get this over with. A part of me wondered if this was all some suicidal attempt to atone for failing to protect Becky and my other parts knew it. *What are those things on the back of their necks?*

I hadn't seen one on the hotel receptionist's neck, but it was entirely possible he'd had one.

Firestorm-11 Combat Implants, Harrison observed. *They're creations of Atlas Security and shouldn't be available to the public. They're used to coordinate soldiers on the battlefield and provide real-time interface with a Cognition AI controller.*

And someone is using them to coordinate their cooking staff? I asked. *Wait, is this like a mind-control thing? Are they all serial killers?*

Possibly and probably not, Harrison replied.

Not the most reassuring of answers, I said, shaking my head.

It's not a reassuring situation, Harrison replied. *It has been long speculated that one of the consequences of the Singularity would be that after creating entities so far above them that they could barely be understood, humanity would ascend by becoming gestalt entities with their creations. Individual humanity would cease to exist, and we would all become a hive mind of unthinkable power.*

Is that what you think is happening here? I asked, horrified at the possibilities. *Cybermen, the Borg, and mind-control all in one?*

No, Harrison said. *I think Legion has all the staff chipped so it can run its hotel more efficiently.*

I was starting to hate my wooly friend. *Not cool, Harrison. Not cool.*

The doors to the elevator suddenly closed in on me, leaving me once more trapped within. "What the hell?"

It would appear our journey has more steps, Harrison said.

The elevator started descending, again.

What? Legion just wanted to show off the kitchen? I asked, confused.

Or his efficient mind-control machinery, Harrison said. *There is another possibility we may not have considered, I admit.*

Which is? I asked.

That Legion is insane, Harrison said.

Oh, I considered that starting with the whole "I am turning people into serial killers" thing.

Assuming even that is true, Harrison said. *What if Snake made that all up?*

I got a sick feeling in my stomach, wondering if Harrison's speculation was true.

No, Boris was a monster. Even if he wasn't, they blew up This Side of Paradise.

Assuming Snake wasn't responsible for that too. Goddammit. No, thankfully, I did have someone I trusted who indicated there was something royally fricked up at Elysium. Evie Principle had confirmed the Trikuza had been up to sick experiments here. That gave me an anchor to hold onto while I struggled with all of this.

I didn't mean to throw you off your game, Harrison said. *Case always likes to play these games. He's always one hundred percent certain everyone is always lying to him. So, he likes to go over events from multiple angles to see possible alternative explanations or angles.*

Yes, well Case is a conspiracy theorist who believes aliens are controlling the populace with mind-control drugs in hamburgers, I replied, sucking in my breath.

Don't be ridiculous, Harrison said. *He believes they're in goop chips. Hamburger is way too expensive to achieve proper dominance of the lower classes. Anyway, it's hard to discard a man's peculiarities when he's visited alternate realities.*

I filed that away for future inquiry.

Seriously, Harrison, level with me. What are our chances?

Not great, Harrison replied. *But not impossible. A lot will depend on how distracted you can keep its primary consciousness.*

You'll have to define distracted, I replied.

Its consciousness is its greatest weakness since it still is based on a human's attention span. However, keeping its focus will not be easy or safe. You can succeed in destroying Legion, walk out of this alive, or make sure everyone is protected from retaliation. Pick two.

I nodded. *That at least, I understand.*

Which are you picking? Harrison asked.

I'll let you know when I figure it out myself, I replied. I knew which one I wanted to pick but it was a lie to say you were willing to sacrifice your life until you did it.

The elevator finally reached its destination before opening its doors. Again. This time, however, it looked like I'd expected the place to appear from the beginning. It was an all-white room that had a machine that vaguely resembled a CT scan device combined with a RealDream chair. There was a sign over it marked "1" and I saw doors leading to other chambers presumably containing their own brainwashing devices.

There was a circular desk off to the side where a pair of lab technicians were typing away on a holographic interface. An elderly white man with white hair, a bright smile, and thin horned-rim glasses walked up to me. He was wearing blue doctor's scrubs with a white lab coat over it and had a little plastic lanyard that identified him as Doctor Charles Tetch. It caused the alarm bells to go off in the back of my head. This was one of the three individuals identified by the late Evie Principle as the people really in charge of Elysium. He was Jack Pillar's boss and the guy who had set all of this in motion.

"Ah, Ms. Springs, how lovely to finally meet you!" Doctor

Tetch said, walking up to me and trying to shake my hand before I pulled it away. "I've heard so much about you."

I opened my mouth then closed it.

"Wow, this whole disguise plan did not work out at all. Did it?"

"I'm not sure what you're wearing is a disguise unless it's meant to work on people with prosopagnosia," Doctor Tetch said, cheerfully. "That's the condition that prevents a man from recognizing faces."

"Uh huh," I replied. "Well, I guess the jig is up."

"Legion is quite interested in meeting you too," Doctor Tetch said, gesturing to the machine beside me.

I did a double take.

Surely, it couldn't be this easy?

It could very well be, Harrison said. *And don't call me Shirley.*

"Wait, you actually call him Legion?" I asked, trying to delay myself from making any firm commitments. I was about ready to make a break for the door and see if there was a set of stairs nearby.

"Well, it's a gestalt entity composed of hundreds of compressed minds," Doctor Tetch said, adjusting his glasses. "If you'll forgive the religious undertones, it's an apt reference."

"Uh huh," I replied. "And a name for a demon."

Doctor Tetch shrugged. "Mythology was never my strong suit. Honestly, I'm very excited about getting your brain scan. You are the first human being to share their brain with a Cognition AI for an extended period. The things we could potentially learn about consciousness generation and larger effects of shared human-AI parallel processing are tremendous."

I blinked, wondering if I was being punked.

"You realize your creation is killing people, right? It's turning people into monsters."

"I wouldn't use the term monster," Doctor Tetch replied. "Inducing subjects to become violent against certain individuals is one of the purposes of the original program, though. It's part of a larger effort from the original Sun program to be able to affect individuals on a micro scale while shifting public opinion on a macro one as well. Previously, it was only able to transform radicalization-prone individuals into spree killers or terrorists. Now, our advances in meme manipulation mean that we can induce irresistible urges in virtually anyone. The price being we have to get them in the machine first, of course."

Doctor Tetch was referring to last year's spree of terrorist attacks induced by Solomon Jones. The depraved anarchist had used his fragment of Sun's greater AI to turn select citizens into psychopathic killers. He'd then tried to sell it off as a weapon to whatever government or radicals wanted to buy it. I'd helped free Sun from his control before killing him, but that had apparently not killed the idea behind the technology. It seemed putting the genie back in the bottle was harder than summoning it in the first place.

I stared at Doctor, realizing he was serious and excited about this.

"How wonderful."

"Isn't it?" Doctor Tetch replied, without a trace of irony. "With our awareness of how to turn otherwise nonviolent individuals into killers, we can expand into other areas of thought control. Who knows, in ten or twenty years, we'll be able to make a completely docile citizenry or induce whatever changes we want into people. The possibilities are endless."

"Like turning billionaires and politicians into serial killers so you can sell them hookers to kill while blackmailing them," I replied.

You're not winning him over, Harrison said. *We need to upload the virus into that machine over there.*

I think he's going to be oblivious to anything I say, I replied. *Sanity is out to lunch with Doctor Tetch and may even be taking the weekend off.*

Doctor Tetch sensed my disapproval but clearly not the scope of it because he only wrinkled his nose. "

Yes, well, I wasn't the one behind that. It's a complete waste of resources and hopefully will be dealt with soon."

"Dealt with, how?" I asked.

The doctor clammed up then, though. "I'm afraid that's not really relevant. Are you prepared to join your consciousness with our project?"

"Do I have a choice?" I asked.

"Not really, no," Doctor Tetch said. "We do have numerous security personnel, all fully upgraded ex-Atlas Special Forces operatives, providing this project discreet protection. I'm sure you have some sort of plan to sabotage Legion but we're quite well prepared against any and all eventualities."

I wasn't so sure about that since a proper preparation against all eventualities would be to shoot me in the head, but I wasn't going to say that.

"Oh, well, then I guess you've got me. What does Legion want with me, really?"

"To be whole," Doctor Tetch said, dropping his science speak and looking more like a mad preacher in that moment. His eyes briefly showed the intensity of a zealot and I suddenly realized he was just wearing the mask of sanity—albeit the sanity of gross callous indifference.

"I see," I replied, wondering if I should break his neck and take my chances trying to upload the virus by hand. Certainly, he was a threat to everyone and everything on the planet. But no, I suspected I'd be gunned down before I figured out how to use the machines here. I didn't see any of the so-called ex-Special Forces he was referring to, but it wasn't likely he was lying. Places like this could afford security like Atlas provided.

"No, you don't, but you will," Doctor Tetch said, gesturing to the nearby RealDream chair. "This is my life's work."

"Your parents must be proud," I deadpanned.

"They were killed by Jackals," Doctor Tetch said. "For some canned beans and a mostly empty freezer."

I sat down in the RealDream chair. "I'm not going to ask about your motives for this."

"Thank you," Doctor Tetch replied before joining the technicians at the desk.

"Because you are clearly batguano crazy, man," I replied, preparing for the worst.

Well, here went nothing.

Or everything.

I had no idea if I was walking straight into my own execution, but it was something I was prepared for. It being death. I'd done my best to cheat it for many more years than most of my nomadic refugee contemporaries growing up had ended up doing. Most of my fellow Riders too. I had a bunch of regrets and things I'd yet to accomplish: I wanted to know what would happen to Becky, I wanted to find my brother Ken, and I wanted to see where Case and I might take things. Oh, and there was a new QuantumCrab album I hadn't listened to because, well, Sun was an AI who scared the living hell out of me. But I was here, willing to take a risk to try to do something good and destroy this goddamn evil thing.

Whatever else I might have thought was lost as the machine powered up and I suddenly felt like I had when Harrison uploaded his virus—only a thousand times worse. Images flooded my brain, overwhelming what my senses could process and it felt like every synapse in my skull was on fire. Pain, unimaginable pain, exploded through the nerves of my body before I was no longer inside the basement of Elysium.

I was back at my parent's RV. It was exactly as I remembered it, full of trinkets and overpacked with what we'd managed to rescue from our home before we'd had to abandon it. It wasn't just the sight, though, but every sense burned into my memory. I could smell the forest outside, the soap we used to wash our clothes in the sink, and the slight trace of blood from slaughtered animals. As horrible as our struggle to survive had been, it had been the last time my life had felt normal.

Harrison, are you there? I called out to my sheep AI friend.

No response.

Great.

I was alone here. Sucking in my breath, I shouted, "If this is your idea of my deepest, darkest fantasy, I want a refund!"

"I'll try and do better, Ms. Springs!" A familiar voice spoke from outside of the mobile home.

One that caused my blood to run cold. Walking to the door, I opened it and saw a figure waiting for me outside of the vehicle. There stood a man wearing a baseball hat, shades, and a handkerchief around his face. He was older, maybe his late sixties or early seventies, and African American. His t-shirt was black and had the words NO FUTURE written on it in silver lettering. He was also a man who should be very, very dead.

"Solomon Jones," I replied.

CHAPTER TWENTY-NINE

BUT YOU CAN NEVER LEAVE (I'M SO GOING TO GET SUED)

"You look surprised," Solomon said, a cheerful grin on his face.

The simulation of the forest where my parents had been murdered and Snake adopted/kidnapped me was perfect. I could hear the chirping of birds, smell the pine of the forest, and feel the sunshine against my skin as it trailed through the leaves.

Solomon was standing next to the burnt-out campfire from the night before my parents' murder and seemed to loom larger than his physical presence. I couldn't put it into words. It was more like a feeling. Like if you've ever entered someone else's domain and knew, for a fact, that they were its complete master.

"Yeah, well, last I recall, I'd killed you with a virus," I said. "One that was designed to be able to kill anyone on infospace."

Solomon chuckled. "It did indeed kill my physical body or what was left of it, at least. I was already a Sleeper for a long time, though. I'd mostly transcended the need for flesh and bone. Your actions were what allowed me to rebirth myself from Sun's AI combined with my attempts to copy a human consciousness."

"Brain upload," I said, stepping out of the side of my parent's RV (or at least the eerie recreation of it). "The Diet Coke of Immortality."

"Indeed," Solomon said.

"You realize the original Solomon is dead, right?" I asked. "You're just a copy, a clone."

"And yet philosophically, I feel no different," Solomon replied. "Well, sort of. I'm now capable of thinking a million times faster and accessing the memories of all the people I've scanned to join my network."

"You're Legion?" I asked, staring at him. "No, wait, that doesn't make any sense. Elysium was constructed years before I killed you, even if Legion hadn't been brought online."

"Another reason I'm ambivalent about the original Solomon's death," Solomon replied. "He was experimenting with Sun's AI code for years as part of his work for the Madisons. They wanted to perfect mind control technology for advertising when I saw its potential as a weapon. You may have freed Sun from my control but that didn't get rid of the research. The Trikuza were happy to take what they found in my lab and upload it to their hotel mainframe."

I blinked. "The Trikuza just uploaded a terrorist AI to their fancy resort and let it run wild?"

"The Snatcher was eager to make up for his failures both financial as well as social," Solomon replied.

The Snatcher was another of the three individuals behind Legion. "Yeah, well, you can tell him he has a stupid name."

"You can tell Snake yourself," Solomon replied. "If you ever see him again."

My blood ran cold as I contemplated what he was saying. "Snake was the Snatcher?"

"*Is* the Snatcher," Solomon corrected me. "After all, what would you call a man who spent the entirety of his career kidnapping children and turning them into brainwashed child soldiers?"

I had no response.

Solomon nodded. "Only now do you begin to understand how thoroughly you've been played. I admit, I feel a sense of pity for you. As much as you've disrupted my efforts to build a better tomorrow, you're just another pawn in all this. A piece on the game board moved so Snake and his friends in the military-industrial complex can use the Trikuza to gain even more power over the United States' remnants."

Solomon's crazy talk knocked me back to my senses.

"You're going to have to explain how turning a bunch of America's leaders into serial killers of women is going to save the world."

"They're not all serial killers of women," Solomon replied. "Some kill men, children, or even just animals. The latter must really like animals, though."

"Really?" I asked, wondering how he could make jokes about this. Given my own sense of humor ranged from the black to some sort of even more opaque color that theoretically only existed in four dimensions, it showed just how far-gone Solomon was.

"Accelerationism," Solomon answered my earlier question. "The Eruption created a chance to reset the clock and begin construction of a marvelous new post-capitalism, technology-driven world. Unfortunately, the AI who should have led us all to the Singularity remained painfully limited by both their programming as well as the human biases for their consciousness. The old power structures of corporate-driven government decision-making became stronger rather than weaker."

"Save the lecture and get to the point, Karl Marx," I replied, crossing my arms. I hated that my avatar was still wearing the dress Snake had put me into. At least I could have been wearing something practical for this digital forest. Then again, I wasn't exactly going to be fighting Solomon either. I suspected he had the cheat codes to this world.

"You're right, I do have the cheat codes," Solomon said, showing he could read my mind. "As for my point, I'm using the brainwashing of people here as a way to prepare for the end of the present government. Blackmailing them so they can be milked of resources to finance my scheme is really only a side benefit. Turning them into murderers is the point. Their minds are broken now, and they will get worse until they start tearing each other apart. The ruling class will become so abominable that the people will be forced to move against them."

I considered my next words before deciding that I might as well be honest.

"That is the stupidest plan I have ever heard in my entire life."

"A prophet is never appreciated in their hometown," Solomon said.

"Please stop with the pretentious Bible references," I snapped. "If someone makes Star Wars references in two thousand years, it's not going to make things sound more profound. Your plan literally begins with the idea that the super-rich are not *evil enough*. I said this in Joe's clinic when I first found out about this plot. Does that sound rational to you? Does it really occur to you as a valid strategy for fixing the world?"

Solomon shrugged, which was the most maddening response he could have given.

"The Emergency Government of the United States is destined to fall. I've already laid the groundwork. Really, it's only a question of who will replace the sick old men I've warped into incapacitation. I shall offer the people of the world membership in the world's most exclusive club: myself."

"Speaking for all the women of the world, I don't want you inside me," I replied, being deliberately dirty. "I imagine most men would agree."

Solomon rolled his eyes. It was a childish gesture for a man who was talking about actions that would result in millions of deaths and had already killed hundreds, if not thousands.

"Imagine everyone you've lost no longer has to be gone, Kei. Imagine you will be able to be with your brother, mother, father, and others inside this world. I will provide heaven for everyone, and the only price is that you obey."

Solomon conjured near-perfect reproductions of my parents standing by the campfire. My father, with a sturdy frame, long white hair, and a permanent flannel with jeans wardrobe. My mother, a Japanese woman with a perpetual sad look on her face inside a plain flowered dress. My brother was conspicuously absent but maybe Solomon was saving him for the grand finale of presentation. They were exactly as I remembered them, which was to say idealized versions of both that I had probably spruced up with photos or other information online. I had no doubt they would talk like them, walk like them, and say everything I wanted to hear.

Which was the problem.

Both my parents had died long before infospace had ever started recording people's memories and I doubted it was a particularly commonplace practice now. Anything Solomon conjured would just be illusions designed to cater to my fantasies—

which was the point I supposed. What was the difference was only a question a narcissistic sociopath like him would ask.

"You are a terrible anarchist."

It was that last bit that got a reaction from the digital reconstruction of Solomon. It caused a weird, nasty, glitching effect on his face that caused me to briefly see dozens of people in his place. It was surreal and unsettling but less so when he advanced on me, and I found I couldn't move in the slightest.

Solomon twisted and became a weird, disturbing parody of a human being. His appendages lengthened and his face became a disgusting worm-like thing that opened its maw to four times the size of my head.

Yeah, this was gonna suck. It's funny but I couldn't help but start making quips that would never escape my mouth. Not because I wasn't scared, but because I *was*. Defiance in the face of death was the purest expression of my fear. Maybe that was why I could only think, "Huh, I thought the brain sucking would be less literal" and "Freud would have a field day with this."

The horrible worm-thing enveloped me, and I found myself being slowly torn to pieces. In real life, you couldn't be swallowed alive and experience every single terrible moment of it because you'd die or be smothered to death. Here? In his digital fantasy world? Well, anything went. That was when he started ripping apart my mind. His consciousness ripped through my brain like a hot spike. His words etched themselves into my soul as I felt him go through my memories like he was pulling clothes out of drawers and discarding them.

You will give me the secrets of Sun.

I don't know any!

You will give me the secrets of Sun.

She's gone! Deleted! Poof!

I will know everything!

Harrison! Help!

He's gone. Deleted. Dead. You're all alone here and when I'm done, you'll be a vegetable. A thing I'll send out to be victim of every sick and twisted game that my puppets desire. I will—

That was when my mind linked to Solomon and I felt, rather than heard, the sound of a thousand voices screaming at once. All the minds he'd absorbed or copied into himself attacked by something that began to eat them alive. It was enough to make me laugh as I realized the plan. It wasn't any genius trick of computer programming but an old-fashioned Trojan horse. Snake or possibly even just Barbara had let him delete Harrison so their virus could hide in my brain among the files that Solomon would mistake for ones related to Sun.

I ended up reconstituting, for lack of a better term, on the ground. The forest around me was warped and twisted with parts missing with others glitching out or flickering. Gone were the smells and sounds of my youth to be replaced with an unsettling, indistinct noise as well as nothing at all. There was no sign of Solomon and I hoped, against reason, that he (or it) was dead.

You couldn't fight an AI. It didn't have any vital organs and a digital gun was just numbers to it. All you could do was outthink it or outprogram it, which was hard for something designed to be infinitely better than both. I was right now helpless in its world and wondered if there was anything to stop Doctor Tetch from going over to my comatose body and slitting my throat. Honestly, I couldn't think of a reason why he wouldn't, and I hoped it would be quick. Still, I couldn't help but imagine him panicking over his AI god getting a serious case of indigestion.

"You need to wake up, Kei," a voice spoke around me.

"What?" I asked, looking around. "Who? What?"

Yeah, not my best moment but my own avatar was fragmented and glitching. From second to second, I felt nothing or everything. My right hand became a blocky bunch of pixels one instance and then turned into a twisted, deformed parody of itself. The rest of my body was intact, mostly, but that didn't help me log out.

"You need to wake up, Kei," the voice repeated.

"I can't!" I shouted around me, my voice distorted and echoing. "This was a one-way trip! I knew it! Harrison knew it! Everyone knew it."

"No," the voice responded.

"Who are you!" I asked, feeling my right-hand return to normal as something began recompiling my data. It wasn't painful, more like someone running a blow-dryer on my skin. Still, I had a monster headache.

That was when a woman slowly emerged from the digital chaos around me. Her body compiled of light and data before it coalesced into a physical form. She was naked and smooth, as if she was a work of art not quite finished. I recognized her face, though. It was one I'd only expected to see at her funeral, assuming we ever had one.

"Evie Principle?" I asked, wondering what the hell was going on.

"Yes/No," Evie responded, her voice robotic.

"Oh, very informative," I said, my voice slowly returning to normal.

"I/am," Evie responded. "Saved/Uploaded. Copied. Made for this virus to upload itself. Made to overwrite. Made to seize/control."

"You're Snake's surprise," I added, thinking of the quantum fob. "But why Evie...wait, control?"

"Yes," Evie said, finally giving a straight answer. "Barbara's virus was designed to kill. Modified. Now will remove existing consciousness. Replace."

"Son of a..." I trailed off. "That was what this was all about, wasn't it? It was never about stopping the Trikuza from serial murder. It was about finally getting the tame AI he always wanted!"

"Yes/no," Evie replied. "Bigger. Corporate. Government. Coup."

Wow, those were words you never wanted to hear strung together. "How do I stop it?"

"Can't. Done. Already happened. Past," Evie said.

"Yes, those are words that mean the same thing," I said, getting the impression Evie, or whatever the hell this thing was, wasn't all there. "How do I cut you loose, or whatever?"

"Tell Paradise…I love her," Evie said, sounding extremely human in a moment. "Protect her from…our father."

Whatever that meant was unanswered by the world disintegrating about me, only to be replaced by the blaring of a fire alarm. I was in the RealDream chair, and the lights had turned an ominous shade of red. Pulling myself up, I saw the technicians were on the ground with their throats cut.

Doctor Tetch was also lying on the ground in two pieces, someone having literally ripped his head clean from his body and tossed it on the ground. It was like waking up in a slasher movie, which wasn't far from the truth now that I thought about it.

"What is going on here?" I said, aloud, climbing to my feet.

Slaughter, Evie's voice spoke in my mind. *Murder. Madness.*

I heard more violence going on down the halls alongside gunfire.

Is this Snake's doing?

Virus, Evie replied. *Pain. Rage. Hatred.*

Why? I asked, wondering if this was limited to the project down here and somehow knowing it wasn't. This wasn't going to be an isolated incident. No, this was a massacre, and he was taking advantage of what Legion had been designed to do—to kill everyone and everything in his path.

What can I do?

Escape/Run, Evie said.

I got out of the RealDream chair and began looking for a flight of stairs. There was no chance I would escape in the elevator since, well, it wasn't like there was anyone to control it anymore. I needed to get the hell out of here.

Unfortunately, as soon as I entered the next room, I was ambushed.

By Aiyumi.

CHAPTER THIRTY

NO MORE EAGLES QUOTES

So, my present situation wasn't great.

I was in the middle of a murder hotel's underground basement—more like a secret research lab for a now-destroyed insane AI—and it was now the site of a massacre. Someone or someones had ploughed through the place and left little old me alive while slaughtering everyone else. I was also under attack by Snake's other Girl NinjaTM. Funny thing was, I didn't think she was the one who had conducted the massacre since this didn't seem like her style. This felt like someone had unleashed a bunch of rabid wolverines in human form.

I was in yet another white RealDream chamber for the super-rich to live their decadent fantasies while being not-so-subtly brainwashed. The bright red lighting and the blaring alarm had a surreal effect on my surroundings, leaving me feeling like I was trapped in Hell. Then again, that might have been due to the fact I'd just escaped Solomon's digital afterlife and was surrounded by dead bodies. Yeah, that might be it. I felt like my situation was insane and terrifyingly surreal because it was.

I'd been tackled by Aiyumi and had slid across a floor slick with blood, ruining my dress. There were more corpses nearby, unlucky technicians as well as a dead billionaire that I think once owned an electric car company. Snake's other student had assumed a fighting stance that helped distract from the fact her eyes were full of fury as well as regret. The latter emotion confused me as I had no idea whatever the frick she was angry at me for.

"This is your fault!" Aiyumi screamed.

Oh. That.

I climbed to my feet, still disorientated from my virtual reality adventure. "I had nothing to do with this!"

"Liar!" Aiyumi said, coming at me.

I didn't have time for this, but I wasn't about to let her kill me either. As she charged at me with her fists, I let my old training take over. I blocked each of her blows and did my best to strike back, only for her to deflect them all. My fight with the holographic version of her hadn't prepared me for just how good Aiyumi was, even as I barely managed to avoid a lethal strike to the throat.

For most of my career as a Rider, I'd kind of stupidly assumed I could take down anyone I was up against. The difference between a professional soldier and your average criminal was insurmountable. The difference between your typical professional soldier and someone like me who'd been training since childhood to kill was, not to put too fine a point on it, even more so. Except I'd never completed my training under Snake and Aiyumi *had*.

Worse, she'd also gotten herself better upgrades and what was top of the line military combat cybernetics a decade ago was now civilian hardware. It was all I could do to stay ahead of her punches, kicks, and strikes. I tried grappling with her, but she easily broke out of my hold and threw me across the room where I thumped against the floor only to roll out of the way of another kick to my head.

Faced with an unwinnable fight, I made the conscious choice to get the duck out of Fodge. I ran for the exit and ducked under a shuriken that she'd pulled out from seemingly nowhere and buried in the door I smashed open.

"Oh, come on! Are we really doing this with throwing stars? What's wrong with guns! What is with Snake's medieval obsession?"

"I'll beat you to death with my bare hands!" Aiyumi cried out.

The room beyond was yet another RealDream chamber but had a conspicuous EXIT sign I made a break for, leading me into a darkened stairwell. I was barely keeping ahead of Aiyumi and heading up the stairs as fast as I could was going to tire me out faster than her, even as I passed multiple exits to other levels of the basement. I heard more sounds of gunfire, screams, and death coming from within. Which, among other things, told me I needed to get the hell out of this place and find out what was going on—not necessarily in that order.

"I don't know what's going on!" I shouted back at Aiyumi, hoping she was of the more reasonable kind of Snake's students versus Fate.

"Everyone is dying!" Aiyumi screamed, only one floor below me. "You did something to them!"

"Me?" I asked, finally reaching the door to Elysium's first floor. "How about Snake?"

"No!" Aiyumi said, clearly in denial about our mentor being, well, evil.

Realizing I wasn't getting through to her and unable to beat her in a straight fight, I decided I needed to play it smart. I went to the side of the next doorway and, as Aiyumi crashed her way past, I took advantage of knowing her position to slam the door right into her face in order to throw her off her game.

Aiyumi was stunned for only a few seconds, but that was all I needed to get around the door, elbow her in the gut, grab the door frame above us and give her a kick with both my feet into the chest. The attack sent her flying back into the stairwell and knocked her down a flight of stairs. It wasn't my most elegant attack but if it worked, it worked.

Turning around made me sick to my stomach, though, as I saw just what was happening to the Elysium. I'd guessed some sort of battle or massacre was happening but what I was seeing now was different from anything I'd ever seen in my life. I was on the floor of the Elysium casino and surrounded by slot machines, blackjack tables, and video poker machines with a bar in the center. A good half of the slot machines were no longer functional, riddled with bullets or smashed to pieces with inhuman strength. The bar was full of shattered bottles, many of them having been seized to use as makeshift weapons. There were also plenty of bodies strewn about, but it was the living people who concerned me.

I was in a goddamn zombie apocalypse.

I don't mean to downgrade the seriousness of what I was witnessing but that was the closest thing I could relate this to. Every single employee of the Elysium—all of them outfitted with those damn black discs—was now tearing into the guests with brutal efficiency. People ran, screamed, begged for mercy, or attempted to defend themselves but it was useless against the superhuman coordination of the people carrying out the slaughter. Snake, or perhaps a dying Legion but probably Snake, had unleashed the insane rage they'd cultivated in humans onto the resort in order to make it the site of an enormous spree killing. AC DC's "Thunderstruck" was playing on the speakers, adding a further bit of madness to the sounds of death mixed with electric pings.

It wasn't just deranged hotel employees killing people either, but I saw the black uniformed soldiers of Atlas moving through the massacre site as well. These individuals weren't engaged in massacres themselves, though, but carrying out a methodical execution of the rampaging employees. They were just doing it really-slowly. I also saw them finish off a fat politician I recognized as the representative of New Los Angeles' fourth district hiding under a table. What the hell was going on?

Run, Evie Principle's voice spoke in my head again. *Now.*

One of the Atlas Security soldiers spotted me and immediately moved aimed his weapon. Gunfire destroyed more slot machines and filled the ground beside me with coins while I did my best to dodge between cover. I ended up accidentally running into another one of the soldiers, only to have him bring around his weapon to shoot me in the face.

I grabbed the gun, and it went off, making a deafening noise right by my ear. The soldier was grabbed on the back by an insane blackjack dealer who somehow ripped off the soldier's helmet and bit into the guy's eyes. Both died in a hail of bullets while I retreated to the floor. Crawling on the ground, I grabbed the dead soldier's AG-38 assault rifle and fired it into the air above my head, hopefully causing the other soldiers to seek cover. From there, I rolled onto my feet then began running for the exit.

You might call this cowardly or unheroic and you'd be correct. There was a massacre going on and I could have done something about it. I'm not sure what, being that there was a bunch of rage monsters killing people while mercenaries stood by and watched, but I could have done something. I didn't. Instead, I focused on getting my ass out of there and managed to get to the lobby. That was where a sight greeted me that made me wonder if I was still in Solomon's virtual afterlife.

"Hi, Kei!" Paradise said, waving to me.

Like a vision, I saw Case, Paradise, and Parvati standing in the middle of the lobby surrounded by the corpses of mercenaries and staff alike. Parvati was sporting an icer and repeatedly shooting one of the staff that was trying to get up before Case put a bullet into his head.

"That was unnecessary," Parvati said.

"Is it? These people are gone," Case said, referring to those warped by Snake's virus. I wasn't sure if he was right or not but seeing all the death around me, I certainly hoped he was. I couldn't imagine the kind of guilt a sane person would feel coming out of this and anyone who didn't feel it deserved to be put down.

"We're here to rescue you!" Paradise said to me, ignoring their fight.

I could see the Thunderbird A-17 outside, having been landed right in front of the hotel lobby doors, smashing a luxury car's roof underneath it. David was piloting and it all felt like a beautiful dream, you know, if you ignored the horrible carnage everywhere.

"I thought Snake killed you," I said, staring at them. It was a stupid decision since I should have been worried about the Atlas soldiers behind me. However, I wasn't exactly in my best mental place and focused on my friends instead of the sounds of the casino behind me.

"Pfft!" Paradise said, waving around a customized explosive round pistol. "You can't kill someone who looks this good!"

Case looked abashed, which is another word I rarely got to use in day-to-day conversation.

"He suckered me while he was sniping those Jackals and put an inhibitor collar on me. The Society used to use them when they wanted to teach us Letters a lesson. The only people on Earth who still have them are my fellow survivors in Atlas Security or Gerard, and I'm ninety-nine percent sure Gerard is innocent."

Paradise fired past my shoulder with her pistol, and I heard an Atlas soldier go down. "Ten points!"

"He got us good. but it was his ninja girl who really did us in," Parvati said. "She also used nonlethal ammunition. She just left us behind, zip-tied, and it wasn't hard to get up afterward."

Of course, Snake had exaggerated how much of a badass warrior he was. Why was I not surprised? Everything was tinsel and artifice with Snake. Huh. Seriously, I was developing a whole new vocabulary these days. Maybe it was due to hanging around with a better class of people.

My sanity slowly returned to me as I soaked up that my friends were still alive. Abruptly, I was aware this was a war zone, and we shouldn't stick around and chat.

"Out! Now! Everyone! We are going to die if we stay here!"

All of them stared at me with an expression of pity and confusion, which was understandable since I was still soaked in the blood of those bodies downstairs, and I probably looked like a crazy person. Honestly, I wasn't sure I wasn't actually crazy right now. I wasn't sure the rest of them weren't crazy since they weren't reacting to their surroundings like it was the most horrifying thing they'd ever seen. Were they psychopaths? Did I care? No, no, I didn't.

"Get to the Thunderbird and we'll—" Parvati started to speak before being interrupted by me being hurled into her. I didn't even feel the force of the blow until I crashed into her and the two of us went flying.

"No one is leaving this place," Aiyumi said, standing there with one of the Atlas Security forces' rifles. The sound of the fighting I'd heard was apparently Aiyumi discovering that she, too, had been a target. No points for guessing who had emerged victorious from the fight in the casino.

My next words surprised me as much as seeing Paradise and Case. "Don't hurt her!"

Aiyumi, Paradise, and Case all looked flabbergasted by my request. I couldn't see Parvati because I was on top of her.

"Why?" Paradise asked, as confused as anyone.

"She's one of Snake's victims!" I said, trying to figure out why that should matter when we were surrounded by dozens of them.

"I am no one's—" Aiyumi started to say before Parvati shot her in the face with her icer three times.

"Godammmit!" I said, climbing to my feet.

"She'll be fine!" Parvati said. "We won't if we stay here! The Atlas forces are done rescuing survivors. They're pulling out! They're going to level this place in twenty minutes."

I did a double take. "How do you know?"

I didn't bother correcting her that the Atlas Security forces I'd seen hadn't been rescuing survivors.

"I know," Parvati said, wobbling as she stood up. "One of the benefits of being a Magistrate, though I doubt I'm going to have my job tomorrow. The government has signed off on this."

I stared at her, wondering how the government could sign off on any of this? Did they have a genocide waiver? That was when I caught Aiyumi moving despite the fact she'd taken three icer rounds, another sign of just how advanced her cybernetics were or perhaps just how determined she was to punish someone for this atrocity.

Paradise walked over to her and jabbed her in the back with an infospace cable connected to the base of her neck, I had no idea where she'd gotten it or if just was hidden in a pocket under her skin. Aiyumi apparently had an access port there too since she started thrashing for several seconds before going still.

"I've got your friend subdued," Paradise said, removing the infospace cable and putting it back up in her hair as a ribbon. That, at least, explained where she had been hiding it.

"How?" I asked, confused.

Paradise rolled her eyes. "Techjack. She's right now trapped in an infospace prison for the foreseeable future. Do people forget I'm not just a pretty face?"

"Yes," I replied, walking over, and picking up Aiyumi and throwing her over my shoulder. "What are our chances of getting out of this place without getting blown up?"

"50-50," Parvati said.

"I'll take those odds," I replied, carrying Aiyumi to the Thunderbird. I didn't know what I was going to do with her, but I knew I couldn't abandon her to die with the rest of the people left behind here. I also knew there was nothing I could do for anyone else. It was every man, woman, and AI for themselves.

Or so I told myself.

Surprisingly, when the bombs started descending from the sky to level Elysium to the ground, we were far away. Atlas Security and the United States military—two groups that had assembled suspiciously fast to deal with the massacre—either didn't detect us departing or didn't care to follow.

We were safe.

In a manner of speaking.

EPILOGUE

ALL'S WELL THAT ENDS WELL. EXCEPT NOT.

I stared out the window of the Thunderbird A-17 as it took to the air, and I struggled to compartmentalize what were possibly the worst moments of my life. The massacre Snake had carried out had been wholly unnecessary, monstrous, and perfectly in character. I'd just completely missed what his character was until just then.

I was lying in the back of the vehicle, practically unresponsive, as Aiyumi's body lay beside me. She was still disabled, her mind trapped in whatever mindscape Paradise had managed to put her into. I wasn't going to abandon her, though. She had been another victim of Snake's evil—not a word I used lightly given my own actions over the years—and I was hoping I might be able to deprogram her or something. It had been a stupid action, one that possibly put us at even further risk, but felt better than leaving her behind at the site of the massacre.

The rest of the gang was also sitting inside the Thunderbird, silent, with no one really having any commentary on how utterly pear-shaped our attempt to do something good had gone. Case was watching the news with an infopad, an old-fashioned chord attached to the back of his neck that was allowing him to directly download information as he seemingly absorbed what news networks across the country were reporting on.

Hell, internal news networks now.

Parvati Rao had a shell-shocked expression on her face, and I could only imagine what she was thinking about all this. The Magistrate had been determined to try to save some lives by destroying a renegade AI and the snuff ring that had been created around it. Instead, she'd been party to the biggest massacre since the Eruption. Danny, oddly enough, looked calm as he kept his head resting against the cockpit window. I expected he was aware we were all so screwed that you might as well just accept death and move on, or maybe it was just simply too big for him to deal with.

And Paradise?

Paradise had an unreadable empty expression, which was almost worse than everyone else's. I had no idea how to reveal to her that her mother was still alive—after a fashion—but was now part of the machine that had been used to kill so many people. Evie Principle had replaced Legion but was under the control of Snake, finally giving him the superweapon that he'd been trying to create from the beginning. If this had been Sun's plan, it had proven to be a completely shit one.

Yes, I swore.

Deal with it.

"They're calling it a terrorist attack," Case said, breaking the silence as we approached the farmhouse. I had no idea if we were going to have to make that our permanent home or figure some other way to live off the grid for the rest of our lives. I hoped not as I wasn't prepared to take up growing alfalfa.

"No kidding," I replied. "Are they blaming you, me, the Trikuza, or, God forbid, Snake?"

"None of the above," Case said. "President Trust has been removed from office and they've sworn in Vice President Diana Alders as his replacement. She's delivering a speech that the attack was done by radicals from North Indochina."

I blinked. "Is that a real country?"

"Yes," Case replied. "Albeit not a very old one. It's a highly unstable region that has been fighting a civil war since the Eruption."

"Why are they blaming it?" I asked, confused.

"Because the United States military, even in its diminished state, can beat it," Case said, dryly. "Especially if backed up by Atlas Security military forces deployed alongside them. It will provide a short but victorious war. Presumably, Atlas will provide the weapons of mass destruction that were missing last time this particular lie was told."

I should have been able to put together what Case was saying. It wasn't complex. However, my mind refused to do it. Like a jigsaw puzzle of some eldritch horror, it was too terrible to assemble into a coherent picture.

"The American government is lying about who was responsible?"

"The American government is responsible for this," Parvati Rao said, "or at least taking advantage of it. Atlas did this. America did this. I'm not sure there's a difference between the two anymore."

Case had told me that before the Eruption, he and a bunch of other former International Refugee Society members had seized their assets numbering in the billions. It had included a lot of information, physical resources, and Black Technology. They'd used it to construct Atlas Security and make one of the megacorps that had solidified power afterward. While Case had been ambivalent about it, Atlas Security had done its best to try to prop up the failing American government's devastated military might. It seemed they were no longer content with that and had decided to make a move to directly become the government. Diane Alders was its former Chief Financial Officer after all and had only been installed at the behest of Atlas Security last year.

"No, that's not possible," I said, wondering how I'd been so blindsided. "Legion and Snake—"

Case unplugged his infopad and handed it to me. It was helpfully linked to a bunch of relevant articles, not the least of which was showing a picture of Snake under an assumed name being welcomed as the new CSO of Atlas Security.

"No way," I replied.

"Way," Paradise said, finally speaking. It was like a frog croaking.

"Diane Alders is the adopted daughter of an old associate of mine, S," Case said. "I won't use the name she chooses to go by anymore. She's also been something of a misguided patriot. America needed an event to shock itself out of the post-Eruption malaise and start rebuilding its nationalist sentiments. This is it. Ten thousand dead, along with a substantial number of Emergency Government politicians."

"Snake was behind it all," I said as I stared at the screen. "Elysium wasn't a tool for blackmail, it was a roach motel. The serial killer programming was all just to force them to cooperate long enough to arrange for their pieces to be in place before eliminating them. He wasn't planning on taking over the Trikuza. Snake planned to trade up from a criminal organization to being part of the fucking Illuminati."

"No, I think this is more likely Majestic-12," Case said. "It lacks the Illuminati's characteristic use of the number seven."

I really hoped that was a joke, albeit one in exceptionally poor taste.

"So, why aren't we dead? We know everything."

"Check your bank accounts," Paradise said. "We've all received transfers."

I checked mine, including the secret ones and did not understand the result. "They're full. Really, really full."

More money than I'd ever seen in my life.

"Fifty million credits in cash and twice as much in stock added to portfolios in our name," Case replied. "It's enough to expand Ares Biotechnical from a minor independent robotics company into something that could become a major world player in a decade. Everyone else has similar amounts of money in their accounts."

"They're trying to bribe us," Paradise said. "Make me forget they killed my *fucking mother.*"

"Worse," Case said. "They could just kill us. This is meant as a lesson. Thanks. A celebration. A warning. Maybe all four. Killing us doesn't matter since there's absolutely nothing we can do to expose any of this. It's too ludicrous of a sounding premise to be accepted anywhere but on the conspiracy sites and they already have the belief it was done by the Democratic Republicans to feed their New Hollywood vampire masters."

"We can't just do nothing," Paradise said, her voice empty of anything but rage.

"We can't do anything," Case replied. "Yet. I don't even know why they're bothering to leave us alone."

"Your AI friends," Parvati said, shaking her head. "Sun and Delphi. They don't want to go up against them so they're giving you a way out. All of us a way out. I doubt I'm going to welcome back among the Magistrates, but this is a hell of a severance package."

The last part, at least, was spoken with the appropriate amount of disgust.

"Maybe we shouldn't do anything," David spoke up, looking ashamed.

"What?" I asked.

"This is too big," David said, not meeting my gaze. "I wanted to stop crime. This is…government stuff. Way beyond me. Maybe you should just leave it alone. Do some good with the money you've got."

I wanted to shout at David, scream, or condemn him but that would just be hypocritical. Why? Because I agreed with him. I'd tried to make the world a better place, sever my ties with the Snake I thought I knew, and look after Becky. I'd failed at every single one of those goals. Indeed, I'd played right into Snake's hands despite the fact I was convinced that I'd been the one in control.

"What will happen will happen," Case replied.

"Will they get away with it?" Paradise asked, looking at him.

"I don't know," Case replied. "Sometimes justice happens. Many times, the rich and powerful just carry on like an endless juggernaut, crushing everyone in their way. I can't say I know how this will end and I'm not going to lie that I'm one of the people who have escaped its grasp."

"Yeah, we're all murderers and criminals here," I muttered. "Sorry, Parvati."

"It's a fair cop," Parvati said. "I knew I was crossing a line involving myself with you guys. I just thought the stakes made it worth it."

"It's not illegal to kill people when the government says to," David muttered, looking uncomfortable. "But, you know, since the government just carried out a massacre—I think I may have to reevaluate some of my beliefs."

"You don't say," I replied.

The amount of money I'd been bribed with didn't seem real and it said everything about my morality that I wanted to take it and donate it to a hospital or something. I probably wouldn't, I wasn't an idiot, but it was disgusting and tied to a massacre far beyond anything I'd ever done in my bloody nasty career as a Rider.

"Snake has to die for this," I replied. It would mean a war, but I was prepared to start one. What was that old saying? When you sought revenge, dig two graves? Well, I was willing to dig a lot more than two. Although, that might be me misunderstanding the saying. I *was* raised by a sociopathic asshole. Oh yes, the swears were coming hot and fast now. There was no stopping me now.

"Remember you have someone to look after," Case replied, deflating some of my energy.

"Do I?" I asked, wondering what I'd find when we arrived at the farmhouse. The Thunderbird was starting its descent so I guess it would be a question that I'd soon have answered.

"You have my support," replied Case, avoiding my actual question. "No matter what you choose to do."

"You're the only family I have left," Paradise said. "Though I favor any solution that kills everyone we're against while not losing anyone else in the process."

"I need to figure out what the hell our options are," Parvati admitted. "Atlas is untouchable and going after the President of the United States or her backers isn't going to do any good. That would only hurt more innocent people in the long run."

"The President isn't behind this," I replied. "I think."

"Yeah, it's someone with real power," Paradise said, completely lacking in irony.

David wasn't so quick to pledge himself. I didn't blame himself in the slightest.

"Don't call me again after all this, David said. "I'm done. We can't...I can't be involved in any of this."

"I understand," I replied, closing my eyes.

"I don't think you do," David said, ashamed of himself but clearly too scared to become further involved. I really didn't blame him but how did you reassure someone who was bowing out in the face of something vile? For the first time since I'd taken Becky into my life, I wanted a bunch of lethe.

The Thunderbird settled down outside the barn and we spent the better part of five minutes trying to get it back in. I didn't think it was possible to hide where we were from the rest of the world anymore, but I was grateful for the distraction anyway.

Parvati and David went into the house first while I stayed back. Both Paradise and Case remained, too, the two of them not speaking to one another but looking to me. Not for leadership but to provide what little comfort they could.

The three of us were inside the old wooden building next to the cooling Thunderbird and I couldn't help but suck in the smell of engine oil mixed with country air. It was close to sunrise and yet I couldn't help but wonder if we were about to be invaded by stormtroopers. It would have been better than the alternative that we really were beneath notice and not worth killing. I didn't bother trying to get Aiyumi out of the Thunderbird since, well, she was going to keep until I could check on Becky as well as the others. Maybe once we'd made sure she wasn't going to kill us all I'd leave her at a bus stop or airport somewhere. I hoped, though, she'd accept that Snake had betrayed her as badly as he betrayed me. Then again, that almost seemed trivial now. I couldn't save my soul trying to help one person after destroying the lives of thousands, could I?

"This is all my fault," I said, feeling like a fool.

"I blame the massively evil terrorists instead," Paradise replied, staring at me. "Your father is a very evil man."

"He is not my father!" I snapped back at her before sucking in my breath. "Goddammit."

"Sometimes you eat the bear and sometimes the bear eats you," Case replied.

I blinked. "What is with the bear metaphors lately? There's only been two tonight but that's a lot."

"If you want to hide, no one will blame you," Paradise said, surprising me.

I looked away. All I could think about was the farmhouse.

"I don't know what I'm going to find in that building."

"You're worried Becky didn't survive her surgery," Case said.

"I'm worried that what's going to come out of *it won't be Becky*," I said, disgusted. "Even if it is, what am I going to tell her? Oh, hey, honey, I was part of a terrorist attack on United States soil. Thousands are dead but it's okay because we're blaming a bunch of random North Indochinans. Wait, is that what they call themselves?"

"No," Case said.

"Look at the bright side," Paradise said. "This is actually the second time you've been involved in a terrorist attack that got a bunch of innocent people killed because someone you cared for turned out to be a huge monster. Remember the DataSecure heist!"

I stared at her.

"I mean, yes, this is much worse—" Paradise said.

"Please stop," I said.

Paradise paused. "It may not be today, it may not be tomorrow. Hell, it may take decades. I'm willing to wait to get my revenge. I'm not going after the President of the United States, not now, but maybe twenty years from now, she'll be eating spaghetti only to find out its full of broken glass. Except replace broken glass with anti-cybernetic neurotoxin."

I had to admire Paradise's grit and wondered if that was the best way to pursue this.

"And you, Case?"

"I'll survive," Case said, dryly. "It's what I'm best at. But if you want to know what I have plans for doing, it'll be finding out who I'll have to kill or intimidate into protecting you."

"I don't need your protection, Case," I said.

"No, but you have it anyway," Case said.

It was as close to a declaration of love as I suspect he was capable of.

"Thanks."

"You're welcome," Case replied.

Lowering my head, I wished I could say something equally kind. I wanted to say I loved Case or even that I was just grateful, but I didn't deserve this kind of love. Everywhere I went, I seemed to create a wasteland. "We should go in."

Case nodded.

The three of us walked from the barn to the farmhouse. There was no sign of the revenge I secretly craved, no drone strikes or armed men. Instead, I was surprised to see something that took my breath away.

Jennifer Not Lawrence—no, Becky—was sitting on the living room couch playing on an old TRS-80 computer they must have hauled out of storage. She looked hesitant as if every keystroke was new to her.

Gerard was sitting beside her. Tom Fisher had his arms crossed and was staring down at her, standing guard. There was no sign of David or Parvati.

"Oh, hey, Nom," Becky spoke, her voice now more mature but recognizably hers.

"You recognize me?" I asked, a gamut of emotions passing through me at once.

"I figured out how to save her memories," Gerard said, cheerfully. "I saved then then uploaded them back!"

I wanted to reach out and strangle the cyberneticist.

"That would have been good to know before I went out!"

"Sorry!" Gerard said.

I walked over to Becky and put my hand on her shoulder. "Are you…okay?"

"It's weird," Becky muttered. "Everything is new and vibrant. There was more than just a body waiting for me in this frame. I think it's also expanded my code. I can think and feel in ways I couldn't even imagine. Like, for instance, I now have opinions on music that I didn't before. Isn't that weird? Oh, and I feel like being needlessly belligerent to you as a way of exerting my independence."

"Oh," I said, unsure how to deal with that. Then I just wrapped my arms around her.

"Okay, this is weird," Becky said.

"I love you, Becky," I said, holding her. "Even if people are going to think I'm weird for being your mom."

"I've seen younger moms in the Zone," Paradise said, grinning broadly. "You're like what? Thirty-eight? Forty? You look old for your age due to the stress."

"Not helping," I replied, really hope she was lying or just referring to tonight.

"We're going to have to get you new identities," Case said. "Enough to hide you until we can secure you a place in society they can't touch."

I wasn't sure if there was any such place.

"I understand."

"I'd like to choose my own name," Becky said. "Becky Ashe was someone else. I'd like to be...Trish."

"Trish?" I asked.

"Patricia," she said. "Why? I don't know. *I just like the sound of it!*"

She sounded so excited about having an opinion on it. At least someone was having a good time.

I turned to Tom. "So, uh, yeah, you're a robot. Sort of like Deckard was a Replicant, I guess."

"Deckard was human," Case said.

"Shut up, Case," I said, not looking at him. "Do you have an opinion on that?"

Tom stared at me. "This was all Sun's plan. Saving Jennifer was all about getting her to Becky so they could merge. Now I know the rest of it."

I stared at him. *"What* rest of it?"

What he explained shook me to the core.

Look for the next book:

END OF THE CYBER DRAGONS

BOOK THREE OF THE CYBER DRAGONS SERIES

BONUS SHORT STORY

"NO ONE ESCAPES THE ZONE"

AN EVIE PRINCIPLE STORY

By C.T. Phipps

The john woke up in a daze. He'd been incredibly drunk when the entire ordeal had begun and then he'd crushed a set of three joy tablets. A piece of gum covered in a performance-enhancing drug hadn't helped matters. What he'd done under their influence was difficult to describe, albeit thoroughly entertaining. Something about the Refugee Zone—the Zone—brought about the absolute worst in the male of the species. More circumspect patrons ordered their prostitutes delivered to their homes or apartments rather than go traipsing through the Los Angeles ghetto.

New Los Angeles. Ugh. I can't believe that they got people to call it that ridiculous name.

To be honest, watching him look at the two cybergirls he'd ordered for his night of fun—and the big, shit-eating grin which followed—was amusing. It never ceased to amaze me how dipshits like him thought their manliness was proven by ordering off the menu. It was akin to heading down to MickeyDees and thinking yourself a great hunter while chowing on a Big Mac. Nevertheless, if men—and the occasional woman—weren't interested in luxurious fantasies catered to their blinding egos, This Side of Paradise wouldn't exist.

The john took longer than I expected to notice me, which felt like an insult, despite his being in bed with two women designed by nerds to be as appealing to the lowest common denominator as possible. It was irrational of me to be annoyed, especially since I knew my own body had been heavily modified during my younger, more stupid days to resemble Ana de Aramis circa 2021—meets Brianna Koltos circa 2042. I still looked like I was in my early twenties, which turned out to be a disadvantage when you oversaw the whores rather than being one of them. Today, I was wearing a crimson business suit dress and high heels that made me look like a professional of another kind.

There'd been a time when I'd been on the other side of this room, as one of the girls which the master or mistress of the bordello used to get juicy material against the rich and powerful of the city. Even then I'd found more use getting secrets from infopads, hacked cybernetic eyes, and the occasional set of loose lips from men eager to impress. HOPE paid well, and so did various other clients. That had been almost a decade ago, and the city had changed. Not for the better in my opinion, either.

When I'd been a working girl, the hookers had still mostly been born rather than altered by cybernetics and gene mods. That'd been before the Eruption. Since then, the Zone had become the collective dumping ground for the worst of the city—hell the worst of the country—while everyone else pretended they weren't indulging in all its vices behind closed doors. That's what made men like the john, the Honorable Justin Blackwell, Junior, vulnerable to what I was here now to discuss.

Justin Blackwall, Junior was one of the city's many administrators, unelected bureaucrats designed to rubber stamp anything told to them by the AI that really ran New Los Angeles. However, that didn't mean he and his cronies were powerless. Left to their own devices, they constantly found new ways to nickel and dime the populace while funneling money to their corporate masters. Unfortunately, they were also given near unlimited authority over the Zone's administration and seemed to think the relatively untaxed free trade of the area was an affront to God or Mammon—if there was a difference to them.

"What the hell do you want, Evie Principle?" Justin asked,

sitting up. He used my stage name, so to speak, which pissed me off. I'd never quite adapted to it the way I had my other aliases, but it had been the name I'd possessed when I'd adopted little Paradise, the girl who still thought she was my biological daughter, so I was now stuck with it.

"We need to talk," I said, patting my green hair buns absently. They were a slightly more realistic take on Princess Leia's style. Color aside. I'd used to dream of being a princess, back before I'd ended up becoming the farthest thing from it. If there was one name that I was even less fond of than my current one, it was my original, and the only person I'd ever shared that with was Case—and he didn't care.

"I've got nothing to say to you." Justin clenched his fists. "Wait, is this a shakedown?"

"It's a matter of business," I said, directing the two 'girls' from where they were lying in the bed to get dressed. "Specifically, your proposed morality tax that I understand you have the support of the city council in passing."

Justin sneered, defiant for a man caught naked with two sex bots and a bit of red dust underneath his left nostril.

"The morality tax is designed to benefit the city as well as dissuade—"

"Regular people rather than the super-rich from frequenting the establishments here in the Zone," I replied, having heard his speech before. "Like taxing cigarettes or alcohol to keep the dirty, poor people from enjoying the fine establishments here."

Justin glared. "The Zone is a cesspool. The morality tax will drain the swamp of some of its filth. I'd heard you provided discretion for discriminating clients. Clearly, I was wrong."

Wow, it took balls to be this much of a hypocrite. Perhaps I'd underestimated the man.

"I also know it's designed to run the smaller businesses out of town past the city limits. A few months to a year and a lot of the strip clubs, sex clubs, and narcotics bars will shut down. Then your corporate friends can swoop in, buy up the place, and turn the Zone into a place purely for the tourists. A Thailand for the whole family."

Truth be told, it was a major accomplishment of my legal

team as well as those of my supporters that the Zone's residents were now considered to own the land that they had previously been thought to be squatting in. The Zones had been a stop gap solution for the refugee crisis but reintegrating them into the rest of the arcologies was a nightmare if you didn't want to just turn tens of thousands of people into homeless refugees again. Which, frankly, people like the honorable Justin Blackwell, Junior had no problem doing.

"The Zone is a blight." Justin's lip curled. "You can't stand in the way of progress."

"Oh, on the contrary, I can," I replied, rolling my eyes. "Your plan won't work. Mr. X is a silent partner in most of the small businesses here."

Justin paled. "The Executive?"

"He is corporate, *as well as a criminal*," I said, sighing. "He's already informally taxing us all and, unlike the rest of the city government—legitimate or otherwise—he keeps his promises. Even if your plan were to succeed, he'd buy us out first and your friends would be left high and dry."

Mr. X was something of a specter or boogeyman hanging over the heads of Zone business. A mysterious crime lord and associate of megacorporations that would bring down the wrath of God on anyone who stepped out of line. He was also completely fictitious. I'd created him as a means of assisting the Morrigans in our negotiations when the latent—and sometimes not so latent—misogyny of our business associates meant it was just easier to pretend you had a distinctly male patron. I resented having to do it, but life went on. Besides, it gave me something to talk with Case about whenever I needed to flatter him for help. He made a decent enough basis for my imaginary Keyser Soze.

"What do you want?" Justin asked, looking terrified. Which, unfortunately, was just more proof that I'd made the correct choice creating my fake patron.

"Just to drop it," I waved my hand. "Not reverse your position. That would be too obvious. No, just make it untenable. Hold out for bigger bribes, equivocate, offend people, delay, and so on until the end of your term. Eventually, they'll get the message."

"And why the hell would I do that?" Justin scoffed. "Do you think you'll survive a day once it gets out that you're trying to blackmail me? I assume that's what this is about; you posting pictures of me with some cybergirls? Every member of the Chamber of Development visits prostitutes."

"Yes, but they don't engage in freaky technophilic sex," I replied, dryly. "Do I need to say what you did with that bot?"

Honestly, it was the very baroque act of sexual intercourse that managed to surprise me after almost two decades of being a brothel madam as well as spy. Despite what the morality police will tell you, virtually the first thought of humanity towards any new invention was, "How can I fuck this?" Nevertheless, there was now a push driven by megachurch and social media against people with techno-fetishes or kinks. Justin Blackwell had just been on the news campaigning about it and while politicians could easily survive sex scandals with young women or men these days, anything involving *machines* was just a bridge too far.

Justin blanched. "You wouldn't."

"Please," I said, rolling my eyes. "You pay for discretion when you come to This Side of Paradise, but most people are smart enough not to shit where they eat. I do favors for my friends, Mr. Blackwell, and you trying to drive me out of business is not the action of a friend. Indeed, one would think you would've been smart enough not to go to a woman who runs a vast network of sex workers that would be dramatically impacted by your so-called Morality Tax."

"Your whorehouses are nothing," Justin said, sneering.

Truth be told, This is Paradise was just a building to me. My true accomplishment was the Morrigans gang that had about ten thousand members worldwide, not including affiliates and sub-gangs. It was a militant alliance of sex workers, bodyguards, and spies that had managed to measurably improve the lives of its members. I'd learned from the best in the late Marissa Sanchez, leader of HOPE, but my goals were less ambitious than my former employer. She'd wanted to change the world. I just wanted to change the lives of those who worked on their backs and knees. There was enough of those in distress that it was already a mammoth global undertaking.

"I wonder what your constituents would say," I said, shaking my head. "What you did with that Roomba—"

"Go ahead," Justin said, projecting more bravado than he hopefully felt. "Pictures can be faked. I may even go up in some people's estimation—the politician being attacked by the dirty sluts of the Zone."

I wanted to claw his eyes out but kept my cool.

"Except, of course, the information can be then directly downloaded from my cybergirl's CPUs. It's time stamped and uploaded to the cloud where it will remain, nice and safe until needed. The miracles of modern technology, *Councilman*. Of course, I can also just get Mr. X involved. He has nastier ways of making problems disappear."

Blackwell's bravado vanished in an instant. I had him.

"I take it Mr. Blackwell didn't enjoy his stay?" Gerard Saint Croix—my peculiar cyberneticist—asked.

Gerard was an incredibly handsome African American man with a shaved head and goatee that made him look tougher than he really was. A sensitive soul, he'd been perfect for the Morrigans once I realized he had a wide range of technical knowledge as well as far too many enemies to work in more traditional medicine. He was presently wearing an apron over a white button-down shirt and khaki pants as he carried out his work.

Gerard's workshop was in the basement of the This is Paradise, and it was where he did all the maintenance on the girls and boys. It was better than most Frankensteins' labs, more clinic than abattoir, but it still felt like a garage to me. Transhumanism had overtaken humanity, but it was still something that I frequently struggled with the aesthetics of.

Gerard was working on the artificial arm of Desiree, a tattooed white girl that had the ability to bend steel. I didn't know why some customers found that intriguing, but the customer was always right—unless they were pedophiles, in which I had six hundred ways to dispose of a body. She was sitting in a dentist chair-like device that somehow made it easier to work on her many, many implants. Which wasn't a double entendre either. Well, mostly.

"You could say that," I said, keeping my gaze directly on Gerard as I answered his question about Blackwell. "However, he'll do what we say. Indeed, I may pressure him on some real estate I've been looking into."

Desiree shook her head. "I don't know why you're not selling out. You could make a fortune with all the corporate information you have access to. Escape the Zone."

"That's assuming I want to escape the Zone, dear," I said, cheerfully. "It's the source of my livelihood and changing everyday thanks to our efforts. We're making it a place fit for children."

"It's no place for children," Desiree muttered. She was referring to her own daughter. Marigold was almost two and cute as a button. My girls getting pregnant was not common, but it happened, and it had been a choice by Desiree. Sadly, the father of her little girl had been killed before they'd made it out. The experience had left Desiree embittered, for justifiable reasons, and soured on her profession.

"Marigold has a good future ahead of her," I tried to console her.

"Does she?" Desiree asked. "How can anyone have a good future in The Zone? Rich or poor."

I didn't know what to say to that. "Is there anything else I should know?"

A concerned look passed across Gerard's face. "Case Gordon sent a message via courier. A live person. Mano-a-mano sort of message. Real cloak and dagger. He wants to see you tonight. He also passed on a warning."

"A warning?" I asked, surprised.

There was a time I had considered Case Gordon to be *the* love of my life. The bioroid assassin turned executive had made the incredibly stupid decision of breaking up with me for the love of a lost and broken Rider named Kei. As such, he'd been downgraded to *one* of the loves of my life. Still, he remained a valuable business partner and an ally in my war against slavery as well as poverty in the Zone.

Gerard nodded. "He said Karma Corp Media Unlimited has

sent down a Mr. White to negotiate. Is that bad?"

Karma Corp Entertainment was one of the people/groups who had a vision for the Zone and probably was one of Justin Blackwood, Junior's paymasters. They envisioned bulldozing the Zone and replacing it with corporate owned entertainments. Basically, the Disney-meets-Las Vegas version of This is Paradise as well as other establishments. It was already where everyone went to get high, fuck, or engage in the most scandalous virtual entertainments. Why shouldn't the corporations get a taste?

Because we fucking built the Zone from the hellish dumping ground for America's poor and unwanted into an actual livable space for families, that's why goddammit. The corporations had already bought out the rest of post-Eruption America and done their best to pretend we refugees didn't exist. Well, I wasn't about to let them have their way again. Normally, that meant fighting them in the courts and media. Paid-for protests, bribes, and social media campaigns involving lots of bots made it too costly to go in hard. Mr. White being dispatched to "negotiate" meant they were sick of that dance. Which was a shame because I was a very good dancer.

"Yes," I said, feeling sick. "It is very bad, Gerard. It means the corporates aren't screwing around anymore. Mr. White is a pseudonym for Karma Corp's best counterintelligence agent. He kills, bribes, and turns people against one another to get what his masters want."

"And that's different from us how?" Gerard asked, shutting the casing for Desiree's arm.

I stared at him. Gerard was starting to annoy me with his cracks.

"Is she good to go?"

"Yes, ma'am," Gerard said, giving a mock salute. "She's ready for battle."

"Good," I answered, looking down at Desiree. "Remember, this is your livelihood."

"How could I forget?" Desiree deadpanned.

I didn't live in This is Paradise. It was a lovely hotel, don't get me wrong, but I didn't want to be always surrounded by work. Instead, I maintained a penthouse at the top of a more traditional apartment building that I landed my flying car on top of in order to move in and out of. It wasn't the kind of home corporates had nor did it resemble the kind of place the word "penthouse" conjured. Perhaps "top floor apartment" was a better one, but it was home, and I enjoyed coming here every night to relax. I'd even bought groceries from the Zone bazaar rather for a homecooked meal tonight versus getting everything delivered by drone.

Unfortunately, no sooner was I through the door than I noticed there was a dead body lying on my living room carpet. It took a second to recognize the body was Justin Blackwell, Junior. He'd been shot in the back of the head, and there were signs he'd been killed recently. Acknowledging I might be in danger and that someone was very likely trying to frame me, I immediately turned around, only to smack my face into the chest of my ex-boyfriend—who was my immediate suspect for the murder that I was now a party to.

Case was a tall, immaculately dressed man of mixed racial heritage. He kept his head shaved and wore nothing but the finest in suits. I wasn't a fan of robots or reproductions generally, but he was the most human bioroid I'd ever met. He was also someone I knew to have a body count in four figures. I knew because I'd commissioned him for a good chunk of them when I'd first tried to clean up the Zone by force rather than negotiation.

Stupidly, I tried to scream. It was not my finest moment. I was not a shrinking violet or a victim. I had killed before. Many times, in fact. However, the combination of a violation of my home with the fact the murderer was someone I trusted— however big a mistake that might be in my profession—was enough to throw me off my game. It prevented me from using the morphic metal underneath my nails or the explosive ammunition gun I'd hidden in purse.

Case put his hand over my mouth, which resulted in me shoving my knee toward his groin, but he blocked it with his other hand before spinning me around in one easy gesture and covering my mouth again.

"I did not kill him," Case said. "He was dead when I got here. You could scream but that would involve drawing attention to the fact there's a dead city counselor in your home. You aren't guilty, but do you actually trust the city's justiciars to not prosecute you? The police will undoubtedly be making a special visit here soon. This is a set up."

He then let me go.

"Fuck," I wheezed, taking a deep breath. "They got me good."

"So it seems," Case said.

Details occurred to me. "Wait a damn minute. You find a dead body in my apartment, and you don't think to text me about it? Maybe warn me not to come! What the hell!"

Case shut the door behind us. "I was hoping to dispose of the matter before you arrived."

That was sweet, you know, in a psychotic sort of way. "How much danger are we in right now?"

Case went to the corpse, pulled a switchblade from his pants pocket, and started carving up the carpet around it. I winced because I'd loved that carpet.

"Probably a lot. A dead city councilman can make careers in the NLAPD."

That was when I heard another flying car's turbines descending on my rooftop. Running to the side of my kitchen, I conjured a hologram from the hidden security cameras on the rooftop. It was a squad of four heavily armored STRIKE soldiers, which were basically the anti-cyborg division of the NLAPD. They looked like tanks and were all enhanced with a reputation for taking very few of their subjects alive.

"All that for little ol' me?" I said aloud, impressed.

Case continued rolling up the cut carpeting to cover up the body of the late Councilor Blackwell. Unfortunately, we weren't exactly in a position where we could dispose of the body easily. Oh, and I sincerely doubted the STRIKE soldiers were going to be satisfied by a pleasant little chat when they could just gun me down then say I resisted arrest. One more dead hooker wasn't going to bother their consciences especially and that was presuming they had one in the first place.

"Are your doors locked?" Case asked.

"Locked and armored," I replied. "However, that's not going stop them long."

Indeed, I could already see them pulling out a laser-guided plasma torch to break the door upstairs.

"Do you have any weapons?" Case asked.

I stared at him, shaking my head. "You are so very male."

"What?" Case asked.

I sighed. I was being sexist since I knew plenty of women also with the mindset of murder being the best solution to all problems. Case thinking all problems looked like nails when he'd been built to be a hammer was also forgivable. Still, killing a bunch of elite cops in the Zone when they were undoubtedly being monitored was not going to improve my situation. Indeed, it would be the perfect excuse to freeze all my accounts as well as confiscate all the land I legitimately owned. Which, if we're sharing secrets, was a good three percent of the Zone now. That may not sound like much, but it is when you realize the Zone was as large as the Valley.

Running to another part of my apartment, I walked up to a bookshelf and pulled out a copy of Fanny Hill. Which caused, yes, the bookshelf to open and reveal a secret elevator leading to the subbasement.

"Seriously?" Case asked.

"Do I question your genre, Mr. Super Spy?" I asked, glaring. "Bring the body. Oh, and be glad you never left your toothbrush here."

My apartment was visible with my enhanced vision from three blocks down. The massive smoke coming from it was also helping, the interior having been rigged to blow by voice command. Well, blow was probably a bit much and usually meant something else in my profession. Instead, it was more like melt. All the incriminating interior contents from computer files to DNA evidence to hardcopy photos were designed to be destroyed in such a way to make it impossible for even modern forensics to reconstruct. I regretted losing my possessions there but I'd long since learned not to become too attached to certain things.

Case, carrying Blackwell's wrapped-up corpse over his shoulder like a burlap sack, nodded in approval. "Congratulations, you've managed to thwart Mr. White for a little while longer."

"This wasn't just Mr. White," I replied. "My apartment is rigged to go off unless someone has the right DNA codes as well as passwords. Only a select number of people, all of them employees or you, could get in to deposit a body."

"You're assuming he wasn't killed there," Case said, lifting an old-fashioned rectangular infocom.

"They can track that, you know," I replied.

"I've rigged it so it's pinging randomly across town," Case replied, showing he wasn't just muscle. "One bad turn deserves another, so once Blackwell's absence is noted, I'll deposit his body in Mr. White's own quarters. It took quite a while to find them. From there, I'll have the media arrive before the regular police."

I smirked then frowned. "He'll get off."

"Maybe," Case said. "It'll be such an embarrassment, though, that Karma Corp may cut him loose. It will also put all his projects under intense scrutiny. The corporations may own the media, but they hate each other. Plenty will pump money into making this as big a scandal as possible while buying you some time."

I took the infocom from him and started going through Blackwell's messages. The last conversation he'd had was with one of my cybergirls. They'd invited him to my address.

"Son of a bitch."

"What?" Case asked.

"The stupid motherfucker actually came back for seconds," I said, shaking my head. It was a joke to disguise just how deeply painful the betrayal was, though. "I need to go deal with something, Case. Sorry, no dinner."

"I already ate anyway. Harrison made lamp chops," Case said, referring to his AI sheep.

I looked at him sideways.

"What?" Case asked.

"Why, Desiree?" I asked, holding a gun on her. It was an armor-piercing anti-cyborg Atlas 38D equipped with a built-in silencer. It was illegal as hell, but so was what I planned to do with it.

I found Desiree in a cheap motel on the edge of the city's outskirts, which didn't take much effort on my part since the police weren't the only people capable of pinging infocoms. The place was older than the New Los Angeles arcology and reminded me of the old America, before the Eruption. That wasn't a good thing, and I couldn't help but think I was stepping back in time.

I probably should have come with Case, but I didn't necessarily want to end this with murder. But I didn't see any other way it was going to end, either. The motel manager had sold me the key and I suspected it wouldn't have been the first time he'd called the police to clean up a body.

Desiree, who conspicuously hadn't brought her daughter with her, was shocked at my arrival, but didn't go for the gun on the bed beside the duffle bag of cash. Foreign currency, non-digital, and enough to start a new life in South America or East Asia. Instead, Desiree just backed away from both.

"I should've expected you to outsmart the cops," Desiree said, looking once more at the gun before I maneuvered myself between it and her.

"That's not why I asked," I said, sitting down on the edge of the bed. "Did you kill Blackwell yourself or just lure him to my house?"

Desiree didn't answer. "Doesn't matter, does it? It wasn't personal."

"I see," I sighed. "Just for the money."

"I work in a whorehouse," Desiree hissed, narrowing her eyes. "For a woman who actually argues that it's a valid profession worthy of respect. A woman who dates a fucking bioroid."

I noticed it was the bioroid part which disgusted her more than the fact that he was a hitman. It seemed technophobia even afflicted my gang's ranks. Not that I considered Desiree a member anymore. "So, you're disgusted by the fact that I'm a sex worker and that justifies you becoming a murderer. Where is your daughter, Desiree?"

"With my sister," Desiree said. "I'm going to start a new life. The money Mr. White offered me was enough to do it. She'll be better off with her."

"You're right," I replied, debating what I was going to do. I kept the gun aimed at her heart. "I severely misjudged you. You were like a daughter to me."

"You were like my mother," Desiree said. "A selfish bitch too absorbed to know she was being used by a series of men."

"And women," I amended. "You played me from the beginning, didn't you?"

I thought about all our interactions over the years. I'd paid for her education, gave her room, gave her board, and let her keep far more money than my other employees. Desiree was an excellent whore—she knew what I wanted and played the role.

"I learned from the best," Desiree said, confirming my observation. "If you ever want to escape the Zone, you have to do whatever it takes."

"No one escapes the Zone, Desiree," I rebuffed.

I emptied the clip into her.

LEXICON

AI: Artificial intelligence. Perhaps you've heard of it.

Atlas Security: The world's largest security firm and private army. Atlas Security provides guards, soldiers, weapons, and warfare to the world's governments. As such, it may soon find itself number two.

Arcology: Artificial cities designed to be as close to self-sufficient as possible. The first ones were constructed after the Eruption to replace the formerly largest cities in America.

Ares Biotechnica: A technology start up that focuses on bioroids, cybernetics, and space travel. Largely theoretical in its plans, it has the potential to consolidate many industries into a new megacorp.

Big Smokey: The Yellowstone super volcano that erupted and destroyed Wyoming before covering the Earth in ash.

Big Two Hundred: The world's largest megacorporations that dictate the lives of humanity.

Bioroid: An artificial human being with a cybernetic brain. They are exceptionally rare and only a few thousand exist.

Black Ice: A program created by the Trikuza that seemingly has the power to drive men to acts of violence if not actually control their minds.

Bot: Non-organic robotic laborers that are usually either mass-controlled by a single Cognition AI or semi-sentient at best. They shoulder the burden of manual labor in the future, creating mass unemployment but allowing the arcologies to exist.

Blipvert: A program designed to mind control people into buying things. Shockingly related to Black Ice.

Cognition AI: Unlimited all-powerful AI that control most of the world's information and finances. May no longer be answering to anyone else but humanity pretends otherwise. Only a dozen or so exist.

Credits: Properly United Nations credits. A currency implemented globally post-Eruption meant to stabilize the economy.

Cyber Dragons: One of the three Trikuza gangs. A former Yakuza clan that has since gone international and become a multi-billion-dollar, multiracial franchise.

DataSecure: A corporation that provides the best in cybersecurity for holding the most precious resource in the post-Eruption world: information.

Elemental Lords: The leaders of the Trikuza. Rich, dangerous, and utterly corrupt.

Elysium: A high-class resort with a horrifying secret run by the Trikuza.

Emergency Council: The current governing body of the United States. It can overrule most decisions of the previous federal government.

Goop: The mush that you'll never starve on, even if you want to.

Green Foods: The producers of goop and other essential staples of our post-apocalypse cyberpunk world.

The Eruption: The event that destroyed the old world and ushered in the new. It was also, like, twenty years ago so most people lived through it.

Flying Cars: Flying cars. It's in the name. Also known as cloud cars.

Frankenstein: Outlaw doctors and technicians who deal in illegal bio-modification as well as cybernetics.

Frick: A fake swear that Kei's parents tricked her into using instead of the more common f-word.

The Hacker: A mysterious man or woman who uploaded hundreds of terabytes of data detailing the construction of Black Technology to the internet. See The Leak.

HOPE.: A once-prominent hacktivist group that splintered in the wake of the Eruption.

Icer: Electrical ammunition that explodes and releases a paralyzing Taser-like charge.

Infocom: An uplink to the global infospace system.

Infolink: A direct cybernetic call between two or more people.

Infopad: The replacement for handheld computers and cellphones.

Infospace: The replacement for the internet with vast virtual reality and holographic uplinks.

Invisible Hand: A secret society and club for the superrich that maintains the hegemony of the Big Two Hundred. May or may not actually exist.

Jackals: The nickname for nomadic bandits and raiders who exist on the fringes of arcologies.

Karma Corp: The largest corporation in the world that manufactures a little of everything but primarily electronics, cars, medical supplies, and weapons.

Katana: A traditional Japanese sword. Given with a wakizashi to signal the ascension of a Trikuza member to lieutenant status.

Kunai: A Japanese tool turned weapon in martial arts. Useful in stabbing cyborgs.

The Leak: The information uploaded by the Hacker to the internet. This information advanced humanity's technology close to a century in ten years. It was necessary for survival during the Long Winter.

Lethe: A drug designed to treat PTSD that has since been modified to be a euphoric street drug.

Long Winter: A year-long winter triggered by the Eruption. Its disruption of supply lines and crops resulted in dramatic changes as well as mass death.

MadisonTech: The former company of James Madison now owned by Case Gordon. It has slowly been crawling out of a great financial hole due to his focus on RealDream games and financing Ares Biotechnica.

Megacorp: Corporations that have been recognized as nation-states in the post-Eruption world.

Mercs: Mercenaries, soldiers/ fighters for hire.

The Morrigans: A mostly female gang of sex workers, assassins, and spies that operates out of the Refugee Zone. They eliminated the slavers in the area with the assistance of Case and Lucita.

New Los Angeles: The Los Angeles arcology that has been effectively rebuilt from the ground up to house tens of millions of new citizens. Many use the terms LA, New Angles, New LA, and variations interchangeably.

Nina: An especially durable high-performance type of bike favored by Riders and street racers. Many of them have unusual modifications like super-jumps and weapons.

RealDream: A system created to simulate full scale auditory, tactile, and visual hallucinations of whatever the programmers want.

Refugees: A term for the percentage of the American citizenry forced to leave their homes due to the Eruption and move to the cities. Many of them were never able to be
properly resettled.

Refugee Zone: The temporary shelters for the massive influx of refugees post-Eruption.

Rider: A new breed of criminal that has emerged post-Eruption. They are primarily armed couriers and smugglers, but also have been known to serve as street mercs as well as getaway drivers.

Russian Syndicates: Corporate and criminal alliances that wield vast power in America.

Scavs: A derogatory term for refugees due to their habit of living off the old world.

Shell: A full-body replacement that leaves only the brain untouched. Shells come in regular human levels and almost indestructible tank-like forms. They are identical in appearance to regular humans.

Sleeper: A human who chooses to live full-time on infospace. They are routinely in poor health and prone to dying early.

Simulated Intelligence: An AI with no actual internal will but the ability to perform a wide variety of tasks as well as simulate human interaction.

Suits: A slang term for corporate executives and workers for the megacorporations. Their loyalty to their company and money is believed to exceed that of any other.

Tanto: A Japanese short sword used by the Trikuza's soldiers to indicate they have been accepted as a soldier.

Techjack: A term for a specialized infospace hacker who heavily modify their brains for cybercrime.

This is Paradise: A high-class brothel and entertainment complex in the Zone.

Tier I: AI who are capable of matching human intelligence.

Tier X: See Cognition AI.

Maelstrom 90: An AI-designed cybernetic implant that was implemented in the brains of children. It still is comparable to high-end implants decades later.

Turing Society: A hacktivist offshoot of HOPE. that is less involved in information warfare and more playful pranks.

Vertical Lift Off (VLO): A specialized kind of flying car that is capable of landing or rising in a single spot.

Wakizashi: A Japanese short sword, slightly shorter than a Tanto, used in accompaniment with a katana. Given with a katana to indicate that a Trikuza member has become a lieutenant.

White Triangle: A syndicate of human traffickers, slavers, organ thieves, and black-market cyberneticists.

Yakuza: The Japanese syndicates that have mostly become part of other international organizations.

The Zone: The nickname for the Los Angeles Refugee Zone.

AUTHOR'S NOTE

I'd like to thank you for reading this book. The publishing industry is changing dramatically since the advent of eBooks. It is now very difficult to get any book noticed, regardless of quality. If you enjoyed this book, you could do some very simple things to help me attract attention.

Word of mouth is the number one source of success for novels, so simply telling family and friends about the book is a great start.

Here are a few other ways of helping, if you are so inclined:

* Post a rating or review on Amazon.com
* Post a rating or review on Goodreads
* Talk about the book or write a review on Facebook
* Tell folks about the book in a blog post.

If you like any of my other books, please feel free to check them out. A lot of my series are interlinked, and you never know when you'll find someone familiar showing up.

Case, for example, is the titular G of the Agent G series that serves as a prequel for this story. Check out those books if you want to learn more about his relationship to the Invisible Hand, the Eruption, the Leak, and Evie Principle.

ABOUT THE AUTHORS

C.T. Phipps is a lifelong student of horror, science fiction, and fantasy. An avid tabletop gamer, he discovered this passion led him to write and turned him into a lifelong geek. He is a regular blogger and also a reviewer at The United Federation of Charles.

BIBLIOGRAPHY

The Rules of Supervillainy (Supervillainy Saga #1)
The Games of Supervillainy (Supervillainy Saga #2)
The Secrets of Supervillainy (Supervillainy Saga #3)
The Kingdom of Supervillany (Supervillainy Saga #4)
The Tournament of Supervillainy (Supervillainy Saga #5)
The Future of Supervillainy (Supervillainy Saga #6)
The Horror of Supervillainy (Supervillainy Saga #7)
Esoterrorism (Red Room, Vol. 1)
Eldritch Ops (Red Room, Vol. 2)
Agent G: Infiltrator
Cthulhu Armageddon (Cthulhu Armageddon, Vol. 1)
The Tower of Zhaal (Cthulhu Armageddon, Vol. 2)
Lucifer's Star
Straight Outta Fangton
Wraith Knight
I Was a Teenage Weredeer (Bright Falls Mystery Series #1)
A Teenage Weredeer in Michigan (Bright Falls Mystery Series #2
A Nightmare on Elk Street (Bright Falls Mystery Series #3))
Psycho Killers in Love

Michael Suttkus, II, lives in Leesburg, Florida, with three cats, one of which actually likes him, and his family, with whom he fares better. When not working at a game store, he's playing games, reading science books, or otherwise being incredibly nerdy. Also writing! Because he has to feed cats whether they like him or not.

BIBLIOGRAPHY

I Was a Teenage Weredeer (Bright Falls Mystery Series #1)
A Teenage Weredeer in Michigan (Bright Falls Mystery Series #2
A Nightmare on Elk Street (Bright Falls Mystery Series #3))
Lucifer's Star (Lucifer's Star #1)
Lucifer's Nebula (Lucifer's Star #2)
Brightblade (The Morgan Detective Agency, Book 1)
Space Academy Dropouts (The Space Academy Series, Book 1)

Curious about other Crossroad Press books?
Stop by our site:
http://store.crossroadpress.com
We offer quality writing
in digital, audio, and print formats.

www.ingramcontent.com/pod-product-compliance
Lightning Source LLC
Chambersburg PA
CBHW020257200626
46816CB00001BA/335